The Sapphire Pendant

Dara Girard

Library of Congress Control Number: 2006923738

Printed in the United States of America.

The characters and events in this book are fictitious. Any similarity to real persons, living or dead, is coincidental and not intended by the author.

Ilori Press
PO Box 10332
Silver Spring, MD 20914

The *S*apphire *P*endant

Dara Girard

ILORI PRESS
Silver Spring, Maryland

Dara Girard

Other Books by Dara Girard

Table for Two

Gaining Interest

Carefree

Illusive Flame

Dedication

To my greatest support— my family. Those who dare to dream. And all the "Kenneths" in the world.

Prologue: late 1800s

The west wind swept over the Caribbean Sea, drumming her fingers along Jamaica's white sands, rushing through its caves with a wicked, echoing laugh.

Sonya Clifton sat by the window, a silhouette in the moonlight. Her revenge was complete; there was nothing left to keep her here. She turned at the whisper of shifting sheets and stared at the man who filled the large bed. His white shoulders were like eggshells against the green bedclothes.

He had said he loved her, but she knew his words to be as tempting and poisonous as the manchineel tree, whose very leaves could cause blisters. She would leave him, this German holidaymaker who toyed with young hearts. Yes, she would leave him, but she hadn't accounted for the memories.

She glanced down at the pendant he had kept hidden under a loose floorboard, unaware that she knew its whereabouts. Her nimble, brown fingers caressed the blue-and-green feather motif and the small sapphires suspended in the rope-chain. She held it up, letting the moonlight fall upon the star-sapphire center—twilight locked in stone.

She draped the pendant around her neck, then kissed the sapphire eye before slipping out the window.

Chapter One

"For God's sake, Jessie, let's get out of here before we're caught," Wendy scolded in a harsh, loud whisper that seemed to bounce off the dark mahogany chairs and glass display cases in the room.

Jessie barely heard the warning, her cinnamon eyes fixed on a display case near the far wall. Its contents whispered to her in a soft, haunting song.

"I must get this back somehow," she muttered, staring at the sapphire pendant that lay seductively in its velvet bed.

Wendy grabbed her arm, eager to leave before either their boss or the owner, Mrs. Ashford, saw them. "So you've said many times." Her blues eyes shifted to the closed door, under which a sliver of light flickered as a shadow passed.

"I promised my father, when he sold it, that I would get it back one day." Jessie swallowed, trying to dislodge the tightness in her throat. Neither her father nor her mother had lived to see her fulfill that promise, but she would do it anyway.

"Well, if you don't have a job, you won't be able to afford it. Susan was looking for you."

Jessie's nagging thoughts quickly disappeared. "Damn." She couldn't afford to get fired again. Aside from having bills to pay, her eldest sister would kill her. She clicked off her penlight, pushed it into her trousers pocket, and headed for the door.

They raced towards the stairs. Jessie suddenly halted at the sight of a striking woman draped in a smoke-colored silk dress, her cunning dark eyes surveying the crowd from the top of the circular staircase.

She took a step back, ready to flee in the other direction. "We'll have to go around the back."

"Why?"

"Because that's Stephanie Radson. She works with Kenneth."

Wendy rested a hand on her hip. "So what?"

It meant he was lurking somewhere nearby, and Jessie always did her best to avoid him. "I want to go out back," she said hastily.

"That's too far."

"Fine, then I'll meet you in the kitchen."

Wendy only shook her head as they parted ways.

Jessie raced down the hall, then halted when she saw Amelia Wainwright, an older woman of indeterminate years, who had two buried husbands and a habit of talking without taking a breath. Jessie moved to duck into a room, but Amelia saw her and waved.

"Oh, good. I was hoping you would be here."

Jessie groaned, then plastered on a smile. "Yes, well—"

"I am so glad to have a moment with you, because I have a question and I was thinking to myself, 'Who do I know that can help me find the answer?' And I racked my brain, and nothing came; I just couldn't readily think of anyone to help me. And then I thought about the last party I attended—I think it was three months ago?—and you did a reading there, saying that Mrs. Ostick would have a new arrival soon. Of course we all thought that finally her daughter was expecting, but instead her son got a divorce and had to move back home, but she did get that new arrival you were talking about. So I thought to myself, 'That's it! Jessie Clifton can help me!' And now here you are." She smiled.

Jessie glanced at her watch. "I'm on duty right now and I have to get back to the kitchen."

Amelia's smile began to fade, and a look of anxiety entered her hazel eyes. "Oh, but it's just a quick question. I won't take up too much of your time. I know how hectic working at a party like this can be. Well, I don't know personally, but I can imagine—"

Jessie shifted impatiently, but kept her voice gentle. "What is your question?"

Amelia glanced up, tapping her finger against her bottom lip. "When I woke up this morning, for some reason, I had to wear this bracelet." She held out her wrist. "I haven't worn this bracelet in years—ever since poor Christopher passed away. He gave it to me, you know. I—"

Jessie shoved her hands in her pockets and rocked on her heels, hoping the woman would get to the point soon. "And what do you want to know?"

"Why did I choose to wear it? What does that mean?"

Jessie sighed, then held out her hand. Amelia took off her bracelet and placed it in Jessie's palm. Jessie ran her fingers over the diamond-and-emerald bracelet, ignoring its cost to focus on its meaning. She let it rest in her hand a moment so that her intuition could read the energy there. She glanced up and read Amelia's face. Once she had gathered all the information she needed, she clasped the bracelet on Amelia's wrist. "You're worried about your health, aren't you?"

Amelia clutched her hands together and nodded, her hazel eyes glistening with unshed tears.

Jessie smiled reassuringly. "There is nothing to worry about. You're only experiencing indigestion. You do not have the same stomach cancer that killed your husband." She patted Amelia on the shoulder. "Now, I suggest you make an appointment with your doctor to put your mind at ease, and tell your cook to stop experimenting with her spice collection."

Amelia stretched out her arms. "How can I ever thank you enough?"

Jessie took a step back and waved the thanks away. "It's nothing, really. I'd better go." Before Amelia could say any more, Jessie rushed past her and hurried through the back door. She raced across the immaculate back lawns of the Ashford mansion like a gazelle running from a pack of hyenas.

She dodged a man carrying a table, jumped over a lady arranging flowers along the house, and slid to a stop in front of the servants' entrance. She adjusted her catering uniform and walked into the kitchen.

Wendy approached her with a paper towel. "Where have you been? You look like a melting chocolate sundae."

"Very funny," Jessie said, wiping the sweat sliding down her forehead. "I got cornered by Mrs. Wainwright." She tossed the towel away, envying her best friend's cool composure. Her olive-toned skin looked a bit flushed, but her black hair was pulled in a strict bun and her uniform was perfect, a lesson she'd learned from her French West Indian parents.

"Don't do that again," Wendy said, turning towards the ovens.

"I won't."

Susan, Montey's chief assistant, pointed at her. "Montey was looking for you," she warned, watching Jessie make her way around the kitchen. "I had to cover for you."

Jessie flashed a sheepish grin. "Sorry, I—"

"No time for excuses." Susan pointed to a carton of shrimp. "Put those in the fridge, then help Carole arrange the hors d'oeuvres." She raised her voice. "Make sure she doesn't eat any."

"I won't," Carole replied in a hurt tone.

Jessie put the carton in the fridge, then joined Carole, whose greedy fingers were reaching for a tantalizing miniature asparagus tart. Jessie slapped her hand away. "Those are for the guests."

"They won't miss just one," Carole argued, popping one in her mouth.

"Montey will notice."

Carole licked her long, slim fingers. Despite having the appetite of a polar bear, she had the figure of a model. Like many others in the Garden catering crew, she was saving money for school next year. "I'll say I dropped it."

"Then you'd better wipe the crumbs off your face."

Jessie smiled as Carole hastily wiped imaginary crumbs from her mouth. She listened to the light music penetrating the kitchen walls. Suddenly the doors burst open, and Amy appeared with an empty tray. Her face was flushed; her green eyes were blazing. She rested against the table and grabbed her chest in a dramatic show of heart palpitations.

"Are you okay?" Jessie asked, concerned.

Carole frowned. "Did Mr. Withers pinch your butt again?"

Amy shook her strawberry-blond head. "He's here," she said breathlessly.

Carole's brown eyes widened, then she grabbed her own chest. "He's here?" she whispered.

"Who's here?" Jessie asked.

The two women looked at her as if she had fallen from another planet.

"Mr. Perfect," Amy replied, forming the words in her mouth as if she were talking about a Greek god who had come to Earth on holiday.

Jessie resisted the urge to roll her eyes. "Oh, is that all?"

Unable to understand her disinterest in one of the most handsome and eligible bachelors on the entire East Coast, the two women ignored her.

Amy took another deep breath. "He is so gorgeous. His pictures don't do him any justice."

Carole reached for another tart, sighing loudly. "I know. He was good-looking in high school, but now..." She shook her head, trying to find the right words. "Now he's downright sinful."

Amy tucked a loose strand of hair behind her ear and leaned closer to Carole. "I asked him if he liked the food, and he looked right at me and said..." She paused, to heighten the climactic moment. "Yes." She fanned herself. "He's got the most beautiful brown eyes, and his voice...I thought I would faint dead away."

Jessie wished she could faint right then, so she wouldn't have to hear anymore about Mr. Perfect, aka Kenneth Preston. She tried to catch Wendy's attention so she would have an excuse to leave, but failed. Aside from the clattering of dishes and the shouted orders, the kitchen hummed with news about Kenneth's entrance.

She couldn't completely blame them. He was a hometown hero, a young man whose ingenuity and skill had brought new pride to Randall County, Maryland. He had been elected CEO of his boss's failing electronics company, and he had made it a multimillion-dollar success, creating jobs and bringing new investors to the area. But what more could you expect from a guy who was every parent's dream? The perfect son, the perfect student, the perfect date, the perfect everything. It made Jessie sick. Of course, it didn't help that they belonged to the same community.

In the Caribbean community, he was an idol. In a county proud of its ethnic diversity, the Caribbean community was quickly making its mark, and Kenneth Preston was its trump card. More times than Jessie could count, her mother would despair, wondering why Jessie couldn't be more like Kenneth. In a culture where your bragging rights are your social currency, Mrs. Clifton would have been bankrupt, had it not been for her two older daughters.

Like Carole, Jessie had grown up in Randall County and had firsthand experience with Mr. Perfect: falling for his charms and easy smile, and thinking him the perfect dream when he was actually the perfect nightmare. He was not what others thought, but attempting to convince anyone of that fact was fruitless, so she stayed out of his way and listened with disinterest to the stories that always circled around him. She knew otherwise. He was an arrogant, uptight jerk who would appear in hell wearing a three-piece suit just to keep up his image. Nobody had ever seen him in short sleeves, and only on rare occasions did he ever look unkempt.

"I can't believe he's not married yet," Amy said.

"Too busy having fun, I guess," Carole replied.

Amy drummed her fingers on the table. "I think he might be suffering from a broken heart. Remember that doctor he was seeing?"

"I heard he got bored with her."

"That was four years ago, and there hasn't been a woman since."

"I wouldn't be too sure. Rumor has it that he's dating his employees."

Amy shook her head. "No way. He wouldn't do that."

"He seems commitment-shy."

"He is a womanizer who collects hearts because he doesn't have one of his own," Jessie said. "Doesn't quite make him perfect, does it?"

They ignored her.

"I wish there were some way to get him to see me," Amy said.

Jessie handed her a tray of hors d'oeuvres. "It might help if you were up there in his field of vision, instead of down here talking about him."

"You're right," Amy replied, missing Jessie's bitter tone. "Oh, but you should have seen his date—"

Susan unexpectedly joined the group, like a camp leader ready to put her troop in line. Her brown face was marred with a frown of displeasure. "Unless you're talking about how many glasses need refilling, or tarts that need to be heated, I suggest you ladies get to work."

Amy lifted a tray and backed out through the doors. Carole was reassigned to filling glasses, and Jessie was ordered to take a tray of glasses upstairs.

She reluctantly headed for the main ballroom through the underground tunnel, instead of the elevator. She hoped to be able to avoid Kenneth as long as possible, and hoped to act professional if she did run into him. She walked through the gray hallways, her shoes pounding against the white tile, and mused about the residents of the house. They probably weren't even aware that such an underground structure existed. It smacked of *Upstairs, Downstairs*. Them and Us. Kenneth had been an Us, and now he was a Them.

Not that she cared. She walked up the stairs, the music and voices growing louder. She wondered what it would be like to have a party in the middle of the week, and to have no worries, except what outfit to wear the next day. She thought of her sisters: Michelle busy at work and Teresa giving piano lessons. They didn't have the luxury of such impromptu soirees. When she reached the door to the main floor, she steadied her tray and lifted her head before entering.

She turned the corner and walked right into Mr. Perfect and the plateful of food he was holding. His meal smashed right into her uniform, like a pie in the face of a clown. Jessie lost her precarious hold on the tray full of glasses, and they fell to the ground with a shattering crash, spilling their contents like a broken aquarium.

"Why don't you watch where you're going?" she said, looking down at her ruined uniform and the broken glass.

He didn't offer her an apology; instead, a sour grin touched his face. "Figures it would be you."

She rested a hand on her hip, annoyed that Amy had been right. He did look gorgeous. His chestnut skin looked ravishing against the gunmetal gray of his shirt and his black trousers. He stood there staring at her with amused brown eyes, surrounded by an air of casual command that only a man blessed with his status could cultivate. She ground her teeth. "What's that suppose to mean?"

"It means that whenever you're around, disaster strikes."

14

"If you had been watching where you were going, this wouldn't have happened."

"Lower your voice," he ordered. "You're drawing attention..."

She lowered her voice to a deadly whisper. "I think what caught their attention was the shattering glass."

"Don't blame me. I'm not the one turning corners like I'm on a secret mission."

"Is that supposed to be some sort of explanation for throwing your food at me?"

"Throwing?" He lifted a dark eyebrow. "You walked right into me!"

She knew he was right, but she was too angry to calm down. She would not allow him the last word. "Well, you shouldn't have held it so clumsily. Or perhaps you could have had your latest concubine—I mean date—deliver it to you."

As if to add credence to her claim, a young woman, dressed in an outfit that could afford Jessie the down payment on a new luxury car, came up to Kenneth and possessively grabbed his arm. "What happened to you?" she asked Jessie, her lovely brown eyes genuinely concerned. Her parents had taught her that "the help" were people too, and she wanted to be sympathetic. She glanced down at the glasses. "You know, you really should get this cleaned up before someone gets hurt."

The woman had such a graceful, feminine manner that she made Jessie feel practically masculine. "That's clever of you to notice," she managed quietly.

She smiled, missing Jessie's sarcasm, and leaned towards Kenneth, her face in a pout. "I want to go home."

"In a minute," he said absently, his amused expression gone. "Go get something to drink."

"But—"

He stopped her with a hard look. She lowered her beautiful lashes and walked away.

"Looks like your date wants her nappy changed," Jessie muttered.

He shoved his hands in his pockets and stared at the ground. "Just for a minute, stop being a smartass and look at your left hand."

She lifted her hand and saw a pencil-thin cut slashed through her palm; a stream of blood seeped through and dripped onto the floor. Pain suddenly registered, but it was quickly replaced with an odd sense of annoyance. "Damn."

Kenneth handed her a crisp, white handkerchief, forcing her to apply pressure. Before she could argue, he turned away. "Clean up this mess, please," he told a passing waiter.

The waiter stopped and stared at the mess as if he had come upon a car wreck and was being asked to provide emergency care. "But that's not my job."

Kenneth nodded and grinned. "Do you want to have a job?" His voice was soft; his threat was not.

The man swallowed. "I'll see what I can do."

"Thank you." Kenneth pointed to a woman in a maid's uniform, who was standing awkwardly in the doorway. "Get me some bandages and antibiotic ointment, please," he said, the hint of an island accent sweetening his words. The woman nodded and disappeared. He took hold of Jessie's other arm. "Come with me."

Trapped in his iron grip, she reluctantly followed him, inwardly groaning as she heard the crunch of broken glass under her feet.

In the powder room, he cleaned the cut, then had her press her hand against his in a fist.

"Does that hurt?"

She snatched her hand away. "Yes, of course!"

"Good. No nerve damage," he explained when she stared at him, outraged. "You've hurt yourself enough times to know the procedure."

"That's not true."

"You were the most reckless tomboy around. What do they call grown tomboys? 'Tommen'?"

"I am not a tomboy."

"Just afraid of being a woman, then?"

A timid knock interrupted her reply.

"Come in," he said.

The maid entered, staring at Kenneth with eyes of worship. She held out the bandages, her hand trembling, as though offering a famous celebrity a handmade gift. "Here are the bandages you needed."

"Thanks." He flashed one of his hundred-watt smiles. The woman blushed and shut the door. He turned to Jessie, and the smile disappeared.

Jessie felt both sickened and mesmerized by how quickly he could turn on the charm. She had to admit it was a gift. His smile made every woman believe he thought she was special, that she was number one in his life. Jessie knew: she had once been on the receiving end of one of those deceptive smiles. "Doesn't it get tiresome?"

He applied the ointment. "What?"

Jessie looked towards the ceiling, praying for patience. "The women."

He sent her an intense look, then began to gently wrap her hand. "You wouldn't believe me if I told you."

Jessie shrugged, indifferent. "You can wrap it tighter, you know," she said, annoyed by his tenderness. She just wanted him to wrap her hand and leave.

"I know. However, I must try to resist stopping your blood flow." He flashed a malicious grin. "The urge is tempting."

She made a face and surveyed the small powder room. Her gaze fell on the hand-painted violet-blossom tiles shipped in from Spain and the cobalt-blue-on-white china basin. She wished the room were larger, since Kenneth seemed to take up most of the free space and air. She could feel the heat from his body reach out and embrace her; the musky scent of his cologne played havoc with her senses. She began to feel lightheaded, which she was certain was a direct result of lost blood and eating only toast for breakfast. The flowers on the walls suddenly seemed to sway from an unknown breeze, and Kenneth felt far away— just the way she liked it. Then he was gone.

"Drink it," Kenneth demanded, shoving a glass of juice in her face.

"But I'm not—"

The glass was on her lips before she could finish her protest. She had the choice to either drink or choke. She chose the former. When she was through, she glanced around and realized she was sitting on a green camelback settee in the hallway, resting against Kenneth. She abruptly straightened.

"Put your head between your knees," he said.

"I'm not going to faint."

"You just did."

"I felt a little weak, but I was fine."

He folded his arms and rested back. "Hmm, I suppose admitting that you fainted would be too feminine for you."

"I have nothing against femininity. I am a woman, after all."

He measured her in one unflattering glance. "Not yet."

"What do you mean?"

He rubbed his chin, suddenly regretful. "Never mind."

"Say it."

He frowned, doubtful. "Do you really want me to explain?"

"If you can."

"Just look at yourself. You're not..." He didn't know how to complete the statement. She wasn't plain. Her skin was a rich dark brown, and her mouth was soft when she laughed, which she never did when he was around. But her eyes were killers, and whenever they flashed in his direction, a rush of heat would shoot through him. Why, he was never quite sure. Fortunately, he always managed to cool it.

No, she wasn't plain, but she wasn't pretty either. In a quick gesture, he lightly fingered the hair floating around her head. Even though she had attempted to pull her hair back in a braid, a few rebellious strands had broken free. He shook his head. "My *belle laide*," he said in a half-whisper.

"What?"

"Are you still reading *Madeline* to practice French?"

"I graduated to *Le Petit Prince*. Now, are you going to explain yourself or not?"

"You don't revel in being a woman. Your hair is always a mess, you hide your body in androgynous clothing—"

"This is a uniform, you idiot."

It hung on her like a sack; the arms were too long, as were the trousers. "And only you can make it look bad. It's like you don't even know the power of a woman's...attributes."

"I don't like fitted tuxes."

"Aside from the way you dress, any man who might be interested in you has to deal with your sharp tongue and nasty temper. The thought makes most men shudder."

"I see." She blinked back stinging, hot tears. It was her own fault. She had asked for honesty and received it in full. "It's nice to know what you really think of me. It explains everything."

He softened his voice, seeing the floating tears. "Jasmine—"

Her voice hardened. "Don't call me Jasmine."

He cradled her injured hand in his—a warm, solid hand that managed to make hers look small, helpless, almost delicate. Oh God, he was touching her, and her traitorous body enjoyed it. "We need to talk," he said.

She didn't want to talk to him. She didn't want to forgive him, like countless other brokenhearted females had. She hated how she had been weakened into bringing up the past in the first place. She had given him permission to carelessly tear at her wounds.

She hated that he could tap her weaknesses, while he kept his well-hidden. He could taunt her or make her feel foolish, but he could never know or understand how it felt to be her—not when he'd been given everything and had taken even more. He was a cunning illusion, trying to make her forget who he truly was. But she never would. She would not be another silent conquest of his deception. Without warning, an overwhelming need to hurt him, as he had hurt her, rose inside her.

She slapped him across the face so hard that her hand stung from the impact. She felt a secret delight when she saw his face become a violent storm, his eyes flashing with uncontrolled rage.

"Go on. Hit me back," she challenged. "I'm woman enough to take it. I know how much you want to. How much you truly despise me, because I know you're a fraud. I can see that temper of yours burning in your eyes, ready for release. Go on and act on impulse and show the world who you really are."

He grabbed her shoulders, lifting her off the settee, and she watched as he tried to keep himself from shaking her. He finally pushed her away from him. Jessie fell backwards, sitting down hard.

For a moment, Kenneth didn't breathe. He wouldn't allow his emotions to settle and take root. He knew the dangerous path down which untamed emotions could lead a man. He had perfected an iron will, which presently sought to douse the flames of his temper. He turned away. "I forgive you," he whispered in a harsh, raw voice that shook from an anger he was unsuccessfully trying to control.

"Don't you dare forgive me," she said, ready to see him break free from his magnanimous armor.

He spun around and grinned wickedly. All signs of anger were now hidden behind devilish eyes. "I forgive you," he said again, knowing this battle was his to win. "Do you want to try the other cheek?"

"You may be able to tame the savage beast, but I'll release it one day."

"Yes, but will you be able to deal with the consequences?"

A high-pitched shriek stopped her reply. "My beautiful glasses! Where is she? Where is that girl?"

Jessie leaped to her feet, alarmed. "Damn, that's Montey," she said in a panicked whisper. She looked around, desperate for a means of escape. She dashed behind a large plant. Kenneth rose to the occasion and moved in front of her and folded his arms, just in time to see Montey approach.

The guy is huge! Jessie thought, staring up at Kenneth's broad frame. He had the body of a warrior: solid arms, legs, and shoulders that could haul weapons and women. Being a big girl herself—and believing him to be one of Earth's lowest life-forms—she rarely noticed his size. *No wonder the jerk is so arrogant.*

Montey stopped in front of him. He was a bulky man with curly brown hair and a fussy mustache that bristled when he was agitated. It did so now. "Hello, Mr. Preston. Have you seen Jessie? I heard that she caused quite a disturbance. I'm glad that she didn't ruin your suit."

"No, she had a little accident."

"That girl *is* an accident," Montey said. "I never should have hired her. I was only doing her sister a favor."

"I'm sure she'll apologize."

"No more apologies. She's fired."

Jessie rested her forehead against the wall and groaned.

"What was that?" Montey asked.

Kenneth kicked the pot. "Oh, nothing."

"If you see Jessie, give her my message."

"I'm sure you could work something out."

Montey gave Kenneth a long, assessing look. "If you think she's such a good worker, perhaps you could give her a job." He spun on his heel and left.

Jessie sat and covered her face. Her shoulders shook. Kenneth reached for her, then thought better of it. "It will be okay."

She looked up at him, with tears of laughter.

"Did you hear him shriek?" she asked between breaths. "He sounds just like my grandmother when she gets angry. I never knew a man's voice could reach such a pitch." She wiped her tears away and sobered. "Damn, Michelle is going to kill me."

He sat down next to her. "Look, I can get you a job."

"Oh, no you don't," she said, shaking her head. She did not want to receive any of his charity. "You've done enough." She shifted awkwardly. "Thanks for hiding me, though."

He shrugged.

She lifted her hand. "And for the bandage. Though I could have taken care of it myself."

He shrugged again.

Jessie looked at him, which was a mistake at so close a range. Up close, she noticed that his eyes were framed by curling black lashes that any woman would envy, and his full mouth entertained a shy smile. She also noticed an imprint forming on the side of his movie-star face: her handprint.

She swore. God had a nasty sense of humor. How could he make a man so beautiful and a woman so plain? "I am sorry about hitting you."

The corner of his mouth kicked up in a quick grin. "No, you're not."

"My temper gets the best of me sometimes," she continued, refusing to agree with him.

He raised an eyebrow. "Only sometimes?"

"I said I was sorry, but that's all I'll apologize for." She rested her elbows on her knees. "I mean, I know that I asked for it, but knowing that someone thinks you're a man doesn't put a person in a good mood."

"I've always thought of you as a woman, Jas. I'm just waiting for you to."

It was a line of bull, and she was falling for it, diving into his delicious chocolate eyes and allowing his words to cascade over her like a waterfall. He was the most convincing sheep-clad wolf she had ever met.

"I still don't like you," she said.

His mouth spread to a full grin, the one he saved for special occasions. Her pulse quickened. She ignored it.

"Fair enough," he said. "I don't like you either."

For a moment they shared a gaze and a camaraderie that began to change into something more intimate as they stared at each other. He unexpectedly brushed a finger against her cheek, then put it in his mouth. "You had whipped cream on your face," he whispered. "I'm hungry."

She rubbed where his finger had been. "Then get something to eat. I don't want you eating off of me."

"Don't worry. I realize poison is deadly."

She sent him a rude glance, which she reluctantly softened with a smile. "Touché." She turned away and stood, breaking the sudden awareness that had come between them. "Looks like your date wants you."

Kenneth also stood, frowning. He watched his date approach. "You might have been right about the nappy thing. She does act like a baby." He turned to see Jessie's reaction, but she was gone.

Chapter Two

Jessie raced back to the servants' hall, but the hostess, Mrs. Ashford, pounced on her before she could escape. Jessie knew that one of the biggest dangers in working in your hometown was that some people never saw you mature beyond a certain age. For Jessie, the age was thirteen—awkward, miserable thirteen. She had become acquainted with Mrs. Ashford when her mother and sisters would collect the leftover food from one of her many parties to feed the homeless.

"My dear girl, what a shame," Mrs. Ashford said in a smooth Louisiana drawl. She grabbed Jessie's arm in a grip as impressive as her tall frame. "You always were one for causing scenes. But I can't have you leaving the house looking like that." She shook her head at the stain on Jessie's uniform. She called one of her servants—Ms. Frey, if Jessie remembered correctly. She was a petite woman who managed to look bored, in spite of all the festivities around her. "Take Jessie to the guest room and give her one of my charities." She turned to Jessie and pinched her cheek. Her face, the color of espresso and just as warm, spread into a smile. "No need to thank me, honey."

Jessie returned the smile. *I wasn't going to.*

She reluctantly followed Ms. Frey's leisurely pace up the steps. They walked down a long wood-paneled hallway lined with large gilt-framed portraits of family members. Jessie despaired of ever reaching the "charity" room when Ms. Frey opened a door. Not a woman of many words, she motioned Jessie to sit in one of the overstuffed couches in the room, situated under a large window. She opened a closet and searched until Jessie became impatient.

"I'm not picky," she assured her.

"Just wait your turn."

Jessie folded her arms and tapped her foot.

Ms. Frey pulled out a flowery two-piece outfit, shimmering with glitter and rhinestones.

Jessie grimaced. "Don't you have anything less...colorful?"

Ms. Frey laid the outfit on the bed. "This here outfit cost her eighteen hundred dollars," she said in a rough voice that seemed incongruous with her small frame.

It looked like something rejected from the disco era. "Can you imagine spending so much on something so ugly?" Jessie asked.

"Well, being rich doesn't give you taste." She stared at Jessie critically. "If you want, I can have your suit washed once you're changed."

"No, thanks. I'll do that on my own. Besides, I no longer have a need for it."

Ms. Frey nodded, handed her a plastic bag to put her clothes in, and shut the door behind her. Jessie stripped out of her clothes and began to dress. She hoped she would be able to reach her car without too many people seeing her. The trousers were a little too short, but otherwise the outfit worked. While rolling up her soiled clothes, she overheard the women in the adjoining room.

"Oh, that looks great on you, Deborah," a voice cooed. "You're so lucky to have such a kind aunt."

Jessie rolled her eyes. The last person she wanted to bump into just then was Deborah Wester. Deborah prided herself on being part of one of the oldest black families in Randall County. Her immediate family was middle-class like Jessie's, but a number of her relatives were wealthy...old-money wealthy. Jessie's family, on the other hand, was part of the small immigrant community that began to grow during the seventies. So although they called the county their own, to some they were still outsiders.

"Thank you," Deborah replied. "You don't think it makes my hips look heavy?"

"You look great in anything," the voice said. Jessie recognized it as that of Deborah's close friend, Tracy Richards.

"I know," Deborah said haughtily. "Unlike some people." Her voice lowered. "Did you see what Jessie Clifton was wearing today? I mean, she should at least get a uniform that fits."

Jessie's ears perked up.

"She looked dreadful," Tracy agreed. "Besides the fact that she was running through the back lawn like a thief."

"Did you hear what she did to poor Kenneth?"

"I know," Tracy said, censoring her tone as if it were a taboo subject. "No class whatsoever."

"I mean, it's bad enough that she and her sisters are ugly—"

"No, they aren't ugly," Tracy delicately corrected. "Just plain."

"Close enough," was Deborah's flippant reply. "I mean, if I didn't have looks, I'd at least try to dress nice. No wonder she hasn't had a date since taking her cousin to the prom."

Both women giggled. Jessie felt her hands ball into fists as shame burned her cheeks. First Kenneth, now Deborah. Didn't they know she was already aware of her physical failings?

"I mean, first, there's her sister."

"Which one?"

"The eldest one, of course, Michelle. She did herself a favor and forgot about men after her separation. I think she's the smartest one of the bunch. She's really clever, but of course she has to be, since she has no looks. Then there's the crazy sister who believes in visions and herbs, but their father probably believed in voodoo or something, so what can you expect?"

"That's not fair," Tracy chided.

Unashamed, Deborah continued. "Then there's poor little Jessie. She always goes around like she's something important, when everyone knows she acts that way because no one wants her. I mean, she can't even keep a job. No wonder she has to tell fortunes on the side to make extra money."

Tracy giggled.

"Plus her entire wardrobe consists of thrift-shop rejects. Why would anyone go out with her?"

That did it. Jessie could no longer hold her tongue. She shoved open the adjoining door, banging it against the wall, and stormed into the room, ready for battle. "As a matter of fact, I can get any man I set my sights on," she announced, with her head held high.

Deborah and Tracy spun around, their mouths dropping open in shock.

Deborah was the first to speak. "What did you say?"

"I said that I can get any man I want," she repeated, enunciating every word so that she wouldn't be misunderstood. The clipped manner in which she spoke emphasized her Caribbean British upbringing.

Deborah had been taught proper social conduct since birth—laughing coyly, standing like a pole, and smiling noncommittally—but in response to Jessie's statement, all these teachings were forgotten. She threw her head back and laughed until tears filled her eyes.

Jessie ground her teeth. "What's so funny?"

Deborah wiped away tears. "You were always so amusing, Jess."

"Deborah, she's serious," Tracy whispered, seeing Jessie's eyes narrow.

"Of course she is," Deborah said, eyeing Jessie's flowery top and trousers.

Jessie placed her hands on her hips. "Looks aren't everything."

"Which is fortunate," Deborah said lightly, "because you don't have any. Now, don't get mad at us. We didn't know you were listening in." She turned back to the mirror and ran a hand down her ample hip.

Jessie knew that Deborah had every right to dismiss her claim. She was every man's dream: curvaceous and exotic with her creamy brown skin, pert nose, almond-shaped eyes the color of acorns, and reddish brown hair that fell in micro-braids down her back. One could easily picture her being carried off by muscular men and fanned with large palm leaves. Tracy, on the other hand, could be mistaken for a life-sized porcelain doll. Her facial bones were delicately carved, as if a sculptor had taken special care; her light brown hair complemented her skin, and her hands and feet were childlike. Men rushed to accommodate her, because she had such an innocent fascination about her.

Meanwhile, Jessie knew that she was best suited for manual labor. Her athletic build would best be put to use building houses or taming horses. She had once been told that she had a lovely nose, but that had been the only compliment about her features that she had ever received. Her eyes were an ordinary brown, and her mouth was simple—not full and luscious or even soft and supple, just simple, like an empty fruit bowl, nothing to comment about. She had deliciously expressive eyebrows and a firm chin, but her hair was always an unruly mess, no matter how she tried to style it. But she wouldn't allow the stark contrast in her features to shake her claim.

"I'm not angry," she lied, unable to loosen her fists. "I just wanted to clear up one misconception." She drummed her fingers on her hips. "I have had dates, and I chose to remain single."

Deborah looked at her friend and grinned wickedly. "When's the last time you've been out on a date?"

"That doesn't matter."

"Right. Because you can't remember. This isn't a big city, Jessie. Everyone knows what everyone else is up to."

"Well, you don't know me. Sometimes I go out of town and meet guys and have fun."

Deborah toyed with one of her braids. "Do you do this before or after a game?" she asked, referring to Jessie's sports activities: tennis in the summer, soccer in the spring, basketball in the fall, and swimming in the winter. "Most of the guys are probably scared that you're stronger than them."

Jessie hesitated. Deborah wasn't far from wrong. She usually intimidated men. Once she had unintentionally humiliated a guy by picking him up when he had twisted his ankle. She brushed that aside. "Look, if you think that you can get any guy you set your sights on, why can't I?"

Jessie thought it was a logical question, but Deborah rolled her eyes. The topic had quickly lost its appeal. "Okay, perhaps you could attract some lower-class guy with no teeth, who would take you out to Bob's Fish and Chips, but you could never get invited to an event like the Hampton Charity Ball. The only way you'd get in is by serving the food."

Jessie's voice turned to ice. "I could get a wealthy man to look at me."

"Not just look. Desire."

"Yes, that too."

Deborah snorted.

Jessie began to fold her arms, but stopped when she heard a tiny rip under her arm. "Okay, you don't believe me," she said, her competitive nature taking hold. "Try me."

Deborah's interest was instantly piqued. "You think you can get any guy you set your sights on to ask you to the Hampton Charity Ball?"

Jessie shrugged nonchalantly. "Yes. I'm smart and funny and…and…" Words suddenly failed her.

Deborah grinned. "And what?"

Jessie returned the grin. "Charming."

"Charming?" Deborah repeated the word as if it were foreign.

"Yes, I can be very charming. Charm has nothing to do with looks, and it draws men like honey." She had never tried it, but she assumed it was true.

"You're wrong. Charm has everything to do with looks. It's a certain glance. A sly grin."

"No, it's about honeyed phrases and compliments. I bet, if given the chance, I could charm any attractive, eligible man I wanted."

Deborah tapped her cheek. "And I was afraid this summer would be boring." She glanced at the clock and grinned. "Okay, then the next guy that asks me to dance is your target."

"But you have—" Tracy began.

Deborah tossed a skirt at Tracy. "Hang this up for me, will you?" She turned to Jessie. "He can't know anything about this. I don't want it to turn into a pity date."

"Of course," Jessie said, offended.

"I want to see if you can get a wealthy guy to ask you to the Hampton Charity Ball."

"Is this a bet?"

"Absolutely."

Jessie thoughtfully chewed on her nails. "What do I get if I win?"

Deborah studied her for a moment. "You know, someone saw you coming out of Aunt Rhonda's art room."

"So?"

"Are you still pining after that little pendant your father sold?"

"That's none of your business."

"It is—if you really want it. I heard my aunt was considering giving it to the Historical Society for their museum, but I could talk to her."

Jessie paused. "What do you mean?"

"If you win this little wager, the Sapphire Pendant will be yours."

A sweet rush of anticipation swept over her. "You could get it for me?"

"I can get anything I want."

She held out her hand. "You're on."

Deborah pointed a manicured finger at her. "But if you lose, you have to be *my* housekeeper for a year. And all my housekeepers wear uniforms, but of course you're used to wearing uniforms."

Jessie continued to hold out her hand. "I'm waiting."

Deborah shook her hand, then glanced at Jessie's outfit, an amused grin on her lips. "You almost look good in that. Put your shoes on and meet us downstairs in the courtyard."

"Fine."

Jessie went back in the guest room and rolled up her old clothes. She tried to smooth her hair back, but a few strands were determined to break free, so she gave up. She glanced at her reflection in the mirror. She knew that she looked ridiculous, like she had fallen into a flower bed and the weeds had attacked her, but she didn't have time to find something else. She stuffed her soiled clothes in the plastic bag and headed downstairs.

She found Deborah and Tracy in the courtyard, as agreed. Deborah was putting on lipstick, while Tracy shaped her nails. Two men collided into each other when Deborah crossed her legs, her skirt falling away to reveal her creamy thighs. Another man crashed into a plant when Tracy looked up at him and winked. Jessie's heart began to pound, threatening to beat her to death for her foolishness. What had she been thinking? Why had she allowed her temper to give her false confidence? There was no way she could charm some man unless he was under the age of eight.

She walked towards them, her bravado severely shaken. There had to be a way to save her pride. Could she plead temporary insanity?

Deborah and Tracy stood up when they saw her approach.

"Are you sure you want to do this?" Tracy asked, reading Jessie's anxious expression.

Deborah nudged her friend in the ribs. She would not allow Jessie any excuses not to her humiliate herself. "Of course she does, don't you?"

It was Deborah's smug tone that prompted her next words. "Without a doubt," she replied. She inwardly swore, knowing she'd lost her last chance to withdraw.

"Excellent." She looped her arm through Jessie's as if they were old friends instead of enemies. "Now, as I am sure you know, picking out the right man is a science." She paused and looked at Jessie expectantly. Jessie obediently nodded, though she didn't know what Deborah was talking about. "I tend to stay away from men standing near the bar."

"But what's wrong with a guy getting a dri—?"

"As for men with jewelry," Deborah interrupted, "personally, I don't go for men who buy jewelry for themselves, because then they won't have enough money left over for me." Deborah stopped suddenly in front of the library. "Now here is a perfect place to browse. Why don't we stay here and see what we can come up with?"

"Sure," Jessie agreed. It seemed like a safe bet. Perhaps she would get lucky and snag some bookish homebody who was desperately in need of companionship.

Deborah sat down on the bench, pulling Jessie down with her. "I'm sure that the next single man that asks me to dance will be perfect for you." She looked down at her watch.

"Expecting someone?"

"Perhaps." Deborah toyed with her hair.

Jessie watched, fascinated, as a man tripped over his own feet while looking at Deborah. She shook her head. Were men really that dumb, or did Deborah have something she just couldn't see?

"So you're certain you want the next man that asks you to dance to be my target?"

"Pretty sure."

There was a niggling doubt in her mind. Deborah's cool demeanor made her uneasy, but that wasn't uncommon. Jessie stretched out her legs and crossed them at the ankles. "That shouldn't be too hard." Just after the words left her mouth, Kenneth Preston walked out of the library. Even from a distance, he had a vitality that struck her like a lighting bolt. As he walked, people stepped aside to let him pass, as if he were royalty. A number of women nudged each other and stared in his direction. It took a few moments for Jessie to realize the true significance of his sudden appearance. Her mouth fell open, and she grabbed her chest to make sure that her heart was still beating.

"Oh, no," she gasped, nearly choking on her words. She silently pleaded for him to pass them, for his date to grab his arm and lead him away. Anything to divert his attention. Jessie leaped to her feet. "I have to go."

Deborah grabbed onto her shirt, pulling her back down, like she would a disobedient pet. "No, you're staying right here," she said behind a smile. She lifted her hand and called his name.

He came up to them and smiled. "I like a lady who's on time. So, Deborah, are you ready for our dance?"

Jessie glared at her. Her voice was laced with ice. "You were already planning to meet here?"

Deborah stood up and continued to smile. "I doubt you two need introductions."

"No." His eyes trailed the length of Jessie's shirt-and-trousers ensemble with sardonic amusement. "Nice outfit."

"One of Aunt Rhonda's charities, no doubt," Deborah mentioned.

Jessie ground her teeth.

"Come on, let's go," he said, sensing Jessie's rising anger. He was glad that for once, it was not directed at him.

"Before you two dash off," Jessie said, taking hold of Deborah's arm with a grip hard enough to make her wince, "I need to talk to you, Deborah."

"Could you give me a few minutes?" Deborah asked Kenneth, fluttering her lashing in such a flirtatious way that Jessie wanted to glue them shut. He nodded, and she turned to Jessie. "What is it?"

"You set me up."

Deborah blinked, becoming the picture of innocence. "Now, why would I do that? He's just a man, after all."

Right. Like Dom Perignon is just a drink; like Kilimanjaro is just a hill. Jessie glanced at Kenneth, who was talking to Tracy, then turned back to Deborah. She began biting her nails. "Look, I'm willing to do this dare with anyone but him."

"Why? Think he's above your league?"

"No one is above my league." She desperately searched for words to explain. "I just…I don't like him."

Deborah lifted an eyebrow. "Impossible. Everybody loves Kenneth. He doesn't have an enemy around. He's absolutely perfect. You know you can't get him, so you're trying to make an excuse."

"That's not true. We've had a mutual dislike for each other since middle school, and I believe we have a good thing going."

Deborah put up a hand and shook her head. "This isn't middle school. You said that you could get any guy, and he's the one that asked me to dance. Are you declaring defeat?"

Jessie shut her eyes. Defeat wasn't an option. "No."

"Good. So you have to get him to ask you to the Hampton Charity Ball."

"But he either goes alone or with some hot floozy on his arm," Jessie protested.

Deborah tossed a braid over her shoulder. "I went with him two years ago."

"My point exactly."

Deborah only smiled, showing a row of perfectly white teeth. "Jealous?"

Jessie focused her eyes on the back of Kenneth's head. "No."

Deborah brushed imaginary dust from Jessie's shoulder. "Good luck, then. You've got stiff competition." She went over to Kenneth and looped her arm through his. The way she laid claim to him made Jessie feel a little sorry for Kenneth's infant escort. "Bye," she called over her shoulder.

Kenneth turned around and casually waved. "See you around. Try to stay away from gardeners."

Both Tracy and Deborah laughed at his attempt at humor.

Jessie stood there, watching them leave, wishing she could crawl into the ground and stay there. Why hadn't she just kept her big mouth shut? Why had she allowed Deborah to get to her? Now she was destined to make an idiot of herself. She had to make Kenneth Preston fall for her and ask her to the Hampton Charity Ball. The guy she had tormented for years; the reason her family had lost the Sapphire Pendant in the first place.

Chapter Three

"Michelle, I'm in trouble," Jessie said, bursting into her sister's downtown office. Her sister owned the Clifton Center for Business and Enterprise, a company that helped establish entrepreneurs. It had started humbly out of their basement, but it now afforded Michelle the luxury of an office on the eighth floor of the exclusive Winfield Building. It had a fabulous view of the downtown area and Catlon Bay. Peach carpeting spread throughout the room, complementing the simple furniture.

Michelle looked up from a contract she was reviewing and frowned. "What happened to you?"

Jessie looked down at her clothes. "That jerk Kenneth spilled his food on me. Mrs. Ashford gave me something else to wear." She felt utterly ridiculous standing in her sister's posh office in an outfit only a color-blind mole or a flamboyant rich woman would wear. She might have been better off just going naked. Her sister, on the other hand, looked stylish, as usual. She had class and elegance that helped to diffuse focus on her face. Like Jessie, she had plain features—ordinary brown eyes and a simple mouth—but her cheekbones were solid, and her eyes had a sparkling intelligence few could dispute. In her classic blue suit, accented with gold earrings and an emerald ring on her right hand, her looks were not an issue.

"I see," she said, going back to her contract. Her blunt, chin-length haircut fell around her face.

"But that's not the problem."

"What is it this time?" Michelle calmly asked, used to her sister's dramatics. She leaned back in her chair and crossed her arms, patiently waiting for her sister's latest story.

Jessie flopped into a chair like a deflated balloon. "First, I was fired."

Michelle fell forward, resting her forearms on the desk. "What? Do you know how hard it was for me to convince Montey to give you that job?"

"I know, I know." Jessie threw her hands in the air in a dismissive gesture. "But it wasn't my fault. Kenneth—"

Michelle shook her head and twirled a pen between her fingers. "Forget it. I don't want to hear it. So now you're unemployed."

"But that's not the problem."

Michelle tossed down her pen and pinched the bridge of her nose. "I can always count on you for a headache. What is it, then?"

Jessie bit her nails. "It wasn't really my fault," she began. "It's just that Deborah was insulting me. I had to do something."

"What happened?"

She leaned forward, resting her elbows on her knees. "She even insulted you too."

Michelle blinked, bored. "What happened?"

"Deborah dared me to get Kenneth Preston to fall in love with me. Well, not in love exactly," she amended. "But I have to charm him. She wants me to get him to invite me to the Hampton Charity Ball."

Michelle frowned, confused. "Why would she dare you to do that?"

Jessie shrugged. "I sort of set myself up," she admitted, looking down at her bitten nails. She had chewed them pretty badly on her way over. "They were talking about me—"

"Who's 'they'?"

"Deborah and Tracy."

"Oh, yes, the brilliant and influential minds of our society," Michelle muttered.

"Will you just let me finish my story?"

"Go ahead, but make it quick; I have an appointment at three."

Jessie glanced at her watch. "It's only one o'clock."

"I know. I'm hoping you'll finish this story sometime before then."

"Very funny," Jessie said, not amused at all.

Suddenly Michelle's buzzer rang. She softly swore and pressed the button harder than necessary. "Yes?"

"Your other sister is here to see you," her assistant replied.

Michelle sighed, resigned. "Send her in."

A few minutes later, Teresa made her entrance, carrying a bouquet of flowers. She had made it a habit of brightening Michelle's office with flowers every week. As the middle child, she had inherited the Cliftons' ordinary brown eyes and simple mouth, but she didn't have her sisters' temperament. Her face was round and soft instead of angular, and she had gentle eyes.

She unwrapped the sheer gold scarf she had tied around her head. "Oh, hi, Jessie," Teresa said. She grabbed a vase from the bookshelf and filled it with water in Michelle's small kitchen. "What are you doing here?" Teresa paused for a moment, then stuck her head out of the kitchen and glanced at her younger sister. She suddenly burst into laughter.

Jessie stiffened. "What's so funny?"

"What are you wearing? I never thought I would see you in flowers."

"And you'll never see me in them again. It's a long story."

"Sit down," Michelle said. "You're just in time to hear your sister's latest spectacle."

"I didn't make a spectacle of myself," Jessie argued.

"From what I—"

Teresa raised her voice. "What happened?"

Jessie sighed. The more she repeated the story, the more ridiculous it sounded. "I bet Deborah that I could charm any guy I wanted."

"Ah, but that's not all," Michelle added. "He has to ask her to the Hampton Charity Ball."

"Do you know how much that event costs?" Teresa asked, arranging the flowers in the vase. "Why would you say that?"

Jessie sighed. "Because she implied that she can and I can't."

"But you can't," Michelle said, trying to help her sister see reason.

"That's not the point. It's about pride, dignity."

Michelle drummed her fingers on the desk. "So you made this ridiculous bet with her in order to save your pride?"

"Yes."

"Go on. I'm afraid I'm beginning to understand your motives."

"So we decided to bet whether or not I could get any guy that danced with her. I really think it would have worked, but she set me up."

"How?" Teresa asked, leaving the flowers in the kitchen and taking a seat.

"She said that the next guy that asked her to dance would be the one. She neglected to tell me that she had already scheduled a dance with Kenneth."

Michelle nodded. "So you're supposed to try to get Kenneth to fall for you. Am I correct?"

"Yes."

"And ask you to the charity ball in a month...correct?"

Jessie nodded.

She rested back and clasped her hands behind her head. "The answer is simple."

Jessie leaned forward, desperate for any advice she could receive. "What is it?"

"Just tell Deborah that you changed your mind."

Jessie fell back in her chair and scowled. Teresa looked up at the ceiling and shook her head, her ponytail swinging back and forth like a wagging finger.

"I couldn't do that," Jessie scoffed. "That would be admitting defeat."

Michelle folded her arms. "It's a stupid dare. Besides, this isn't high school. What could she do to you?'

"She could gloat. Besides, if I lose, I have to be her housekeeper for a year and wear a uniform."

She held up her hands. "I'm sorry. I was wrong. This *is* high school."

"But if I win, I get the Sapphire Pendant."

Her sisters stared at her in silent awe.

Michelle finally shook her head, irritated that she had briefly entertained thoughts of winning. "It won't work."

Jessie turned to Teresa. "What do you think?"

Teresa thought for a moment, smoothing out her brightly colored gold-and-purple dress. The gold bracelets on her wrists gently clinked together. "Anything is possible. I think it's a sign. Gran Sonya had to seduce someone to get it, and now Jessie has to seduce Kenneth to get it back."

"Charm, not seduce."

Michelle snorted, resting her chin in her hand. "Since you two have obviously made up your minds, I can get back to work." She lifted up a business plan in front of her.

Jessie snatched it from her and scanned it. "The idea is good, but the plan will never work. I suggest you send them back and have them tighten their mission statement."

Michelle took the plan. "Don't think that because you took a few night classes in business, you are now an expert."

"She was only trying to help," Teresa said.

Jessie crossed her legs and swung her foot. "You don't think I can succeed in anything, do you?"

"That's not true," Michelle said.

"You blame me for losing the pendant. Dad wouldn't have had to sell it if it hadn't been for me. And you hate me for not keeping a job long enough to get it back."

Michelle scribbled down something. "You're wrong. I don't hate you and I don't blame you."

Jessie didn't believe her. "I will get it back. I have to."

Michelle shook her head.

"I need to do this, Mich," Jessie said, determined to make her sister understand. "It's our heritage, and I want to prove to Deborah and all the other hoity-toity girls that we can get guys too." *And I want to prove to you that I'm not a failure.*

Michelle lifted her head. "Why do you say 'we' like that?"

"They were insulting you too. And they think Teresa believes in voodoo!"

"Hey!" Teresa protested.

Michelle shrugged. "So what? They think all island immigrants are into that. It's just ignorance. Deborah and Tracy are no better or worse than we are."

"They're prettier and richer than we are," Teresa said.

"So?"

Jessie pounded her knee. "It's the principle."

Teresa nodded her head. "If it's important to Jessie, it should be important to us too."

Michelle glanced at both of her sisters and rubbed her forehead. She softened her voice. "Look, love, I know how much you want to win this dare, but…have you looked at yourself in the mirror lately? You're not exactly gorgeous."

Teresa rolled her eyes. "Mich, you're as tactful as a rock."

"What?"

Jessie slumped into her chair. "Was that supposed to make me feel better?"

Michelle shrugged. "I'm being honest."

"Dad said that charm and grace are more important than looks."

Michelle tapped a pen against her desk for a few moments, then flashed her sister a bland smile. "Jessie, let me tell you a little secret about Dad that I found out."

"What?"

"He lied to us."

Both Jessie and Teresa groaned. "You're so negative," they chorused.

"I'm not being negative." Michelle stood up and came from around her desk, addressing her sisters as if they were clients heading towards a bad business venture. "I'm being realistic."

"You sounded just like Mum," Jessie teased.

Michelle bristled at the comparison. Their mother had grown up with a harsh, well-intentioned nanny and had been schooled with strict headmasters in England, causing her to be a disciplinarian and a realist. Unfortunately, her emphasis on obedience at times overshadowed her genuine love for her children. Though Michelle loved her mother, she didn't wish to be compared to her.

"Kenneth Preston is a very attractive man," she continued. "He has a lot going for him: money, looks, and women. Deborah set you up because she knows you will fail. She couldn't even get him in college. He invited her once to the charity ball, and that was it. He's been surrounded by women all his life. What makes you think that you can catch him?"

"I have to try," Jessie said in a quiet voice.

"He's just a man," Teresa added. "Why couldn't she get him? Do you think he's too good for her?"

Michelle rested back against the desk and crossed her ankles. "Don't put words in my mouth. I'm just stating fact. We weren't born yesterday. We all know how the world works. The pretty girls get the princes, and we get the paupers." She suddenly grinned. "Fortunately, both are made exactly the same."

Teresa shook her head. "Oh, Mich, will you be serious?"

"I am being serious." She turned to Jessie. "You don't even like him. You never have."

That's where she was wrong. "That is beside the point. I hate losing, and my honor is at stake."

Michelle thought for a moment, adjusting the cuffs of her jacket. "Honor can be bought, you know."

"What are you talking about?"

She folded her arms. "I'm willing to pay Kenneth to go out with you."

Jessie jumped to her feet like a spring. "Have you gone completely mad?"

"No. You have. This is one of the silliest situations you have been involved in. Why can't you grow up?"

Jessie rested her hands on the desk. "Why? So that I can become a coldhearted workaholic like you?"

"As opposed to a hotheaded, lazy—"

"I am not lazy."

"If you could keep a job—"

Teresa pushed Jessie towards a chair. "You're both being childish."

"You're right." Michelle smoothed down her hair, containing herself. "I'm trying to help you, Jess. You shouldn't embarrass yourself just because some stupid girl insulted you. I don't want to see you get hurt. Just forget about the whole thing."

"I can't."

"Why should she?" Teresa asked. "If she wins, we get the pendant back for free."

Michelle glanced at the ceiling. "I wish you'd stop encouraging this."

"It sounds exciting." Teresa sighed wistfully. "It's about time one of us set our sights on a man."

"What for? So that we can prove to people who don't matter that we count?"

"No. I truly think that Jessie and Kenneth were meant to be together."

Michelle covered her face with her hand and moaned. "Why?"

"I saw their children as clear as day in a vision."

Jessie cringed. "Oh, not that again."

"Dad told me that my visions were real."

"Dad was a dreamer," Jessie reminded her. "Remember, he thought stones had magic."

"So do you. You can read them and tell fortunes."

Jessie shrugged. "A simple parlor trick. I size people up and tune into their fears. Anyone can do it."

"No, they can't. Your gift is real. Your fortunes usually come true, and Dad also told us a lot of things that came true."

Michelle dismissed the statement with an impatient gesture. "Coincidence."

Teresa sighed in defeat. She stood and went to the neglected flowers in the kitchen. "I don't know why you don't think that Jessie can pull this off."

"I have explained my reasons."

"I know. Okay, so we're not the best-looking girls." She placed the vase on Michelle's desk, then sent her sister a sly grin. "You married James."

Michelle froze at the name of her estranged husband and nervously twisted the ring on her finger. She pushed herself off the desk and went to grab a book from the shelf. "He was a mistake." She opened the book and began flipping through its pages.

"So? He married you and he was *gorgeous*," she said, dragging out the last word like a lovesick teenager.

Jessie gave a low whistle in agreement. "I didn't know a man could look that good. You really hit the jackpot."

Michelle snapped the book shut. "But as you can see, I also went bankrupt."

"Are you ever going to tell us what happened?"

"I told you that we were not compatible."

"That was evident from the beginning, but you still married him."

"Wealthy James Winfield," Teresa remembered. "Mum and Dad were so proud. I miss him."

Michelle shoved the book back into place. "Look, we are not discussing me or my…or him. We're discussing Jessie."

"We're not expecting Jessie to date Kenneth, just charm him. If you could charm a handsome devil like James, then obviously you can give her some pointers."

"James was an accident." Her sisters stared at her, unconvinced. She tried another angle. "Jessie, do you think that Kenneth is going to forget that you've always tormented him?"

"'Tormented' is a harsh word," Jessie said.

"How about 'harass'?"

"Oh, come on Mich, that was in high school," Teresa protested.

"All I'm saying is that I wouldn't fall for a woman who bumped into me and made me drop things, set weird objects on my chair, glued my books together, hid my homework, or put pepper on my food."

Jessie pulled on her fingers. "He liked the pepper."

"That's not the point. You made his life hell."

Teresa grimaced. "Yes, I guess 'torment' would be a good word."

"He made my life miserable too," Jessie defended. "If Mum wasn't comparing me to either of you, she was comparing me to him. 'Why can't you be smart like Kenneth?'" she mimicked. "'Why can't you be graceful like Kenneth?' And he knew I was the one who harassed him, but he never told on me."

Michelle shivered in mockery. "Ooh, what an ogre."

"And he offered to tutor you in French your senior year so that you could pass," Teresa added.

Jessie grew quiet. That had been the year she had fallen in love with him; the next year, she would hate him with a passion that still burned. "What's past is past. I am going to win this bet for the sake of the pendant."

Teresa placed her hands on her hips. "Jessie's right. We have a chance we may never get again."

"So you'll help me?" she asked, raising her eyes to meet Teresa's.

"Yes."

Both women turned to Michelle expectantly. Michelle shook her head. "Okay, I'll help for the sake of the pendant," she said with reluctance. "But I think we're going to regret this."

Chapter Four

To say that Kenneth was in a bad mood the next day would be to underestimate the seething anger he kept hidden underneath his cool features. Why was that woman able to get to him? Ever since yesterday's meeting, he had not been able to get Jasmine out of his mind—her messy black hair, or how she had tried to blink away the tears he had inflicted from her eyes. He had gone too far, but so had she. They just seemed to bring out the worst in each other. And yet he remembered that brief moment of amity, her soft smile and how good it felt to know that it was meant for him…only him. He yanked at his tie and looked down at a profit-and-loss report. He had to focus. He had to stop thinking about her, stop thinking about her hands, how her lips would feel on his, or her…He swore.

"That's not the kind of welcome I expected, Mr. Boss," Nathan Phillips greeted him, closing the door behind him with artistic flair. He had been Kenneth's college roommate and was now CFO at Radson Electronics and Software. His easy smile and charming personality proved a healthy balance for Kenneth's more serious nature. "Hey, thanks for letting me borrow your car the other day."

Kenneth shrugged. "Do we have an appointment?" He glanced at his watch, which usually alerted him to such events.

"No, but we do need to talk." Nathan sat. He adjusted the lapels on his bright-green jacket, a surprising complementary color against his cocoa skin.

"Is everything on schedule?"

"The programmers' meeting went very well. We discussed why there might be a delay in running programs on our systems, and R&D

is already proposing a new project, which we could get funding for." He stretched out his legs and crossed them at the ankles. He stared at his reflection in his shiny black shoes and straightened his tie.'"But of course you knew that, since you were there."

Kenneth studied his friend for a moment with a mixture of amusement and annoyance. "Right, so what do you want to talk about?"

"Invis Electronics."

Kenneth was thinking of purchasing the small electronics company. "Yes, what about it?"

"I want to handle it." Nathan kept his hard, hooded gaze on him. Most people turned away from him at this point, but Kenneth merely smiled, amused that his friend would attempt to intimidate him.

"I'm handling it. What could your reservations be? Granted it's been losing revenue because of some antiquated thinking, but I can fix that with good management. The company has a long history, strong sales, good location—"

"I know, I know."

"Brooke went on a site visit. I will later. We've done a thorough analysis of the company's strengths and weaknesses. I've met with the owners—"

Nathan sat up, ready to defend his case. "I'm not challenging your methods or implying that you haven't done your homework. I just have doubts. I think I should devote my time to this project so that you can do other things. Look, I have college degrees, just like you, and it would be nice if you'd actually let me use my knowledge for once."

He returned to the report in front of him. "Brooke recommended the company after months of searching, so I'm already supervising her to handle it. Things seem to be going as planned."

"Yes, that's what I'm afraid of."

Kenneth gave Nathan his full attention. He wouldn't agree with him, but he would listen. He nodded, gesturing for Nathan to speak.

Nathan stood up, ready to display the cunning charisma he used in getting financial backing for a company endeavor. "Try to see the big picture." He fanned his hand through the air. "You have a lot on your plate." He began to count them off on his fingers. "Meetings, conferences, presentations, a social life that's in desperate need of CPR."

Kenneth didn't blink. Nathan continued, "Plus the board isn't completely behind you on this. Some want you to consider the bid from Draxton."

"I'm not selling the company."

"When the board votes in August, you may not have a choice."

He sighed. The last meeting had been disappointing. Despite his success, he knew he would always have to prove he was worthy of their trust. The privately held company was not used to outsiders running the business. "We will not sell."

Nathan licked his lips. "That's all well and good, but the truth is that I've heard rumors that IE—"

"You know what I think of rumors," Kenneth said, narrowing his eyes. The wrong information could destroy a company, and any successful person knew there were people ready to see you fall. "I have my informers."

"I know, but you—"

"Brooke has assured me that everything is okay. I will handle things in due time."

"Why wait? Why not just let me handle it? Why do you have to handle everything yourself?"

"Because I can."

Nathan shoved his hands in his pockets and sighed fiercely. "Sometimes I think you take the nickname Mr. Perfect too seriously."

Kenneth returned to his computer and began typing.

Unfazed, Nathan continued. He rested his hands on the desk and lowered his voice. "The computer delays will only give them more fuel."

"I will handle it."

"Let my brother Rodney look into it. You can trust him to do a good job."

Kenneth nodded. "I wouldn't have hired him if I thought otherwise."

"You need to spend more time covering your back. Despite what you think, you're still not completely welcome here. There are many people hiding knives…like Stephanie and Brooke."

"They are not a concern."

"Their father owned this company; they should have our jobs. Hell, the only reason I'm here is because Radson thought he owed my father a favor and he gave us shares in the company. I'm there for you, but you act as if you trust them more than me. Even though—"

"I don't trust anyone," Kenneth interrupted, his voice suspiciously neutral. "However, I don't make accusations unless there's a reason to."

Nathan opened his mouth to say more, but finally shook his head in defeat.

"Hey, Jessie, you're looking glum," Wendy said, performing a crossed-leg stretch in preparation for their tennis match. "Still upset about getting fired?"

"I shouldn't be. Waitressing isn't the greatest job. Remember when we had to dress up like fairies for Catherine McBride's first birthday?"

"I still have nightmares."

They both cringed in remembrance.

"No, I'm not upset," Jessie said. "I just have a lot on my mind, so I'm not in the best of moods." She flexed her ankles.

"*Bien.*" Wendy pulled a sweatband over her hair. "You're at your best when you're in a bad mood."

"Thank you for your show of concern."

Wendy grinned. "You know, we're catering another event in a week. I could talk to—"

"Thanks, but for now, my catering days are over."

"You know, if you need a companion, Bruce and I still have some puppies left."

Jessie glanced at the half-naked man dousing himself with water. "Did you have to bring him?"

"I didn't *bring* him. He's not a dog."

She opened her mouth, then closed it. She didn't like Bruce, who only grunted when spoken to and loved himself more than anyone. The reply was too tempting. "I can't afford a puppy anyway."

"They're free."

Jessie laughed. "I can hardly feed myself, but thanks anyway." She sighed. "I made an idiot of myself again."

"How?"

"I bet Deborah that I could get Kenneth to ask me to the Hampton Charity Ball."

Wendy stared. "Kenneth? The man you've hated forever?"

Jessie glanced at her bandaged left hand. "Yes."

"She set you up, didn't she?" Wendy asked, used to Deborah's conniving ways.

"Yes…no. I should have known better."

"Fortunately, if anyone can pull it off, it's you. We both know how much you hate losing."

Jessie smiled, feeling her confidence heighten. "Yes, so let me start by beating you."

It was a strenuous and exhilarating game. Towards the end, Jessie was soaking with sweat, but her mind was clear and her trembling muscles were alive. Somehow she would figure out how to manage her social life. Then she saw him: the one flaw in her future plans.

Kenneth was jogging around the park, with the sunlight falling on him like a spotlight. He wore a light, long-sleeved shirt and sweatpants. His body was well-hidden, but she knew he had a great physique. She remembered the broadness of his shoulders. She imagined the muscles in his back constricting and relaxing, rivers of sweat sliding down his chest like water over rocks. He had everything. Why would he look at her? How could she ever try to capture his attention, especially after being mean to him for so long? What could she possibly do to get his attention?

"Jessie! Look out!"

The warning came too late. Jessie saw the green blur of the tennis ball coming towards her, then darkness.

She felt like she was floating, being cradled like a baby in the arms of a cloud. There were voices: one anxious, one soothing. She pushed them to the back of her mind, not wanting to interrupt the peace she felt. She released a sigh of contentment. The arms put her down, and she felt a light, feathery touch on her forehead. Then a hand slapped her across the cheek. Her eyes flew open; she glared into Kenneth's smug face.

"Did you enjoy doing that?" she demanded.

His eyes were alive with devilment. "More than you would know." His face suddenly grew serious. "How does your head feel?"

"Fine." She sat up, but had to grab onto his arm when the world began to spin.

"You need to go to the doctor to make sure that you don't have a concussion." He pulled a blade of grass and a leaf out of her hair. "I'd offer to take you, but I know how much you enjoy my presence."

She was going to say something biting, but instantly realized that this was the perfect opportunity to change her ways. "No, I wouldn't mind."

Kenneth paused, his eyes worried. "You must have hit your head pretty hard. It actually sounded like you were being nice to me."

Jessie clenched her jaw and attempted a smile. "Are you going to take me to the doctor's or not?"

He lifted her in his arms as if she were a sack of flour. There was no romance or care in the gesture.

"Put me down." She tried to wiggle out of his grasp. "I can walk, you know."

He nodded, casually shifting her weight. "I know. You'd better stop wiggling, or I may drop you."

"Just let me down."

He abruptly loosened his grip, and Jessie frantically circled her arms around his neck to keep from falling to the ground like a rock.

He laughed with masculine pride, tightening his hold. "Now look who's hanging on."

"Will you please—"

"Just be quiet, or I'll throw you over my shoulder instead."

"You wouldn't."

He lifted an eyebrow.

"Yes, you would," she amended in a dry tone. She turned away from him and noticed a couple watching them with curious intensity. As they drew closer, she recognized them: Montey and his wife.

"My dear girl, are you all right?" Annabelle asked, coming up to them.

Montey frowned, masking his concern. "She's a walking accident, I tell you."

"Montey, hush. What happened?"

"She tried to butt a tennis ball with her face," Kenneth replied.

Jessie was outraged. "That's not—"

"But she'll be fine," he continued.

Montey's frown deepened, and Annabelle looked at Jessie as if she were ready to offer her last rites. They walked on, muttering to each other.

Jessie buried her face in his neck. "Montey already thinks I'm a complete flake, and now this proves it. Can my life get any more embarrassing?"

Kenneth didn't respond. He couldn't. He was vexed that he liked the feeling of holding her. She felt so solid, yet soft, and her skin was warm against his, like the pleasing comfort a blanket gives on a chilly night. He enjoyed how her head fit perfectly against his neck, the smooth slope of her nose, the electric brush of her eyelashes; the touch of her hair against his face felt like a whisper of hidden gentleness.

He glanced down at her. Her whole body had a healthy, glossy sheen of morning dew. He bit his lip, struggling with the urge to taste her, nibble on her ear. She had pretty ears—intricate, small, refined. His thoughts quickly jumped to other areas he could nibble on. Her chest was pressed against his own.

He felt his lower body tighten and inwardly groaned. He had been alone too long to start fantasizing about her. If she discovered that he had any attraction to her, she would probably slug him. Annoyed with himself, he unceremoniously let her go when they reached his black BMW, causing her to stagger against it.

"You'd think I was some sort of disease," Jessie said, regaining her balance. "I didn't ask you to carry me."

He opened the door. "Just get in the car."

She stared at him for a moment, wondering why his mood had become so sullen, and then finally got into his car.

Chapter Five

She didn't have a concussion, but she was going to have a nasty bruise.

"Where do you want me to take you now?" Kenneth asked, leading her to his car. He decided to let her walk this time, and placed plenty of distance between them.

"Home, I guess." Her plan wasn't working. Anytime she tried to get close to him, he moved away. In the waiting room, when she had sat next to him, he had stood up to look at pictures; when she went to talk to him about a particular picture, he said he wanted to read. Now he walked parallel with her, making sure there was a car between them. She didn't know the next step to take.

"You guess?" he said. "You don't know?"

"No, I don't know, all right," she snapped.

He opened the car door.

She bit her lower lip and got in the car, slamming the door. Damn it! Why couldn't she just be nice? Here she had the perfect opportunity to charm him, and she was snapping at him like a crab. There was no way she was going to get Mr. Perfect to ask her to the charity ball at this rate. Her head was killing her, and her annoyance wasn't helping. She shut her eyes and tried to collect her thoughts.

The car seat was comfortable, and she was in danger of falling asleep in exhaustion and defeat. The car reflected its owner: neither had any visible flaws. It smelled fresh, and had clean gray carpets and spotless windows. No doubt he tended to its maintenance daily, unlike her own car, which screamed for attention by refusing to start on cold mornings. She wondered what name he had given it. She shook her head and winced. She had to focus. She had to think about something on which to compliment him.

"Thanks…for doing this," she said, rubbing the back of her neck.

He shrugged.

"I know how much you dislike me, so I want you to know that I really appreciate it."

He sent her a sharp glance, but still said nothing. He put the key in the ignition, then paused. "I suggest you put your seatbelt on."

Her charm wasn't working. She rested her head against the window, wondering how other women would handle the situation. They definitely wouldn't be talking about seatbelts right now. "Ah, what's the point? Flying through the windshield might do me some good."

Her attempt at flippancy only annoyed him more. "The point is that I don't want to see you flying through the windshield and getting blood in my car." He reached across her and grabbed the seatbelt with a vigorous yank.

Jessie sniffed. "It figures you would say something like that."

His eyes locked onto hers like handcuffs. "Why?"

She didn't reply. For one panicked moment, Jessie thought she would go into cardiac arrest. He was so close—too close. His sleeve softly brushed her arm, and his completely male scent enveloped her senses. His eyes were mesmerizing and melting her body's normal defense system. They continued to stare at each other. Their breaths mingled in the air, like a kiss waiting to be shared. The mood was quickly broken when Kenneth turned and connected the seatbelt.

"That's better," he said in a rough tone.

She only nodded, thinking she must have hit her head harder than she had thought to be entertaining such ideas.

She rested her head against the seat. Perhaps she could get his sympathy by playing the poor invalid. She placed the back of her hand to her forehead, as she'd seen some heroines do in the old movies Teresa liked to watch. "My head aches so much."

"You've been knocked out by worse," he said flatly. "Fortunately, you have a hard head. But if it's a killer, there's some aspirin in the glove compartment."

Jessie felt her face grow hot, but she successfully kept her mouth closed. That callous reply, though typical, was not what she was aiming for. She counted to ten. By eight, her temper had cooled. She tried another tactic.

"You know it was really...comforting to have you as my rescuer. You're very strong." She nearly gagged on the saccharine tone and silly words, but she had heard Deborah use the technique successfully on occasion. "I mean, I know I'm no lightweight."

He adjusted his rear-view mirror. "Yes, you can say that again. You don't look heavy, but you're pretty substantial."

Jessie took a deep breath. "Yes, but you didn't complain."

He turned to her, surprised. Jessie smiled and lifted an eyebrow, attempting to look coy.

Kenneth's jaw twitched, then he made a sudden U-turn.

"Where are you going?" Jessie asked, holding onto the door handle as the car spun in the other direction, its tires squealing in protest.

"I'm taking you back to the doctor's. You're acting funny. They must have missed something."

"I'm just trying to be nice."

"Like I said, you're acting funny."

Jessie's eyes flashed. "Listen here, Mr. Perfect—"

He suddenly grinned, relieved. "Ah, yes. This is the Jasmine I know."

"My name is Jessie. Why do you enjoy provoking me?"

"Come, now, just the sight of me annoys you."

She stared out the window. "That's not true."

"It's been true since I've known you."

"No, it hasn't." She tried to rub away the tension building in her neck.

"Now you're making your headache worse," he accused. He opened his glove compartment, and a handful of condoms fell into Jessie's lap.

"What the—?" Jessie picked up one of the colorful assortment. "Haven't we been busy!"

"They're not mine," Kenneth quickly explained. "My friend's car was in the shop, so I let him borrow mine."

Jessie couldn't ignore the red that colored his cheeks. She shoved the condoms back into the glove compartment and closed it.

"Wait, I didn't get the aspirin," he said.

"No, that's all right. My headache is gone." She checked his sun visor, then hers.

"What are you doing?"

"Checking to see what other surprises you might have. Edible panties, licorice whips, maybe some KY Jelly."

Kenneth's color deepened. "You're not going to find anything. I'm a pretty dull guy."

"So at what time did you tuck in your date the other night?"

"She was just a favor." He didn't know why he felt the need to explain. "Her parents are family friends and want her introduced to the right people."

That gave her an idea. "Speaking of people, you haven't seen my sisters in a long time."

"I've seen them both recently."

"Oh. Well, how would you like to come over for dinner sometime?"

He turned to her, suspicious. "Why?"

"Because it's a nice thing to do."

He looked back at the road. "I know that, but why are you asking *me* in particular?"

She stirred uneasily in her seat. "I want to thank you."

"You already have."

"I mean formally. I'm not too bad a cook...or, if you want, Teresa could cook an excellent pepper-pot stew."

Kenneth tightened his grip around the steering wheel. He had a wild desire to say yes, just to shock her, but he knew she was up to something. After falling for a number of her pranks, he knew the pattern. "It's a nice offer, but I'm really busy at the moment."

"Of course," she said, attempting to appear nonchalant. Inside, she was burning like a lit oil spill. He was turning her down, rejecting her like a bad credit card. She felt like crawling out the door and scraping her pride off the road. He probably never would turn Deborah down, or Tracy, or the infant he took to the Ashford mansion. "You could have just said no, instead of offering a lame excuse that you're busy. We're not friends, so you don't have to use your nice-guy act with me."

"Nice-guy act?" He smiled blandly. "Now, what's that supposed to mean?"

"It means that I, unlike most people, know the truth."

He rubbed his chin, trying to loosen his tightening jaw. "And what would that be?"

"That you're a fake. That you're hiding the real you under a facade. You play the game all other guys play, but you disguise it so cleverly. You use people—"

He changed gears with more force than necessary. "I've never used anyone."

"You used me."

He softly swore, but kept his voice level. "Look, you've got it all wrong. You always have."

"I don't want to talk about it."

He stared at her, incredulous. "You're the one who brought it up."

"Will you please look at the road?"

He did, glancing up at the street sign. "Aw, hell, I'm going the wrong way." Again he made a sudden U-turn.

"Do you always drive like this?" She held onto the door handles, her knuckles pale from strain.

"Only with you in the car."

"I'm glad to know I have such an effect on you. I'd probably crash into a tree on purpose."

"Jasmine—"

"Don't call me that!"

"Why not? It's your name, isn't it?" He paused. "It's a beautiful name."

She laughed without humor. "Yes, my father had a sense of humor."

"What's wrong with being called Jasmine?"

"How would you like me to call you—"

"Don't," he warned, knowing the name that was on her lips.

It took an extra amount of restraint not to call him Kenny, the name for which he had given two boys bloody noses. No one could figure out why it bothered him so much.

"Then you understand," she said.

"Fine, then. *Jessie,* we need to talk—"

"I don't want to talk about it."

"That's because you enjoy being angry with me. You don't want to know the truth."

"The truth is that you hurt me like no one ever has, and you betrayed me." Her voice was almost a whisper. "That's all I need to know."

Kenneth stared ahead at the smooth surface of the road until flashes of stars fell between his eyes. He squinted. Oh, hell, he wasn't breathing again. He took a deep breath. Many thoughts crashed in his mind, but he couldn't find the words to express them. They always came to the edge of discussing what had happened, but somehow she always pushed it to a standstill. It lingered between them like the scent of a rotten dish, at times faint, but still hanging in the air to be remembered.

They spent the rest of the drive in silence. Kenneth turned on the radio, but neither listened to the soothing sound of the steel pan filling the air, too wrapped in their own thoughts to care. He dropped her off in front of her house, drumming his fingers on the steering wheel, determined not to say another word.

"Thank you," she grumbled, opening the door.

She broke his resolve with those two words. Though they were spoken reluctantly, he felt that maybe he had a chance to redeem himself. He grabbed her hand.

Jessie's first instinct was to pull away, but she didn't. She looked down at his hand and wondered if she had suffered a concussion, something to explain the strange fluttering in her stomach and heart. She turned to him, her eyes questioning.

"I know I'm asking too much of you, but one day—it doesn't matter when—just one day, would you allow me to explain what happened?"

She opened her mouth to say no, that no excuse he gave would make her forgive him, but instead of a cutting remark, she found herself nodding. His face split into a brilliant grin—his special grin.

"That doesn't mean I'll believe you," she said.

He let her hand go, and just as quickly as the smile had come, it disappeared. "And don't expect me not to know you're up to something."

She winked with teasing malice. "It gives me a strange pleasure to know I can still make you nervous."

"Don't think I won't figure it out."

"I'll let you do that."

Jessie didn't know why his suspicion annoyed her. She got out of the car and walked up the porch steps of the house she shared with her sisters. Her calm demeanor hid the anger inside. How dare he be so confident that she was up to something! Okay, so she was up to something, but he had no right to suspect her.

Both Michelle and Teresa met her at the door as Kenneth's car wheels accelerated, kicking up gravel.

"Wendy called me and told me what happened," Michelle said.

"We brought your car home," Teresa added.

Jessie nodded, then winced. "Thanks."

"Are you all right?" She put her arm around Jessie's shoulders.

Jessie shut the door, feeling suddenly drained. "I'm fine." Why couldn't she have had a romantic accident, like getting hit by a car while saving a child's life, instead of getting knocked out by a tennis ball?

"So, how did it go with Prince Charming?" Teresa asked.

"It didn't go anywhere. I asked him over for dinner, but he refused." That fact still stung.

Michelle laughed. "He was probably afraid you would poison him."

"Michelle!" Teresa scolded.

"Well, at least you got his attention," she said, leading her sister into the kitchen. "I have to say...that was very clever of you."

Jessie scowled. "I didn't do it on purpose."

"I know. That's what makes it so perfect." She gently pushed her into a chair. "Wendy told me that he carried you off the court into the shade of a maple tree. She said it all looked very romantic. I'm sure you would have enjoyed it too." She grinned maliciously. "Had you been conscious."

Chapter Six

The shower's hot water stung his skin without mercy. Kenneth stuck his head under the rush and closed his eyes in a fruitless attempt to douse his temper—or whatever it was that made blood rush to his brain and other parts of his anatomy. Damn that woman! She was taunting him, and she was the only woman who could. It didn't make sense.

He shut off the shower and grabbed a large towel. He wrapped it around his waist, then went to the mirror and wiped off the condensation. He stared at his reflection through the haze. She thought he was a fraud; she was too close to the truth. He turned away and turned off the lights.

He toweled himself dry, threw the towel in the direction of his bed, then watched it slide off and land on the floor. He went to his dresser and began to change. For all he had accomplished, there were certain things he could never change. No amount of money could alter his past. That fact still bothered him. Once dressed, he went downstairs to his desk.

He just wanted a chance to explain, but he knew there was no excuse that would make her forgive him for first standing her up on prom night, and then seeing him with another girl on the same evening. Unfortunately, he couldn't tell her why; he wasn't sure he could trust her. He wasn't sure he *wanted* to trust her. He sat at his desk, burying his face in his hands when the memories came back, as they always did, unwanted guests of his battered conscience.

He remembered the pale peach walls of the high school, and resting against them as security passed. He had successfully avoided them and found Jessie at her locker before the class bell rang.

"We need to talk," he had said.

Her hair was short at the time, and she had worn a baggy tracksuit. Her eyes, once so lively, were dark. "Leave me alone."

He had grabbed her wrist, desperately hoping she would give him a chance to explain, hoping that he could miraculously come up with the perfect word or statement that would make her stay. "Jas, please don't go. Give me a chance to—"

"Let me go, or I'll hurt you," she had warned.

He had wanted her to hurt him, to pound his chest and get all the anger out of her, so that he would get a chance to explain. But her eyes had blazed with such anger that he had known it was hopeless. He had released her wrist and watched her run down the hall, wiping away tears with the back of her hand.

He let his hands fall to the desk and stared up at the ceiling, waiting for the memories to fade away, as they always did.

The doorbell rang while he was reading *Business Week*. He ignored it, focusing on Beethoven's heavy piano concerto blasting from his speakers. It was the only music that was able to drive certain thoughts from his mind.

The doorbell rang again.

He turned down the volume and went to the door. "Who is it?" he asked, seeing nothing but a small blue cap through the peephole.

"It's me, Uncle Ken," a soft voice replied.

He opened the door and stared down at his ten-year-old niece. She stood on the doorstep with a huge green backpack and a suitcase with a handle that was threatening to break. The suitcase itself was being held together by packing tape stretched twice around the middle. His eyebrows shot up. "Ace, what are you doing here?"

She lifted her suitcase and went inside. She was a sturdy-looking kid with a proud heart-shaped face and sharp brown eyes, which she hid under a blue baseball cap—today turned backwards. "I came for a visit."

Kenneth shut the door behind her and scratched his head. "Your father didn't call to tell me that he was sending you."

"Well...that's what I'm here to talk about."

"I see." He took the suitcase from her; the handle immediately ripped and the bag fell to the ground. Kenneth pushed it against the wall with his foot. "Are you hungry?"

"A little."

"Come on, then."

Fortunately, his housekeeper kept his fridge full, so he was able to make her a chicken sandwich and lemonade. He put the food in front of her, sat down and waited for her to explain. When she didn't say anything, he spoke. "Okay, what's going on?"

Ace avoided his gaze. "Yum. This sandwich is very good, Uncle."

"I'm glad you like it." He rested his forearms on the table, prepared to stay there until he got the entire story. "A year has passed by, and I'm still waiting."

Ace reluctantly put the sandwich down. "All right. I admit it. I ran away."

It wasn't the first time, but she had never run to him before. Her father lived in Georgia, which was quite a distance from this Maryland town. "How did you get here?"

"Greyhound."

"They just let a kid take the Greyhound across states?"

Ace shrugged. "Hey, as long as you have the money, they don't ask questions. From there, I took a taxi."

"Where did you get the money?"

She took a bite of her sandwich and chewed for a moment. "I saved. I had a job."

"Doing what? What kind of job would they give you?"

"Retrieving stolen items."

Kenneth stared at her for a moment, hoping he had misunderstood her. "What?"

Ace licked her lips. "Promise you won't get mad."

He sighed. He must have spent all his anger today. "Just tell me."

Her words came out slowly. "You know how people, when they lose things, they'll put up reward money?"

He nodded.

"I figured that if I returned their things to them, I'd get the reward money, but I'd have to steal it first."

Kenneth covered his face and groaned.

"You aren't angry, are you?"

"Strangely, no."

"I gave it all back," she said, after a relieved sigh. "I just took little things, like jewelry and pets. Pets were the easiest, because animals like me."

Kenneth rested his chin in his hand. "Business is closed permanently now, right? Nobody's dog is suddenly going to go missing?"

She lifted her sandwich and took a large bite. "Nope. Now that I'm here, I'm fine. I'm really glad to see you." She smiled, looking like a chipmunk with its cheeks filled with nuts. "I'm—"

"Don't talk with your mouth full."

She swallowed. "Dad does."

"Well, I'm not talking about your dad. I don't want you to."

"I'll do anything you say," she promised. "I am really glad to see you."

"I know, little dove." He patted her cheek. "I'm glad to see you too, but your dad's probably worried about you."

Her smile quickly disappeared, like a passing wind. "Nah, I left him a note."

"How long were you planning to visit?"

"Not long. Perhaps five years or so. Then I can get a real job and move out."

Kenneth fell back in his chair, as if a boxer had hit him with a mighty punch. He wouldn't overreact. He would have a mild stroke, maybe a heart attack, but he wouldn't overreact. "You mean you've come here to stay?"

"Just till I'm grown," she assured him. "I won't be any trouble, I promise."

"What's wrong with home?" He knew the answer, but asked anyway.

Ace's serious eyes grew hard, making her look much older. "Because I hate it there. Anyway, Dad doesn't want me. I was a mistake, remember?"

Kenneth stood to get something to drink, his mouth suddenly dry. "Your father wasn't thinking when he said that."

"That's because he was drunk," she spat out in a bitter tone. "He's always drunk."

Kenneth banged his cup against the counter, annoyed that it was plastic. He felt like shattering something. His younger brother had a serious alcohol problem, but no one could seem to get through to him. He shook his head. "Ace, I'm a busy man. I don't know what to do with kids." He poured his drink and took a healthy swallow.

She came over to him and touched his sleeve. "I won't be any trouble. I don't eat much, and I'm clean, and I'll help out. I'll be so good, you won't even know I'm here." She looked up. Her eyes pleaded with him.

Kenneth stared out the window, shaking his head. He loved her, but she wasn't his. He remembered the first time he'd held her, felt the soft curls on her head and looked at her tiny brown eyes, hoping the world would be kind. He'd wanted her, but couldn't have her, and as time passed, he knew it had been for the best. He had been young and struggling, and hadn't had much to offer.

Now he had the money, but not the time or the temperament. He couldn't be a father. What if he unintentionally hurt her? He would never forgive himself. But he couldn't send her back right away. He needed to think of something.

She tugged on his sleeve again. "Please don't make me go back." Her voice shook, but she steadied it. "I came all this way. Please."

He took off her hat. Her hair needed to be washed. Her jeans hung over her shoes, and her shirt smelled musky, like it hadn't been washed in a while. He cupped her chin and stared into her face. His voice lowered. "It got really bad, huh?"

"Dad sprained his ankle because he was so drunk that he tripped over his slippers and fell down the stairs." She covered her mouth and laughed, but it wasn't a beautiful sound; it attacked Kenneth's ears like nails against a chalkboard. He knew her pain and the terrible demon that trapped them both.

"Well, you won't see me doing that," he replied grimly. "For now, you can stay here. But I can't tell you that it will be fun."

Ace nodded. "I'm glad I'm here. I hate my dad."

"No. Don't say that." Her words were like a lost echo in his mind.

"Why not? It's true."

"Because it hurts your spirit."

"Really?"

"Yes, really." He gave her back her hat. "And you're here because you're visiting me. Nobody needs to know you ran away."

"Okay."

"Why don't you take a shower before going to bed?"

Ace backed away from him, embarrassed. "I must smell pretty gross, huh?"

He gave her a lopsided grin. "We all smell gross once in a while, but don't wash your hair yet. When Ms. Rose comes, she can help you with that."

Kenneth showed her where she would stay and the toiletries. When she was ready for bed, he tucked her in. She wrapped her arms around his neck. "I'm so glad I'm here with you."

He held her close for a moment, inhaling the clean scent of Ivory soap, wishing he could repeat the same sentiments. If only he could offer her more than her father did. He loved his niece, but she posed a problem: a painful reminder of things he couldn't change, a reminder of a past that would always haunt him. And the possibility that he might not be good for her. He kissed her forehead. "Go to sleep."

She rested back on the pillows and did.

Kenneth went to his bedroom and moved a game piece on his chessboard. He had been playing himself for two months and seemed to be at a standstill. He stared at the board. What was he going to do with her? School was closed for the summer, and she wasn't sociable enough for camp. There were camp counselors somewhere, still recovering from their encounter with Ace Preston.

He had to find someone to look after her while he was at work. Ms. Rose was busy enough. He couldn't put an extra burden on her. He would have to tell his assistant to find someone, someone discreet who wouldn't use this family situation to their own advantage, someone who could take Ace's tricks…but most of all, someone kind, someone she could trust. He turned off the light and climbed into bed. He would speak to Ms. Mathew tomorrow.

"I blew up in his face like a volcano. I can't seem to help it," Jessie complained at breakfast two days later. The summer's warm breath seeped through the open window of the breakfast nook where the three sisters ate. The morning sun peered through like a stray cat, while the overhead fan gave a gentle wind and enhanced the smell of chamomile tea and blueberry pancakes.

"Could you pass me the salt?" Michelle asked Teresa.

Teresa gave it to her. "Could you hand me the butter?"

"Sure."

"These eggs are delicious."

"Thanks." Teresa went on to discuss the ingredients she had used.

Jessie watched the dull exchange for a moment, then pounded her hand on the table, rattling the dishes. "Isn't anyone listening to me? I've got a problem."

"The problem is that destructive temper of yours," Michelle said, calmly salting her eggs.

Jessie narrowed her eyes and clenched her fist. "I don't have a destructive temper."

Michelle sniffed. "Right, and I'm Cleopatra. Everyone knows the Clifton sisters have tempers." She raised her teacup, as if offering a toast. "It's our claim to fame."

"He's a fraud."

"That's not the point. You need him to fall for you, and you've already lost time. You'll have to ask for a job. I think a couple of administrative positions have opened up."

"Work for him? No way."

Teresa poured syrup on her pancakes, then took a bite. She chewed thoughtfully. "You need to have an excuse to see him."

"He's the reason you were fired, so he owes you a job," Michelle said. "I heard that he has a position he must fill. I didn't get the details, but it sounded interesting. Just say you'll take it."

"Yes. This is a great opportunity. Try not to lose your temper, and something good might come out of it."

Jessie frowned. "Like what?"

"You might get employed again, instead of hanging about here,"

Michelle said. She stared at Jessie critically. "You'll have to borrow one of my suits."

"I'm not wearing a skirt."

"No one is asking you to," Teresa said soothingly. "But at some point you'll have to show some leg." She lifted up a leg of Jessie's sweatpants. "You have nice ones."

"Maybe even some cleavage," Michelle added.

Jessie glared at her.

"In spite of all the baggy clothes you wear, I know that you have breasts."

"I am not—"

"Let's take this one step at a time," Teresa interrupted. "Everything will be revealed in due time."

Michelle laughed. Jessie scowled.

After breakfast, Michelle helped Jessie put on a nice cream suit and pulled her hair back into a bun. She put on a dab of lipstick and highlighted her eyes. Jessie looked at herself in the mirror.

"I look like you!" she cried.

Michelle frowned. "What's wrong with that?"

"I'm supposed to attract him, not try to take his job."

"You're going for a job interview. You need to look efficient."

"Teresa, say something," Jessie pleaded.

"The makeup could be stronger." She grabbed the tube of lipstick.

Michelle shook her head. "If you go there like a painted doll, the assistant is going to see right through you and not let you in."

"A little makeup won't hurt," Teresa said, applying more lipstick. "Now, remember to look inviting."

"How?"

"Use those expressive eyebrows of yours, and flutter your eyelashes."

"And moan and whimper," Michelle added sarcastically.

Both sisters glared at her.

"You're not helping," Teresa said. "Have you forgotten what's at stake?"

"Her pride, her dignity, her self-respect, her—"

Teresa turned to Jessie. "Just remember to smile. Give him compliments."

"And if all else fails," Michelle said, brushing some lint off her shoulder, "knock him over the head and hope he develops amnesia."

Chapter Seven

The lights were cruelly bright in the elegant ladies' room of Radson Electronics and Software. The harsh overhead glare made Jessie's face look like a mannequin, and already strands of hair were escaping her bun. She sighed and attempted to brush the strands back into place. She was about to swear in frustration when she noticed a little boy in a large, baggy T-shirt and a baseball cap. He snatched something from a woman's purse and stuffed it into his pocket. He quickly looked left and right, then headed for the exit. Jessie grabbed his sleeve before he could make his escape.

"Hey, what's the big deal?" the boy asked, trying to pull free.

Jessie stared closer, noticing the boy's serious brown eyes. "Wait a minute—you're a girl."

"Yeah, what of it?"

Jessie held out her hand. "Give it here."

The girl smoothed out the wrinkles in her shirt. "I don't know what you're talking about."

"Perhaps the police could refresh your memory."

The girl forced a cool smile. "Look, I wasn't hurting anyone."

Jessie kept her hand held out.

The girl sighed and handed her a wallet, a necklace, a broach and a tube of lipstick.

Jessie was reluctantly impressed. "You've been busy."

"It's been a busy day. Please don't tell anyone. It's harmless fun. You know, people shouldn't carry so many things around with them. It gives a girl ideas." Her eyes slid away. "Come on, you understand. If you don't tell anyone, I can make it up to you. I know people."

"Just don't let me catch you doing it again."

She smiled. "You won't regret it."

Jessie grabbed the back of her collar before she could leave. "Just give me back my watch."

The girl laughed in triumph. "Just testing." She placed the watch in Jessie's palm. "You're good."

"I know."

The girl gave a tiny salute, then rushed out of the room.

Jessie put the items in the Lost and Found, then headed for Kenneth's office.

"I'm here to see Kenneth Preston," she told the assistant, a formidable yet attractive woman dressed completely in brown, with her hair pulled back in a braid so tight that it gave her face a cheap facelift.

The woman stared up at the unthreatening female before her. She didn't look like the typical silly fluff that came around to haggle her boss, with their short skirts and tight blouses, but she wouldn't put it past her. "Do you have an appointment?"

"No, but—"

"Then I'm afraid he can't see you." She went back to typing.

"Ms. Mathew—" she began, reading *Glenda Mathew* on the desk.

"*Mrs.* Mathew, if you please," the woman corrected. "I haven't been married for twenty-eight years to be called '*Ms.*'"

"I'm sorry, Mrs. Mathew, but it's important business." The woman gave her a look that said *I've heard that before.*

Jessie leaned closer, lowering her voice to a conspiratorial tone. "Listen, there's a lady claiming that she'll file a paternity suit against Mr. Preston. I've been able to dissuade her from spreading her story, but I have to talk to him about it. It's a very delicate matter. I hope that I can trust you to keep this situation to yourself."

The woman's eyes widened. "Of course."

"May I please speak to him?"

The assistant picked up the phone, muttered a few words, then replaced the receiver. "Wait over there," she ordered, pointing to a row of chairs. "He'll be ready to see you in a few minutes."

Jessie couldn't believe it had worked. Kenneth must be a busy guy for a lie like that to succeed. She took a seat, sinking into the too-soft leather cushions, and picked up one of the magazines on the side table.

"I had the best date ever last night with Kenneth," she overheard an employee say.

"Couldn't have been as good as mine," another woman replied.

Jessie lowered her magazine to the bridge of her nose. The first woman was tall, in a willowy way, with handsome features; the other woman had a friendly face and hair so stiff that it looked like it was in danger of breaking off.

"So where did he take you?" Willow Woman asked.

"To that new Thai restaurant."

The other woman lifted her nose a notch higher. "Well, he took me to see a play that just opened."

Jessie shook her head. Dating his employees, just like the rumors said. Had the guy no morals? She turned to glance at the assistant to see if she had overheard. But instead of seeing her typing, Ms. Mathew was staring straight at her.

"For the *third* time, he's ready to see you now," she said tartly.

"Oh." Jessie tossed the magazine down and stood. "Thank you."

She took a deep breath and said a silent prayer before opening the door. She desperately hoped that she wouldn't twist her ankle in the stilts the fashion industry called high heels. She opened the door, then stood paralyzed. She had expected to see an office. This was a presidential suite at a luxury hotel. It was the size of her living room and expertly decorated in the colors of green and gray. It had an inviting fireplace, with a glass coffee table and a charcoal leather couch facing it. Jessie didn't doubt that he put all three to use.

It wasn't only the office that rendered her speechless, but the man who filled it with his magnetic presence. Kenneth sat casually on the edge of his desk, looking down at his computer, dressed in a dark suit that accentuated his strong build. He suddenly looked like a stranger to her, a ruthless tycoon who could easily destroy a company with the flick of his wrist. He turned to her, and his keen brown eyes bore into hers.

Kenneth shoved his hands in his pockets. "I'm not really in the mood for games today. What do you want?"

"I...I..." For some reason her mouth and brain wouldn't connect. Perhaps Deborah was right: there were certain men out of her league.

"What are you doing here?" Kenneth rested an arm over his knee. "Glenda said that you had a delicate issue to discuss with me."

Jessie slowly shut the door and went towards him, unsure if she felt unsteady on her feet because of the heels or the look Kenneth was sending her. The hostility coming from him was as tangible as hot coal, and just as scorching. He had every right to look at her with distrust, and she didn't know how to change it. As she approached the desk, she discovered why he had been sitting on it. A little girl spun around in his chair.

Jessie stopped and stared; the girl did the same. "You!" they chorused.

"You two know each other?" Kenneth asked, curious.

"No," Jessie said.

"Yes," the girl replied.

Kenneth rubbed his chin. "Which is it, yes or no?"

"Yes," Jessie corrected.

"No," the girl said.

Kenneth frowned.

"We met in the ladies' room," Jessie said, noticing that the girl's knuckles had gone pale. They quickly relaxed.

"I see. Well, this is my niece, Ace," Kenneth said absently.

Jessie reached out her hand. "Nice to meet you."

Ace grinned, pleased with the gesture. "She thought I was a boy at first. Most people think I'm a boy, but I don't mind."

"Why do they call you Ace?"

"My father wanted a boy."

Jessie smiled. "That figures. My grandfather wanted a boy too. Until I was thirteen, he called me Jay. I got mistaken for a boy all the time. It was really funny to trick people and see their faces when they discovered I was a girl."

Ace giggled. "It's true. Once I joined this secret club that was supposed to be all boys. But I dropped out because it was boring."

"I know. Have you ever—" She stopped, noticing that Kenneth was

watching her with an odd expression. "But that's not why I'm here."
Kenneth stood, his eyes wary. "Why are you here?"
Jessie glanced at Ace, then back at him. "Perhaps this matter would be best discussed where she can't hear it."
"Probably," he said, resigned.
"Nice to meet you, Ace," Jessie said.
The girl smiled. "Right."
Ace tugged on her uncle's sleeve, then whispered something in his ear. His eyebrows shot up and he shook his head. Ace continued to talk until he closed his eyes and groaned. He ushered her out of the room, but not before she was able to give Jessie the thumbs-up sign.

He asked Jessie to sit, and took a seat behind his desk. He did so with such grace and efficiency that Jessie could only stare. She had never seen him this way, so in command and in control. She had known he had it in him—that behind his friendly facade and devastating smile lived a darker, colder side—but she'd never seen it before. It was similar to witnessing a beloved pet turn into a ferocious predator. And he was definitely a predator. His eyes gave away nothing except his determination to know what she was up to.

Jessie walked towards the offered chair, accidentally tripping over the rug. She looked down and saw the gigantic head of a bear displaying its teeth. She let out a little squeal, then she noticed that it was not a real head that was ready to bite her exposed ankles. Her imagination was getting the best of her.

"Are you okay?" Kenneth asked, standing.

"I'm fine." She took a seat. He resumed his seat as well.

"Do you want a drink?" he asked, watching Jessie fidgeting in her chair. She looked left and right, as if she expected the walls to crush her.

"Uh...no, thanks." She tried to smile, but her mouth wouldn't move. *Charm him, charm him*, her mind kept telling her, but she didn't know how to begin. She couldn't do it, she suddenly realized. She was a plain jock, an ex-waitress who lived with her sisters. She couldn't charm this man, this stranger with an intelligence and ambition that had given him financial success. He was clever; he had outwitted her before, hadn't he? She couldn't ask him for a job. Her pride wouldn't allow her to bend that low.

She stood. She would have to come up with another plan. "I'm sorry I've taken up your time."

"Sit down." He said the words softly, but the command was clear. She hesitated, but sat. She fought the urge to bite her nails.

"You're wearing one of Michelle's suits, aren't you?"

She glanced down and fingered the lapel of her jacket. Oh, God, was it that obvious? "Uh, yes."

He watched her with intense eyes and put his fingers together, forming a steeple. "Do you need money? Is that why you're here?"

Jessie shook her head. "No, no, no. I'm, um…" Why couldn't she just say what she needed? She wished she were Michelle, with her calm gaze and smooth voice. Or as pleasant as Teresa, with a ready smile and gentle eyes. Or even someone with the seductive powers of Gran Sonya, with her brilliant mind and dangerous body. But she was Jessie, the only woman around who could annoy him. She rubbed her temples, a headache dancing against her skull with foolish abandon.

Kenneth let out a fierce sigh and stood. "Why do you do this?"

"Do what?" she asked, watching him as he poured a glass of water.

"Get so anxious that you give yourself a headache? On the field, you're as cool as lemonade, but off, you're a bundle of nerves." He handed her the glass and aspirin.

"Thank you."

After she swallowed, Kenneth took the glass from her and held her hand. "You still bite your nails, huh?"

She pulled her hand away and frowned at them. "I'm trying to stop."

He scratched the back of his wrist. "Why are you here?" he asked again, tucking away a layer of his hostility.

She decided to stall a little longer. "You look different."

He had begun to sit, but paused and looked at her. "What?"

"I can barely recognize you in this." She gestured towards his attire.

"That makes two of us. Just a minute ago, I thought Michelle had walked in here, but of course she wouldn't have her hair all over the place."

Jessie's hand flew to her hair. She could feel the rebellious strands.

"Damn."

"So you don't like my suit?"

"I didn't say I didn't like it. You just look different."

"Of course. It's my armor. It helps to look intimidating in this line of work. The kind boy-next-door image doesn't go far." He took off his jacket and tie and rolled up his cuffs. "There. Now I'm the guy you've hated since—"

"I don't hate you," she cut in.

"Why are you here?" he asked. This time, his tone left no room for excuses or delays.

Jessie crossed her legs and leaned forward, deciding to be blunt. "You owe me a job."

"I do?"

"Yes. If it hadn't been for you, I'd be employed right now."

He leaned back. The chair creaked softly under his weight. "I doubt that."

"You said you had positions, and I know there's one especially for me."

"What are you talking about?"

"The job that recently popped up—I want it."

Kenneth sent her a dubious expression. "You want the job that badly?"

"Yes."

"Why?"

She cleared her throat. "That's a good question." One she hadn't practiced an answer to. "Um…because I want to try something new. I'm a fast learner and, um…very responsible."

He rubbed his chin. "I'm surprised word went around so fast. I had hoped to keep it quiet. So who else knows?"

Jessie frowned, unsure why the position would be a secret. "Just Michelle, I think."

Kenneth nodded. Of course. Because Michelle had once run a temp company, she would be aware of different people and vacant positions. She was very trustworthy with her selection. However, he was surprised that she would recommend her sister for the job of looking after Ace.

"Have you done this type of work before?"

"I've done almost everything before. You can test me if you want."

A corner of his mouth lifted. "I think that would be a little hard to do, don't you think?"

Jessie didn't think so, but agreed with him anyway.

Kenneth rubbed his hands on the arms of his chair. "I won't deny that this is surprising, especially considering…" He let his words trail off. He rubbed his chin until it ached. When he looked down at his palm, it was red. He spread his hands flat on the desk and tried to choose his words wisely. "You probably know that I'm desperate, and that's why you've come. Besides, Ace instantly liked you, and she doesn't usually like people. She has requested, or rather demanded, that I hire you."

Jessie furrowed her brows. "What does Ace have to do with anything?"

"Well, you're going to look after her, right? It's important that she likes you."

Jessie stared at him in stunned silence.

He continued. "You can stay at my house, or commute, if you want. I don't care. I'm rarely there. Ace usually wakes up around eight. From there, you can schedule your day together." He folded his arms. "You will be well compensated, and I will pay for any activities you two do together. I just don't have time, as you probably can guess. Can you start next Monday? I'd like to have the weekend to get things in order."

Jessie was speechless. There had to be some sort of mistake. She was being hired to look after his niece? Like a nanny?

"Don't act surprised. You knew I was desperate enough to hire you."

She found her voice. "No, I didn't." She frowned; that hadn't been much of a compliment.

He picked up three pens and lined them up, side by side. "Now that that's cleared, what's the real reason you're here?"

"I told you. I need a job."

He nodded. "I know that. What I really want to know is why you're here in *my* office."

She found it much easier to lie to him when he wasn't looking at her. "I'm trying to change my ways."

He sent her a doubtful glance, then draped his tie around his neck and began to arrange it. "I'm giving you this job because in spite of our differences, you've never betrayed me. You've hated me, but never that. The Cliftons have a good reputation when it comes to integrity. I hope that you won't prove me wrong."

Yes, the Cliftons had integrity; the Prestons, however, did not. "I won't."

He slipped into his jacket and looked up to study her face. His brown eyes were hard. The shark was back. "Because if you do, you will regret it." His voice held a silken thread of warning.

"Don't worry. I know what you're capable of."

He sighed. "Ace is very important to me. I trust that any dislike you have for me won't affect how you treat her. She's..." He stopped, refusing to give any more information than was necessary.

"You can trust me," Jessie said, eager to reassure him.

His eyes continued to pierce hers until Jessie could feel the hairs on the back of her neck begin to itch. "Is that a promise?"

"Yes."

He watched for any telling reaction. "I mean it."

She held up her hand, as if ready to say an oath—anything to redirect his gaze. "She will be like my own daughter. Any tricks or pranks will be purely instructional, I promise."

Kenneth's mouth softened into a smile, and Jessie had to blink to make sure that she was talking to the same person. "You held up your hand like that when you caught me writing my brother's paper for him."

"You were always trying to cover for Eddie." She bit her lip, unsure whether to ask the question that had been gnawing at her since she had seen his niece. She decided to ask anyway. "Is Ace Eddie's child?"

"Yes. He's trying to get back on his feet," he said simply.

"You know, you're not doing him any favors by taking up his responsibilities. I mean..." She let her words trail off.

Kenneth had redirected his gaze, placing paper clips in perfect order, side by side. Jessie sensed that he controlled the situation without the need to look up. He made it clear that her opinion was of no importance to him. Jessie wanted to say more, but fought not to. It wouldn't be the first time they had both helped Eddie. Hadn't he convinced her to sacrifice her future for his brother's? And wasn't she the one who had been so young and blinded by love that she'd agreed? She pushed back the anger. Now wasn't the time for those memories.

The moment of quiet crackled with an untamed energy between them.

After a few moments, Jessie stood. "I'd better go."

His head shot up, as if he had forgotten she was in the room. He rose from his chair and went towards her. "So, is this a truce?" It was after he said the words that he realized how important it was for him. Perhaps if they had a truce, he could silently indulge in his fantasies about her. She wouldn't seem so off-limits. She looked good in cream. Cream made him think of milk; milk made him think of...

Jessie took a step back. His eyes had developed an odd, yet mesmerizing gleam. Not to mention that the closer he got, the more she had to look up at him, and the more she could smell his cologne. "You could say that."

He took a step towards her. "Let's shake hands, then."

She took another involuntary step back. "Sure."

He flashed a knowing smile and held out his hand. She stared at it for a moment, then took it. His grip was warm, firm, and strangely gentle. She hadn't expected him to hold her hand with such care, and she could feel her heart begin to beat in a strange pattern, not from anxiety, but something much more disconcerting: desire. She tried to snatch her hand away, but he held it. "Truce?" he asked, as if to make certain.

"Truce."

He let her hand go. "Good. Now that we have a truce, I can do something about your hair."

Stunned by the sudden change of conversation, Jessie watched as he retrieved a tiny comb from the inside of his jacket and began to comb back her hair.

"You keep a comb in your pocket?" she managed to ask.

He glanced down at her, his eyes mischievous. "Have you forgotten how vain I am? Don't worry, it's clean."

She felt heat rise in her cheeks. His vanity was something she always accused him of. He never showed signs of vanity. She just assumed he was vain because he was so good-looking.

She'd never had a man comb her hair before. It was a deliciously pleasant experience feeling his fingers and the comb slipping their way through her hair like a fish slicing its way through a current: solid, smooth, sensual. She stared at his chest, resisting the urge to move closer to him, resisting the urge to ask herself why she was letting him do this.

He stepped back and tilted his head to one side to study her. "Much better."

"Do you have a mirror in there?" She nodded towards his inner pocket.

"I'm afraid the window works better in cases like this."

She went to the window and grimaced at her reflection.

He came up behind her. "You don't like it?"

"No, it's not that. You did a good job."

"Then what is it?"

"I look like Michelle."

He shrugged. "Don't worry, it won't last." He sat on his desk. "Now that I've done you a favor, can you do one for me?"

"I'll try." She stared out at the city moving busily below, watched the fluttering trees of Long Creek Park in the distance and the still waters of the bay.

"Could you tell me what you're up to?"

She kept her gaze on the distance, trying to gather courage from the water, the sky, and the ancestors who had captured the men they had wanted. She swallowed, then turned and walked towards him. "All I want is a job and a second chance." She moistened her lower lip.

"A second chance at what?"

She lifted his tie and let it fall between her fingers. "That's up to you."

He began to smile. "If I didn't know better, I'd think you were trying to seduce me." He blinked, then threw his head back and laughed. "Now that would be the day, wouldn't it? The day Jasmine Clifton tried to seduce me." He laughed harder.

Jessie tried not to scowl. "Yes, isn't that hilarious?" She spun on her heel and walked towards the door.

He stood. "I'm not laughing at you. It's just the thought. It's like me falling for you." He began to laugh again.

Jessie opened the door. *Let him laugh.* He'd always found her amusing and insignificant; that's why he had used her. She grasped the chain at her throat, a sapphire flashing through her thoughts. She would charm him, then she would make him pay.

Dara Girard

Chapter *Eight*

Brooke Radson walked into the dining room and stared across the ornate mahogany table at the woman eating seared halibut on sliced potatoes. She wished the bitch would just drop dead. Unfortunately, there seemed no hope for that. She looked disgustingly healthy for her age, with a smooth brown face nearly free of wrinkles; short-cropped hair, dyed to the perfect gray; and an elegant physique maintained by a strict diet and exercise routine. Brooke could have admired her, and would have, if the woman's dark brown eyes weren't so hollow, didn't look so haunted.

Brooke took a seat. "Hello, Mom."

Her mother smiled back in her cool, placid way.

She spread the lacy cloth napkin on her lap. She could bear it if her mother at least had a drinking problem. Then she could be cliché—a middle-aged socialite with a drinking problem. She would even accept her smoking too much or spending too much money, but she did nothing, absolutely nothing—no parties, no organizations, no groups. She just stayed in the house, like a modern-day Miss Havisham, a ghost of her former flighty self, loving a man who had another woman filling the greater part of his tiny heart. Thank God she hadn't inherited her mother's ineptitude in choosing men. They were, at best, excellent accessories, and at worst, useless pets. And she treated them all accordingly, from her first boyfriend to her latest, Derek Allen, the owner of Invis Electronics.

He would fit perfectly into her plan, and he wasn't bad in bed, either. Too bad only one man could claim the title of being the best lover she had ever had, and at the moment, he would probably love to

79

see her strangled.

She smiled at the thought. Poor fool. He should have known how much she loved being a bitch, especially since she could get away with it. She was cute, with wide, brown eyes, so innocent that they deceived the shrewdest people; and a round chin and baby-fat cheeks, which helped her to dimple prettily. She had known that was her greatest asset when she had used it to get her cousin Trent into trouble.

She hid a scowl and looked up when she realized the woman in front of her had decided to speak. "Excuse me?"

"How is work?"

She gently stabbed her halibut, keeping her temper. She didn't know why the woman even asked. She had never been interested in the company, and had barely blinked when Dad had given it to an outsider. "It's fine, thank you."

She flashed another placid smile.

Brooke lowered her eyes to hide her disgust. The entire house could crumble to the ground, but as long as Winifred Radson was told things were fine, she assumed they were. Fortunately, Brooke was not that stupid. Radson was in the wrong hands and she would make sure that error was corrected. It was the impetus to make sure that the county's power was held in check. She loved Randall, with its diverse ethnic groups and mixture of cities and suburbs, but as in any society, a sense of balance had to be maintained.

African Americans were already a minority, and she did not want them polluted by the growing power of the island immigrants. They had their exclusive councils, scholarships, stores, and businesses. She couldn't allow them to reap the riches her ancestors had sweated for with their blood.

She glanced around the room, her eyes falling on a hand-painted porcelain Japanese Imari plate. It was a dish found in grand European homes dating from the 1680s to the 1740s. Would her great-great-grandfather have hoped this for his descendents? She loved the sense of power in acquiring things. It was this obsession that had led her to smuggling diamonds inside antiques—the thought of possessing something she shouldn't. Plus it was extremely profitable.

A low feminine voice interrupted her thoughts. "Hello, Mom,

Brooke."

This time Brooke smiled for real. She loved her sister, Stephanie, the woman who had really taken care of her growing up. She was beautiful, with dark eyes that were too clever to be pretty, a striking physique, and a sharp tongue that made most men wary. Brooke wasn't worried; most men didn't deserve her. Yes, Stephanie was perfect, except for one glaring fault: she was too kind. She had let Dad shit all over her, still loving him although he had given her company to an outsider and cared about a mother who was no better than a zombie. Fortunately, Stephanie also had a love of success and money, and they both wanted Radson to make money.

Stephanie touched her hand, her eyes apologetic. "Brooke, I owe you a bracelet."

"What are you talking about?"

"I picked up the wooden bracelet from Mrs. Donovan, as you requested, and I put it on because it matched my earrings. I thought it was a good way to keep it with me, but I seem to have misplaced it. I'll check the Lost and Found at work. Otherwise, I'll just get you another one."

Brooke only nodded. She pushed herself away from the table.

"You haven't finished."

"I've had enough." She stood. "Excuse me." She walked away, keeping her hands relaxed, reminding herself that it wasn't wise to kill the only person you love, no matter how much you wanted to. Stephanie had lost her bracelet—a bracelet filled with enough diamonds to house a sultan. She would not panic.

Her entire plan depended on the payment she had received from the South African mining company in exchange for computer cycles. Diamonds were the perfect payment because they left no money trail. However, without them she wouldn't be able to bribe the board members and get rid of the current CEO.

She saw her mother's cat, Cally, licking her silky white fur on the side table. The cat looked up at her with wary green eyes. Brooke stroked the cat until it began to purr. She suddenly pushed it off the table. It squealed in surprise, then ran off. Good: she could still tame and trap. She would have to use this skill to the best of her ability. She released a sigh and smiled. The bracelet would be returned to her in due time; she always got what she wanted. She even had God wrapped around her finger. Stephanie had probably put it in a drawer in her office or something; if not, she would place an ad, and of course there was Jack.

She had time before anyone asked for payment. The vote was months away. Fortunately, the diamonds were only one part of her plan to destroy the perfect man.

Chapter Nine

I belong in a disaster movie, Jessie thought, sitting in her sister's office later that day. The echo of Kenneth's laughter still rang in her mind. She had wanted to speak to Teresa, but she was with a piano student, so Michelle would have to do...even though she was as comforting as a scorpion. "Why doesn't anything in my life ever go right?"

Michelle impatiently shuffled through a couple of papers. "What are you talking about?"

She kicked off her shoes and took a seat. "I've been hired to look after his niece. I'm a damn nanny. Can you believe it?"

Michelle's head came up. "How did that happen?"

She shrugged. "I don't know. I went there thinking I was applying for a vacant position with his company, and the next thing I knew he was telling me he was glad that Ace liked me."

"Ace?"

"Yes, that's the kid's name. I met her when..." She trailed off. The less said about their introduction, the better. "She's going to be a handful," she finished lamely.

"How do you know?"

Jessie wiggled her hands. "She has sticky fingers."

"Oh."

"I start on Monday." She swung her foot. "Now, I ask you: how am I supposed to win him over if I'm with his niece and he's away at the office?"

"That's a question you should ask Teresa."

"Teresa's busy. I'm asking you."

Michelle sighed. "How old is the kid?"

"Eight or nine, I guess. That's another thing. You know I'm not good with kids. I'm not very patient."

"There's nothing wrong with learning a new skill." Michelle drummed her fingers. "You know, this might work to your advantage. You can appear domestic."

"Domestic, me? How?"

"Let me think." She tapped her chin. "You could cook. No, he doesn't deserve that kind of punishment. You could play an instrument, if you'd ever learned one, or…"

Jessie narrowed her eyes. "This is not helpful."

"You'll just have to hope he thinks of you as his Jane Eyre."

"His what?"

"Jane Eyre, the governess in Charlotte Bronte's novel." She stopped when Jessie's eyes glazed over. She picked up a pen. "Never mind."

Jessie rested her head in her hands. "I've never admired men who fall for their staff. There's something sort of incestuous about that."

"You need to charm him, not admire him."

She furrowed her eyebrows. "This sort of makes me his servant, right?"

"Don't look at it that way. Think of it as strategic planning. You know, in the time of Jane Eyre, the role of a governess—"

"It's okay." She wasn't in the mood to listen to the history of hired help. Jessie brushed her foot against the carpet. "He…he wants to talk about what happened."

Michelle went back to her papers. "What happened?"

"About the prom."

"Oh, that," she said, with a dismissive gesture.

Jessie stood, annoyed by her sister's disinterest. "Not everyone can turn off their emotions like a switch."

Michelle shook her head sadly and sat back in her chair. "See, that's the difference between you and me. A statement like that is meant to hurt, but it doesn't, because it isn't true. Of course I have feelings, though limited, I admit. They're just not ready to rise up at the smallest provocation. You enjoy being a victim, otherwise you would let go of the fact that Kenneth teased you about not having a date for the prom.

Jes, that was how many years ago?"

Jessie turned away and looked out the window at the boats in the distance, bobbing up and down on the water. "It was more than that."

Michelle put her pen down and pushed her papers aside. "What are you talking about?"

"He was supposed to take me." Jessie's toes curled into the carpet. "But he stood me up." *If only it were that simple.*

Michelle's voice cooled. "Kenneth was supposed to take you?"

Jessie spun around. Her sister's voice always grew soft when she was angry. "I didn't tell you because I was too ashamed."

"He's the one that should have been ashamed." She tucked a strand of hair behind her ear with a quick angry movement. "I remember how you sat there in your lovely yellow dress, waiting for your mysterious date to come, and how devastated you were when he didn't. I thought you'd made him up. Did he ever explain why?"

Jessie walked to her chair. "I never gave him the chance."

"Why not?"

She groaned. "Not everyone can explain their actions."

Michelle rested her chin in her hands. "So you've been angry all this time, wallowing in self-pity, when he probably has a perfectly good explanation?"

"The explanation seemed pretty clear when I saw him with another girl. And I mean *with* another girl."

"Hmm…that doesn't sound like him."

Jessie smiled with sweet sarcasm. "Of course it doesn't sound like him. He's perfect."

"I'm only thinking." Michelle stood and sat on the edge of the desk. "I've never really had the chance to know Kenneth, but one thing I do know is that his heart is good."

"You're wrong, Mich."

"Rarely, and not about this. For some reason, he frightens you."

She folded her arms. "Don't be ridiculous."

"He still does, and I don't know why."

"You're—"

She held up a hand. "Just listen." She pushed Jessie into a chair. "It's really very simple." Jessie rolled her eyes. Michelle had said the same thing when she was describing trigonometry. "Back then, you couldn't believe that a guy like Kenneth would be interested in you. Remember the first time you saw him?"

Jessie nodded, but Michelle continued anyway.

"It was September or October, and you were kicking a ball by yourself. He was in his yard across the street, creating a structure out of twigs. You accidentally kicked your ball into his yard, and it fell right on top of his building. He stared at the ball and his ruined creation for a long time, then picked it up and came towards you. You were terrified, because you thought he was going to be angry."

Jessie let her arms fall. "I wasn't terrified."

"So I guess it was only the ground under you that was trembling?" She continued before Jessie could protest. "Anyway, he handed you the ball and said, 'If you wanted to get my attention, all you had to do was say hello.' Then he smiled, and you stuck out your tongue and ran back into the house." Michelle smiled, remembering the moment. "Even then, you couldn't accept him being nice to you."

"I couldn't believe he didn't get mad. How can anyone be that nice? He didn't even swear. Hell, I would have. It's unreal."

"It's not his nature to get angry, and you have a hard time accepting that."

She glanced away. "He does get angry."

"How do you know?"

"I just do. Everyone gets angry at times," she added, not wanting to give away too much. "But I think you're right about other things." Jessie crossed her legs and swung her foot. It was irritating, but sometimes her sister's brutal honesty was good. It was a trait they had all inherited from their mother. Michelle, however, seemed to have received an extra dose.

"Of course I'm right."

"Your modesty is enviable."

Michelle shrugged.

"It was too incredible." Her mind flashed back to when he'd come up to her that cool autumn day, a time when things should be dying or passing by. It was a time when her youthful heart had begun to bloom. He was a lanky older boy with a bright grin and warm eyes offering friendship to a tough eleven-year-old girl. She hadn't been able to believe that he liked *her*. She wasn't a clever student, and was boyish and plain, she didn't think there was anything special about her that would captivate the attentions of someone like him. But for one semester, she had believed that he truly liked her, only to discover the true extent of her attractiveness.

Her voice was soft when she spoke. "He never liked me, Mich. Not the way you think."

"Of course he did. I didn't blame him. You were talented and courageous. You made me proud."

Jessie shook her head. Her mouth quirked at her sister's attempt at flattery. "You thought I was young and lacking in direction."

"You still are, but I know what you're capable of. A girl of hidden depths."

Unfortunately, none of her potential had risen to the top this morning. She sunk lower into her chair. "When I saw him today, I froze. I couldn't even open my mouth. If it was any other guy, I could do it, but not him."

"Let me tell you a secret about Kenneth that will make this easier for you."

"This isn't a trick, is it?" she asked, cautious.

"No." She leaned forward and lowered her voice. "One day, Kenneth and I were watching a nature film in biology about an orphaned wildebeest that couldn't find another mother to nurse him. So the little baby just curled up alone, and we knew it would die. The room was basically quiet, with some compulsory snickers, but I turned to Kenneth, and in the glow of the screen, I saw tears in his eyes. He blinked them away before the lights came on, but then I knew."

Jessie frowned. "Knew what? That he was a sissy?"

"It was sad," Michelle said defensively.

Jessie smiled. "Did you cry too?"

"You're missing the point."

"What's the point?"

"He is like anyone else. He has his own hurts, fears, and joys. He's just a man, Jessie. And luckily, as a woman, you have everything necessary to catch him. You just need the confidence."

Jessie fell into silence.

Michelle sat behind her desk to resume work. "By the way, don't tell Kenneth this story."

"Why not?"

She glared at her. "Because if he doesn't kill you, I will."

"This is so exciting," Teresa said at dinner, after Jessie had explained the situation. She wiggled in her seat, like a child ready to open birthday presents.

Michelle took another helping of curried goat. "Why is everything so exciting to you?"

Jessie ignored her. "He said that I could either commute or live in his house."

"In his house? Are you serious?" Teresa rubbed her hands together. "It gets better and better."

"What are you planning to do?" Michelle asked.

Jessie toyed with her food. "I'll commute, I guess."

Teresa waved her fork. "Wrong answer. You're going to stay there. It's perfect. That way, you have more opportunities to bump into him."

Michelle and Jessie stared at her. "*Bump* into him?"

"Yes." Teresa gazed up at the ceiling fan. "Draped in a silk robe, you go down to the kitchen for a late-night snack, and there he is— wearing just his red boxer shorts and a milk mustache. Your eyes meet, your lips part, then—"

Michelle groaned in disgust. "Oh, no. Have you been reading those sappy romance novels again?"

Teresa smiled sweetly. "Yes, I took them from your bedroom."

Properly rebuked, Michelle made a face and began to eat.

"So what are you planning to pack?"

Jessie shrugged. "I don't know. Clothes, books..." She rubbed her temples. "I'm not sure I want to stay at his place. He probably uses it as a harem or something." She still didn't like the fact that she was going there as a nanny. She didn't like any situation that put Kenneth in control.

"I seriously doubt it." Teresa stood up. "Let's go see what we have to work with."

"What's the rush? We have all weekend to decide."

"Yes, but why wait when you can start now?"

They left the table and went to Jessie's room. Michelle opened the closet, and Teresa opened a drawer while Jessie just sat there bouncing up and down on the bed.

"I wish you'd stop shopping at the Salvation Army," Teresa said, lifting a worn flannel nightdress.

"Look, I don't expect Kenneth to see me in my nightdress, so what does it matter? I'm supposed to try to charm him, not seduce him."

"You never know. Seduction might be faster." She tossed the nightdress on the bed. "You'll just have to borrow some of Michelle's."

Michelle turned. "Why mine?"

"Because you have the best nighties of all three of us. The way you shop, one would think you had stock in Victoria's Secret."

Michelle rested a hand on her hip. "I like the material."

Teresa grinned. "Yes, and men buy Playboy for the articles."

Michelle left the room.

"I don't see why we have to put so much emphasis on my clothes," Jessie said as Teresa went through her wardrobe.

"You have to think of this as a championship game," she said, trying to appeal to Jessie's competitive nature. "To play, first you have to have the right gear. You wouldn't wear a helmet to play tennis, right?"

"No."

"So in charming a man, some of your attire has to be more alluring."

Michelle returned with two silk nightdresses. "Stain them and die." She gently placed them on the bed, as though laying out diamonds.

Jessie frowned. "How could I possibly stain them?"

Michelle opened her mouth, then shook her head. "Still a virgin, are you?"

"What does that have to do with anything?"

She nodded. "Question answered. Just be careful."

Teresa went through some more clothes in Jessie's closet, then folded her arms. "It's official. We need to go shopping."

"You're just trying to find an excuse," Michelle said.

Teresa smirked. "Like I ever need an excuse. Jessie cannot charm a man in these." She picked up a worn tie-dyed T-shirt as though lifting it from a rubbish heap. "Let's shop."

It would have helped if Jessie knew how to shop. She roamed around the women's section like a fish caught in seaweed—she didn't know which way to turn. She was used to grabbing whatever fit and hoping it matched what she had. She glanced at her sisters, who were quietly arguing about what she should wear. Michelle wanted a conservative, old-money look, while Teresa wanted a modern look with a New Age flair.

Jessie wasn't sure which look she favored. A cream, crocheted ballet blouse caught her eye. She liked the soft feel and simple style. She picked it up and held it out to her sisters.

"What about this?"

They looked at her in surprise. "You must be joking," Michelle said. "You could never pull that off."

Teresa touched the hem of the blouse. "It's just a little too feminine for you. Don't worry, we'll come up with something."

Jessie glanced at the blouse once more, then put it back. Her sisters were right. She'd probably end up looking like a man in drag.

Unfortunately, in the end, they could not agree on anything. Michelle bought herself a blouse, Teresa bought a skirt, and Jessie purchased a pair of gym socks.

"That was a waste of time," Jessie grumbled on the drive home. "How am I supposed to charm him with a pair of socks?"

"Easy," Michelle said. "Wear them and nothing else."

"If you weren't driving, I'd hit you."

"You can just borrow our clothes," Teresa said. "We have other things to focus on."

"Like what?"

Teresa sent Michelle a conspiratorial grin, but neither said anything.

Chapter Ten

"No, no, no! I will not let you put that on me!" Jessie said, ducking Teresa's attempts to put a mud mask on her face.

"It will tighten your pores."

"My pores are fine."

Teresa frowned. "Stop being a baby. It's painless."

"No."

She waved the jar. "It's for the pendant."

Jessie sighed, glanced at Michelle, and surrendered. She groaned as her face hardened. "This feels awful. Why do women do this to themselves?"

Teresa buffed her nails. "Because it's worth it."

"You'll thank us later," Michelle said. "Now, where are the hot curling irons?"

Jessie stiffened. "No!"

"Stop shouting," Teresa scolded. "You'll crack your face."

"No hot curlers." She held out her hands as Michelle came towards her. "You burned me last time."

"Oh, quiet," Michelle said. "I was only ten at the time, and you had annoyed me." She found it and plugged it in. "Now, just keep still or my hand might slip...again."

An hour later, Jessie stared at Michelle, incredulous. "You want me to spray perfume where?"

"In your underwear drawer," Michelle said. "Don't look appalled. Imagine how good you'll feel opening your drawer and smelling the scent of roses. You need to get in touch with your sensual side."

She glanced at the lavender Teresa had set about the room. "I'm trying."

"Remember to look at him when he talks," Teresa said.

Michelle added, "But don't stare."

"Speak your mind."

"But don't interrupt."

"Smile."

"But not too often."

"And relax."

"But never show it."

Jessie rolled her eyes. "Thanks. That sounds easy enough."

On Sunday night, they helped her pack, using one of Michelle's expensive cases.

Teresa held up a bottle in Jessie's face. "This is called lotion," she said slowly. "You use it on your body to keep it soft and moisturized."

Jessie snatched it from her, offended. "I know that."

"It would be nice of you to show it, then."

"Try to remember to iron your clothes," Michelle said.

Teresa began, "As for your makeup—"

"I don't wear makeup," Jessie cut in.

"Don't force me to point out the obvious. At least try these." She handed Jessie some rouge and lipstick. "It won't hurt."

Jessie shook her head. "This whole thing is not about looks, it's about charm."

"Like I said, it won't hurt." She put the makeup in the bag. "I'm also giving you lullaby oil, mango juice, and papaya cream for your face."

"Thanks," she grumbled. "At night, when I get hungry, I'll think of eating them for my snack."

"Now try to get a good night's rest," Michelle said. "There's no need to arrive at his place with bags under your eyes,"

Teresa nodded. "And don't be nervous."

"I'm not nervous," she lied. Her heart was already beating out a SOS. *Save me from my sisters. Save me from myself and my own foolish pride.* How could anyone think clothes and some makeup could suddenly change them? Kenneth had already seen through her "Michelle" disguise.

"It will be all right," Teresa said.

"Unless—" Michelle stopped when Teresa nudged her in the ribs. "You'll be fine."

They both said good night, then left.

Jessie sat on the bed and tugged on her necklace with anxious fingers. What had she gotten herself into? She went to her full-length mirror and ran a hand over her face. Why couldn't God have given her some looks?

She tried to pout, as she had seen models do in magazine ads, but ended up looking like a scary aunt waiting for a kiss. It was no use; even though she had all the features necessary to be pretty, she was ordinary. And what was wrong with that? She had been that way all her life and her parents had taught her that all things created had beauty.

She ran a hand down her body and flaunted it in the mirror. She had a nice figure, if you were into round hips, strong arms, and a full chest. She fell down onto the bed, and the mattress bounced up and down under her weight. This bet wasn't about looks, anyway; it was about charm and confidence. If only she could find some. She fell back on the bed and stared at the ceiling.

Damn it, she had done it again. She had gotten into a situation where she would ultimately end up the loser. All because of false pride—and a false hope that she was better than she actually was. She'd been that way over ten years ago, and to her disgust, she was still the same way again. The family failure…the family disappointment.

But what if she could win the bet? What if she surprised everyone and succeeded at something nobody thought she could? She would be a heroine. The Sapphire Pendant would be back in their possession, and generations of Cliftons would live to tell the tale of how Jasmine Clifton had won it back. She had to win. She could not deprive Clifton descendants of their heritage.

She had to get over the memories of his betrayal. She wasn't that girl anymore; she was a woman now, with a woman's cunning. In a month, she planned to hold the pendant in her hand. Jessie stood and went to the collection of stones she kept on a bookshelf. She glanced at the rich blue of a labradorite, the deep red of a fire opal, a brilliant amber, and a somber topaz. She ran her hand over the collection, then grabbed a pink tourmaline, a stone known to relieve nervous tension and enhance self-esteem. She lay on the bed with the stone resting in her palm and let the healing energy sweep through her. Calm soon descended.

"Okay Dad, I'm doing this for you," she whispered. "I'm going to charm Kenneth and get the pendant back, and then you can be proud of me. You too, Mum." She blinked back tears, gripped the stone in her fist, and sat up. She would succeed. She had no other choice.

Her bedroom door opened a crack. Michelle peeked in. "You know, it's not too late to change your mind."

Jessie picked up a pillow and threw it at her.

The sky that Monday morning was as indecisive as Jessie's mood. The sun reluctantly made an appearance through a stream of clouds, only to decide that it would much rather sleep, leaving the day warm but gray. She was thankful for the half-hour drive to Bedford, a community known for its huge houses and affluent residents. It gave her time to practice the smile she would use. She silently rehearsed what she would say and what delicate hand gestures she could use.

As she drove up Kenneth's meandering gravel drive, she expected to see a magnificent mansion with pillars and huge windows. Instead, she approached a simple two-story, white-and-blue colonial home with lively green bushes and magnolias lining the walkway. Behind the house loomed a forest, like a protective mother hen.

She checked her reflection in the rearview mirror. She had taken extra care with her looks, ironing her blue blouse and making sure her jeans were clean and without holes. Michelle's curls had given her hair a nice bounce, and Teresa had outlined her eyes with a smoky purple eye pencil to make them appear brighter. Overall, she thought she looked pretty good, considering what she had to work with. She was ready to dazzle Kenneth with her charm.

She got out of the car and walked up the drive, feeling the gravel crunch underneath her sneakers. She rang the doorbell and waited, a smile plastered on her face. Unfortunately, Kenneth didn't answer. Instead an older, medium-sized woman opened the door. She reminded

Jessie of a kangaroo with her bouncy enthusiasm, animated wide mouth, and light brown eyes.

"Oh, thank goodness you're not one of those silly girls after Kenneth," she said in a faint Georgia accent, giving Jessie a once-over. She narrowed her eyes. They disappeared into slits in her slightly wrinkled brown face. "You aren't, are you? He's got enough trouble without some woman filling up his time."

"I'm just here for Ace," she assured her.

"Good. I'm glad to hear it. I'm also pleased you're not family. His family could drive a nun to hell. I'm Freda." She held out her hand and gave Jessie's hand an enthusiastic pump. "Good." She nodded in approval. "A nice, sturdy girl. You didn't give me one of those dead-fish handshakes. Can't stand those either. Makes me want to reel them in and fry them. " Freda looked down at Jessie's suitcase. "I suppose you're going to stay here at the house?"

"Yes."

"Good. I just made up one of the guest bedrooms for you. Mr. Preston said that you probably wouldn't stay, but I made it up for you anyway." She winked. "Glad I did, aren't you?"

"Yes, very glad."

"Come inside, dear, come inside." She grabbed Jessie's elbow and yanked her inside like a naughty child caught doing mischief. She closed the door behind her with her foot. "Follow me. Try not to touch anything. I just finished dusting and polishing."

Jessie snatched her hand back from a sculpture she was about to examine. "Looks very clean."

When she stepped into the living room, her eyes fell on the chocolate couch stuffed with red pillows one could cuddle into, then her gaze shifted to a fireplace perfect for cold nights. She glanced up at a skylight that let the sunlight through like a welcomed guest, then looked at a patio perfect for lazy Sunday afternoons. She walked over to a small oak desk in the corner of the living room, inhaling the scent of baked bread and jam that floated through the air.

"So, what do you think?" Freda asked, clasping her hands together with pride. "Not bad for a bachelor, huh? Mr. Preston decorated it himself."

Jessie felt strange hearing Freda refer to Kenneth as Mr. Preston, since she was old enough to be his mother. She hoped he didn't expect her to adopt such a habit. "It's really nice."

"More than nice, I'd say." She straightened a picture frame. "It's downright homey. Like you, I was surprised. You'd think a man would at least have a stuffed deer head somewhere, a rifle, or even a stuffed fish. You know how men love killing things, but not even a stuffed flea is to be found in this house. God bless him."

No, Kenneth didn't have stuffed animal heads, but he did have trophies and plaques placed about the house, like a narcissistic shrine. At least that fit his personality.

Jessie shrugged, knowing Freda was waiting for a reply. "Kenneth was never into things like that."

"Oh?" Freda looked at Jessie as if seeing her for the first time. "You know Mr. Preston well?"

Too well. Jessie cleared her throat and chose her words carefully. "Well, no, not really. Um…we used to go to school together."

"Oh, I see. Old schoolmates." She smiled, widening her mouth an incredible distance. "Well, isn't that nice?" She glanced around the room. "Let me tell you that everything is in order. You don't have to worry about leaking roofs, creaky floors, or dirty pipes. Mr. Preston always makes sure that this place is in perfect condition, in case someone needs a place to stay." She briefly raised her eyes upward. "Which happens enough with his family. He's just so kind and generous."

And perfect, of course. "Doesn't he come home?" Jessie asked, following Freda to the kitchen.

"Sometimes, but usually he stays at his office."

Jessie silently groaned. Great. He was either a workaholic or a womanizer. Neither scenario was encouraging. It was hard to charm an invisible man.

"Mr. Preston had me stock the fridge in case you came." Freda opened the refrigerator to back up her claim. It was overflowing with food: boxed juices, fruit, vegetables, and kids' snacks. She closed it and opened the pantry. It also bulged with enough crackers, crisps, and cookies to create a food avalanche. "And he said that chocolate chip cookies were your favorite, so I picked up a few."

"That was kind of you."

"No. Don't give me the credit," Freda said, brushing away the praise. "It wasn't my idea."

Jessie tried to smile. She should be grateful. It was a kind gesture on his part, but the fact that he remembered her favorite cookies annoyed her. It chipped at the shield she had cultivated against him. Yes, they were at a ceasefire, but she still didn't like him. She couldn't afford to like him. She knew where that had gotten her before.

Freda led her upstairs to her bedroom. "Your bathroom has fresh towels, and we have a state-of-the-art intercom system." She described how to operate it and talked about other domestic issues before finally handing Jessie the keys to the house. She then dug into her pocket and handed Jessie a piece of paper. "Mr. Preston said that you can reach him at this number if you have questions or concerns."

"Thanks." Jessie folded the paper. "Freda, may I ask you a question?" .

Freda puffed up a pillow and straightened out the bedsheet. "Sure."

"Why do you call him Mr. Preston? I mean…you're older than him."

"Because he's my boss."

"He made you call him that?"

Freda shook her head, disappointed. "You young people throw away simple traditions. Sure, he wanted me to call him by his first name. He said it made him feel funny to be called Mr. Preston, but that's just too intimate for me. Next thing I know, I'll forget my place and start treating him like a son."

"Does he call you Freda?" She assumed so, since he called his assistant Glenda.

"No. He calls me Ms. Rose." She grinned with pride.

In spite of herself, Jessie grinned back.

When Freda left, Jessie took off her shoes and closed the door. Then she did what she always did in the presence of a new bed: she ran and jumped on it. She sunk into the soft cotton blankets and sighed. She buried her head in the feather pillow and relaxed on the sheets. She rolled on her side and studied her new surroundings. The room was painted a soft yellow and whispered kind words about its owner, murmuring of the care with which the room was prepared. A sturdy sleigh bed filled the room, facing a green couch covered with a cream cashmere throw. There was also a bookshelf with an assortment of hardcover and paperback books. She sat up and let her feet sink into the plush carpeting, as if she were barefoot in a valley.

Jessie stood and began unpacking, but soon abandoned the activity to glance out the window and look at the forest. She opened the window and rested on the windowsill. She had to give him credit. It was a lovely place, and he had finally acquired the trees he had loved since childhood.

She sat on the couch, and a fresh pine scent engulfed her while the cushions wrapped their arms around her, as if in welcome. She closed her eyes. She could stay in the room all day and think about a perfect tennis game, running along the beach, Kenneth…

Her eyes flew open. Where had that come from? This was all a farce—the room as well as the reason she was here—and she couldn't forget that. She stared at the pillow she was hugging and pushed it away. She rubbed her arms as if trying to rid herself of an annoying perfume. She went back to the bed and quickly finished unpacking, then went downstairs.

Chapter Eleven

"Hello?" she called.

"We're in the kitchen," Freda called.

Since Jessie had forgotten where the kitchen was, she ended up in the living room and then the dining room before reaching the kitchen. There she found Ace eating her breakfast and reading the classifieds while Freda washed dishes. The kitchen smelled of ginger muffins and strawberry marmalade.

Freda glanced at her. "Finally found us, huh?"

She laughed at herself. "Yes, thank goodness."

"Uncle's house really isn't that big once you get used to it," Ace said.

"I'm glad."

Ace studied Jessie for a moment. "Uncle Ken said that you and I are going to do a lot of fun stuff today."

Jessie took a seat. "Yes, we are." She eyed the muffins in the middle of the table, hesitated, then grabbed one. She cut it in half, spread some marmalade on top, and took a bite. "Oh, Freda, this is delicious."

Freda laughed. "Don't give me the credit. I didn't make them."

"You must tell me the name of the bakery where you got them," Jessie said, taking another bite.

"They aren't from a bakery. Mr. Preston made them this morning."

Jessie nearly choked; the delicious muffin had suddenly become a hard stone in her throat. She was enjoying something that Kenneth had made? She finally swallowed after two attempts. "He probably used a box recipe."

"Nope. It's the old Preston recipe," Freda admitted. "He won't tell it to me, no matter how I try to trick him."

"He made it just for me, because it's my favorite," Ace said, licking her fingers.

Jessie put the rest of the muffin down, losing her appetite. This profile of Kenneth didn't fit her perception, and it annoyed her. He was a jerk, not an uncle who woke up early to make muffins for his niece before he left for work, not a man who offered his housekeeper respect by addressing her by her surname, not a guy who remembered the favorite cookies of a girl he once knew.

"Well, I've got to go and run some errands," Freda said, taking her purse and coat from off of the table. "I'll see you two later."

They said their good-byes, then Ace asked, "Are you and Uncle Ken friends?"

No, we are enemies who have agreed not to stab each other all summer. "Sort of."

"He wasn't very happy to see you last time. Did you just return to town or something?"

"No. It's just the way we are. We pretend not to like each other, but way deep, down we did...do."

"Oh." She adjusted her cap. "That makes sense. Do you know if he has a girlfriend?"

"Why do you want to know?"

She touched the marmalade on her plate with the tip of her finger. "Can you keep a secret?" She sucked her finger.

Jessie crossed her heart and held up her hand. "Definitely."

Ace smiled at the solemn gesture. "I'm hoping to convince Uncle to let me stay with him, so I figured I have to get her to like me, just in case they get married or something."

"Why do you want to stay here? You have a father."

Ace took another swipe of the marmalade.

"Isn't he well?"

Her eyes slid away. "No. No, he's...he's sick, so I need to find a new home."

"What does he have?"

Ace swirled her finger on the plate, spreading the marmalade around. "Will you get mad if I don't tell you?"

Jessie rested her arms on the table. "No, I just thought that perhaps I could find someone who could help." She lifted the girl's chin. "I used to know your father when he was young."

Her expression became guarded. "It's weird to imagine Dad young. Did you like him?"

Jessie chewed her top lip. Eddie Preston. She remembered a young man with his brother's arrogance and his mother's good looks. No, she hadn't liked him. But honesty wasn't necessary right now. "Let's just say I'm happy he had you. Because if I hadn't known your father, your uncle might not have let me have the job."

Ace nodded her head, and her face relaxed. "So do you know?"

"Know what?"

She sighed dramatically. "If Uncle has a girlfriend."

"No, I don't." Jessie's head began to pound as an icy fear crept over her. She hadn't even thought about that. What if he had a girlfriend that he was already considering taking to the charity ball? She would never have the guts to steal a man from another woman, even for a bet. Besides, how could she compete with the type of woman he liked? What about the two women at his office?

"Hello?" Ace snapped her fingers in front of Jessie's face. "Are you all right?"

Jessie shook her head like someone who had been hypnotized. "Sorry, I was just thinking of..." *My stupidity.* "No, I don't think he has a girlfriend. If he did, everyone would know about it."

"Why?"

"Because a lot of women want to marry him."

Ace nodded. "Yeah. Uncle is a good guy and he's rich. It always helps if a guy's rich."

Jessie decided to switch the topic. "So, Ace, what's your real name?"

"Syrah," she grumbled. "Alias Shiraz. As in 'Try a sparkling Shiraz with wild duck.'" She kissed the tips of her fingers.

Jessie smiled. "It is unusual, but it has a certain flair. Do you mind if I call you Syrah? I like it better."

She shrugged. "No, I don't mind. So what do I call you?"

"You can call me Jessie."

Syrah bit into her muffin. "Do you mind if I call you Aunt Jessie, sort of like you were family or something?"

"No, I don't mind."

Syrah adjusted her cap. "So what do we do first?"

"What do you like to do?"

"I like to play sports and watch TV and go to movies and eat pizza and go out and…"

Jessie held up her hands in surrender. "Okay, okay, okay. I get the picture. I see you also like to read the classifieds." She gestured to the paper Syrah had tossed under her chair.

"Yeah. I…like to see what people are…selling."

"That's nice."

"Right now I need to find a job."

Jessie reached for the remainder of her muffin. *Who cares who made it? It tasted good.* She'd insult its creator another time. "What for?"

"So that I can earn my keep." She picked up her milk. "You know, just in case Uncle gets into a bind. I want to make sure there's enough money around. I have some left over from my trip, but not enough."

Jessie folded her arms. "How old are you?"

"Ten."

"You know, ten's pretty young to be worrying about taking care of your uncle. He's a grown man."

"My dad's a grown man, but that doesn't mean anything."

Jessie paused. *Eddie must be really sick.* That was unfortunate. He had always gotten into trouble, but he had been a healthy kid. Life had a way of knocking you about. "Well, I know for a fact that Kenneth—I mean, Uncle Kenneth—will be able to provide for you."

"I know, but I need a job," she said firmly.

"For now, let's just focus on being a kid, okay?"

Syrah shook her head, her serious eyes determined. "No, you don't understand. I need to have money of my own."

Jessie relented. "All right. How about this week, you focus on being a kid, and next week, I'll help you look for work? Sound good?"

Syrah hesitated, then reluctantly said, "Okay."

In her room, Syrah grabbed her sneakers and pulled them on. She didn't need a stupid babysitter, but Aunt Jessie needed a job, and she owed her. She began to tie her shoelaces. Yeah, Aunt Jessie needed a job; too bad it wouldn't be watching her. She had plans that didn't include anybody else.

She grabbed a sock from her drawer and turned it inside out, letting its contents fall on top of the dresser. She loved the sound. It was like the pleasant ring of coins falling on a countertop. Sure, she had promised Uncle that nobody's dog would go missing. She hadn't lied; she wouldn't steal pets. Jewelry, however, was another thing completely. The day Aunt Jessie had caught her, she'd been able to hide some stuff in her shoes. Good thing, too. She hated working and ending up with nothing.

She picked up a bracelet, then toyed with a ring. They weren't exactly beautiful. The bracelet had a bunch of large beads that shook like maracas, and the stone in the ring was kind of small. But since someone had bought them in the first place, they would probably want them back.

She sighed. She couldn't wait until someone placed an ad in the classifieds, because when they did, she'd be ready.

The day progressed smoothly. Jessie and Syrah played Frisbee in the front yard, ate their way through a pepperoni pizza, then went to the arcade and played games. Towards the evening, Jessie took Syrah with her to the park so Jessie could play tennis with Wendy.

"So who's this?" Wendy asked, offering Syrah a friendly smile.

Syrah hid behind Jessie and looked at the woman with suspicion. "My name's Ace."

"Her real name is Syrah," Jessie corrected.

Wendy raised a brow. "Like the wine?"

"Yes. She's visiting her uncle Kenneth."

Wendy's eyes lit up. "As in Kenneth *Preston*?"

"Yes."

"*Oh, la, la.* I'm impressed. How did you manage that?"

She sent her a warning look. "It's a long story."

Wendy turned to Syrah. "Well, any relative of Kenneth's is a friend of mine."

The girl didn't smile.

Undeterred, she leaned towards her. "How would you like to have a do—?"

"She's not interested," Jessie cut in.

Wendy gave her a classic French shrug. "It was worth a try." She handed Jessie a book.

Jessie read the title. *"How to Flirt?"*

"It works. That's how I got Bruce."

They turned to the man flexing his muscles for a passing female jogger.

Jessie looked at the cover and frowned. *Which means it doesn't work properly*, she thought.

"Your friend seems okay," Syrah said as they returned to the house.

Jessie smiled at the grudging respect in her voice. "Yes, I like her."

She took off her hat and wiped the lip with her hand. "Is she married?"

"No, but she has a boyfriend."

She put the cap back on. "And you want a boyfriend too?"

Heat rushed to her cheeks. "Why do you say that?"

"Because she gave you that book."

"She was trying to be funny."

"Oh…" Syrah considered the statement, then her face spread into a grin. "Oh, I get it. You like Uncle."

She shook her head. "That's not it at all. She just wants…she…well. Don't worry about it." She tugged on her wet shirt. "I'd better get showered. I'm all sweaty. Your uncle should be home by now."

Syrah watched Jessie open the door. "I can help you if you want."

"I am not interested in your uncle."

"Fine. Why don't you come up to my room and play a game, or, um…we could watch TV or something. You don't smell that bad."

"Thanks, but I'd prefer not to smell at all. I feel grimy." She went inside.

In a perfect world, she would have entered the house and had the opportunity to shower and change. Then, completely refreshed, she would greet Kenneth. But it wasn't a perfect world. She entered the house with a sticky T-shirt, with her hair plastered to her head, and she saw Kenneth sitting with a woman that put sugar to shame.

Rodney Phillips used his Street Nerd T-shirt to wipe his glasses and squinted at the computer screen. It was amazing the things a guy would do to get laid. He couldn't believe he'd gotten into this mess. Fortunately, disbelief didn't automatically lead to regret. He certainly didn't have any.

He shoved his glasses onto his face, then quickly decoded the numbers in front of him. Everyone was entitled to do something shady at one point in life. As long as no one got hurt, what did it matter? He had always been a good kid. Where had that gotten him? Nowhere. Twenty-one, and his first sexual experience had cost him a hundred and twenty dollars. He still wasn't sure if he had gotten a fair deal. It didn't matter anyway. The second time wouldn't cost him a thing.

This time he had a woman who was truly interested in him—and not just any woman: Brooke Radson, prime, unadulterated female. He remembered seeing her in the hallways at Radson, and being ashamed of his dirty thoughts when she brushed past him. Her scent always lingered in the air, making him rise and salute every time. It disturbed him, because she was so cute. It was like lusting after one of those princesses in Disney cartoons. But hey, she was still a woman, and there was something sexy about her, despite her wide eyes and dimpled cheeks.

He'd nearly crashed into a plant when she had first said hello to him. Guys like him didn't get noticed. He'd spent his entire life blending into the background. And in a family of seven, that hadn't been too hard. He hit the Enter key and scowled. He would never forgive his parents for having so many damned kids. It was uneconomical, and it made him feel like part of a mob. He was the loner in his family, while his older brother, Nathan, was the playboy, handsome, confident, and leaking charisma like a snitch leaked information. He had broken his first heart at the age of five.

Nathan liked to tease him about his love affair with the computer. He wouldn't be teasing him now. Geeks were gaining power, and the computer was a ticket to success. It wasn't guys like Nathan or Kenneth

Preston who ruled the world. They only had the illusion of power; guys like him controlled it.

Guys like him helped create the systems that offered a sense of security—but with a few keystrokes, he could crash that security from its tower. He lightly ran his fingers over the keyboard. The sense of power caused beads of sweat to form on his upper lip. He had the power to create and destroy right at the tips of his fingers. No, he had no regrets. He wasn't doing anything deadly, just making a little side profit with a South African company and impressing a girl in the process. He sat back in his chair, easing the tension in his groin as he thought about Brooke in his bed. Yep. Life was good.

Chapter Twelve

Jessie stood paralyzed in the hall, imagining sweat dripping from her and forming a puddle at her feet. She stared at the cutest woman she had ever seen. A woman so cute that she looked edible.

"I'd like you to meet Brooke Radson, my executive assistant," Kenneth said. "This is Ace and Jasmine."

Brooke grinned, showing brilliant white teeth. She dimpled prettily. "Hi, Ace, Jasmine."

"It's Jessie." She shook Brooke's outstretched hand, hoping not to crush the delicate fingers.

"But Kenneth just said—"

"He was wrong. Don't worry, it's not uncommon."

"Oh." Her eyes took in Jessie's disheveled state with the grace of one pretending not to notice. "It's nice to meet you."

Nice isn't the word, Jessie thought. She looked at her complete opposite with disgusted admiration. Her gray dress draped a soft feminine figure; wide, appealing brown eyes were framed by perfectly arched eyebrows. And her full cupid lips looked so kissable that Jessie wouldn't be surprised if Kenneth jumped her once she and Syrah left the room. She sat, poised with the nonchalant arrogance of having the right degrees from prestigious schools, and glowing from the privilege of being part of the right class.

Jessie felt her unfinished degree hanging over her. Here she was, standing in front of Kenneth, looking like a gym sock, and Brooke looked as if she were a pageant contestant. Jessie resisted the temptation to ask her what she would do if she won the crown. She was as sweet as a kitten. No amount of charm could disarm that.

"You're Michelle's sister, right?" she asked.

"Yes." She was always just Michelle's sister to people like Brooke. She wasn't the "smart" sister, after all. She looked at the papers on the table, determined not to be intimidated. "So what are you two working on?"

"We're trying to negotiate a contract with Trans Moore," Kenneth said. "We want them to use our software."

"That sounds great. You know, I always thought the best way to negotiate was to—"

"I'm sure you've got a great strategy," Brooke interrupted, with a gentle smile. She rested her antique beaded handbag on her lap and pulled out a pen. "But this is big business. We can't afford to make any mistakes." She glanced pointedly at Jessie's tennis racket.

Ouch. The kitten had claws. Jessie narrowed her eyes, suddenly noticing that there was no kindness in the wide-eyed gaze.

"I'd be happy to listen to your strategy when I have time," Kenneth said absently.

Jessie took a step back, ready to leave. "Thanks."

"We had the best day, Uncle," Syrah piped up, touching his hand.

He pulled his hand away. "I'm glad to hear it. When dinnertime comes, you can tell me all about it. Right now I have to finish some work here."

"Okay." Syrah lifted her shoe and pretended to scratch her ankle. Jessie saw her wipe the dirty bottom of her shoe on her hand. She went up to Brooke. "It was nice to meet you." She held out her dirty hand.

Brooke successfully covered her disgust and shook the tips of Syrah's fingers. Once the girl had turned, she discreetly wiped her hands on a tissue.

Syrah pulled Jessie's sleeve. "Come on, let's go."

"That wasn't very nice of you," Jessie told her as they climbed the stairs.

"I don't care," Ace said. "I don't like her."

"You don't like anyone."

"I like you and Uncle."

"Which makes your taste questionable. What don't you like about her?" Jessie asked, shamefully glad that Syrah agreed with her.

"She's fake."

"She could be your uncle's next girlfriend, for all you know." And he would deserve her. *Two well-made frauds.*

She shook her head. "Nah, she's not his type."

Jessie playfully poked her in the back. "How do you know that?"

Syrah threw a smug grin over her shoulder. "Because he called her Brooke."

"So? That's her name."

"Exactly. Uncle always changes people's names. Like he calls me Ace or Rah and he calls you Jasmine, not Jessie."

"He only does that to be annoying."

"No, it's 'cause he likes you. I told you, if you really want him, I can help you."

"Forget it."

When they entered Syrah's room, the large window greeted them with a panoramic view of the forest. Stuffed animals fought for space on the bed, with some balancing precariously on the edge. Next to the window sat stacks of puzzles, board games, and books. In the closet, a basketball, soccer ball, and rollerblades peeked through.

Syrah followed her gaze. "Uncle took me shopping this weekend."

Jessie nodded. The room, in spite of its crammed quarters, was incredibly neat. Not a chair or drawer was out of place. All her clothes were neatly put away, and her shoes lined the room.

"Are you expecting a military inspection?" she teased.

Syrah took off her shoes and socks, then pushed them against the wall in line with the others. "What?"

"Your room is so neat. When I was your age, I had things all over the place. It would drive my mother crazy."

Syrah smoothed out a wrinkle on her bedcover. "It's not good to be messy."

"You know, it's okay if some things aren't perfect."

"I know," she said in a quiet voice, straightening a picture next to her bed. She checked for dust on her lampshade.

Jessie began to bite her nails. "Does your uncle expect things to be this neat?"

She shrugged, nonchalant. "I just don't want to make him mad. I like to be clean anyway."

"I'm sure he won't mind a little mess," Jessie said. Syrah shifted her attention to the window. "Why don't you write your father and tell him what a wonderful day you had?"

She turned to Jessie with eyes so devoid of feeling that Jessie felt a chill sweep through her. "No."

Jessie cleared her throat, surprised that such a harmless suggestion had caused such animosity. "Isn't there anyone you can write?"

Syrah continued to stare at her, daring her to show any amount of pity. "No."

Jessie began to sit down on the bed, but stopped, remembering how Syrah had smoothed out the wrinkles. She decided to sit at the writing desk near the far wall. "You know, I have a sister who loves to get letters. She'll even write you back. Have you ever gotten a letter before?"

Syrah adjusted her cap. "No."

"Not even birthday or Christmas cards?"

"No. Besides, cards are no big deal unless they have money in them."

"Oh." Jessie had no response. Syrah's eyes were too much like her uncle's: fierce and penetrating. She needed to find a way to soften that expression. "It's nice to get letters." She opened a desk drawer and took out paper and a pencil.

Syrah shoved her hands in her pockets. "That stuff isn't mine."

"I'm sure that your uncle made sure it was there for you to use. He put you in this room for a reason. It has a great view and a lovely writing desk for you to write letters."

Syrah still looked unconvinced.

Jessie stood and held out the pencil and paper. "I have to go shower and change. When I get back, please have a letter ready so that I can give it to my sister. She's even better with secrets than I am."

Syrah stared at the items, the cold in her eyes turning to worry. "Are you sure she'll write back?"

"Yes." *Even if I have to force her.*

She slowly took the items. "Is she as nice as you?"

Jessie hesitated. "Most times."

Syrah sat at her desk, smoothed out the paper and lifted the pencil to write. "Okay. What's her name?"

Jessie meant to say Teresa, but instead said, "Michelle."

Half an hour later, Jessie stared at herself in the mirror. The water cooled on her back as the steam from the shower dissipated. "I'm doing it wrong," she muttered to her reflection. "I'm supposed to be focusing on the man, not the child. But Syrah worried her. There was a deeper need to please Kenneth that went beyond wanting to make him proud. Had Kenneth gotten angry before about a messy room? Had Syrah accidentally unleashed the tiger Jessie had always suspected was there? She knew he could be heartless. The question was: how heartless?

She turned off the light and left the bathroom. Syrah would eventually go back to her father. She had to stop imagining herself in the middle of some family drama that probably didn't exist. She had to focus on Kenneth. She had to charm him. A snake charmer didn't think about the creature, just the dance. And she would make him dance to the tune of the Sapphire Pendant.

She remembered her father telling them the story of the pendant and the other antiques he worked on at Fedor Malenkov Jewelers, filling their minds with tales of murder and undying love. To him and his ancestors, jewelry had a special magic—objects swelling with secrets and stories. They had loved curling up on the couch, resting their heads against his cotton shirt, his deep voice drawing them to faraway lands as his large, scarred hands painted pictures in the air.

There had been many trips to the county's crown jewel: the Historical Society's museum. It boasted an assortment of artwork, jewelry, and writings that celebrated the cultural diversity of the county. In August, Mrs. Donovan would be donating the Arand necklace, a piece of jewelry rooted in the history of Randall, which would soon be visible for all to see and admire. It was an event her father would have loved to see, illustrating how history speaks through our adornments. The event would celebrate the cultural diversity of the county giving residents of all walks of life a sense of community.

She wrapped her hand over the gold chain on her neck. Her fingers pulsated with the memory of her first piece of jewelry and the story it held.

Very soon she would create a new history for the pendant that generations would hear. The story would begin tonight, on a summer evening, when she tangled with a kitten and charmed a serpent.

When Jessie returned to Syrah's room, she saw the girl sitting on the bed, staring down at her completed letter. In the room that held so much material wealth hung a sadness Jessie couldn't understand.

"I'm back!" she announced, trying to evoke enthusiasm.

Syrah looked up, her voice solemn. "I wrote the letter." She handed it to her.

"Great. Michelle's going to love it."

She glanced at Jessie's sweater and handbag. "Are you going somewhere?"

Jessie pushed the letter into her bag. "I'm going to my house. I eat dinner with my sisters. Teresa's a better cook than I am."

Syrah looked stricken. "But why can't you eat here?"

"Oh, I'm sure that your uncle wants to spend time alone with you, since he's been gone all day."

Syrah's hands trembled as she searched for words. "But—but I want you to stay."

Jessie squeezed her chin. "I'm coming back, love. You're acting as if I'm abandoning you. Tomorrow we'll have a wonderful time."

She shifted from one foot to the other, then back again. "Can I come with you?"

"But you haven't seen your uncle all day."

"That's okay."

Jessie kneeled and held her hands. "Are you afraid of him?"

She quickly shook her head. "No, I'm happy to be here."

They seemed like hollow words, but they sounded sincere. Jessie stood. "You can come another time. Don't look at me like that. You'll have fun with your uncle. Come on, let's go see what he has planned for dinner."

By the look of things, it appeared that he planned to have Brooke for dinner. Not that she could blame him. The little kitten had crossed her silk-clad legs so that they were touching his. She leaned toward him, as if she was aiming to dive into his lap. A tasteful amount of cleavage peeked through her top. Kenneth didn't seem to mind.

Jessie coughed. "Excuse me."

Kenneth looked startled; Brooke looked annoyed. "Can I talk to you a minute?" Jessie asked Kenneth.

"Sure." He tossed down a paper and stood.

"Stay right here," she told Syrah. "And no tricks."

Syrah smiled.

"I mean it."

Her smile grew wider, but she nodded.

Jessie led Kenneth to the corner of the family room, wedging herself between a large plant and the couch. She suddenly felt small in his presence, like a chipmunk in the presence of a hawk. Unfortunately, being backed up against the wall didn't ease her discomfort.

He had loosened his tie and unfastened the top two buttons of his blue shirt—the only indication that he was in a relaxed mood. He rested his hands on his hips. For the first time, he looked at her with interest—not hostility, disappointment, or annoyance. It was a little disconcerting not to see those familiar emotions in his eyes. She briefly allowed herself to remember a time when they weren't so civil to each other, a time when she had dreamed of him looking at her just like this and kissing her. She rubbed her forehead. She couldn't think of that foolish girl she had been.

His gaze grew concerned. "Are you getting a headache?"

Jessie let her hand fall. "No." She managed a smile. "At least I hope not."

"Is there a problem?" He inhaled her scent. She smelled fresh and alive, like a spring morning. He had to plant his feet in order not to step closer.

"Not really." She cleared her throat. "I was wondering what you had planned for dinner."

He shrugged. "Whatever you two want is fine with me. Just tell Ms. Rose."

"I'm going to my house to eat, so you will have to think of something for you and Syrah."

He rubbed his chin and stared at Syrah, who was tugging a loose thread on her shirt. "Can't you just take her with you?"

"No, I have to go home."

He turned back to her. "I hired you to look after Ace."

She stiffened. "Yes, I'm very aware what you *hired* me for. And I don't believe taking her home with me was one of the stipulations."

He sighed fiercely, glancing at Brooke. "But I have work to do."

She glanced at Brooke as well too. "I'm afraid *work* will have to wait." She lifted a brow. "You could just give Syrah the requisite bread and water and keep her in her room."

His fingers tapped his hip, and his eyes became unreadable. "I thought we had a truce."

"This isn't about us. She's feeling really displaced right now and she wants company."

Kenneth took off his tie and crumpled it in a ball. "That's why I hired you."

"I'm her companion, her nanny." She tried not to choke on the word. "Not her mother."

His lip curled. "And I'm not her father, so don't look at me as if I'm the one letting her down."

"Oh, relax. I'm sure she doesn't want you as a father. Nobody could live up to your perfect standards." She rubbed her nose. "So how often do you inspect her room for cleanliness?"

He frowned. "What are you talking about?"

"Aside from the room, I'm sure you don't consider it abnormal to pull away when she touches you. Are you scared her dirty fingers will soil your clothes?"

His frown deepened. "Are you feeling all right?"

"I'm fine."

"That's debatable."

She narrowed her eyes. "What isn't debatable is that she doesn't even want to be with you."

His jaw tensed. "She said that?"

"Not exactly—"

"Then I suggest you don't make that assumption."

Their eyes clashed in silent battle, Jessie's dark brown eyes slicing through his light brown ones. She suddenly scowled and shook his shoulder. "Breathe."

He took a deep breath.

"I hate when you do that."

He shook his head. "I'm not going to argue with you."

"Good. Circular arguments are tiresome." She rested against the wall. "Now, I know that you don't want her here, but she's a good kid and she wants to please you."

He stroked the leaves on the plant next to them. His voice was low. "And I know you have the worst possible opinion of me, but I have things I must get done."

"You'll have to prioritize."

A branch snapped in his fingers. "Don't overstep your bounds by telling me what to do."

She felt the brief sting of the temper he tried so hard to control. She decided not to provoke it further. "Fine."

He ran a tired hand down his face. "I'm sorry I was short with you. I just have a lot on my mind." He tossed the broken branch in the pot and stared at the soil. "I know you're trying to help, and I admire you for that."

Jessie ground her teeth. Damn. It was hard to hate him when he was like this—so apologetic, so human. She could almost feel the way he was able to collect his anger and tuck it away.

"You're entitled to being short every once in awhile. I could offer you lessons for a fee."

There was the hint of a smile. "Hmm."

She took his chin and forced him to look at her. She needed to read his eyes, knowing that they would belie his calm voice. She was right. His eyes smoldered with a fire that was not only fueled by anger, but by a volcanic desire she hadn't anticipated. She tried to step back, only to remember that she was against the wall. A delicious shudder raced up her body. She looked away.

His voice was low, calling to something deep within her. "Are you surprised, or embarrassed?" He fingered a loose tendril against her cheek.

Jessie kept her eyes averted.

"Or perhaps disgusted?"

No, not disgusted—she felt powerful. That wonderful intangible force that could be intoxicating in its command. He wanted her. That gave her control. She was free to indulge in the temptation standing before her. She could discover what he tasted like, how he felt. She took a step toward him to brush his lips. He abruptly moved back so that she ended up kissing his chin.

His mouth spread into a cruel smile. "Ah, so that's the game you're playing. I hadn't pictured you as one of those."

Her sense of power disintegrated. Blood rushed to her face as shame surrounded her. Her throat tightened, forbidding the passage of words or an explanation.

She slipped past him and made a quick exit, offering Syrah a hurried good-bye and Brooke an insincere one. She ran down the front steps, gulping in the cool night air, blinking away the hot tears in her eyes. She kicked a stone out of her way. She had been an idiot to think...*I must have read his eyes wrong.* She must have misunderstood the sensuous gleam she had seen.

She had underestimated him...again. He was used to playing games, used to misleading women by showing an attraction he didn't feel. His rejection made that clear. How could she have been stupid enough to believe that he was attracted to her, that he would want *her?* The memory of her actions made her feel ill. She had nothing to tempt a man like him, yet her foolish pride had allowed her to fall in his trap again.

Again she had given him the power to reject her, just as she had years ago. But it wouldn't happen again, not for a stupid bet. She would just tell Deborah that he was involved with someone else—that wasn't really losing, was it? She would get the pendant another way. She would work for it, even if it took years. She didn't have the skills to manipulate him. She didn't have his ruthlessness. Michelle was wrong; he was no ordinary man.

She walked to her car, then searched for the keys she had haphazardly thrown inside her handbag. After a few moments of fruitless searching, she rested her forehead against the hood. *Some grand exit.* If she had been in a horror film, she would be dead. Some murderous fiend with a chainsaw in one hand and a garbage bag in another would have done his dirty work. She would have deserved it. Hell, she would have welcomed it, because she had failed. She had failed her parents and her sisters. She threw down her bag. "The family loser," she said, disgusted.

She closed her eyes and listened to a car speed past in the distance, heard something scurry under a bush. The sound of tinkling metal interrupted the cry of a crow. Then she heard the grating of a key in her car door. A hand covered her mouth before she could scream.

"Relax, Jas, it's just me." Kenneth removed his hand. "Why are you standing out here?"

There was no reason to reply. She was wallowing in self-pity, reliving her failures. What did he know about failure? She took her handbag from him and opened the door. She tossed her bag on the passenger seat and got in. Kenneth grabbed the door before she could slam it shut. He rested his forearms and chin on the frame and looked down at her with a lazy grin.

"You and I have a lot in common, you know," he said casually. "We both like sports and we both like games." He paused. "But do you know the one problem with games?"

Jessie started the ignition.

"Someone has to lose." He closed the car door and walked away.

Chapter Thirteen

When Jessie reached home, the spicy scent of stewed chicken with peas and rice greeted her. She dropped her handbag in the foyer and went into the kitchen, surprised to see that her sisters were halfway through dinner.

"I was only a few minutes late. You could have waited for me," she said. She glanced and noticed that a plate hadn't been set out for her either. "What's going on?"

"What are you doing here?" Michelle asked.

She took a seat. "I always eat dinner with you."

Teresa placed a plate and utensils in front of her. "We expected you to eat with them."

"Oh." It was a logical deduction. Of course, she couldn't tell them that she hoped never to see Kenneth again. Or if she did, she hoped an angry mob would be leading him towards the gallows like the beast that he was. "The food's better here." She piled her plate and began to eat. After a few seconds, she glanced up. Her sisters were watching her. "What?"

Michelle delicately dabbed her mouth. "We're waiting to hear a report."

"There's nothing to say. His house is nice."

Teresa cut her chicken. "Is the child difficult?"

"No, she's wonderful. Unfortunately, she wants to stay with Kenneth." Jessie retrieved Syrah's letter from her bag and handed it to Michelle. "She wrote you a letter."

Michelle stared at it. "Me? Why?"

"I asked her to. I think she needs someone to talk to, someone she feels safe with. Besides, I thought you could use a friend." Michelle's job had been her life since her separation and the death of their parents. "You will respond, won't you?"

"Of course I'll reply." She snatched the letter. "I'm not a complete ogre, you know."

"I know. That's why when she asked me if you were nice, I said that when the moon was full, you are at your best."

Michelle laughed. "At least I don't have your temper."

Teresa shook her head in disagreement. "Oh, please. I'm the only one born without a temper."

"Remind me to write you a reality check."

Teresa put down her fork. "It's true. Jessie's temper's like a bonfire. You turn into a glacier, and I stay mellow."

"Like an undercurrent. You trick people into believing they're safe until you're ready to drown them."

Teresa rolled her eyes and began to eat.

Michelle placed Syrah's letter beside her, then clasped her hands. "Enough about Teresa. How's Mission Impossible going?"

Jessie lifted her glass. "If I throw water on you, will you melt?"

"I'm sorry. Bad joke. But how is it going?"

"Nowhere." She groaned. "I met Brooke Radson."

"Bright woman. She's given Mrs. Donovan excellent advice on running her antiques shop," Michelle said.

"Aside from being brilliant, she's beautiful. The kind of woman you want to kiss and kick at the same time. I can't compete with her. I thought I had a chance when..." She trailed off.

"When what?" Teresa urged.

She bit her lip. Shame rushed back to her, as fresh as before. Her eyes fell. "I tried to kiss him." She glanced up. "He moved away."

Michelle frowned. "Why were you trying to kiss him?"

"Because he looked like he wanted to kiss me."

Teresa leaned forward. "What kind of look was that?"

"Never mind," Michelle said before Jessie could reply. "What did he say when he moved away?"

Jessie shrugged. "I didn't give him the chance to say anything. But when I was leaving, he said, 'The problem with games is that someone has to lose.'"

Michelle nodded. "Clever man."

"I'm glad you think so," she said bitterly. "Perhaps you should have accepted the bet."

"Sorry, *I'm* too clever for that."

Her jaw tightened. "I'm doing this for us because I thought the pendant was important. I don't see you doing anything to get it back."

"I'm saving."

"Hell, if you had just stayed married, we could have bought it back."

Teresa touched her hand. "Jessie, that's not fair."

Jessie kept her gaze on Michelle's cool face. "What's not fair is that she thinks this is all some sort of joke. I wanted to win. I wanted to do something important and I failed again. Is that what you want me to admit? That I'm a failure? That nothing I think of is logical and of any importance?"

"You're not a failure," Michelle said. "Yes, I do admit that I don't understand the way you do things, but you do them with such conviction that I have to give you credit. However, I do not believe in degrading myself for something that can be obtained in another manner."

"It's too late to turn back," Teresa said. "If she loses, she has to be Deborah's maid for a year."

She looked thoughtful. "Will she pay you?"

Jessie stared at her, outraged. "Michelle!"

"That's not the point," Teresa said. "I believe Jessie can charm Kenneth. She just needs help in how to do it. Give her tips."

Michelle took a sip of her drink. "You just need to gain his trust. You can't just throw yourself at him when the mood strikes you."

"I feel like striking you right now."

"Jessie," Teresa warned.

"I didn't throw myself at him, as she'd like to suggest. I was subtle and, I thought, alluring." She glared at Michelle. "You said I had everything necessary to attract a man, so I thought he might want to kiss me. I was wrong."

Michelle buttered a roll. "I doubt you were wrong, but you have to gain his trust before he'll become vulnerable."

"Kissing is not about being vulnerable. People do it all the time."

"When you care about someone, it's different."

"You think he cares about me?"

"Always has."

She rested her chin in her hands. "I see Dad wasn't the only dreamer."

Michelle shrugged and bit into her roll.

"Perhaps you can try to arrange something for all of you to do together," Teresa said.

Jessie shook her head. "He's too busy."

"He comes home in the evening, doesn't he?"

"At this point, it seems that he either doesn't come home or brings company."

"So challenge him to something," Michelle said. "Nobody's been able to resist a challenge from you."

Teresa waved her hand. "No, don't challenge him. You're too competitive as it is." She folded her arms. "This will have to be your last dinner with us."

"Why? You're my strategic team."

"Dinner is the perfect time to put on the charm."

Michelle wiped the corners of her mouth. "Unless something gets caught in your teeth. Or you choke…"

Teresa shot her a warning glare. "Be quiet." She turned to Jessie. "Listen to me. Eat dinner with him. It's the perfect time to see how his day was and to chat. Then perhaps you can wheedle your way into his trust."

"Under false pretenses, of course," Michelle muttered.

Her sisters ignored her.

"Just remember your manners. Don't reach across the table for anything."

"Don't talk with your mouth full," Michelle added.

"Don't put your elbows on the table."

"Don't slurp your soup."

Jessie licked her fingers. "I have been housebroken. Thank you."

Teresa handed her a napkin. "Don't do that either. You have to be charming, graceful, and above all feminine."

Michelle crossed her arms and leaned forward. "Which means: don't lose your temper."

She didn't lose her temper for an entire week. Unfortunately, whatever charm was, she obviously didn't have it. The food was divine; the company was not. Kenneth brought his work to the table, spreading out pens, papers, manila folders, and calculating devices as if he were in a work room instead of a dining room.

On several occasions he would further disrupt the dining experience by accepting both business and family calls at the table. He would nod his head when Syrah spoke, but both she and Jessie knew that his mind was elsewhere. Though his behavior vexed her, for the first two days, Jessie said nothing. She tried to catch his attention with a coy smile or a sly glance if he looked at her, which was rare. Nothing worked. On the fourth day, she tried to engage him in conversation as he wrote his bills.

She licked her lips. "Is there anything I could help you with?"

"No."

She spotted an advertisement from Macy's with a cashmere blouse circled twice in black. "That's a lovely blouse. It would make a great gift."

"It's for my mother," he muttered.

She lifted the ad and looked closely. In the margin was a woman's scrawl detailing the size, color, and style. "Her birthday's coming up?"

"No, she just wants it."

"Why don't you wait for her birthday?"

He sent her a brief glance. "Because she wants it now."

"And as the ever-dutiful son, you'll buy it for her."

He licked an envelope and sealed it.

She sighed. His relationship with his mother was none of her business. She shifted her gaze to a catalog from the University of Maryland. "Are they already asking for donations?" she asked as he wrote out a check.

He didn't raise his head. "My nephew goes there. He needs money for another semester."

"What is he studying?"

He shrugged.

"What year is he?"

"A sixth-year junior."

Her eyebrows flew up. "A what?"

He tore out the check. "He's had trouble deciding what to do."

"For two extra years? Why are you paying for his indecision? Make him get a job and pay his own tuition. He'll make up his mind fast. Trust me."

He took a deep breath, then slid his checkbook across the table. It stopped in front of her. "Whose name is on this?"

She chewed her lip. "Yours."

"Then whose business is it?"

She took another helping of corn.

It was now day seven. Jessie stared at Kenneth's bent head. Enough was enough. She had to do something to get his attention. She stabbed her peas, trying to think.

"It's been so nice to have you eat with us, Aunt Jessie, hasn't it, Uncle?" Syrah asked.

"Sure," Kenneth said, not taking his eyes off the figures in front of him.

Syrah grinned at Jessie, offering her the same embarrassed expression parents give when their children are misbehaving in public.

Jessie's patience snapped. "You know, it's not polite to bring work to the dinner table when you have a guest."

"You're not a guest."

Jessie continued to stab into her vegetables. She wouldn't get angry. She wouldn't imagine the peas were little Kenneths rolling around on her plate. She had to engage him in conversation, talk about something that interested him.

"I was thinking of this great idea for your negotiations with Trans Moore. I heard their president is a sucker for—"

"Thanks, but I'm really busy right now."

It took Jessie a moment to realize that Kenneth had just made his statement the other day to help her save face. He really wasn't interested in her ideas, which wasn't surprising. Nobody usually was.

"Can I be excused?" Syrah suddenly asked. "I finished all my food."

"How about dessert?" Jessie asked.

"I'll get it later."

"Okay."

"Did you eat your vegetables?" Kenneth muttered.

Jessie scowled. "If you looked up from your papers, you'd see that her plate is wiped clean."

Kenneth glanced up, noted the plate, then went back to work. "Oh. Then go on."

"Thanks." Syrah stood, then stared at them, as though uncertain she should leave them alone together. She had the expression of a trainer worried about leaving two prized lions in the same pen.

Jessie grinned. "We'll be fine."

Syrah pushed in her chair and ran upstairs.

Jessie glared at Kenneth's bent head. "If you want to do your work, why don't you just leave the table?"

"I think you're forgetting that this is my house," he said coolly.

"What's so important that you can't even spare a few moments at the dinner table?"

"It's called work. I'm sure you're familiar with it."

Jessie clenched her teeth. "What's that supposed to mean?"

He began writing down some figures. "It means that I don't have the luxury of losing my job."

"You're the one who got me fired."

"And who can you blame for your past dismissals?"

"You're just a greedy bastard that only thinks about money."

He tapped his pencil against his chin and looked up at the ceiling pensively. "Oh, yes, that's right. I don't keep my business aboveboard for the numerous employees I have, for the community I helped revive, or to make sure that my family lives comfortably. I do it all for the bottom line." He pointed the pencil at her. "Thanks for reminding me."

Arrogant pig. "You don't need to be sarcastic."

"Is that what I am? I thought I was being honest."

"If you don't want to eat, you should go somewhere else."

He returned his attention to his papers. "You're not my wife and you're not my girlfriend, so don't believe you have the authority to tell me what to do in my own home."

She pushed food around on her plate. "Unlike the other disillusioned girls pining after you, I have no desire to be either."

His lips twisted into a cynical smile. "Oh, so that attempted kiss was my imagination?"

Heat burned her cheeks. She didn't know if it was from shame or temper, and she didn't care. She put down her fork with deliberation. "No, I briefly forgot I'm not your type. You're a very deep and spiritual man. You look for the special qualities of a woman, like how long her legs are, or the size of her chest. While I—"

"Like to play games." He waved his pencil. "Don't throw your insecurities about not being pretty or smart onto me."

She could feel her hands tighten. Why was it so easy for him to open her wounds and expose her, leaving her scars bare to bleed? "That's not true." Jessie pounded her fist on the table, her wrist hitting a forkful of food. It flew through the air, landing on Kenneth's crisp white shirt.

Jessie winced as she saw the food slowly trail a path down his shirt, like a lazy slug. "That was an accident."

Kenneth removed the fork, scraped the food away, and put it on his plate. He gathered all his papers together and shoved them in his briefcase. He then lifted a spoonful of mashed potatoes and aimed it at her.

Her mouth dropped open. "You wouldn't," she whispered.

He nodded. "Yes, I would." He let the spoon go. A big splat landed on her shoulder.

She scooped up the mashed-potato glob and glared at him. "That was a mistake, Mr. Preston." She grabbed a handful of baked beans.

He gestured to her hand. "I believe you'll regret that, Ms. Clifton."

"I doubt it." She flung the beans at him, but he ducked, and they splattered the wall behind him.

"Your aim was bit off."

She grabbed her juice and threw it in his face, soaking him. She lifted her chin. "How's that for aim?"

He took a napkin and wiped at the juice sliding down his face. He took a handful of mashed potatoes and formed it into a ball.

"I was very good at dodge ball," she said. She ducked when he threw the ball at her. "Ha! Missed me!" She laughed, only to have the ball hit her in the face.

Kenneth grinned. "I was also good at dodge ball. I could fake out any opponent."

Jessie wiped her face and threw the remnants at him. Kenneth moved to another part of the table and grabbed a handful of vegetables. She grabbed more baked beans. They stared at each other, ready for the battle to begin.

"We don't have to do this," Kenneth said.

"I know." She fired.

And the battle began. They grabbed and threw whatever was close, aiming and firing at random. Neither would admit that after a few moments, it became enjoyable, that they had almost forgotten what the argument was about. It was the thrill of the game that mattered; it was a way to vent their mutual dislike and attraction to each other.

"All right, that's enough!" Kenneth said after a few minutes of battle had passed.

Jessie threw a biscuit. It hit him on the forehead and landed on the table. She picked up a mixture that had congealed together on the table.

He seized her wrist before she could throw it, forcing her to drop the mixture. "I said that's enough."

She yanked her wrist free. "Fine."

He stared at her. She had an assortment of food over her face and clothes and looked like a contestant on a kids' TV show. He imagined that he didn't look much better.

"Look at the mess you created," Jessie said, surveying the damage. The beautiful dining room had been turned into a kindergarten cafeteria. Food stuck to a painting, hung on chairs, and dotted the floor.

"Me? You started it."

"It was an accident." She pointed a finger at him. "Your spoonful was pure revenge."

"Yes. You deserved it."

"I deserved it?" Her voice cracked.

"You need to control that damned temper of yours."

She walked up to him, ready to tell him off, but she slipped on some peas and crashed into him. He stepped back and slipped on some juice.

They both landed with a thud.

"Oof!" he said.

"Did you hurt yourself?"

"Would you care?"

"Not really."

He rubbed the back of his head, feeling the beginning of a lump. "Then, no, I didn't." He looked up at her. She was too close, damn it. He could feel the shape of her thigh between his legs, and it didn't help that her breasts were crushed against his chest. Their shirts were wet, leaving only a thin layer of cotton to separate him from her nakedness. He could see the outline of her bra. He inwardly groaned. He stared up at her for a moment, watching a glob of mashed potato slide down her cheek. He wiped it away with his thumb. Even though her face looked a mess, he still had a wild desire to kiss her.

"What are you up to, Jasmine?" he asked, his breath warm against her face. "What type of revenge are you seeking? Emotional blackmail, perhaps? Do you wish to ruin my reputation?"

She pulled away from him, aware of their closeness and the feel of his pounding heart beneath hers. "Is that possible?"

He sat up and wiped peas from his forehead. "Would you like it to be?"

"No."

"No pranks or tricks up your sleeve?"

"No. I don't want to hurt you."

The corner of his mouth quirked. "That's a dangerous statement to believe. Are you willing to shake on it?"

"Yes."

She held out her hand and he shook hers. When he let go, her hand was covered in mashed potatoes. She watched as it slipped down her palm and plopped to the floor.

"You disgusting—" She stopped and patted the side of his face, smearing the potatoes on his cheek. "Thank you for your trust."

He began to reach for her, his eyes glittering with the playful promise of revenge. He halted when he saw something glittering around her neck.

Chapter Fourteen

"**H**old on. What's that?" he asked in an odd voice.

Jessie sat back and looked down at herself. "What's what?"

He lifted the necklace from her neck. His warm fingers brushed against her skin, sending goose bumps up her arms.

"Is this what I think it is?" His voice was hoarse.

"What do you think it is?"

He slowly shook his head. "No, let's not play games now. Not now. Just answer me."

Jessie clutched the necklace in her fist. "It's nothing."

"This is the necklace I gave you." His eyes pierced into hers. "Why are you still wearing it?"

Jessie began to stand, but Kenneth grabbed her wrist. "Answer me."

Her voice was soft. "Do you want it back? Is that it?"

"Do you want to give it back to me?"

She let her hands fall in her lap.

He stared at her in disbelief. "I can't figure you out. You act like I'm scum, and yet you still wear the necklace I gave you years ago." His eyes fell on the necklace. "That stupid, dented piece of crap."

She covered it from his disgusted gaze. "It isn't a piece of crap."

He leaped to his feet. "I forgot; that's the title you reserve for me. The guy who worked hard to save enough money just to give that to you, because you meant a lot to him. I'm the worst person in the world, because I hurt you. Well, here's a news flash: you hurt me. I discovered that because you were so quick to despise me, that deep down you already did."

"You gave me every reason to despise you." She unlatched the necklace. "Do you want it back?"

He pushed a chair hard against the table, causing a glass to topple and crash to the floor. "I don't know why I bother. Even a rock isn't this dumb."

Jessie inwardly flinched. He was right. She could no longer pretend to misunderstand what he was saying. "It was the first piece of jewelry anyone had ever given me." She held it up in front of her. Her parents had thought her too boyish for such things. "I wore it out of hope, a fantasy...that on some level, what happened between us was real."

"It was real."

She ran a hand down her arm. "No, it never existed."

"Jasmine—"

"It started out as a dream. A guy was going to take me to the prom. Not just any guy—Mr. Perfect."

Kenneth winced, glancing away.

"I didn't tell anyone because I wanted it to be a surprise. I wanted to see my family's face when you walked through the door. I dreamt of how people would stare when I arrived at the prom with you. I sat and waited. My family asked me what I was doing, and I told them that my prom date was coming. He never did." She bit her lip, not sure whether she wanted to laugh or cry. How pathetic she must have looked. "My mother called up my cousin, and he took me. I made excuses for you in my mind, some of them quite imaginative. You would have been impressed. Then, on the drive home, I saw you on Lover's Hill, making out with another girl as if your very existence depended on it."

He rubbed the back of his neck. "It wasn't what you thought."

She rolled her eyes. "It doesn't matter what I thought. I know what I saw."

"Just listen for a minute." He pulled out a chair and sat down. "It was going to be everything you'd dreamed of." He began to count on his fingers. "I had the tux, the limo, the corsage, the tickets, the dinner reservations. I remember that the day was clear and I vowed you'd have the best prom ever. It was only an hour before I was to meet you when everything changed."

Her heart began to pound. Here came the truth—the reason she had been avoiding all these years for fear that she would forgive him. "What happened?"

Kenneth opened his mouth to explain, but no words came forth. The truth was that his father had come back into his life. He had threatened to tell everyone that Kenneth was the illegitimate son of a drunk if he didn't give him money. Kenneth had been so ashamed that he couldn't look at anyone...be with anyone. Until Regine offered herself to a young man who felt his entire world had collapsed on him.

"Could you...?" He silently swore. Here at last was the perfect opportunity to explain, and he couldn't. He couldn't give her what she wanted, what she deserved: the truth. "Could you just accept that I wanted to be there?" He clasped his hands together and let his gaze fall. "But I couldn't see anyone, least of all you. I was staring up at the stars, thinking of what I would say to you when Regine came and discovered my weakness."

She wiggled her eyebrows. "Lucky girl. I didn't realize you had any."

He met her gaze, pleading with her to understand. "Everyone does."

She pounded her fist on the table. She was sick of his dishonesty. "Why can't you just admit that you used me? I'll understand. I've been angry this long. I know you didn't want to take me. It's the deception that makes it worse." She took a deep breath and relaxed her hands. "I understand ambition and I understand the price of family loyalty. What I don't understand is why you need to pretend to be something you're not."

"I never used you," he said, his tone hard. "I'm sorry I missed the prom. I'm sorry you saw me with Regine, who had nothing to do with you. What I don't understand is why you act as if I betrayed you. We were friends; I messed up. Why wouldn't you just let me make it up to you?"

"Because you can't make up for betrayal with a dinner date."

He rested his head back and threw his hands up, exasperated. "How the hell did I betray you?"

"You broke a bargain."

He sat up. "What?"

"You convinced me to give up my scholarship so that Eddie could have it. You wanted Eddie to be given a chance. Remember? You said I'd get other chances and that I didn't have to worry. You said you'd make it up to me, which I thought was the prom. I was so stupid that I believed you, and I spoke to Eddie and my sponsor to let him have the money instead of me. But did I get any other offers? No. So my father had to sell a treasured family heirloom in order to pay for my schooling." She laughed bitterly. "Which was a waste, because I never completed it anyway."

He frowned. "But I never told you to do that."

"Yes, you did. You said how wonderful it would be if Eddie had my opportunity. We talked about it for nearly an hour."

Color drained from his face. He looked ill. "I was just talking, Jasmine. I had no idea you would take me literally."

She gripped the edge of the table. "Of course you did. You knew how much I loved you. You knew that I would do anything for you."

He looked horrified. "That's not true. We were friends. Maybe you had a crush, but you were young and—"

"I was young and I had a heart, and you broke it. Was I so insignificant to you that you couldn't even see how I felt?"

Her heart crashed to her feet when she saw the look on his face. He hadn't known. All this time she had thought he had spitefully captured her heart and broken it, when he hadn't known he had captured it in the first place. False pride laughed at her again. How could he have known? He had never really seen her. Plain, boyish jocks didn't care about stupid high school dances. They were just pals and would understand. She glanced up at him. He was too still. She jumped up and shook him. "Breathe."

He continued to stare at the wall.

She shook him harder. "Stop that or I'll punch you."

He took a deep breath and began to cough.

She fell back into her chair. "I wish you wouldn't do that."

He didn't hear her. His voice was quiet, as if he were in a dream. "I could never figure out why you hated me so much. What had I done that—"

She shrugged, wanting to make light of it. "Well, it's all over now."

"Why didn't Eddie tell me?"

"Who knows?" *Who cares?* She wanted to forget everything. "It's okay."

He shook his head. "No wonder you hated me if you thought me capable of that. You thought you were in love with me and I..."

She touched his sleeve. His face was so anguished; she could almost see the painful memories flash in his eyes. He remembered his sadness and added hers. "I shouldn't have told you."

"I should have known."

"You couldn't have known. How would an eagle know a blade of grass worships him?"

She would forgive him, but she would never trust him. How could he have known he was the first love of a young girl desperate to fit in? Their past was a setup meant for heartbreak: French lessons in the park, on the bay. She sighed, forgiving the foolish girl she'd once been. "It didn't matter anyway."

"It does matter," he said, with a vehemence that shocked her. "You were my best friend. You were the only one who...You were all I had, the only person I could share my thoughts with. He knew that, and he turned us into enemies."

His best friend? She didn't understand what he was saying, but she knew he couldn't blame Eddie. "No, *I* turned us into enemies. I played the woman scorned and enjoyed it. I never gave you the chance to explain, because..." Her voice fell. "I didn't want a reason to care about you again."

"And now?"

"Now what?"

He shoved his hands in his pockets. "Can you care about me again?"

She narrowed her eyes, cautious. "Be friends?"

He nodded.

She chewed her lower lip, unsure.

"Jasmine, remember when you used to collect stones?"

"Yes."

He held out his hand. In the middle of his palm sat a turquoise stone. "You gave this to me." He came around the table and stood in front of her. "You're not the only one who had hope."

"Kenneth, I didn't give you this."

He looked down, stunned. "You didn't?"

She tweaked his chin. "Gotcha."

"Up to your old tricks." He grinned. "I should have known."

She stared at the floor, not knowing what else to say.

His voice changed, "Jasmine, it's nice to see you again!"

She glanced up, startled. "I'm sorry?"

He hugged her and spun her around. "It's been a long time!" He kissed both her cheeks. "How long has it been? Ten, twelve years? You look great. What have you been up to?"

Jessie laughed. "What are you doing?"

"I haven't been up to much. I've been helping this company widen its profit margin. Radson Electronics. You might have heard of it?" He lifted an eyebrow, inviting her to play along.

She smothered a grin. "Oh, yes. I think so. Michelle talks about it all the time. I'm glad you're working there. I know how hard it is for you to keep a job. I, on the other hand, work for this crazy workaholic, looking after his niece. Fortunately, I'm having so much fun; I don't mind finding paper clips in my salad."

His eyes burned into hers. "I missed you."

I missed you too. "Yeah."

He hugged her again. She'd remembered this most about him. He had always been affectionate: pulling her hair, kissing her forehead, grabbing her hand. It felt good to be in his arms. Too good.

She wrinkled her nose. "This is disgusting. We're covered in food."

He shrugged. She could feel the muscles in his chest move against her. She briefly shut her eyes. "Who cares?" he said. "I just got one of my best friends back."

One of his best friends? Doesn't he have enough friends? She pulled away. "So you've conquered your only enemy."

He laughed. "Not quite. Some board members want me to resign; some family members would like me dead—"

She widened her eyes alarmed. "What?"

"Inheritance. And then there are the women."

"Women?"

"With the probability of sounding vain—yes, women. But you can help me." He rested against the table. "As friends, let's make a promise that we'll warn each other about bets, dares, or pranks concerning one another." He flashed her a conspiratorial grin. "You know, it will be a great relief to have you on my side. You wouldn't believe the amount of women who bet that they can get a date with me."

Damn. "Oh, really?"

"Yes, you wouldn't comprehend the lengths some women will go to." He lightly touched her chin, then let his hand fall. "I'm glad you're not like that. You wouldn't go after some guy just because of a stupid bet."

She swallowed hard. "That's right." The gentle glow in his eyes made her want to reveal all, but she said nothing.

"Good." He turned away. Jessie squeezed her eyes shut and silently swore.

"This place looks awful," he said. "Ms. Rose is going to have a heart attack when she sees it."

"I wouldn't want that. I like her."

"I'm glad. She's American, but she cooks Caribbean food like a dream. Do you still like 'dip and fall back'?"

"Yes."

"I'll make sure she makes it for you."

His kindness hurt. "You should go to bed. I'll clean up. I don't mind." She needed time alone to think anyway. Physical labor always helped to clear her thoughts, and she definitely needed to clear them. She silently groaned when he said, "Neither do I."

They filled two buckets with soap and water. Kenneth mopped the floor while Jessie scrubbed the table and chairs. They both wiped the walls, "accidentally" splashing each other once in a while. Morning slipped through the windows by the time they finished.

Kenneth rubbed his eyes and yawned. "Wow, it's amazing what we can get done when we're not arguing with each other."

"I'm…sorry about everything," Jessie stammered.

"You don't—"

"I mean everything." *Like the fact that the only reason I'm talking to you now is because of a ridiculous bet.*

He draped a brotherly arm around her shoulders. Jessie had to resist the urge to lean into him. "Now that I've got you in this remorseful mood, you probably wouldn't mind paying for the cost of my dry cleaning."

Jessie elbowed him in the ribs. "You still have a tux you owe me."

"I have my old prom tux upstairs."

"Can you still fit into it?"

He gave a world-weary sigh. "No, I got fat."

She laughed. "The only place you got fat was in your wallet."

"Yes. And I have to be at work in three hours."

Jessie looked at her hands, then pulled at her cheeks. "Mashed potatoes and peas cannot be good for the skin. I can feel my face hardening."

"No, your face always looks like that."

She punched him in the shoulder. "I thought we were friends."

"Sorry." He rubbed his shoulder. "Old habit. I'll remember next time." He unbuttoned his shirt.

"What are you doing?" Her voice came out as a squeak.

He stripped off his shirt and looked at his shoulder. "I'm looking to see if you left a mark." His eyes were bright with merriment. "Were you expecting something else?"

"No." She touched his shoulder and noticed a tiny bruise. "Oh, damn, did I do that?"

He pulled up his shirt. "Probably not. You punch like a girl."

Jessie met his eyes, ready for battle, but was quickly assuaged by the teasing gleam there. A tingling sensation entered her stomach. She licked her lips, which had suddenly become dry. Slowly the distance between their lips began to close.

"Uncle Kenneth," Syrah called from the hallway. They pulled apart before she entered the room. "I had a nightmare and couldn't find Aunt Jessie—" When she saw Kenneth and Jessie, her mouth dropped open.

"We, uh…" Kenneth looked at Jessie for help.

"It's an ancient ritual practiced by a small tribe…uh…to cover yourself in food for good luck," Jessie improvised.

Syrah nodded her head. "Oh."

"We just wanted to check it out." She tugged on her shirt. "I'd better go change."

Kenneth grabbed her hand before she could leave. His voice was soft, brushing against her ear like a caress. "Good morning, Jasmine. Sleep well."

She was in deep trouble, deeper than she ever thought possible. What had happened to her integrity? Jessie got out of the shower and changed. Not only had she made a promise she was already breaking, but she was falling for him again. With no reason to hate him, she had nothing to protect herself.

But she had a duty. She couldn't put her own foolish desires in front of her family again. If she had cared about how much her parents had wanted to send her to college, she wouldn't have given her scholarship away. She couldn't let her family down for a man who would never return her affections. Damn it, she had to win for her father, for her family. She couldn't bow out and admit defeat, not when she had made such progress.

Life was a battle that left a few casualties. Kenneth wouldn't necessarily be a casualty. He would understand her need to get the pendant back. He had to. It was a risk she needed to take. She rested against the door. But it still felt wrong.

Chapter Fifteen

It was nearly noon when she woke up. She pulled together an outfit (one of Teresa's blouses, which was a little too big, jeans, and a light sweater), then noticed that the hamper where she had carelessly thrown her clothes was empty. She ran downstairs and found Freda loading the washing machine.

"Are you washing my clothes with his?" she asked, noticing one of Kenneth's shirts dangling out of the machine.

Freda sent her a haughty look. "You don't expect me to do a separate load for you, do you?"

"I didn't expect you to do it at all."

"Well, I am."

"Thank you, but…" She let her words trail off, but Freda understood clearly.

She grinned. "If your unmentionables start to multiply, I'll separate the clothes."

Shamefaced, Jessie went into the family room. She found Syrah putting together a puzzle.

"Sorry I'm late," she said. "You should have woken me."

"That's all right. Uncle was late for work too." A wicked grin spread on her face. "You should have seen his face when he saw what time it was."

"I'm sure it was very entertaining." The thought of Kenneth brought heat to her face. Not just the thought of him, the memory of him, the feel of his arm around her shoulder, his chest against hers. The warmth he offered when they became friends. He was an unfortunate pawn, but there was no other choice. Still, she definitely had to talk to Teresa.

"Get your shoes, Syrah. I have to run some errands."

Jessie glanced at the gray two-story building as she parked. It was built in a traditional country-home style with a wraparound porch and arched windows. The garden was its most alluring aspect, exploding with blush-colored roses, pink tulips, and stone urns spilling over with purple geraniums, irises, and peonies. It had been their mother's joy. At times she could see her mother's orange cartwheel hat bent over a bud peeking through the soil. Now Teresa tended to it just as faithfully.

Jessie checked the time. Teresa usually didn't have students until later in the afternoon. She hoped that schedule hadn't changed. As they walked up the drive, they noticed a redheaded girl weeding.

"Hey, can I help?" Syrah asked the girl.

"Sure." She looked up at Jessie. "If your mom will let you."

"I'm not her—" Jessie began.

"Can I?" Syrah interrupted.

"Okay."

Jessie left Syrah in the garden and walked into the house. The smell of magnolias and daylilies scented the air.

"Well, look who's here," Teresa said, putting down a sheet of music. "What's going on?"

Jessie sat on the couch. "Since when did you have other kids weed the garden? You never let me weed."

"That's because you couldn't tell a weed from a flower. Denise is bored and driving her mother crazy, so I thought I could make her useful. Besides, later I'm going to make some body creams."

Jessie glanced at the clock. "Don't you have a student this afternoon?"

Teresa smiled sadly. "Not anymore, I'm afraid. Patricia has decided that she wants to learn to play the trombone."

"I'm sorry."

She brushed the pity away with a wave of her hand. "I'm used to it. When you're free, I need help clearing the garage. Michelle has been complaining that it's a safety hazard."

"I'll see when I have a free moment." *Which might be sooner than you think.*

"So what are you doing here?"

She bit her thumbnail, then stopped. "I need your advice. I'm in big trouble."

"It can't be bigger than—"

"It is." She took a deep breath, then said in a rush, "I think I'm falling in love with Kenneth again."

Teresa waved her hands as if trying to free herself from a cobweb. "Wait a minute. What do you mean by *again?*"

"When he was tutoring me, I fell in love with him. After the prom, I hated him, but now that we've made up, I think I'm falling for him again." She buried her head in her hands. "I can't believe I'm so stupid. You would think one heartbreak was enough. I know he doesn't think of me that way. I'm just a pal, someone you kiss on the cheek and pat on the back." She looked at her sister. "But when I look at him…"

"I don't see what the problem is. Just charm Kenneth for real. It won't be hard. You were meant to be together."

"I'm not in the mood to hear about your visions."

She sighed. "You never are. So what do you want to do?"

"I want to stop feeling this way. I want to charm him. I want him to want me and want to win that bet."

"So it's his friendship or the pendant?"

She pinched the couch cushion. "I've put friendship over family honor before. It wouldn't be fair to do it again."

"We only want you to be happy. We'll save enough to buy the pendant back. The unfortunate question is: could you stand being Deborah's maid for a year?"

Jessie rested her chin on the back of the couch. She could save a friendship and torture herself, secretly loving him while she lost the pendant and her dignity. He wasn't worth that much. She raised her head. "No, I have to win. I refuse to fall in love with him and be like the hundreds of other women who want him." She straightened as her conviction grew. "I don't want him, I want the pendant. That's all that matters. Besides, it's a harmless bet." Jessie chewed on her nails, her conviction wavering. "He doesn't have to know about it, right?"

"Right. Besides, if you kill him with kindness, even if he does find out, he'll forgive you." Teresa held up a hand as a thought struck her.

"Wait right here."

Teresa came back with a small bouquet of daylilies. "I was going to put them in the dining room."

"What are these for?" Jessie asked, taking the bouquet. It smelled sweet and looked like bursting sunbeams.

"A gift for him."

Jessie handed it back to her. "I can't give a man flowers."

Teresa pushed it away. "Why not? They're beautiful. Men like flowers too. For all you know, you may start a trend." She grinned.

"I don't know."

"Then find out. Stop stalling."

Jessie glanced down at the flowers again and inhaled their scent.

"If I were you, I'd bet on love. A year can go faster than you think."

True, but unrequited love can make a year feel like eternity.

Jessie headed for her car. "Come on, Syrah."

Syrah leaped up and raced after her. "Are we leaving already? Do we have to?"

Jessie stopped and stared at Syrah, who was covered in dirt. "I have to deliver these flowers."

"Can I stay here and help Denise weed? We've got more to do, and…" She lowered her voice. "I may even get paid for it. Then we'll go and get ice cream. She said that her mother can drop me home later."

Teresa came out onto the porch. "It's okay," she said.

Jessie tugged on Syrah's cap. "Be good, then. I'll tell your uncle where you are."

"Thanks." She ran back to the garden.

Jessie sat in her car and stared at the bouquet of daylilies, then glanced up at the building. Like a proud mother, the sun polished the glass windows of Radson Electronics and Software. She sighed. She might as well get it over with. She felt ridiculous going through security with the bouquet, and totally idiotic when she got in the elevator and people complimented her.

"Oh, those are lovely flowers. You are so lucky," one woman said.

"How do you know she's lucky?" another replied. "He's probably trying to get on her good side." She pulled Jessie's collar so she could whisper in her ear. "Don't let him bribe you with flowers, dear. Wait for the jewelry."

Jessie smiled weakly. "Uh, right."

The elevator stopped on the third floor, and two women Jessie recognized stepped on: Willow Woman, who she discovered was named Claire Barker, and her friend, Janet Perez.

"I had the most fabulous date with Kenneth the other night," Claire said.

Jessie frowned. That couldn't be right, Kenneth had been home most of the night. Perhaps she meant early evening. She mentally kicked herself. It was none of her business.

"He is so generous. He took me driving near Catlon Bay, and we had dinner on the water."

"Well, that couldn't beat the time he spent with me." Janet grinned. "We didn't go anywhere at all."

When the elevator stopped on her floor, Jessie had half a mind to go back to her car and throw the bouquet away. But that was being petty. What did she care how he spent his spare time? He was a man, not a saint.

She stepped off the elevator and saw Kenneth coming out of his office. He spotted her, and his face lit up with such delight that even Mrs. Mathew stared at him. Jessie felt her body tremble at the impact of his bright eyes and arresting smile. She couldn't believe they were meant for her.

"Hi, Kenneth," a smooth voice said.

She looked behind her and saw Brooke dressed in a tailored designer suit, returning his smile. Her body immediately went back to normal. She sighed. *Figures.*

The soft chatter seemed to die down as he came towards them. He walked past Claire and Janet without even a nod. Jessie thought that was rude, considering he was dating them, but she reminded herself that it was none of her business. She sidled to the wall, so it wouldn't be so obvious when he passed by her.

She glanced down at the bouquet and sniffed it. Perhaps she should take them home and rest them on the windowsill. They were like sun catchers. As she considered this, a shadow fell over her. She glanced down at a masculine pair of brown shoes. Her eyes slowly trailed up.

Kenneth looked down at her, his eyes so warm with pleasure that they melted her insides. "What are you doing here?" he asked.

"I...uh, brought you these." She shoved the bouquet into his chest, afraid her sweaty palms would drop them.

Claire, Janet, and Mrs. Mathew watched them as if they were at a movie. All they needed was a tub of popcorn. Brooke smiled kindly at her, then left.

He took the flowers and stared at them. An enigmatic expression crossed his face.

Jessie brought her fingers to her lips, then stopped. "You don't like them, do you? They're from our garden, so they're not professional."

He smiled and kissed her lightly on the cheek. "They're beautiful. Come on." He took her hand. Jessie thought she would burst into flames at the sudden heat that curled itself around her. She had to remind herself that being attracted to him did not mean she was falling in love with him.

Kenneth looked at Mrs. Mathew. "Hold my calls for now, please." He turned towards his office. Janet and Claire blocked the way. "Do you need something?"

"Uh, no," Claire said. They didn't move their eyes, which were focused on Jessie.

"I assume you have work to do," he said tersely.

His tone broke through their paralysis. "Oh, certainly." They sent Jessie one dismissive glance and walked away.

"She's probably a relative," she heard Janet mutter.

Kenneth ushered her inside his office and shut the door. "A woman's never given me flowers before."

Jessie sat down, her hands nervously fluttering in her lap. "You don't have to pretend if you don't like them."

He took a flower from the bouquet, cut off its stem with a penknife, and placed it in her hair. He rested his hands on the arms of her chair and gazed down at her. His face eased into a smile. "I like them very much," he said, his voice like silken oak.

Jessie stared at his lips, wanting them to be on hers, wanting to touch him and tangle with the tiger he kept hidden underneath. "I'm glad."

He drew away. "I'm afraid that I don't have a vase anywhere."

"Oh, that's okay. It doesn't—"

He snapped his fingers. "Wait a minute." He went to his kitchen, emptied out a milk carton, cut a hole at the mouth, filled it with water, then placed the flowers inside. "That's better."

"That was clever."

"I knew that B.E. degree would come in handy." He placed the flowers on the windowsill. "That was very sweet of you."

Jessie grinned sheepishly. "Out of character, huh?"

He paused and gazed at her pensively. "No, not at all." He took a seat behind his desk, undoing his tie. "So where's Ace? I hope she didn't get on your nerves, forcing you to drop her body off somewhere."

"No. We like to play this game called Scavenger. I dropped her off in a field with a map and a compass, and we'll see if she can make it here." She laughed at Kenneth's startled expression. "That's a joke."

He shrugged. "I knew that."

"Actually, she's a busy girl. She's made a new friend and found herself a job weeding."

"A job?"

"I couldn't talk her out of the notion. Don't worry, it's with my sister Teresa."

"Ah, good. So you're free to go to lunch."

Jessie started. "Uh, I didn't come here to weasel a meal out of you."

"Why not? Other people do." He grabbed his coat from off the back of his chair.

"I just don't think we should be seen eating together."

He paused in the act of putting on his jacket. "Why not?"

"Because I don't want to be seen as just one of your women."

His warm gaze turned hard and flat. "Hmm. That *is* a problem." He placed his coat back on the chair and sat down.

His sudden change in mood filled her with regret. She didn't want to ruin their already-fragile relationship.

"Wait, that didn't come out right. I'm not judging your lifestyle or anything."

Kenneth looked at her disappointed. He turned to his computer. "Okay."

She hated when he looked at her that way. "I mean, everyone knows you like women." She tried to sound understanding. "There's nothing wrong with that."

He rested his elbows on the table and toyed with his watch. "I see, and just how many women do I have?"

"How would I know?" Why did he have to make her feel like some foul-smelling thing he'd discovered under a bush? She was just being honest.

His eyes challenged hers. "Well, you seem to know more about my social life than I do." He took off his watch and swung it on his finger in a circular motion. "Tell me about it."

"You're dating your employees, for example."

He dropped his watch on the table and swore, hoping he hadn't cracked its face. When he was certain it was okay, he returned his attention to her. "What did you say?"

"I overheard Janet and Claire talking."

"About what?"

"About you."

He leaned back in his chair and looked up at the ceiling. God, did no one have anything better to do than listen to or create rumors? No matter how quietly he tried to live his life, he could not escape them. "So what have I been up to?" He tossed his watch up in the air. "Have I gone to Catlon Bay again?"

"Yes."

He slid his watch back on and said, "Jasmine, what kind of restaurants are there around Catlon Bay?"

"Seafood restaurants, of course."

"Funny that I would take someone there, considering that I hate seafood." He pinned her to her seat with a penetrating gaze. "Or had you forgotten that?"

She sat back, momentarily rebuffed. She *had* forgotten about that. And now that she thought about it, most of their claims weren't plausible. Aside from the fact that he was usually in his office, he didn't like Thai food either and wouldn't have had time to eat with Syrah and then have a hot rendezvous with Claire.

He clasped his hands behind his head. "I once heard that your sister Teresa was seen flying on Halloween."

"Don't be stupid."

He shrugged. "That's what I heard."

"Lies."

He nodded. "Yes, people have a funny habit of telling them."

"Okay, your point has been made." She stood, wanting to fall through the floor.

He let his hands fall. "So are we going to lunch or not?"

In her surprise, she tripped over his rug. When she regained her balance, she asked, "You still want to go to lunch with me?"

He slipped into his jacket. "Sure. You behave like a twerp every once in a while, but I can handle it." He opened the door. "Let's go."

Jessie took off her sweater and left it on the chair. The day was hot enough.

When they got outside, they squinted from the blaring sunlight. The sidewalk was bursting with businesspeople out for lunch, tourists grabbing refreshments from street vendors, and kids rolling past on bicycles and skateboards. Jessie felt herself relaxing in the summer fun, but it slowly died as people watched them. Women stared, nudged, and whispered when they saw Kenneth. She knew they couldn't help themselves; his classic male presence was magnetic. Even she sent quick glances his way.

She glanced up and halted, staring at the building ahead.

"What's wrong?"

She began to walk. "Nothing."

He looked around, then understood. He caught her wrist, stopping her. "When was the last time you were in there?"

She could feel herself being seized by memories as she looked at the familiar oak doors of Fedor Malenkov Jewelers with its elaborate glass etching. In the show window, gems lay on dark velvet with the same enticing promises as ladies in the red-light district. A few pieces sat there: an antique amethyst choker, an Edwardian diamond pendant, a set of wedding and engagement rings, and pearls in elaborate yellow-gold settings. "I don't know."

He let her wrist go. "You can't avoid it."

She averted her gaze. "It's the past now."

"Doesn't your cousin BJ work there?"

"Yes. He was taught the trade."

"I always thought you'd follow your father."

She turned to him. "Me?"

"Yes, you were fascinated by stones and gems."

"I loved the stories, but I never had the skills to be a jeweler."

He walked towards the door. "Since we're here, we might as well say hello."

She grabbed his arm. "No." She didn't want to see BJ, the son her father never had. He was a little older than her, a large, solitary man who spoke little. Seeing the shop was difficult enough; she didn't want to step further into the past by talking to him.

The door suddenly chimed, and a little woman with a large purple head-wrap stepped out. She had a smooth brown face and keen, dark eyes. She spotted Jessie and smiled. "Going in or going out?"

Jessie took a step back. "Neither."

The woman lifted a brow; a knowing smile hovered over her lips. "It's not there, you know."

"What isn't there?"

"The pendant. You want it, don't you? You want to know where it is?"

Jessie quickly looked at Kenneth, hoping she wasn't giving him any ideas. "I already know where it is," she said casually. "Safe with the Ashfords."

The woman blinked and frowned. "Oh, I see. Of course." She shrugged. "Say hello to Teresa for me."

"A friend of your sister?" Kenneth asked, watching the strange little woman walk away.

"Yes. Her name is Bertha," she said absently, wondering why she had mentioned the pendant. She shook her head. The woman was odd anyway.

"That's Bertha? I thought she'd be scarier than that. I heard she turned a man into a—"

Jessie moved her hand in a quick dismissive gesture. "Never mind what you heard. It's probably nonsense." Most of her sister's friends had rather interesting reputations.

"Are you sure you don't want to go in?"

"Yes."

Kenneth didn't argue with her. Instead, he took her hand. "Fine. You're going to love this place. It has the best food and the best view you could imagine."

Jessie was so taken back by the affectionate gesture that she tripped on the uneven pavement.

"I'm sorry," he said, steadying her. "Am I walking too fast for you?"

"No, you're fine." She was the one on hormonal overload. She had to get a grip.

As they passed a Mexican restaurant and a lovely Greek bistro, Jessie became increasingly curious about their destination. Her curiosity soon grew to worry. What if he took her to some place where she couldn't read the menu or pronounce the food? She really wasn't in the mood for making a bigger ass of herself. Her anxiety had reached its peak when he finally stopped in front of a hot dog stand at the opening of Long Creek Park.

"Here we are: Le Chien," Kenneth announced. "And don't worry, it's all on me. Order whatever you like."

Jessie looked at him, stunned. She didn't know if she should be outraged or amused. She chose the latter, inwardly laughing at how much she had worried. "Oh, thank you," she cooed. "You're so generous."

"Ah, Mr. Preston, it's great to see you again," the hot dog vendor said. He smiled, offsetting his hook nose. "I see you've brought a friend."

"Yes," Kenneth said. "I want you to give her the best you have."

"Certainly." Two bright hazel eyes focused on her. "That's a beautiful flower." He gestured to her hair.

Jessie touched the flower with self-conscious fingers. "Thank you."

"What would you like to order, madam?"

She looked at the list of items as if she were at a five-star restaurant. "I'm not sure." She turned to Kenneth. "What would you suggest?"

"Well, his rack of lamb with Dijon mustard crust is excellent," he said, pointing to the hamburger list. "However, I prefer his beef and broccoli." He gestured to the hot dog section.

"That sounds good."

"Two orders, please, with everything but onions." He glanced at Jessie for confirmation.

She nodded.

"Certainly, sir, and would you like an appetizer?" He pointed to his assortment of chips and cookies.

"Crostini sounds good." He picked up two bags of potato chips.

"And something to drink?"

Kenneth turned to Jessie, who was thoroughly enjoying this game of make-believe and the man who was playing it. "What are you in the mood for, darling?"

"A chilled bottle of merlot would be divine."

He turned to the vendor. "You heard the lady."

The vendor nodded. "Of course." He fixed their hot dogs and handed them their cold sodas. "That will be two hundred and eighty-seven dollars."

Kenneth reached for his wallet and suddenly looked worried. "I hope I have enough."

The vendor grinned. "So do I, though you do make a good dishwasher."

He smiled and handed him the money. "Thanks."

"Good day, and come back soon."

Kenneth gave Jessie her lunch, then held out his arm. "Now let me take you to the table that I reserved for us."

Jessie looped her arm through his, as if she had done this many times before. "Wow, you really must be important to reserve a table here. Some people are on the waiting list for six months."

He sent her a sly glance. "I have my ways." He led her to a clearing in the trees, where a fountain squirted water from two unicorns. He gestured to a wooden bench under a maple tree.

"Here we are."

"The view is lovely," Jessie said, taking a seat. She placed her drink and chips beside her, then unwrapped her hot dog. She took a bite and closed her eyes, inhaling the scent of the trees, the grass, the bun, and Kenneth's musky cologne. She opened her eyes and stared at the fountain, suddenly feeling the need to cool off. "Hmm, you're right. The food is delicious. I'll have to tell all of my friends about this restaurant. Though I doubt we'd be able to afford it."

Kenneth stared at her for a moment, his eyes sweeping her face as if seeing her in a new light. He turned to the fountain. "I wasn't sure how you would respond."

"Afraid that you might end up with ketchup on your head?"

"That did cross my mind, but somehow I knew." He unwrapped his hot dog and frowned at it. "People always want the extravagant, showy things, things that don't mean anything except to the people you're trying to impress. But this means a lot to me. Grabbing something from *Le Chien* and coming here is one of my favorite things to do. You couldn't get this fresh air cooped up in some fancy restaurant."

Jessie took a sip of her drink. "I always thought it was the company rather than the place that was important."

He paused with his hot dog halfway to his mouth. He shot her a stunned glance. "Is that a compliment?"

She thought for a moment, then laughed. "Don't worry, it won't happen again." She patted herself on the back when Kenneth smiled at her. Compliments were definitely a charm requirement.

They finished their lunch in silence, not wanting to disturb the almost-magical harmony that rippled around them. They watched two couples walking their dogs, a group of kids playing soccer, and some people sunbathing on the concrete slab around the fountain. It was a perfect summer day, with the sun gently spreading its rays and the cool breeze from Catlon Bay playing the leaves like a musician would a violin.

Jessie didn't realize she had dozed off until she woke up and found her head on Kenneth's shoulder. He had a solid shoulder and wide enough to carry all the responsibilities he had inherited, yet soft enough to rest on. She checked the corner of her mouth, hoping that she hadn't drooled on him for one reason or another. She hadn't. She inhaled his scent. He smelled like ketchup, fresh leaves, and a masculine scent all his own so intoxicating that it made her head heavy. She soon realized the reason was that his head was resting on hers. She sat up, waking him up.

"Sorry about that," she said.

He ran a tired hand down his face. "No need to apologize. Neither of us slept very well last night." He blinked at his watch. "I'd better get back to work."

She smiled wistfully, not wanting the time to end, not wanting him to leave her. She shyly took his hand, and he curled his fingers around hers. "Thanks for lunch," she said.

"You're welcome." He didn't move from where he was sitting. She didn't move either.

He nudged her. "See those two squirrels by the tree? Let's see if I can call them." He made a high-pitched squeak between his teeth. The two squirrels stopped and stood on their hind legs, listening. He made the sound again, and they came towards them, as if greeting old friends. Kenneth reached in his pocket, pulled out some nuts, and tossed them to the squirrels.

Jessie laughed. "You still carry nuts in your pockets?"

A squirrel jumped up next to him. Kenneth gave him a nut. "A bad habit of mine, I guess."

"Aren't you afraid they'll bite you?"

"They've never bitten me. We're old friends." A secretive smile appeared on his face. "When I was a kid, I used to—" He suddenly stopped. He couldn't share his past. He liked Jasmine, but he couldn't trust her. He couldn't trust anyone. Everybody thought he was Mr. Perfect, and that was the image he had fought to maintain. He had to, since he had nothing else. "Never mind. We'd better go." He got up, tossed the rest of the nuts on the ground, and walked toward the street.

Jessie followed, wondering why he had suddenly wanted to leave. "Are you okay?"

He halted so abruptly that she crashed into him. It was like hitting a brick wall, and it took her a few moments to reorient herself. He turned to look at her and then glanced at something in the distance. He frowned.

Jessie glanced in the same direction, but only saw a group of kids. "What is it?"

"They won't let him play," he said, watching a group of children dismiss another child from their group. The child held a soccer ball under his arm. "Excuse me for a minute."

Kenneth jogged towards the boy. He tapped the boy on the shoulder and asked him some questions. The boy only nodded. Kenneth pointed to himself and Jessie. The boy at first looked suspicious, then smiled.

Kenneth came back over to her. "I need you to do me a favor—"

"Yes, I'll do it."

Kenneth smiled wickedly. "You know, that's a dangerous practice."

"What?"

"Saying yes to a man when you don't even know what he wants."

"I know what you want."

He quirked a brow. "You do?"

She ignored the teasing tone. "You want me to be referee."

He tweaked her chin. "I like a woman who can read my mind."

She tweaked his chin. "I know."

He took off his jacket, dropped it on her head, and went to the boy. Jessie took the coat off her head and hugged it close to her. *Damn, damn, damn.* She really liked him. She enjoyed having Kenneth as a friend. It wouldn't stay this way—it couldn't—but she would treasure it for now. She wondered if Gran Sonya had felt the same conflict about the German she had seduced. Had there been any regrets? Any heartache? She shook her head. She didn't wish to dwell on it. There was no turning back this deep in the game. She swung the coat over her shoulder and approached the pair.

In the distance, Tracy watched her, then raced to her car.

"What do you mean you saw Kenneth and Jessie in the park together?" Deborah stared at Tracy, shocked. "Get off of me," she told the seamstress pinning her dress. The woman took her pins and hurried away.

Tracy kept her voice low, not wanting to draw attention from other customers. "I was taking a walk around the fountain and I saw them," Tracy said. "They seemed really cozy. Her charm seems to be working."

"You must be wrong. You saw him with someone else."

"It was definitely Jessie. I could recognize that wispy hair anywhere."

Deborah folded her arms and began to pace. "What was she wearing?"

"A regular blouse and jeans."

Deborah gathered the billowing skirt of her dress and sat on the platform. "It's impossible. How could that plain little…" She looked up at Tracy and narrowed her eyes. "Are you sure—?"

"Positive."

Deborah ran her fingers through her hair, her mind racing. She could not allow plain Jessie Clifton to upstage her. There was no way she—Deborah Elizabeth Wester—could lose. How could she tell her dear Aunt Rhonda—the aunt she hoped would leave her a hefty inheritance upon the unfortunate event of her death—that she had lost the Sapphire Pendant in a bet with one of the crazy Cliftons? It would be so humiliating. She had to think of something.

At that moment Stephanie Radson came into the store. Deborah looked at the woman with growing interest. She'd been to a few of her parties, but they were far from close. Fortunately, that wasn't essential to making her plan work. Nobody could say Stephanie was as pretty as her sister, but she had all the qualifications (education, family connections) to be a catch for the right man. Besides, Stephanie always seemed to be at Kenneth's side for business; why not for pleasure as well?

Deborah raised her voice a notch, just enough so Stephanie could hear, but not enough to be gauche. "Thank you for telling me about Kenneth Preston, Tracy. It's so nice to know what he's been up to." As she had hoped, Stephanie tilted her head in their direction.

"Why are you talking so loud?" Tracy whispered.

She stood, smoothing out the skirt of her gown. "I mean, if Jessie can convince Kenneth to take her to the Hampton Charity Ball, then she wins the bet and the pendant. That's only fair. There's nothing I can do. He's just a pawn in our little game."

The door chime rang.

Deborah turned to the entrance and smiled with triumph. Stephanie had gone. She had succeeded in leveling the playing field.

Chapter Sixteen

"**D**aniel, this is my friend, Jasmine," Kenneth said, rolling up the cuffs of his sleeves. Jessie began to correct him, but decided to let it pass. "You can call her Jas for short," he continued.

Daniel smiled, lighting up his chubby face. His round, gray glasses framed eyes the color of molasses and stood out against his pecan skin.

"It's nice to meet you," he said, his voice higher than she'd expected. She supposed his large build disguised the fact that he was probably a preteen.

After introductions, the game was underway. At first, Kenneth was lenient with the boy, but he soon discovered that in spite of his size, Daniel was a good player. While Jessie was watching, two girls came up to her.

"Can we play?" one asked.

Jessie glanced at Daniel and Kenneth, then shrugged. "Why not?" She turned and waved her arms to get their attention. "Hey, guys! We have new players."

"Let them come," Kenneth said. "Daniel and I can take them."

Soon more kids started to come and ask if they could play. Before they knew it, Jessie and Kenneth were organizing twelve kids of various ages and sizes into two different teams. One kid brought a football, so tag football was born. An older kid offered to referee, giving Jessie the opportunity to play. To even the playing field, Kenneth and Jessie played on different sides.

At one point, Jessie got a hold of the ball and was close to making a goal when Kenneth tackled her to the ground.

"Hey, this is not tackle football," Jessie said, trying to push him off her.

"Oh, it isn't?" He wiped a smudge of dirt from her cheek. "Sorry, forgot about that."

Naturally, she had to seek revenge for such forgetfulness. While he was running to catch a toss, she stuck her foot out and sent him flying forward. He looked up at her and grinned, his eyes bright. All he said was "Touché."

Jessie's team won, and soon the sound of the ice cream truck caught everyone's attention.

"Ice cream for everyone!" Jessie announced. "It's on us." She patted Kenneth on the back and mouthed, *Meaning you.*

All the kids cheered and ran towards the white truck covered with pictures of summer treats.

"Still up to your tricks," Kenneth said, walking towards the truck and the crowd of kids.

"I knew you would offer anyway."

He took out his wallet and counted the bills. His spirits dampened slightly. Of course she knew. He was Mr. Dull, Mr. Nice, Mr. Perfect. "I'm predictable."

"No, I can read your mind."

He stopped and stared at her. "What am I thinking right now?"

She squeezed her eyes shut. "You're thinking, 'I want to buy Jessie a Firecracker Popsicle.'" She opened one eye for confirmation.

He grinned. "Not even close." He jogged towards the ice cream truck and created order amongst the kids, who were eager to get their requests heard. He looked like a troop leader, except he didn't seem frazzled or impatient. He made sure that every kid was serviced, remembering their names and their orders. He accepted their thanks as they walked away.

When he returned to Jessie, he found her in an alcove surrounded by bushes. She sat under a large oak tree, enjoying its shade. He handed her the Firecracker, then stretched out next to her and rested on his elbow. He watched a cardinal dart through the sky and the clouds floating past with their white sails flying.

"You're dripping ice cream down your arm," she said.

He looked down and saw white drops falling from the bottom of his cone.

She handed him a handkerchief.

He frowned at it. "What is this?"

"Don't pretend you don't know what it is. Didn't your mother make you to carry one around?"

He wiped his arm. "Yes, I just didn't expect you to have one." He sucked the bottom of his cone, then quickly finished it. "That was good."

"Mine was better."

"At least my lips aren't blue."

She made a face.

He rested his head back, closing his eyes as the sunlight fell through the trees. It scattered across the ground like diamonds. Jessie stared at him, the arrogant slope of his nose, the feathering of dark, curling lashes against his cheeks. He looked beautiful, simply taking the simple pleasure of lying on the park lawn. She wondered why he didn't always look like this, why there always seemed to be a shield between him and the rest of the world. No matter how genuine the smile, he seemed far away, but here the real Kenneth seemed to slip through the mask. Why did he feel the need to pretend?

He suddenly opened his eyes; they clashed with hers. She meant to look away (*Look but don't stare*, she heard Michelle say), but she couldn't. Her eyes wanted to drink him in before the mask was set in place, to marvel at the amber specks in his brown eyes, at how large his irises were.

He sat up, but their gaze never wavered. For the first time, she didn't see him as a crush or a pawn or an enemy to conquer. She saw him as a man, a man she wanted—desired in a purely feminine way. This was no schoolgirl crush, with thoughts of holding hands and sweet kisses on the bay. This was carnal lust rushing through her veins. She wanted to ravish his full, sensual lips, to run her hands up the contours of his chest and find out just how perfect he was.

He was close enough to touch, but she didn't move. She'd never even kissed a man before. She had tackled a man, even wrestled one, but kissed one? Never. And she had never been given the opportunity to practice. She had practiced once by using the inside of her elbow, but she was sure the real thing wasn't the same. She would probably make an idiot of herself and end up kissing his chin again. She was almost willing to risk it. But what if he pulled away like before? She licked her lips. She would have to find out.

He didn't pull away, but the kiss proved to be a disappointment. That was it? Two lips pressed against each other? She drew back.

The corner of his mouth kicked up in a grin. "You've never kissed a man before."

She took a deep breath. Her face felt as though it was on fire. "Go ahead and laugh."

"Why would I laugh? I feel honored."

She stared at him in disbelief.

"This is going to be fun."

"Fun?"

"Yep." He cupped her chin and rubbed his thumb over her lower lip. "Open your mouth a little." He began to smile. "I said a little: like this." He demonstrated. "Understand?"

She did. "I feel silly."

"You won't in a minute. You're going to enjoy this. Now kiss me again."

The difference was a puddle versus the ocean. She delved into the sweet softness of his lips, the warm wetness of his mouth. Her hunger grew with each passing moment. She leaned into him, her fingers running through his hair, her hands sliding down his spine and roaming the expanse of his back. Although his mouth was as soft as the grass beneath them, his body was rigid as steel.

It annoyed her that at such a moment of pleasure, he still could be distant. She wanted him to lose control. She darted her tongue in his mouth. His resulting groan only hinted at the passion she'd tapped into. He wrapped an arm around her waist, bringing her close, the buttons of his shirt biting into her chest. He suddenly pulled away and stared at her, his eyes a storm of conflicting emotions.

"Trust me," she whispered against his lips.

His mouth covered hers like an avalanche—overwhelming, fast, and furious. She fell backward, her fingers grasping his collar and bringing the heat of his body on top of her. She could feel the tiger prowling, pacing back and forth, still locked in its cage. Despite his control, she could feel her body respond to him, feel the hardening of her nipples, the gathering moisture between her legs. She wanted him.

"We should go," he murmured.

She nibbled on his lower lip. They quickly forgot the comment. The loud honk of a passing car jerked him back, reminding them where they were.

He jumped to his feet and pulled her up next to him in one effortless tug. "We have to go now." He picked up his jacket and walked away.

She followed.

Oh, God, what must he think of me? She was supposed to be subtle, suave, charming, yet she had jumped on him as though he were a new mattress. No, that was a bad analogy; it only led to dangerous thoughts. What had happened? What was wrong with her? She would never be able to look at him again without thinking of his mouth. What a mouth! She wouldn't mind having it explore all her erogenous zones. She squeezed her eyes shut.

She didn't expect to be like that, a woman that thought about sex every time she looked at a man. She didn't love him or anything, and she wasn't brought up to want a man solely for his body. It wasn't proper. She was overexcited because it was her first time with a man, any man. She had to make allowance for that. She just wasn't sure how to act. She glanced at him—the granite jaw, piercing eyes. The mask was back in place. She would be casual about it.

"It was the weather," she muttered as they rode the elevator. It had to be the heat and excitement of a game.

He turned to her. "What?"

She stared ahead, still unable to look directly at him. "I left my sweater in your office. I was just reminding myself."

"Oh." Kenneth stepped out of the elevator, then held the office door open for her. *He should apologize.* She had offered him a simple kiss, and he had turned it into much more. Too bad he wasn't going to; he didn't feel in the mood to be a hypocrite.

Jessie grabbed her sweater off the back of the chair, eager to leave, then she stopped. She wouldn't run away from him. She had to behave as if it were no big deal. She looked at a stack of memos on his desk, then leaned over to see what he had on the screen.

Kenneth sat down and offered her a dry smile. "Can I help you?"

She looked at him. "You're typing letters?"

"Yes."

"Why? Don't you have someone to do that for you?"

He glanced down and saw a grass stain on his shirt. He would have to change. "I can do it."

"That doesn't mean someone else can't. Ask Mrs. Mathew."

"I'm sure she has better things to do."

"Then ask Janet, Claire, or Brooke."

He rubbed his chin. "It's complicated."

Jessie rested her hands on the table and leaned forward. "How complicated?"

He hesitated. His eyes focused on the way the front of her shirt fell forward, revealing her cleavage. "Take a seat."

"Why?"

Why? Because when you lean over my desk that way, I can see right down your blouse, and it's damned distracting. "I just thought you'd be more comfortable."

"I'm fine, thanks."

He tried to glance away, but his eyes kept returning to the delicious crevice between her breasts. He saw a trickle of sweat make a river down her neck and rest in the ravine. He wondered what she tasted like there.

"Let's just say that I'm doing someone a flavor—" He shook his head. "A favor."

Jessie leaned closer. "Meaning?"

He decided to stare at the computer screen. "Okay, to be honest, a guy who helped me with some capital asked me to hire his daughter and her friend. Their résumés looked strong, so I said sure."

"And they've been a useless piece of furniture ever since," she concluded.

"I wouldn't say that. Stephanie and Brooke came as an extra bonus."

"Because their father owned the company?"

He nodded.

"It's not fair." Jessie pushed herself off the desk. Kenneth sighed, wiping the beads of sweat that had formed on his forehead. "I work hard, trying to go above and beyond my duty, and I get fired, while they get cushy jobs."

He shrugged.

Jessie looked at the pile of papers on his desk. "I can do them for you."

"No, I can do them myself."

She gathered the notes together and took them. "You're welcome."

"My handwriting's a little messy."

She squinted at one of the letters. "A little messy? A rat has better penmanship."

He leaned back in his chair. "This, coming from a woman whose handwriting was so bad that teachers thought she was writing in a foreign language?"

Jessie flinched. "I know. My mother used to make me write in those stupid handwriting books." She stuffed the papers into an empty manila folder. "You know this will cost you another expensive lunch."

"I know." He groaned. "Next time would you not order the wine?"

She grinned and opened the door.

"Jasmine." He straightened his desk set. "Look, I'm—"

She walked up to his desk, tossing down the manila folder. "Don't you dare apologize."

He blinked, then his mouth spread into a sensuous grin. "I hadn't planned to."

"Good." She leaned across the desk until their noses touched. "Because I know you're not sorry." She kissed him, softly and slowly.

"I'm not." She drew back and picked up the manila envelope, hoping he didn't notice her fingers trembling.

"You just made a big mistake," he said in a deep tone.

She boldly met his eyes. "I did?"

"You shouldn't have done that."

"Why not?"

He came from around his desk. His eyes had a sheen of purpose. "Because you're playing with fire."

She raised a brow. "So are you."

"I like the heat."

She sent him a mischievous grin. "And I like to play."

"Then we're even."

He claimed her lips and crushed her body to his, this time letting his hands roam free. He wouldn't let her go anytime soon, not when he'd waited so long to visit the delights she kept hidden from view. His hands loosened her blouse from the constraints of her jeans and slid up her shirt, capturing her breasts.

Jessie moaned, closing her eyes. Nothing would distract her from the exquisite pleasure. His lips were gentle and soft, like the touch of candy floss against the tongue, melting into the same sweetness. She had expected to feel wild, naughty, and reckless in his arms. The sense of security was unnerving. How could she feel so safe in his arms? Safe, in the arms of a man who had probably held numerous other women this way? She pushed the thoughts aside. All that mattered was this moment and the new sensations she'd never even imagined.

He pulled her down on the floor and drew her blouse over her head. She rested back on the rug, ignoring the coarse feel against her skin. She quickly unbuttoned his shirt, eager to explore him and discover things she didn't know. She silently swore when she discovered he had on an undershirt, but let her hands trail a path down his chest, watching the muscles constrict under her fingers. Her curious hands descended to the hard bulge in his trousers.

"You'd better watch those hands," Kenneth warned, against her neck, "or you'll get more than you expected." He unlatched her bra and captured her hard nipple his mouth, allowing his tongue to roll around her nipple. Jessie bit back a moan, not wanting to alert anyone outside the office to their activity. She arched her back, rubbing her lower body against him.

The buzzer rang.

"Trouble's coming," Mrs. Mathew warned. "Tanya's on her way."

Kenneth swore; Jessie jumped.

He grabbed his shirt, buttoned it, and stuffed it into his trousers with such speed that he could have broken a world record. Jessie, unable to find where Kenneth had thrown her top, barely had enough time to duck behind the couch before the doors swung open.

"Why haven't you called me, Kenneth?" Tanya asked in a petulant voice.

"Was I supposed to call you?" His voice was cool. No one would have suspected he had a half-naked woman behind the couch.

She stomped her foot, like a child ready to throw a tantrum. "Yes, to invite me to the ball."

"Oh, right. I'm not even sure I'm going, so you're free to go with someone else."

"But you have to take me. I've got this dress you're going to love." She began to describe the dress in detail.

"That sounds great," he interrupted. "A gorgeous dress like that shouldn't be wasted on me."

"But Kenneth—!"

"I have work to do now. I'll ring you later."

"You promise?"

"I'll try."

Jessie heard him lead Tanya to the door and close it.

A moment passed before he came over to the couch. He rested his hands on the back and grinned down at her like a smug Cheshire cat. "You definitely are an athlete. I never saw a woman move so fast."

"You've done this before, haven't you?" she asked, envious of his neat attire. His appearance gave no hint to what he'd been up to.

"No, I'm just a fast learner."

She doubted that, but didn't wish to pry. "Was that the infant?"

"I'm afraid so."

She began to stand, but decided against it. She continued to cover her bare chest. "Could you please hand me my clothes?"

He shook his head, his face thoughtful. "No, I don't think I will. I like you this way."

"Kenneth!"

"Come on, don't be shy."

She glared at him.

He sighed dramatically. "All right." He retrieved her things. "Why don't you get a top in your own size?" he asked, tossing it to her.

"I need my bra too, please."

He held it out in front of him. It was a nice peach color. "I think I'll keep it as a souvenir."

Jessie slipped into her top and held out her hand. "You'll have a black eye as a souvenir if you don't hand it over."

He draped the bra around his neck. "I just might risk it."

She lunged for it, but he held it above his head, out of reach. She leaped up and tried to grab it. He switched it to his other hand.

"Give it back."

His arm slid around her waist, drawing her close. "Keep jumping. I like the sensation."

She stilled. "You're impossible."

She tried to tickle him, but his grin only grew wider. "I'm not ticklish, remember?"

"I'm warning you." She reached for it again.

He switched hands. "Come on, Jas. I'm sure you have plenty of others. This would be my first."

The door swung open.

Kenneth stood still, giving Jessie the chance to grab her bra. But she snatched it so fast that she lost her grip and it sailed across the room, landing on Mrs. Mathew's clipboard.

"Mr. Preston, I have your—" She stopped and glanced down at what was in front of her.

Jessie yanked it off the clipboard. "I beg your pardon."

Mrs. Mathew took a step back, her features a model of composure. "Forgive me, Mr. Preston, I didn't realize you were occupied."

"We're almost done here," Kenneth said, as though finishing a meeting with a business associate.

She nodded and closed the door.

Jessie refused to look at him. She fastened her bra and adjusted her shirt, then attempted to smooth back her hair. When she felt she had dealt with the embarrassment of the situation, she turned to say good-bye. She didn't get the chance. Kenneth was doubled over in laughter.

"It's not funny," she said.

He glanced at her and laughed harder.

She bit her lip, refusing to be so immature. "Kenneth—"

He leaned against the wall and held his sides. "Only her eyebrows moved," he gasped.

She covered her mouth to stifle her giggles, but didn't succeed. Soon they were holding onto each other, weak with laughter. All they had to do was look at each other, and the laughter would start again.

"I think I should go," she said into his chest.

He nodded.

She grabbed the folder and her sweater, then raced out of the room, careful not to look at Mrs. Mathew as she passed her desk. She stepped into the elevator and took a deep breath. When she turned, she saw Kenneth standing in his office doorway, imitating Mrs. Mathew's expression. She burst into laughter once more as the doors closed, ignoring the curious stares.

Kenneth fell down on the couch. She was up to something, he could feel it. He had learned early that tenderness was earned, not given. And Jasmine had given too freely for a hot dog and popsicle. Yes, she definitely was up to something...damn her. But the fact was that he didn't care. He didn't care at all. His face spread into a grin. Whatever scheme she was up to, he definitely liked the process.

He rested his hands behind his head and stared at the ceiling. He wanted her. He wanted her like an art thief craved an original Van Gogh, like a hacker craved an encrypted code. He wanted her wet, dry, dressed, naked—he especially wanted her naked, preferably in his bed, but he could be creative.

He shut his eyes, still able to remember the taste and smell of her. He rubbed his chin. He had to be careful; he couldn't let it go too far. Unfortunately, it had already awakened the longing in him. He'd fed a tantalizing morsel to the hungry man within him. He shook his head. He couldn't forget that he wasn't like other men. He had an image to maintain, secrets to keep. The next time he had her, it would be under cover of darkness. He would have to plan it right.

The buzzer on his desk rang. He growled and leaped to his feet. He hit the button. "Yes?"

"You have a call," Mrs. Mathew said.

He coughed to discourage himself from laughing, remembering the look on her face. "Okay."

"Your brother Eddie is on line three."
All good humor died.

Chapter Seventeen

He hated talking to his brother, but he had discovered that avoidance was just as stressful. He counted to ten, then picked up the line.

"What do you want?"

Eddie laughed. "Is that any way to speak to your flesh and blood, man?"

"Would you prefer silence? What do you want?"

Eddie slipped into the dialect of their youth. "I have fi get money,"

It had the expected effect, transferring Kenneth from a powerful executive to a young man who would do anything to protect his family. He turned towards the window and watched the traffic down below. "Is what 'appen to the money mi give you last time?"

Eddie's voice lifted to a whine. "I told you I'll pay you back when I get the chance. Come nuh, man, I have fi have it. Me ina worries."

"Fi what?"

"Rent. A little jill is all me want."

Kenneth let his eyes fall on the daylilies sitting on his windowsill. They seemed to be watching him and cautioning him behind their sunny smiles. He didn't believe Eddie, but he couldn't say no. He couldn't let his brother suffer when he knew he could help him. "I see." He sighed, sickened by his own weakness, sickened by how quickly his brother could trap him in the tentacles of their past, reminding him of the young man he used to be, a young man who had envied Eddie his daughter, his mother's love, and his freedom. "Awrite."

"Thanks. Okay, me gone."

Kenneth sat up in his chair. "Wait, now. Is that all?"

Eddie paused. "Yeah, I think so."

166

He ground his teeth. "Aren't you missing something?"

"Uh…?"

Kenneth sighed, exasperated. "Like a dawta, perhaps?"

"Oh, yeah, Shiraz. Look, uh, I trust her wid you."

Kenneth tightened his grip on the phone. "It's not about trust. She's not my child. You need to take care of her."

He could almost hear his brother's mind working, trying to make up excuses to have Ace stay longer.

Eddie switched to Standard English, the language in which he did his best scheming. "Things aren't at their best right now, Ken. When everything is sorted out, I'll come get her."

Kenneth stroked the petals of the flowers with his thumb. "She told me you're still drinking."

"The kid's got a big mouth. I cut it down, Ken, way down."

"You don't need to do this."

"I'm trying. I don't drink much."

"You're not supposed to drink at all."

Eddie's voice hardened. "Hey, don't start acting like mi fadda." He quickly regretted his words, knowing what an insult they were. "Me sorry." He coughed. "I mean, I'm sorry. Ken, I didn't mean it. Kenneth? Kenneth, are you there?"

"I'm here."

"I'm sorry."

Like always. "Hmm."

Eddie let out a deep breath. "Just give me time. I'll mend everything."

"Not too much time."

"So when are you going to send the money?"

Kenneth ripped off a petal, then stomped on it. Why couldn't his brother get his priorities straight? Why couldn't he get through to him? Sometimes he wasn't sure whether he hated his brother or just the addiction.

"I'm going to pay your landlord directly," he said.

"What?" Eddie's voice lifted in surprise and hurt. "You don't trust me?"

He had learned early not to trust him with money. "No."

Eddie's voice turned surly. "Well, if you can find it in your heart to send some money for food, I'd appreciate it."

"I'll make sure you get food. How's your job?" Eddie wrote a syndicated column about the joys of life. The irony never escaped them.

"I'm living. No worries. So are you going to send the money?"

"I'll take care of things."

"Thanks." He hesitated. When he spoke again, it was not as an indigent brother, but man to man. "In spite of what you think, I am trying, but I'm not much of a fighter." He laughed bitterly. "We all can't be perfect like you."

Kenneth gripped the phone. "You of all people know I'm not perfect."

"Maybe."

"How come you never did tell me about Jasmine giving you her scholarship?"

"I'm a Preston. Appearances—I'm sure you know a little something about that." Eddie hung up.

Kenneth held the receiver until it began to buzz, then he put it down and sighed. Appearances were all his life was about.

What had caused her to be so bold? Jessie wondered, returning to Kenneth's place. Never in her life had she been so brazen, so sassy. God, it felt good. She tossed her bag on the couch and held her head as a nagging thought struck her. She had told him to trust her. She shouldn't have said that. She'd unwittingly pointed to her Achilles' heel: the Clifton word of honor. She swore. If he ever found out about the bet, he would remember her words and use them against her. Then once again the Clifton honor would be at risk because of her. She groaned, recognizing the truth: she had lost the pendant again.

Instead of mentally kicking herself, which she decided to leave for the evening, she typed his letters. She had just completed the stack when Teresa called.

"So did it work?" she asked, excited.

Jessie hit the print icon. "What?"

"The flowers, you ninny."

Jessie sat back and rested her feet on the desk. "Like a magic potion. He even took me to lunch." *And kissed me until my skin tingled.* "Right now I'm typing some letters for him."

"Excellent! You may pull this off after all."

She shook her head. "No, I won't." She lowered her voice. "The bet's off."

"Why?"

She rested a hand on her forehead. "Because I kissed him."

Teresa gasped. "You kissed Kenneth Preston? On the mouth?"

She sat up. "Yes, where else?"

There was a pregnant pause as they both imagined the many possible places.

"Never mind," Teresa said quickly. "That's great!"

Jessie stared at the computer monitor, blinking back tears of frustration. She had lost even before she had begun. "No, it's not. I told him to trust me. If I continue with the bet and he finds out, everything between us will seem like a lie. The Clifton word would be a sham."

Teresa sighed, understanding the dilemma. The integrity of a family name was sacred. "Oh, but you're so close."

"I know."

"Michelle will be proud." Teresa paused. "But what if he never finds out? You could win the pendant and still keep him as a friend. Nobody else knows about the bet, and if you win, I doubt Deborah will tell anyone."

"I don't know." Jessie felt a shadow descend. She looked up and saw Freda glaring down at her.

"Uh, Teresa, I'll call you another time. I've got to go."

"Okay. Syrah's at Denise's house, but she'll be home for dinner."

"Great." Jessie placed the receiver down, stood up, and smiled. "May I help you, Freda?"

Freda did not return the expression. "Sit down, Ms. Clifton. I want to talk to you."

She sat. "Is there a problem?" It was a silly question. Freda's lips had all but disappeared.

Freda sat down, arranging the pleats in her skirt. "I'm not going to pretend that I didn't overhear your phone conversation; nor will I pretend that I'm not disappointed in you."

Jessie opened her mouth to defend herself, but Freda continued, "I've seen a lot of women try to wheedle their way into Mr. Preston's affections." She held up both hands, as if trying to fend off something. "Now, I try not to get involved, but I cannot be silent this time. Whatever little plan you've concocted is working. You've won. He called me up to ask me to make 'dip and fall back,' because it's your favorite."

"Freda, I—"

Freda's wide mouth tightened to a thin line. "I will not make this meal unless your feelings are sincere. Unless your presence here is without pretense."

Jessie sighed, helpless to come up with a solid explanation. "It's complicated."

"Deception usually is."

She bit her lip. "I don't want to hurt him."

"But you will. Everyone usually does." She stood. "Dinner will be served at seven-thirty. We'll have chicken."

Silenced and defeated, Jessie watched her go.

Syrah came home soon after and told Jessie about her day while they washed up for dinner. Later, they began to set the table.

Freda came into the dining room and frowned at them. "What are you doing?"

"Just trying to help," Jessie said.

She snatched a plate from her. "You do your job and I'll do mine."

Silently Syrah and Jessie went into the family room to wait until Kenneth came home. Time passed. He didn't come.

"I guess Uncle's working late," Syrah said, during the second round of checkers.

Freda closed the blinds. "He's probably not coming home tonight."

"He could have called, at least," Jessie said.

"Mr. Preston is used to being a bachelor," Freda replied gruffly. "He's not used to unnecessary ties. Why don't you two eat dinner before it turns to ice? He can take care of himself."

Jessie stood.

"How come Freda is in such a bad mood?" Syrah whispered as they walked to the table.

She glanced at Freda as she plumped the pillows. She'd never have guessed that she would end this wonderful day making a new enemy. "She's had a long day."

"You're angry at Uncle, aren't you?" Syrah asked as she took off her robe for bed.

"No, I'm not angry," Jessie lied. "I have no right to be angry."

"Uncle likes to work. It makes him happy."

Syrah was right. That didn't stop Jessie from wishing that Syrah would be angry with Kenneth too. He gave her toys, but never his time. Anytime she got close to him, he would move away or give her a quick pat on the head, as if he were trying to keep some distance between them. Had he been so hurt in the past that he couldn't accept even the simple affections of a little girl? "Your uncle needs a hobby. Like spending time with you."

Syrah shook her head. "Oh, no. I don't need him to be with me. I'm all right." She changed the subject. "Do you think your sister will write me back?"

"Yes, she's very dependable that way." Jessie watched Syrah hang up her robe and saw that the hem of her nightdress was fraying and there was a tear under the sleeve. "Don't you have another nightdress? That one's torn."

"Nah, I really like it. But one day I'm going to save enough money to buy a pair of pajamas." She got under the covers. "Really nice ones made out of soft cotton with ice cream cones or clouds on it."

"I'm sure your uncle would buy you a pair if you told him."

She shook her head. "Nah, he's busy as it is." She pulled up the covers. "It's nice to have a dream, though."

"Yes."

"Do you have a dream, Aunt Jessie?"

Her present dream seemed to be slipping away from her. Perhaps she'd never have the pendant in her hands again. "I never thought about it, really."

"I have lots of dreams and I think about them all the time." She smoothed out her blanket and lowered her voice to a whisper. "One of them is that Uncle will let me stay with him."

"You know, you have other relatives who—" Jessie stopped, because Syrah was already shaking her head.

"No, Uncle Kenneth is the best. I only want to stay with him."

"I know you love him, but it's okay to admit that he gets on your nerves sometimes."

She scowled, offended. "Uncle never gets on my nerves. I love him more than anyone in the whole world."

"And I'm sure he loves you."

"I know he does," she said, with the arrogance of a child. "I just wish he'd get married, but he never will."

"Why not?"

Syrah shrugged. "Don't know." She studied her for a moment. "Would you like to marry him?"

"We've discussed this."

She sighed heavily. "I know, I know. You're not interested."

"Right."

"Do you plan to get married someday?"

Jessie sat down on the bed. "I never thought about it." She laughed. "Personally, I don't think there's anyone besides my sisters who could put up with me."

"I can put up with you."

Jessie playfully tugged on a pigtail. "You're one of the few."

Syrah patted one her pillows and laid her head down. "I'm never getting married."

"Why not?"

She shrugged, then buried herself under the covers.

Jessie sat on her bed and tried to immerse herself in a mystery novel, her ear cocked, waiting to hear Kenneth's car drive up. It never came.

She closed her book when she realized that she was still on page two. She leaned her head back and imagined him having a late meeting with Brooke, who wore a skin-tight leopard-print dress, while a fire roared and food sat on silver plates provided by the Garden catering company. In between talks of contracts, they fed each other sautéed apples, deviled eggs, or pâté on radish flowers. The thought of Brooke's dainty paws near Kenneth's mouth made Jessie want to spit fire.

This afternoon meant nothing, she reminded herself. *It was just a bit of fun.* She pounded her pillow. She didn't care at all. She really didn't. She buried her head in the pillow, but sleep was far away.

The next day, she received a frantic call from Wendy that buried any thoughts of Kenneth. "We need more hands!" she said.

"What are you talking about?"

"Montey's about to have a heart attack. Two people called in sick. We're desperate. Tell me you'll come."

"Will he pay me?"

"Of course."

She could always use the extra money, now that she would have to save in order to purchase the pendant herself. "I'll be right there. Where are you?"

"Donovan House."

Fortunately, Syrah didn't object to spending the day with Denise. Jessie grabbed Kenneth's old tux, annoyed that she hadn't dry-cleaned her own, and sped to the Donovan House. She silently asked for forgiveness as she broke a few traffic laws.

The Donovan House was an impressive structure, its style influenced by gothic castles and Italian villas. It boasted arched windows, gleaming balconies, and lovely landscaping. Since Ms. Donovan owned an antique shop, she could claim the best pieces for herself and usually did. Inside, eighteenth-century tapestries hung on ivory-toned wallpaper. Oak floors gleamed against the aged glow of vintage mahogany furniture. In glass vases, giant white lilies held up their regal heads.

For all its beauty, Jessie only had bad memories of the Donovan House. When she and her sisters would come to visit with their mother, the two eldest boys would lock them in strange rooms and leave them there for hours. Since the house was built during Prohibition by a successful bootlegger, it was equipped with many secret passageways, allowing the bullies endless places to play their tricks.

The torment never bothered Michelle, who pretended she was poor Jane Eyre locked in the Red Room, and Teresa would cry, but Jessie would pound on the doors until her fists swelled. Eventually, they discovered ways to escape their confinement.

Even though she was grown and the two bullies had left the state to wreak havoc on the unsuspecting city of Chicago, Jessie was still afraid that one day they would pop out of nowhere and perform their pranks again.

The first person she saw when she entered the kitchen was Montey. His mustache twitched like a mouse, and his face had turned bright red from rising panic.

"Everything's going to be fine," she assured him.

He shoved a tray of stuffed mushrooms into her hands and pushed her out the door.

She graciously assumed her duties, happy to be back in her element. A few guests smiled and absently thanked her.

Wendy sidled up to her. "I'm so glad you could make it." She frowned. "Are you shrinking, or is your tux too big?"

"It's the tux." Jessie tugged on the jacket. " I borrowed it from a friend."

"God, your friend must be enormous."

Jessie ignored the comment. "I'm glad you called me. I desperately needed something else to do."

"Is Syrah giving you trouble?"

"No, it's nothing like that. She's at my house right now with Teresa."

Wendy lifted a brow, a knowing smile touching her lips. "So it must be Kenneth, then."

"I think he's avoiding me."

"Uh, oh. That means…crap, Montey's staring at us." Wendy jerked her head at the man, who was gesturing wildly for them to keep working. "I'll talk to you later."

Jessie moved through the crowd like a ghost. She loved how the guests treated her like a piece of furniture and would say outrageous things in her hearing. During the course of the event, she learned about the marital problems of two local families, the sexual preference of a prominent judge, and the financial crisis of a developer.

The biggest news she overheard was the donation of the Arand necklace, said to have been created by the Arawak Indians of Jamaica and brought to American soil by a Scottish slave who helped found Randall County. He was also believed to be a distant relative of the Donovans. Jessie dismissed most of the chatter, but one conversation snagged her attention.

"Have you heard about Brooke Radson?" a woman asked her associate.

"Of Radson Electronics?"

"Yes, who else?"

The two women lowered their voices. Jessie stepped closer.

"It seems that she might be going down the aisle again."

"Again? You mean she was married before?"

"Yes. It was a small scandal, of course. The man was...well, her father didn't approve, and it was quickly crushed."

"I've heard that she has her eyes set on—"

"Hello, Jessie," Stephanie said, taking a mushroom from the tray.

Jessie sent her a cautious glance. Stephanie had never approached her before. She smiled politely. "Hello."

"It seems you've caused quite a buzz at the office."

"Me? Why?" She lifted her chin, though they were basically the same height. She felt as if the other woman were looking down at her.

"The flowers. Nice touch. Wish I'd thought of it myself." She glanced around the room. "So are you and Kenneth...?" She let her words trail off; she was too well-bred to make assumptions.

"We're friends."

"Just friends?"

"Yes, but when it becomes any of your business, I'll let you know."

"I know what you're up to, and it won't work. I suggest you go back to where you came from." She assessed Jessie's tux in one unflattering glance. "Oh, I see you already did."

The warning stung. Stephanie already knew she had lost, but Jessie refused to step down. "So what do you do?" she asked.

"When what?"

"When two sisters are after the same man? I'm afraid you are trailing behind."

Stephanie's lips tightened. "You don't know anything."

"That's right. So you have nothing to worry about." She held up her tray. Stephanie glanced at it, then walked away.

Jessie watched her go. How could she possibly know what she was up to?

Wendy came up to her. "You're supposed to be working."

"I know, but I've been dodging claws."

"Whose?"

"Stephanie's."

She grimaced. "Good luck."

"I don't need luck. I need nail clippers. She knows—" They both spotted Susan and quickly parted ways.

Jessie disappeared into the crowd and noticed a book under a chair. Something shiny stuck out of its pages. She bent to pick it up.

"Leave it alone," Susan said. "You're not being paid to do the housekeeping."

Jessie abruptly straightened. "I only thought—" Susan's steely glared halted her explanation.

She measured Jessie's uniform. "Do we need to go over the dress code again? Tuxes are not to be oversized or touch the tip of your shoes. Your trousers are swallowing them."

"I'm sorry. It's on loan. It won't happen again."

"Good. This is your last chance. Get to work." Susan turned on her heel and left.

Jessie mentally lifted a hand in quick salute, then approached another group, offering them the tray and a big smile. The smile fell when she saw Kenneth. He stopped with his glass at his lips. He excused himself from the group and asked her for some more hors d'oeuvres. He discreetly dragged her into the hallway, where they would not become fodder for the rumor mill.

He led her to a room unimaginatively called the Blue Room for the obvious reason that everything from the hangings on the windows and the four-poster bed to the carpet was a dark blue.

"What are you doing here?" they both asked once Kenneth had shut the door.

"I'm working," they replied in unison.

"Stop that," Kenneth said.

He looked wonderful. She held her tray with both hands, resisting the urge to jump him. "I didn't do it on purpose."

"Why are you here?"

She gestured to her tux and tray. "I'm in a play. Guess what role."

"Where's Ace? In the kitchen?"

"No, she's with my sister." She rested her tray on the ground, afraid to put it on the antique desk, which held an inkwell and porcelain box.

"You already have a job. What are you doing here?"

She shoved her hands in her pockets and rocked on her heels. "I can always use the extra money."

He folded his arms. "If you're really strapped for money, I can raise your salary."

"No, thanks." She would not look at his mouth.

"Fine, then I'll make it a loan."

"No." Oh, why couldn't she hate him again?

"You're being stubborn."

She smiled at his frustration. "I know."

He tugged on her jacket. "This is big on you." He rubbed his chin. "And it looks oddly familiar."

"It should. It's yours."

His mouth softened to a grin. He rolled up her trouser legs so that they didn't cover her shoes like excess icing on a cake, then he did the same with her sleeves. She looked at his bent head, wanting to ask him if he'd come home tonight, wanting to know if he remembered what had happened between them, if he cared. She bit her lip and said nothing. He straightened her bowtie.

Jessie rested her hands on her hips. "Now all you have to do is wear my prom dress, and we'll make the perfect pair." At least that's what she was about to say before he kissed her.

It was reassuring, comforting, caring. She wrapped her arms around him, wishing their action could be expressed in words. He drew away.

Her voice was an urgent plea when she said, "Please don't—" then stopped.

"Don't what?"

Don't hurt me. Don't make me love you. But that was ridiculous. She would never give him the power to hurt her again. She knew the type of man he was, knew about the many women in his life. "Nothing."

He caressed her cheek. "Okay."

She looked up at him, a series of questions in her eyes. He merely offered her a smile. He opened the door, checked to make sure that no one was around to see him exit, then left. He didn't come home that night either.

Chapter Eighteen

Brooke rested her foot on the glass dining table and opened a bottle of nail polish.

"Honey, you should put a robe on."

She glanced towards the bed, at the gray-haired man who filled it. He looked like caramel wrapped in gold cellophane. Derek Allen was a handsome man. Unfortunately, he was a sexual bore. "Why do I need a robe?"

"Because you'll get cold."

She wasn't cold at all. She loved being naked, especially when she had a male audience. Men were such visual creatures; it gave her all the power.

"Please, honey."

She loved the begging the most.

"All right." She slowly walked to the closet, making sure the light hit all her attributes at the perfect angle. She arched her back so her breasts would fall just so. She grabbed her robe and wrapped it about her, loving how the red silk clung to her form. It was better than what the hotel offered. "There. Better now?"

"Much."

"I could really use a drink."

He began to change. "I'll get you something, and I saw the perfect necklace for you in the gift shop."

She followed him to the door. "You're so good to me."

His hand slid up her side and cupped her breast. "You make sure this deal with Radson goes through, and I'll be even better."

She kissed him, her eyes falling on the rich mauve carpeting of the hall, and then to the cream of the walls. Suddenly a warning of danger shot up her back. She'd received that sensation before from only one man. She drew away.

Derek looked at her, concerned. "Are you okay?"

She tugged on the sash of her robe. "I'm fine. Go get that drink for me."

He smiled and walked to the elevators.

Brooke took a deep breath before she turned. Nathan leaned against the wall, his cocky arrogance filling the air between them, his devastating smile sending a tremble through her. The door next to him opened, and a husky female voice called to him. He sent Brooke one long, sweeping look that revealed nothing, then disappeared inside.

A few hours later, Brooke watched the setting sun polish the dining table a rich cocoa. She glanced at Stephanie as she tucked into her tiramisu. She clasped her hands together. "I thought you should know something," she said.

Stephanie looked up. "What?"

"Nathan saw me with Derek Allen."

"So?"

"He happened to be holding my breast."

Stephanie choked and glanced pointedly at their mother, who acted as though she hadn't heard a thing. "You shouldn't say such things at the table."

"Oh, please. That woman wouldn't know if a bee flew up her—"

"Mother, why don't you finish your dessert in the sitting room? You can watch the sun set."

Winifred smiled. "That's a lovely idea." She left.

Stephanie signaled the maid and pointed to her mother's plate. "Take it to her in the sitting room." When the maid left, she glared at Brooke. "I wish you would treat her with more respect."

"Why? She wouldn't know the difference."

"Mom has always been rather absentminded, but she's not a complete idiot."

"The stress being on *complete*," Brooke said under her breath. She didn't wish to argue.

"Now what's this about Nathan seeing you?"

"I was having a little fun."

"Can't you control your hormones for one minute?"

"Relax, honey, it doesn't change anything."

"It's called conflict of interest."

"There's no conflict. We aren't buying IE anyway. We all know we are selling Radson."

Stephanie set down her fork. "That's for the board to decide."

Brooke smiled gently. "We are the board. Don't forget, Uncle Lamar could always use the money, Mom does whatever we tell her, and Aunt Rita and Cousin Trent can easily be swayed. And then there's us."

"You're forgetting Nathan and Kenneth."

Her smile widened. "No, I'm not."

"Like it or not, right now they're in charge. They have a big share in the company."

"But not big enough to fight all of us."

Stephanie lowered her eyes and turned her plate. "They have done a lot for this company."

"Our company. Think how much money we'll make."

"I don't think Dad would have wanted us to sell."

"Well, Dad's dead."

Her gaze flew up. "I'm aware of that."

"Let's not argue. Did you place the ad about the bracelet?" she asked softly, hoping to use guilt as a weapon of distraction.

It worked. Stephanie looked contrite. "Yes. It will run next week."

"I'm sure someone will return it soon."

She hesitated, then said, "You shouldn't have let Nathan see you."

Brooke took a sip of her drink, studying her sister. "I hope you're still not carrying a torch for that man."

Stephanie picked up her fork and took a bite.

"I thought I showed you years ago the type of man Nathan is. You deserve better."

"My statement was made as a professional observation."

Brooke relaxed, glad that Stephanie's feelings for Nathan had passed. "Ah, but emotional is the best way to play. You'll need to get to Kenneth before Nathan does. I'll tell you what to say and how to approach him. Remember to appear sincere and you'll have nothing to worry about."

"What about Nathan?"

"Don't worry about him." *Soon he won't be a problem at all.*

Kenneth tossed down the report and swore. He glanced up at Stephanie and Nathan. "Thank you," he said, signaling their dismissal.

Stephanie left. Nathan stayed behind.

"This is proof," he said.

Kenneth drummed his fingers on the desk. "Proof of what?"

"That they're dangerous. Brooke is literally in bed with the head of IE. If we'd bought them, they would have milked us dry."

"She's still learning. Besides, you heard Stephanie—"

"What I heard was a woman talking about her *sister*. Do you think she wouldn't lie?"

"Nate, the issue is over. Brooke fell for the head after she discovered they would be a bad prospect. This is their father's company. They wouldn't do anything to jeopardize it."

"Maybe not. But they would jeopardize you."

"I'm doing what's best for the company. They can't fault me for that. They may not like me personally, but professionally we're all working towards the same goal: maintaining the dream of Frank Radson."

Nathan paced, jingling the change in his pocket. "If only everyone were as loyal as you." He stopped and rested against the desk. "I know you're letting Stephanie work on the programmer's delay, but I'd like to let Rodney have a crack at it as well. He's a clever kid, and everyone's been pleased with him."

Kenneth tapped his finger on the desk. "If it will give you peace of mind, go ahead."

He smiled, grateful for the small victory. "Thanks. You won't regret it."

The raw, earthy scent of cologne first alerted Stephanie to the occupant of her office. The prickles of attraction she'd tried for months to ignore shot through her with a renewed fury when she saw Nathan sitting in the corner. It was the mixture of masculine vitality and intellectual cunning that she found so seductive. Too bad he hated her guts.

She walked to her desk. "May I help you?" she asked, using the cool voice she had perfected for all colleagues.

He stood. "Your performance was Oscar-worthy, Ms. Radson."

"Everything was explained—"

He nodded. "Yes, the script was faultless. I congratulate you."

He had every reason to distrust her. He was a womanizer and a cad, but she found his loyalty to the company and its CEO admirable. She had to protect her sister, but she didn't want him to hate her. She gripped a pen, gathering her courage. "If you have any concerns, perhaps we could schedule a time to go to lunch and discuss them."

He sent her a look of such disgust that her stomach tightened. "I'm sorry, Ms. Radson, but when I fall off a bicycle, I just get a new brand." He spun on his heel and left.

Stephanie released her hold on the pen and let her gaze fall.

Syrah liked Denise, but thought her mother was weird. Mrs. Shelton was always cooing and awing over old junk. She took them to flea markets, rummage sales, and antique shops, acting like a food addict searching for the next buffet. Syrah strolled around Donovan's Antique Shop while Denise tried to persuade her mother not to buy an ugly table lamp. She made sure to keep her hands in her pockets, promising herself that nothing would "accidentally" disappear. She turned down an aisle stacked with old dishes.

"So do it," a woman said in a harsh whisper. "I'm sure you know how to cover yourself. You computer guys are so smart. Pretend to do the job for them and continue to do the job for me."

Syrah peeked around the corner and saw Brooke talking to a skinny black guy with tiny glasses sliding down his nose. She supposed he was tall for his age, but his shoulders were so bent that she wasn't sure.

"I'm willing to do what you want," he said, his voice deep with anxiety. "I just want to know when—"

Her voice turned sweet. "How many times do I have to tell you not to worry?" She trailed a finger along his jaw, making him smile. "When the time is right, you'll get what you want." She kissed him.

Syrah jerked her head back in disgust. At least she knew Brooke would leave Uncle Kenneth alone, since she had that dork. Relieved, she turned and went outside to wait for Mrs. Shelton to drop her off at Aunt Teresa's.

Jessie stared at the business plan in front of her: her unofficial Plan B. She had created it during her first night class. Perhaps she could run away somewhere and implement it, start fresh, create a new identity. She hastily closed the binder when she heard a key in the front door.

"I got a letter!" Syrah said, running up to her. "My very own letter!"

Teresa followed. "Michelle had me deliver it today."

"I wasn't sure she'd write back," Syrah said, jumping from one foot to the other. "Can I open it now?"

"You don't have to ask permission to open your own letter."

"I don't want to rip it. It looks so pretty." She ran her hand over the envelope's geometric designs.

Jessie went over to Kenneth's desk and opened a drawer. "Let's see if your uncle has a letter opener we can use." She found one and handed it to her.

Syrah carefully ripped it open, then raced up to her room.

Teresa walked around the room. "Wow, this place is nice." She admired a plaque on the wall. "I'm impressed."

"Since he's never here, I'm thinking of turning it into a museum. How much do you think people will pay to see this?"

"He's a busy man," she said gently.

"He should have at least called and told Syrah that he wasn't coming home. She was very disappointed."

Teresa tilted her head, trying not to grin. "And what about you?"

Jessie shrugged, trying to be nonchalant. "What about me? I don't care."

Teresa's grin appeared, despite her efforts. "Yes, and I bet you dream about his kiss every night."

"You'd lose." *She pictured him naked and doing a lot more than kissing.*

She shrugged and headed for the door. "Hey, anything I can do to help, just tell me."

"I will." Jessie waited for the door to close, then returned to what she had been working on. She was mulling over her mission statement when she heard the front door open. She glanced up and saw Kenneth enter the room. She was so happy to see him that she leaped to her feet. She immediately sat back down, realizing how silly that was.

"You're home early," she said, trying to sound nonchalant. She knew it was a silly statement. He hadn't come home for three days. She picked up her binder.

He laid his briefcase down and shrugged out of his jacket. "Yes. Is that a problem?"

She ran nervous fingers over the binder cover. "No, of course not. But since you didn't come home last night…" She trailed off. It was none of her business.

He gave her a sideward glance. "Miss me?"

"Like a headache."

He undid his tie. "Hmm, someone's in a fighting mood today."

If only she could fight the useless emotions she felt for him. They were just friends, and she would act like it. She noticed his eyes were tired, and his good humor was not as genuine as in days before. She pointed to the pile on his desk. "I finished your letters."

"Thank you." He sat down at his desk. "If you must know why I'm home, it's to get some work done."

"Isn't that what your office is for?"

He sent her a quick grin. "Funny, I thought so too. But that opinion seems to be in the minority." He didn't feel like explaining the many interruptions that cluttered up his day. He had too much to get done. For one thing, he needed to figure out why so many of his programmers were having a hard time running programs. Nathan thought he trusted Stephanie and he wanted to put his faith in Rodney, but Kenneth trusted no one. He would figure this out himself.

He put his briefcase on the desk. "Where's Syrah?"

"She's up in her room, writing a letter."

"Good. Have you two been getting on?"

"Except for the puddle of blood in the kitchen, we get on well." She tucked her feet under her and watched him open his briefcase. "So you spent all night at work?"

"Yes."

"Why?"

Because he didn't want to come home. He didn't want to see Syrah and witness Eddie's neglect on her face. And he didn't want to see Jasmine and remember how close to chaos he had come.

"I'm not judging you," she said quickly when he remained silent. "But it would be nice if you would let us know when you're not coming home. Syrah was disappointed."

He sounded surprised. "Was she?"

"Yes."

He scratched his cheek. "And what about you?"

Jessie ignored the question. She leaned towards him, her voice eager. "You know, you should try to make an effort to bond with her a little bit more. You never interact with her."

"Why should I?"

"Because she's—"

His stormy gaze stopped her words. "I'm not her father, nor do I plan to be."

"I know that." She scowled. "What's wrong with Eddie, anyway?"

He turned away with impatience. "What does it matter? You're here to look after Syrah. That's all you need to worry about."

"I *am* looking after her. I'm looking after a little girl who desperately loves an uncle who barely looks at her. Why are you covering for Eddie, anyway? Since you don't want her here, she might be better off with him. You're only raising her hopes."

He took out some papers and slammed the briefcase shut. "She belongs here with me right now."

"You just admitted you're not her father."

He spun around. "Sometimes I damn near wish—" He stopped and took a deep breath. "The problem with this argument is that you don't have all the facts, but you're right. I'm not good for her. I admit that."

"I never said—"

"There are few things you need to say, Jas." He rubbed the back of his neck. "Don't worry, she'll go back to her father soon enough."

She uncurled her legs and chewed her nails. "What is wrong with Eddie?"

He set his briefcase on the floor.

"Syrah says he's sick," she continued.

Kenneth picked up a pen and began scribbling down some notes.

"Pushing her away isn't going to solve anything."

He threw his pen with such force that it bounced against the wall and flew in the opposite direction. He pinned Jessie with a glare so venomous that her blood chilled. "This conversation is over."

She wanted to nod, but couldn't move her head.

His low voice cut through the silence of the room. "I know she's not safe here. I know that she belongs with her father, and she will. Do you have anything else to say?"

"No," she said in a choked voice.

"Good." He returned to his work.

Jessie stared at him, wondering if any action might set his anger loose. She had once wanted to provoke his rage; now she wasn't so sure. She narrowed her eyes. Then again, a Clifton never backed away from an argument. And yet there was something inherently dangerous about his calm that would make his anger twice as frightening.

He abruptly dropped his pen and pressed his palms against his eyes. "Jasmine, don't look at me like that."

"Like what?"

He let his hands fall and turned to her. "Like I'm the big, bad wolf and you're Snow White."

The corner of her mouth quirked. "You're mixing your fairy tales."

"You know what I mean."

Her gaze fell. "Yes."

Silence descended.

He muttered something under his breath, then sat down next to her. She moved away, because she didn't want him to sense how she felt.

He said, "I didn't mean to—"

Not again! Her eyes flew up to meet his. "Stop apologizing for being human! How can we have a nice, healthy argument if you apologize all the time, especially when you're right? I know I'm overstepping my boundaries and I know you're doing the best you can, so you have every right to be vexed with me."

"I'm not vexed."

"No," she said slowly. "The word is angry."

Some dark emotion flickered in his eyes. "No, I could never be angry with you. Ever."

"Yes, you could."

He held her gaze. "No."

She only smiled.

He lifted a brow. "You enjoy provoking me, don't you?"

"I'm not sure yet."

He nodded and turned, his mouth twisting into a smile or a grimace; she wasn't sure which. She did know that his mask was in place, fastened by his iron will. She could almost feel the energy it took to guard his emotions, to make sure he didn't reveal too much. But what could be too much? He had his personal demons that he kept hidden, but for all his controlled anger, she sensed no cruelty in him, felt no survival instinct to flee when anger slipped through the fissures of his mask. No, she would never fear his anger. It made him all the more human.

She watched him as he rested his elbows on his knees, his thoughts elsewhere. "Kenneth?"

"What?"

"I did miss you."

He said nothing, then suddenly turned and rested his head in her lap. "I didn't miss you at all."

She stared at him, stunned, then hit him on the arm. "Well, thanks a lot."

He lifted her blouse. "Are you wearing my favorite bra?"

She slapped his hand away. "No."

"I still can't look at Glenda without grinning. I'm afraid she might think I'm flirting with her."

"We wouldn't want that, would we?" she said dryly.

"No, she looks like a *B* cup."

"Kenneth!"

He looked pensive. "However, I do like variety." He cupped the air. "It's more the shape than size that's alluring."

"She's married."

"Which makes them all the more attractive—a married woman's breast has that special forbidden quality."

"You're ridiculous."

He glanced up at her. "Remind me to give you the building entrance code so that you can visit me anytime you want. We can be ridiculous together any time we want to."

"Kenneth!"

He yawned. "I love that office. You know, when I was first appointed CEO, I slept there. The job was my life, and I couldn't afford to fail. I couldn't let Mr. Radson down." He closed his eyes and smiled. "Hmm, that's nice," he said as she gently stroked his hair. "No, don't stop. Yes, that's better. Thank you." He rubbed his cheek against her thigh. "I remember the first time I met him. I'd seen him carrying boxes from his car, and I offered to mow his lawn. Unfortunately, I scared the poor man. I shouldn't have sneaked up behind him like that.

"He spun around and dropped all his boxes. I picked them up for him and introduced myself, while he stared at me as if I were a mugger. He asked me all these questions about myself. I must have answered them correctly, because from then on, he was my mentor." His voice began to drift off. "I know some of the board members don't trust me, but I'll eventually show them that Mr. Radson was as much family to me as he was to them…" He fell asleep.

She considered waking him, but decided against it.

Half an hour later, he jumped up so suddenly that Jessie shrieked.

He looked at her, stunned. "Did I fall asleep?"

"Yes."

A light blush of color entered his cheeks. "I didn't mean to do that."

"It's okay, Samson, your hair is still there."

"It's not that I don't trust you—"

"Of course you don't trust me. You don't trust anyone."

Since that was the truth, he didn't argue. He stood and picked up her binder. He flipped it open and scanned its contents. "What's this?"

She reached for it. "My plan to become an independent consultant."

He blocked her hand, still reading. "In what?"

"Business."

He glanced up. "Why?"

"Because it's lucrative."

"Hmm." He nodded and closed the binder. "It's a nice plan, but it's not you."

She frowned. "I can do it. I've taken night courses and everything."

"I don't doubt your knowledge. It's…" He searched for words. "You're not the business type."

She folded her arms. "You mean I'm not like Brooke or Stephanie."

He nodded in agreement. "No, you're not."

"And what would you have me do? Serve desserts for the rest of my life?"

He sat down and stretched out his legs. "I'd always thought you'd design and create jewelry like your father, or at least work in the field as a clerk in the store. You know so much about stones and the history of different jewels. You're honest, free, artistic."

"It's not a practical profession."

"So? Who says you have to be practical? You'd make a decent living. You don't have to be like Michelle and go into business, or teach people like Teresa. You're Jasmine. Do what you're supposed to do."

If only she knew what that was. "I already told you BJ is keeping the tradition."

He tossed the binder on the couch. "You could do other things. Do a reading for me. You used to do readings for everyone except me."

"I didn't bring my stones with me."

"Bring them over tomorrow. I'm willing to pay you."

"No."

He looked disappointed, but shrugged. "I'm sure a lot of other people would pay."

"Yes, I know, but that's just entertainment, not a real career."

"You're making excuses. You could use your knowledge in other fields. You could be a jewelry historian or a gemologist."

"I'm not making excuses. I don't want to go into the field."

"Why are you so scared to be like your father? He was an admired man and good at his trade."

And that's all it was—a trade. Like a mechanic or a plumber. He'd had no great ambition to design the next Peacock Throne, an extravagant piece made up of diamonds, emeralds, and rubies. Or to own a store of his own. He had been content to fix the clasp of a bracelet, reset a pearl ring, or create simple broaches and earrings to sell to ordinary people. And then there were the stories (from the Kohinoor seized by Persia's Nadir Shah to the diamond necklace that led Marie Antoinette to the guillotine) he told his stories to passing strangers, engaging them so completely that they missed buses and dinner reservations. She loved her father, but she wanted to be more than something ordinary and forgettable.

"I'm not like my father."

"You're just too scared to be who you are."

She laughed. "Oh, that's rich, coming from you."

His jaw tightened. "What does that mean?"

"You take care of your brother's child, pay your relatives' bills, and suffer through a job you hardly enjoy."

"I enjoy my work, and my family needs me."

"I think you just need them to need you."

"You don't know anything about me."

She tapped her chest, her tone rising. "I know that you live a lie every day and that you have no business telling other people how to live a life you're too afraid to live."

His eyes hardened, but his voice grew soft. "And I know that you try to act brave on the outside, but inside you're terrified of who you are. Go ahead and try to be a carbon copy of Michelle. Try to be tough and cool. Just like your other jobs, you'll fail at that too."

She clenched her teeth. "I'm not a failure."

"I didn't say you were."

She snatched her binder and stood. "You didn't need to."

He wrapped an arm around her waist and pulled her onto his lap. "Where are you going? I thought you liked to argue."

"I changed my mind." She elbowed him in the ribs and jumped up.

He feigned disbelief. "You mean you lied to me?"

"I didn't lie."

He stood. "Then why are you walking away?"

"Because I want to."

He grabbed her arm and spun her around. "Chicken," he said, in soft challenge.

She dropped her binder, then quickly shifted her position, tossing him over her shoulder. He fell on his back. "I don't suggest you do that again.

He grinned up at her. "I'd like to offer you a challenge."

She rested a foot on his stomach. "You're not in the position to offer me anything."

"I guess I'll have to change that." He yanked on her leg and brought her down hard. Before she could recover, he pinned her arms to the ground and straddled her. "That's better."

She struggled beneath him. "Get off me."

"Now, that's a first," he said, thoughtful. "Never heard that before."

"Kenneth!"

"Tsk, tsk, tsk." He held her with careless strength. "Is that all the fight you have in you?"

"You weigh tons."

"Here's my challenge. You make a piece of jewelry, and I'll buy it."

She stopped struggling and stared at him, confused. "Why?"

"I'm interested to see what you'd come up with."

"I'm not a jewelry maker, I'm a businesswoman."

He stared at her for a moment, then stood, frustrated. "No, you're not."

She tripped him and jumped on him before he could recover. "I may not be Michelle or Brooke, but I'm smart and I can be ruthless."

He didn't fight her. The position was too comfortable. "No, you can't. You have too much passion. All someone has to do is look in your eyes and see what you feel."

"That's not true."

He suddenly rolled on top of her, his elbows resting on either side of her head. "Right. So when are you going to kiss me?"

"I don't want to kiss you."

"*Now* you're lying." He pressed his mouth to hers and immediately felt a pleasurable sense of release, of coming home. "I lied too," he whispered. "I did miss you." He brushed his lips against hers, then halted when he felt her knee positioned at a very dangerous angle against his groin.

"Let me up," she said.

"Are you still angry?"

"I will be."

He wasn't too concerned. He knew he could move before she did any major damage. He opened his mouth to respond, but stopped at the sight of a pair of jeans. Syrah asked, "Are you fighting or making up?"

He quickly rolled off Jessie and stood. "I was just showing Aunt Jasmine some fighting moves. Right?"

She grabbed her binder and hit him on the top of the head. "Yes, and he lost."

Syrah watched Jessie leave and slam the front door. Damn, they were arguing again. Why did adults like to argue so much? She would have to find a way to fix things. She wanted them to like each other. Perhaps she could give Aunt Jessie something and make her feel better.

She raced to her room. There she searched through her drawer and grabbed her special sock. She'd been able to return the ring and a broach, but nobody wanted that ugly bracelet. She picked it up. Since no one else wanted it, Aunt Jessie might as well have it.

Arrogant jerk, Jessie fumed, kicking gravel in the driveway. She wasn't scared of anything. How dare he imply she was trying to be Michelle. Her business plan was sound. It was a great idea; she was smart. She walked towards her car. The man had an ego the size of Greenland. Who was he to tell her about herself? Did he honestly think she wanted to spend her life with her father's reputation? Her father had been a man people openly admired, but privately thought a little strange.

Granted, Dad loved his work and made a decent income, but it was nothing extravagant, not something that people would look at in awe and talk about for years. Did he think she wanted to be like her antisocial cousin, locked in the shop all day with metal and gems? She wanted to be noticed for something, to make a difference somehow. Their lives were not for her, and Kenneth—the man of many masks—had no right to imply that it was.

She kicked a large stone that turned out to be the top of a boulder. She stubbed her toe and swore, jumping up and down as she rubbed her sore appendage.

"Aunt Jessie, are you okay?" Syrah asked, coming up to her.

She gently put her foot down. "Yes, love. Thanks."

Syrah adjusted her cap. "You and Uncle were fighting, weren't you?"

"Yes." Jessie bit her nails. "It must make the house very uncomfortable for you."

"Nah. It's sort of funny to hear you two fighting. When my parents used to fight, it wasn't funny at all. My father would swear, and my mother would throw things. That usually happened when Dad was drunk."

Jessie's heart constricted painfully as the truth showed itself. "Does he still like to drink?"

"A lot." She suddenly covered her mouth and looked at Jessie in horror. "I wasn't supposed to say anything. Don't tell—"

"Don't worry." Jessie knelt in front of her and held her shoulders. Her voice was gentle. "Is that why you came to your uncle?"

Her dark eyes hardened. "I'm not going back ever. Not ever."

"No one's telling you that you have to."

Syrah hesitated, then said, "I want you to have this." She took out the bracelet and slipped it on Jessie's wrist.

"Oh...wow." It was an ugly brown bracelet that looked like a child's beaded project; it rattled, as if it were filled with pebbles. "It's...very special." She hugged her. "Thank you."

Syrah stepped back, uncomfortable with Jessie's affection. "No problem."

Jessie watched Syrah return to the house, then glanced down at the bracelet as she faced the root of her anger. She wasn't angry with Kenneth. He was right. She had always been fascinated by stones and the craftsmanship of jewelry, but she had never thought she had the skill. She didn't want to be a faded copy of her father; he already had

BJ. She had been scared and had never had the courage to try.

Dinner was a disaster. It was not the food itself (chicken with lemon sauce), but Freda was determined to punish Jessie for her deception.

"I thought about your business plan," Kenneth said, leaning towards her. "If you want to go ahead with it, I'll help you make contacts,"

Freda tossed Jessie's plate in front of her, forcing him to sit back.

"How was the 'dip and fall back' Ms. Rose made?" he asked, glancing at Jessie's plate.

"I didn't make it," Freda said.

Kenneth stiffened. He wasn't used to an order being ignored. "Why?"

"There wasn't enough salt." She glared at Jessie.

"But I made a specific request—"

"It's all right," Jessie said. "What she made was delicious." *Chicken...again.*

He glanced at them, then shrugged, determined not to make an issue of it. He picked up his fork and continued on his original topic. "You'll have to sell yourself, of course." He twirled his fork, searching for the right words. "In consulting, you not only sell knowledge, but your experience and...image."

"I know that. I'm not asking you to believe in me."

"You've barely touched your food, Ms. Clifton," Freda said. "Not *rich* enough for you?"

Jessie's cheeks burned. "No, I'm not very hungry."

Kenneth rubbed his chin, oblivious to the drama before him. "I just think you should focus your energies on something you're good at. You don't like people enough to be a consultant."

Freda blocked his view. "Let me refill this."

Jessie reached for her glass, but Freda got to it first. "I don't—"

"I hope it's pure enough for you. I know you only want the best." She refilled the glass, then banged it on the table, causing everyone to jump.

Kenneth sat back in his chair and glared at her. "Ms. Rose, what's gotten into you? You can't talk—"

"It's all right," Jessie interrupted. She didn't want Freda reprimanded for her loyalty.

Kenneth studied the two women, then sent Jessie a knowing smirk. "Like I said, you just don't get on with people."

He said the words lightly, but they fell on her like rocks, grating on her raw nerves. It was too close to the truth. "That's right. I'm so antisocial that I shouldn't be seen in decent society. I think I should go." Jessie pushed herself away from the table and excused herself. She grabbed her coat from the hallway closet and opened the front door.

Kenneth slammed it closed, all levity gone from his voice and eyes. "Okay, what's going on?"

"Nothing." She rubbed her temples.

"See? Now you're giving yourself a headache."

"I'm okay." She moved towards the door.

He grabbed her shoulder, stopping her. "Stand still." He massaged the back of her neck. Jessie tried to remain stiff, even as his fingers softened the tension within her. "We're friends, aren't we?"

She nodded.

His voice was gentle. "I was just offering advice."

The warmth—not just from his hand or tone, but also his gaze—seemed to spread throughout her body, seeking to calm the worrying thoughts in her mind. She placed a hand on her forehead. If she wasn't careful, his kindness was going to make her start to cry. "I know."

"But you're not going to tell me what's wrong?"

"I just want to go home."

He swung her into the circle of his arms and lifted her chin. His eyes filled with regret. "Did I hurt you by bringing up your father? I know you loved him very much. I'm sure you still miss him."

She did miss him. He would know what to do. And if he were still around, she would have more time to succeed at something that would make him proud.

Her voice was barely a whisper. "I've failed him in everything."

"That's not true."

Jessie squeezed her eyes shut, but the tears came anyway. She rested her head against his chest, allowing herself one moment of weakness. She drew on his strength, expecting it to feel strange and unnatural—she was a strong, independent woman, after all—but it felt right. He felt right. She needed his comfort and safety.

Jessie pulled back, holding her head down, ashamed of her tears. "I'm getting your shirt all wet."

"I have others." He wiped a tear away with his thumb. "Come on, tell me what's wrong, Jas."

She glanced up at him and suddenly knew what she had been fighting against all her life: a dream she felt she could never have. She wanted to be a woman in every sense of the word—strong, but not afraid of her weaknesses and honest about her desire to have someone else to lean on. A woman who loved and was loved. A woman not ashamed of her longing to have a husband and family and a career she enjoyed.

But women like her weren't supposed to have such wishes. Their plain faces and sense of power rebelled against such simple, ordinary desires. They were happy with themselves, and didn't care if they never had a date or received gifts. They were the natural spinsters and old maids who enjoyed being "the aunts." They were the rocks, the foundations you could depend on, not the weepy females who clung to men and stained their shirts with tears.

The revelation of her heart was both a pain and a relief. At that moment, the pendant no longer mattered; Kenneth did.

But that couldn't be. She grasped the doorknob, ready for escape. "I have to go," she said and darted to the freedom outside.

Chapter Nineteen

Jessie burst into the house while Michelle and Teresa cleared the dinning table. They stared at her in surprise.

"What happened?" Teresa asked.

Michelle put a plate down. "What are you doing here?"

Jessie fell into a chair, folded her arms, and laid her head down. "Freda hates me and I hate myself."

Her sisters shared a confused look, shrugged then sat.

"Start from the beginning," Teresa said, patting Jessie's back.

"Freda overheard me talking about the bet and thinks I'm a money-hungry hussy."

Teresa gasped appalled. "Did she say that?"

"No, but it was implied. But it's worse than that. It's the most horrible thing in the world."

"You're in love with him," Michelle said.

Jessie raised her head, her eyes wide. "Is it that obvious?" She groaned. "How awful. How embarrassing." She covered her face. "I can't see him again. What if he suspects? He'll feel sorry for me."

"He won't suspect anything. I've discovered that most men aren't that clever when it comes to women's feelings."

"You must despise me."

"Why?"

Jessie sat back in her chair. "Because for the second time my selfishness has cost us the pendant. I have no honor."

"You have honor. You have maintained the Clifton integrity by realizing that using someone in order to get what you want is wrong."

Teresa spoke up. "But what about Deborah?"

Michelle frowned. "What about her?"

"Jessie will have to be her housekeeper for a year."

"It won't be that bad."

Jessie rested her head down and groaned. "How did I get myself in this mess?"

Michelle smiled. "Let me remind you, shall I?"

"Shut up, Michelle," Teresa said. "You could tell him the truth and hope he takes you anyway."

"He's not supposed to take me out of pity. That's cheating."

"Deborah won't know."

"I'll know. Besides, he might not take me. He might be furious and never talk to me again."

Michelle sighed. "Let's take this step-by-step. First, tell Freda the truth. Once you tell her the truth, it will get easier."

"I hope so." Jessie doubted it. But the truth had to come out eventually. There was no use holding onto false hope. It was just as damaging as false pride. She could write a book on it. She rested her chin in her hand.

"Nice bracelet," Michelle said.

Jessie stared at her surprised. "You like it?"

"I didn't say I liked it. I said it was nice."

Teresa took her wrist and ran her fingers over the beads. "Did Kenneth give it to you?"

Jessie shook her head. "No. Syrah."

"Looks expensive."

"I'm sure it's not."

They fell silent.

"Do you think she loved him?" Jessie asked.

Michelle glanced at her. "Who?"

"Gran Sonya. Do you think she took the pendant because she loved the German and not because of revenge?"

Michelle frowned. "But that would defeat the whole purpose. You can't fall for the man for which you vowed vengeance. She didn't steal a lock of hair or a note scribbled in his hand. She had no desire to be sentimental. She took his most prized possession. She wanted to teach him a lesson and she did. The Sapphire Pendant is a symbol warning us of the duplicity of men."

"Then how did Dad end up with it?"

"Perhaps because he had three daughters."

Jessie bit her nails, her voice mumbled. "I wonder if it was meant for something else."

"Like what?" Michelle asked.

"I don't know." She shook her head then let her hand fall. "I don't know anything right now. My mind is mush."

"You'll feel better when this is all over," Teresa said.

Jessie raised her brows. "Over? I'll be scrubbing Deborah's toilets for a year."

Teresa gave her an impish grin. "Maybe."

"What do you mean by maybe?"

She only smiled.

Jessie looked at Syrah as the girl slept with her head buried under the covers in the dark hush of the room. She kissed her on the cheek then went into her bedroom. She would miss her. She got dressed and climbed into bed, determined to talk to Freda tomorrow. But she ended up staring at the ceiling instead of falling asleep and changed her mind.

Jessie grabbed her slippers, wishing she had a robe. She felt naked in Michelle's pink silk nightdress. It whispered promises she couldn't fulfill. She hoped that she didn't bump into Kenneth. She grabbed a long sleeved button down shirt and put it on.

She went to Freda's room, which was towards the back of the house. As she walked down the hall, she saw light peeking from under the door and heard the murmur of voices from the TV.

She knocked softly on the door.

"Who is it?"

"It's me. Jessie. I really want to talk to you."

There was a pause, slow heavy footsteps then the door swung open. Freda appeared with her head wrapped in a bright purple scarf, a large T-shirt saying 'Dangerous', and fluorescent green fuzzy slippers. "Okay, talk."

"May I come in?"

"No."

She sighed. "Freda, I'm not what or who you think I am." She threw up her hands in a hopeless gesture. She saw Freda's frown increase and looked down to see that her shirt had opened to reveal her seductive nightdress.

"Right," Freda said doubtfully.

Jessie pulled the shirt around her. "Look, this is my sister's nightdress. Trust me. I couldn't seduce a cat to eat tuna."

Freda rested her hip against the door and folded her arms, her eyes beginning to glaze over.

"I'm not after Kenneth's money," Jessie said, pulling at the buttons on her shirt. She took a deep breath. "The truth is I accepted a bet to charm Kenneth to ask me to the Hampton Charity Ball. If I won, then I'd get the Sapphire Pendant which was sold to send me to college. It's an important family heirloom. I know that means nothing to you, but please let me explain."

Freda nodded.

"Most people think only humans have emotions like pain, joy or fear, but others believe all things are alive. My father was one of those people. He didn't think things were alive as we are, but that they live in their own way. A way we cannot understand. He also believed that those who did not have an inner truth were in danger of becoming soulless. Of having their spiritual selves taken by the many forms of evil that roam the Earth.

"The story of our family heirloom is a tale of an ancestor taking the sapphire pendant of a callous holidaymaker who left tears in his wake. Through her act she was taking part of his soul because my family believes that when you possess something it becomes a part of you. So to my family the pendant remembers and teaches us many lessons because it is something that lives and will continue to live on no matter how the world changes.

"There are stories that my people came fully formed from the insides of a petrified tree when the God of Whispers cried because no one could hear his voice. When we came forth we honored him by using the natural treasures of the earth to speak. That's why giving jewelry and other ornaments means so much—it speaks for the giver and receiver showing love, affection, demonstrating power or even corruption.

"It is no accident that in our family there is always one who has an affinity with stones, metals and gems. It is so someone is always listening to the whispers carried through the wind and settled in the ground."

Jessie shook her head a little embarrassed. "Whether the tales are true is of no importance now. It has carried us through tribal wars and slavery so that we know we have a right to exist though others may not think so. Through our stories we will always know who we are. The Sapphire Pendant's importance is not only its value or even the act of Gran Sonya but for its voice, its symbolism."

Jessie sighed unsure she had made any sense. "I know it was stupid to try and retrieve it through a bet, but at the time it seemed like the best way to get it back without spending years to save to buy it back." She chewed her nails. "I used to hate Kenneth because-- well it doesn't matter now. But I don't hate him anymore so... I don't want to marry him or anything," she said in a rush. "I don't need his money. I know that everyone believes he's Mr. Perfect, but he's not--he's vain, a workaholic and he says *I* have a temper." She sniffed. "But he--"

"Come inside and sit down," Freda interrupted.

Jessie halted with her mouth open then nodded. She chose a paisley couch near the window. Freda sat down on the bed and lowered the volume on the TV. She turned to Jessie with a shrewd look.

"You really had me worried for a while. I'm usually not a bad judge of character, but now I'm sure you're okay. So what are you going to do now?"

"What do you mean?"

"I mean you're in love with the man, what are you going to do about it?"

Jessie waved her hands, heat burning her cheeks. "It's just lust. I don't know him well enough to love him."

"It just might do you good to believe your father's stories. So they will give you courage."

Jessie frowned. "I have courage."

"Just not enough to love." Freda shook her head and stood. "I'm too old for this. Do what you will." She pushed Jessie out of the room. "Now go away so I can sleep."

Jessie began to speak, but the door closed in her face.

She stared at it for a few moments then turned. Did she have a sign on her forehead: I'M IN LOVE WITH KENNETH PRESTON? It was horrible. Didn't her heart know better? She had been down this road before. Was she a complete masochist?

Jessie ripped off her shirt and crumpled it up. Damn it, she would not make a fool of herself again. She refused. She fought the urge to stomp down the hallway like a spoiled child. The very idea was ludicrous. They were friends, for however long that would be, then it would end.

She glanced over her shoulder at Freda's door. It was lust, it had to be. Sure she wanted to be married someday, but not to him. She just wanted sex. Who could blame her? He was like a set of keys to a woman locked in prison. Falling in love was for romantics; she was a realist. She wanted his body—that's all--no matter how ashamed her mother might have been. She turned and crashed into what she at first thought was a wall.

She took a step back and her heel caught on the hem of her nightdress. She fell back landing on her bottom with a thud.

"Are you all right?" Kenneth asked, flipping on the lights.

She narrowed her eyes against the glare. "I'm fine." She stood, rubbing her sore behind.

"I thought I heard someone sneaking round down here."

"I wasn't sneaking," she muttered resentfully.

Kenneth's eyes trailed the length of her nightdress. "Oh, I guess you lost your way. My room is upstairs."

She gasped and grabbed her shirt.

Kenneth snatched it from her. "No, don't put that on, it will ruin the effect."

"That's the plan."

"What for? You look good." He licked his lower lip, his eyes resting on her cleavage. "Yum."

Jessie folded her arms. "Stop that. I look ridiculous." She glanced down at herself. "It's too long. Too tight in some places and too loose in others." She frowned at his green long sleeve pajamas. So much for Teresa's boxer shorts scenario. "How come you never wear short sleeves?"

Kenneth furrowed his brows. "What are you talking about?"

"It's summer time and you're wearing that." She gestured to his pajamas. "Even when you were younger you always wore long sleeves." It used to drive the neighborhood kids crazy seeing him in a buttoned up shirt when the day was hot enough to melt coal. They used to joke that he probably swam in a suit.

His finger trailed a sensuous path along the scooped neck of her nightdress. "But we're not talking about me right now."

She seized his hand, feeling her body grow warm. "Don't do that."

He rested his other hand on her shoulder, his teasing tone gone. "Are you feeling better?"

She lowered her gaze, embarrassed. "Much."

"No more tears?"

"Sorry about that. I-"

He placed a finger against her lips. "I believe you once told me not to apologize for being human. I was glad to be there. "

She met his eyes. "I'll be there for you too if—" She couldn't finish.

He handed her the shirt and stared at her for a moment, his dark eyes calling out to something deep within her. "Good night."

Jessie touched his arm as he turned. "I have a few minutes if you want to talk."

He laughed. "You wear something that good and you think I want to talk?"

She slipped into her shirt. If he didn't want to talk, she wouldn't force him.

"Good night," he repeated.

"'Night." She watched him disappear into the darkness, taking all his secrets with him. She couldn't blame him. Didn't she have her own secrets she had no wish to share? They were alike in that respect. They each asked for trust without offering any.

She reached for the light switch. Kenneth unexpectedly appeared out of the darkness like an apparition. He grabbed her hand and led her towards the back door. He opened a closet and handed her his shoes

Dara Girard

and a long coat.

"Put these on," he said.

She slipped into his oversized shoes and wrapped his coat around her. She inhaled its musky scent. It was as intimate as being in his arms.

He opened the door and took her hand. "Come on."

The moon was bright enough to light their path, but Kenneth still used a flashlight to guide their way through the trees. Jessie didn't ask him where he was taking her, not wanting to disturb or analyze his strange mood. She would rather enjoy the warm summer night, the sound of old leaves crunching beneath their feet, crickets singing merrily, and the moonlight painting their way.

He finally shone his flashlight on a little cottage. He unlocked the front door and turned on the lights.

Inside revealed a furnished room that had light cream colored chairs, gleaming hardwood floors that were softened by an area rug and a bed overstuffed with pillows.

"Oh, it's beautiful," Jessie said, eyeing the bed with special interest.

Kenneth grinned, reading her expression. "You can go ahead."

She turned to him. "What?"

He folded his arms. "You still like jumping on beds, don't you?"

She shifted uncomfortable. "It's a silly habit."

"So? I keep peanuts in my pocket."

"You're right." She kicked off her shoes and leaped on the bed, landing face down. It was like falling into feathers. "Oh this is heaven," she mumbled, sinking her head into the mixture of silk and cotton pillows. "I'm sure you put this bed to good use." She regretted her words once they left her mouth. She wasn't sure whether to apologize or let it pass. Her uneasiness grew as a cold silence followed her remark. She turned to him, expecting to find him glaring at her with hard eyes, but instead he was fingering a small sculpture of a person reading.

"I'm sorry," she said. "I don't mean to judge."

"It's been my experience that people who say that, usually do."

Jessie sat up and straightened the pillows. "I wish at times I could cut out my tongue."

Kenneth slanted her a glance. "Vex me enough and I might do it for you."

She smiled relaxing at his light tone. "You're a true friend."

He turned off the lights. "Sometimes I sit out here to think alone with my trees," he said in a quiet voice. "Lay on your back, I want to show you something."

He laid down next to her then hit a button on the side table. Suddenly, the ceiling began to open, displaying the starry sky and a bright moon that looked low enough to touch. Jessie stared speechless.

"The night's not black enough," Kenneth said. "On some nights you can see which stars twinkle and which don't."

"Stars really twinkle?"

"Haven't you ever looked up at the stars before?"

She rested her hands behind her head. "Not like this. It's beautiful."

"Yes." He paused. "You know stars help us know the location of satellites. See satellites..."

She nudged him with her foot. "Don't ruin this moment by talking about satellites."

"Sorry." He was silent then said, "One day I'm going to buy a book on astrology and figure out what I'm looking at."

"I'll buy it for you."

He turned to her the moonlight reflecting the surprise on his face. "Don't be ridiculous, Jas."

She frowned. "I'm not being ridiculous."

"I can afford to buy myself a simple book."

"It's not about whether you can afford it, I just wanted to—" She searched for words.

"To what?"

"To give you a gift."

"Why?"

The man was infuriating. Why should she have to explain why she wanted to give him a gift? It was something people did. Jessie slid off the bed. "Don't worry the feeling has just left me."

He grabbed her nightdress. "Where do you think you're going, hothead?"

She spun around. "Hothead?"

"I thought you said you had time to talk."

She slapped his hand away. "I'm through talking with you."

He pulled on her nightdress until she was forced to sit. "I'm not."

He held her to him. "I'm sorry I brought up your father."

"It's okay. I shouldn't be sad. We had one of the largest "home coming" parties in the community. I am happy for them."

"It's okay to miss them too."

"They wouldn't want me to feel sad. They would be disappointed."

Jessie sighed. *But then again that would be nothing new.*

"I had a grandmother who died a few years back. Her funeral was very somber, she came from somber people."

"Methodist?" she teased.

He smiled. "Yes. I had to force myself to cry. Everyone was so impressed by her weeping grandson, but inside I felt ashamed."

"That you couldn't cry?"

His voice fell. "No, that I hated her."

She looked at him startled. She couldn't imagine him hating anyone.

"But that was a long time ago," he said, leaving no room for questions. "When I'm here the past and future cease to exist. All there is, is now. I glance up at the sky and see all the possibilities." He fell quiet then said, "If you could have anything, what would it be?"

"The Sapphire Pendant," she said without thinking.

"That sounds familiar."

"Dad talked about it enough. Every time I feel a warm summer breeze and look up at the sky I think about it. Especially on nights like this. The pendant is a family heirloom. Mrs. Ashford has it now."

"The one your father sold?"

"Yes."

"Oh."

"What would you want?" Jessie asked before they both sank into melancholy thoughts.

Kenneth was quiet for so long she wasn't sure he would answer. "I can't tell you."

"Why not?"

He shook his head.

"Let me guess then. You already have a great job, an enviable position in the community, respect, a loving if not somewhat selfish family, money, women who adore you. No, I can't figure it out but..." She lifted his hand and kissed his palm then closed his fingers. "There."

"What was that?"

"Whatever you want it to be."

He gazed down at his hand. "That was sweet."

She covered his mouth. "Shh! It's a secret."

He laughed and the solemn mood lifted. "I need to go away for the weekend."

"Why?"

"I have to talk to Eddie."

She chewed her lower lip. "I know what's wrong with him."

He kept his gaze averted. "He just needs time to focus," he said defensively. "To prioritize. He's not as bad as...He's not that bad."

"You can't heal him. He has to do that himself."

"I'll be back by Monday."

"Okay." She sat up.

He still looked down. "Will you miss me?"

She wanted to lie. It would be so easy to lie. 'No, I wouldn't miss you,' she could say. 'You mean nothing to me.' "Good friends are always missed."

"Jasmine?" His voice was low, but she could feel it reaching out to surround her in the darkness.

She stared at one of the shadows in the corner. "Yes."

He placed his hand against the slope of her neck. "Do I need to ask?" He was closer now, his breath warm against her skin.

"No."

He didn't waste any time. Within moments she was on the bed and naked in his arms. His body covered hers—a powerful silhouette of passionate hunger—slowly melting her in his heat.

"Kenneth, I—"

He effectively stopped her words with his mouth, forcing her to leave the rest trapped in her throat. She released an encouraging moan of pleasure. His mouth engulfed her as his hands roamed free. Her body immediately responded to the mastery of his fingers against her flesh. They skimmed from her stomach to her thighs to her breasts, seeking to explore every aspect of her.

Jessie sought to do the same, her fingers slid under his collar, stroking the curling hairs on his chest.

"This is unfair," she breathed, placing kisses along his jaw.

"What is?" His voice was muffled against her throat.

"You're still dressed."

He impatiently removed his clothes and tossed them on the floor. Jessie's hands greedily reached up to see what the darkness hid from her eyes. His body was impressive: a solid form of muscle and strength that could intimidate as well as overwhelm, but she felt no fear as his body crushed hers; his skin hot as it moved against her own.

Kenneth dared not think. He couldn't believe this was real. Did the night sky deceive him or was this fiery woman, touched by the glow of the moon, really naked in his arms, trembling from the same passion that kept his body hard? Were the celestial gods forgiving him his secrets; forgiving him his shame and finally offering him this one night of pleasure? He moaned aloud when her hands grasped the inner part of his thigh.

His lips moved to her neck and Jessie shut her eyes. Her body responded to his masculine exploration, but in her mind she saw him with someone else. She saw his lips caressing the neck of a teenage girl who had curly brunette hair, who liked to wear heavy eye shadow. She saw his hand reach for her blouse as they made out on Lover's Hill...

How could she fool herself to believe she was anything more than just one of his women? Hadn't he admitted to his weakness? What would happen in the morning? Would she just be another conquest? She could imagine her label listed in his black book: secretary, *check*, waitress, *check*, lawyer, *check*, plain little virgin, *double check*.

She had wanted an excuse to hate him and at this moment she did. She hated him for pretending to be her friend then treating her like all the others. How many women had he brought to this cottage and had told the same story? She had been foolish before to think she was "the one", the special person in his life, and had let her hormones control her mind. She wouldn't do that again.

Jessie shoved him away, leapt out of the bed, and wrapped his coat around her.

"Where the hell are you going?!" Kenneth caught her around the waist before she reached the door.

"I'm leaving."

He tightened his hold as she struggled to free herself. "Why?"

She hated his strength, hated how weak she felt in his arms. "Because I'm not going to be one of them."

"One of what?"

"Your women."

Kenneth spun her around. Jessie could see his anger as though it were as visible as the moonlight. "Damn it Jasmine! What's the game? Give me the rules so that I can play too. Or am I suppose to lose?"

"The only game player is you. I fell for this years ago. I thought you cared about me."

"I did care about you."

"Sure we were friends. And we're still friends, except now it's different. Now you're horny and I'm within arms reach. Then once it's all over, I become the nanny again and you the rich employer. And we're supposed to still be friends because it's just sex after all, right? It doesn't mean anything. So when I see you with another infant at a party, I'm supposed to nod and smile and understand because that's what women like me do.

"We're supposed to be thankful that a least *someone* would be willing to sleep with us. Well, I am grateful. Men like you make dreams come true. You notice women like me and make me feel special for just one Cinderella moment. Then the clock strikes twelve."

"Right," he said, his velvet voice edged with steel. "And women like you are so wounded that you surround yourself in self-pity and use it both as a shield and as a weapon. You've been mistreated by life because of your looks and personality or some other flaw that you exaggerate to carry around as the bane of your existence.

"You wallflowers stay on the outside pretending to watch and observe, but you judge and label. You don't see people. You see titles: Beautiful. Talented. Conniving. You look at guys like me and we're immediately the enemy because we've attained everything you haven't. We are everything you wish to be.

"But people like me are not real to you. We're trophies. Something to show off. Something to attain. All that time I spent with you. I learnt everything about you. Your favorite color, that wasps scared you, your favorite dessert. What did you learn about me? How long my eyelashes are, how tall I am?"

"I know your favorite color."

"Yet you forgot what food I ate."

Jessie turned away.

"Is there anything about me that you could tell me that half the city doesn't already know?"

She hesitated.

"No, you can't because you don't care. I don't think you ever did." Kenneth rubbed his forehead. "You know for a while I did believe you lost the pendant because of me. Because you loved me." He stumbled over the words. "But the truth is I was the perfect scapegoat. You never wanted to go to college and when the Caribbean Council awarded you the money to go to school you panicked. You had no idea what you would do. Sure you would like the sports program, but books and studying for another four years? No way. Then you saw your perfect out. You could give it away and still make yourself look selfless.

"So you did. You gave it to Eddie and with no money you had no way to go to school. But you didn't count on your parent's dismay. You thought that since Michelle and Teresa had gone to school you'd be free, but that wasn't the case. They had been determined that their youngest would go too and they'd do whatever it took. So they sold the pendant. And what has bothered you all these years was that you lost the pendant because you had lied to yourself and to all those you loved. Not because of me."

Jessie folded her arms. "And what do you know about love? You don't have to give an ounce of it to anyone. Everyone meets you and loves you. You don't have to do anything for it, but show up. You write a check here, give a pat on the head there, and that's as far as your emotional vulnerability will stretch you. Not that I blame you. Why do more than you have to?" She tapped him on the shoulder. "But you are loyal. I will give you that. You know your brother is an alcoholic, but you'll take care of him and make sure everything looks good. Nothing can stain the Preston name. You'll do anything for appearances; even sacrifice your niece for it."

Kenneth tightened his jaw. "Yes, I'm heartless, but I find it interesting with people like you who profess love all the time. What have you ever sacrificed for love, for honor?"

"Plenty."

He grabbed her shoulders. "You're a hypocrite and a liar." His grip tightened as his voice deepened into huskiness. "How can you claim to love someone and then seek revenge in this way? To torture a man by using the power of your body, knowing that he wants you, teasing him and then withdrawing...I don't have women and you know that. You know I'm not the type of man to go from one bed to another, that I'd never knowingly hurt anyone." He brushed his lips against her forehead then said softly, "Sometimes I wonder if I should give you a real reason to hate me. You'd like that, wouldn't you?"

"Talk like that is beneath you."

"What?" He raised his tone in surprise. "First I'm a cheating, heartless dog and now I have standards? Make up your mind, Jasmine."

"I have. I do want you." She held out a hand when he pulled her close. "But I don't trust you."

He paused. "Why?"

She was glad for the darkness so that he couldn't see her face. "Because this will mean more to me than it will to you."

He brought her hand to the front of his trousers. "Can you deny what I feel when you hold it in your hand?"

She held him for a moment then pulled away. "That's just..."

"Lust? No. Whatever you feel, I feel it too. If you knew the risk I am taking just to be with you, you'd understand."

"Yet you don't trust me."

"I do."

"Then tell me why it couldn't have been me that night on Lover's Hill," she challenged. "Didn't you know I would have gone anywhere with you? I would have done anything. Why didn't you come to me that night?"

"Jasmine—" His voice broke. "It's complicated."

"I'm listening. I want to understand. Was she prettier, willing to put out more? Just tell me the truth so I can understand why it wasn't me back then, but why you want it to be me now. What has changed? You can have any woman you want. Why me?"

Kenneth briefly shut his eyes, wishing he could shut out the pain of his past as well. Could he risk telling her the truth? Just for one moment? So that this aching need, which had become a throbbing pain, could find release between her soft thighs? But he had too much to conceal, too many people depended on his secrecy. He couldn't betray them no matter what.

He felt a slow anger beginning to build. It was always like this with Jasmine. She always wanted more than he could give her. "You want the truth? Yes, she was prettier than you and she gave me what I wanted without question. She didn't need or want anything from me and I liked that. I needed that. I'm not perfect," he said in a ragged whisper. "You of all people know that. I wasn't perfect then and I'm not perfect now. I can't give you the answers you want. If that's a problem then you should go because I'm not changing. There are plenty of Regines out there. They make a man's life less complicated."

"I see."

Kenneth lowered his voice. "You know I want you. So it's your choice."

"I know. I wish—" Jessie bit her lip then turned and raced to the door.

He listened to her feet pound across the dry leaves as if a deer in flight from a predator. He sighed, glancing up at the stars, wondering if someone up there was laughing at him.

Chapter Twenty

Jessie woke the next morning, feeling the sun mocking her with its brightness. She sat on the edge of the bed and saw a note under her door. It read:

We'll talk when I get back. There's something you should know. Miss me.

   Kenneth
PS Kiss this spot. I did.

She smiled in spite of herself. There was a lot she would remember about last night, but most of all their vulnerability. It had frightened her. Why couldn't they trust each other? Why did she demand it instead of give it? Kenneth was right; love was not about being selfish.

She looked at the sun as it chased shadows across her room, its brightness no longer seeming to mock her. She lifted the blinds and stared at the trees: tall noble witnesses, whispering, their many secrets, to each other in the morning breeze.

"I do know about love," she said. "I risked winning the pendant for him, didn't I? That proves it."

The trees stopped whispering; the sun found solace behind a cloud.

"Cowards," she murmured, turning to the bed.

And yet she'd saved face again. By declaring herself the loser she wouldn't have to try to win and face failure. Then she would work for Deborah, knowing in her heart that she hadn't really lost because she hadn't tried. She frowned. Her pride was a tricky monster. Kenneth was right; she did see him as trophy. But she also loved him. If she wanted to prove it, she would have to tell him the truth—risking it all.

He had failed. Hopelessly. He wished he hadn't gone. Kenneth hit the steering wheel and swore as he drove back from his brother's place. It didn't matter that he had set his brother up in a nice apartment; made sure he always had food in the fridge and checked in every now and then to see he had managed to keep his current employment. The alcohol was winning. Eddie had been sober enough to speak coherently, but needing a drink so badly that his hands shook like a patient with Parkinson's. Kenneth had congratulated himself for keeping an emotional distance from the situation until he saw a wine bottle in the recycling bin. His calm snapped.

"Why the hell are you doing this?" he demanded, waving the bottle in his brother's face. "Explain it to me because I don't understand. You have everything a person could want. What do you need this for?"

Eddie sounded tired. "It helps me to think."

"What do you need to think about? You've got a daughter, a job, and a nice place."

"So what?"

"You have responsibilities you have to take care of."

"Is that an order?"

Kenneth turned away. Jasmine was right, he couldn't bring Syrah back here until Eddie sobered up. He had spent so much of his life doing everything he was supposed to do or what people expected him to do, he had forgotten what he needed to do. Right now he had to protect Syrah. His gut clenched. He didn't like how the words sounded. Eddie wasn't a bad guy. He wasn't a monster. He drank, he was lazy, but he loved his daughter. He was her *father* that was the role God had given him. What right did he have to break up that bond? Especially, because he knew he had a selfish desire to claim Syrah as his own.

"You need to take care of her."

"What are you going to do?" Eddie mocked. "Take her away from me?" "Is the man who has everything going to take the one thing *him bredda* has to claim in this world, take the one thing that is of any importance? Is Mr. Perfect going to take *him brother* to court and risk him pristine image by admitting the truth about me, maybe even about him mother? Does he think he could do better?" Eddie laughed. "Both of us know that isn't true. If you wanted, you could drop your seed and get one of your own. But you're too afraid of your secret."

"I'm not afraid."

"How's Leticia? Are you still paying for a little nightly comfort? Afraid that regular women will be too disgusted by your...breathe Kenneth."

He did.

"I love my daughter," Eddie said. "She can be a pain in the ass and I need a break sometimes, but she's still mine." He tapped his chest. *"My* child, not yours! Mr. Preston was good to us, but he wasn't our true father. Blood means something. Remember that."

Kenneth shook his head. "After all that bastard put us through, how can you think of him as a true anything? Did the liquor wash away your memories?"

He shrugged. "It helps."

"Do you remember what he did to us? Don't you remember what his drinking did to him?"

"I'm not going to fight what we are or who we are."

Kenneth tossed the wine bottle in the bin. "I'm not this."

Eddie smiled cruelly. "Are you sure about that?"

"Yes."

"Then why don't you take a drink right now?" He retrieved a beer can from a lower drawer and popped open the top. "Go on. Take just one sip. See what happens. See if it doesn't find a home in your veins. See if it doesn't fill the hollowness inside. You can only keep up the charade for so long before you snap. Before your true nature sneaks up behind you and chokes you...that's when this," he lifted the can, "will be there for you. To help you cope with it all. You can't run from fate, Kenny."

"This isn't my fate."

Eddie smiled again, bringing the beer to his lips.

Kenneth brushed aside the memory and tightened his grip on the steering wheel. He felt an overwhelming sense of hopelessness. He hated seeing a young man so brilliant, fight such a cunning demon—a demon so clever it appeared to be a solace. He couldn't send Syrah back there. He rubbed his hands against the steering wheel until his palms burned. He'd failed his brother and Syrah...and his mother. Eddie was her favorite.

Jasmine would be sickened by the man his brother had become. The man whom she had altered her future. He felt guilty he had even suggested the scheme in passing. No matter her reasons, she'd listened to him and lost the pendant for what? Eddie didn't even care about his future. Kenneth tapped the steering wheel, thoughtful. He would get the pendant back for her. Maybe it would give her the courage to live life the way she wished. It would let her realize she had a freedom of choice, something he'd never had.

He had expected to hate her after she left him that night. He had raged a bit and thought of going to Leticia, but couldn't. Jasmine's honesty stopped him. She was afraid because she cared about him. He knew the fear. He felt it too. He admired her honesty. Nobody challenged him the way she did. No one sought to shatter the mirror image he showed to the world. It was dangerous for a man with secrets, but it made him feel alive—if only for awhile.

When he reached town, Kenneth went to the office instead of returning home. It would be too much of a strain to show a happiness he didn't feel.

"Hello, Mr. Preston," Mrs. Mathew greeted.

He affected a casual smile. "Hello."

"I should warn you about your office."

"At this moment nothing could shock me," he said, opening his door. His emotions had become numb. Nothing could bother him.

He was wrong. His office had been turned into a flower shop. Bouquets, plants, and single roses lay everywhere. Their perfume soaked the air like an overzealous sales clerk with a new fragrance.

He stood stunned in the doorway. "What is this?"

Mrs. Mathew stood behind him, peeking into the room. "They started arriving late Thursday then early Friday."

Kenneth picked up a bouquet of chrysanthemums. "Why?"

"I think it has a lot to do with the fact that you have yet to choose a date for the Hampton Charity Ball." She went to her desk to retrieve the messages.

He put the bouquet down and glanced up when he heard a light knock on the door. "Come in."

Stephanie walked into the room. "I spoke with Draxton."

"We're not selling."

"That's for the board to decide. They've sweetened the deal. " When he didn't reply, she took a seat and glanced around the room. "I see that the annual hunt has begun." She crossed her ankles. "Who will you take this year?"

"I haven't decided," he said absently, retrieving papers from his box. It wasn't like Stephanie to chat on frivolous subjects.

"I hope it won't be Jessie Clifton."

His head shot up. "Why not?"

She pulled lint off her trousers. "Because of the bet."

"What bet?"

Her eyes clashed with his. "The bet she made with Deborah."

He loosened his tie. "Bull. Jasmine isn't like that."

"Oh no?" She raised a brow. "You didn't find it odd that after all these years she suddenly wanted to work for *you* of all people? That she suddenly wanted to be your friend? Has she stroked your ego so much that you've forgotten to be cautious? I hate to be the bearer of bad news, but to her you're just part of the game. Rumor has it some sort of pendant is at stake. I heard Deborah say so herself."

His heart raced. "I don't believe you."

She stood. "Suit yourself," she said as she left.

Kenneth stood paralyzed as everything came into focus. Why Jasmine had strangely become cordial. Why he had seen her conversing with Deborah as if they were old buddies. Why she had been so eager to be his friend. Why he had felt she was up to something. Why she had suddenly changed her mind about sleeping with him. He grimaced. Of course. Sleeping with him wasn't part of the deal: no witnesses.

But she had sounded so sincere. So honest. He'd thought her feeling had been for real. How she must have silently laughed at him as he stood vulnerable before her. Kenneth threw his briefcase on the couch. He was more annoyed than angry. He glanced down when pain shot up his arms and saw his hands clenched, his nails biting into his palms.

No. He was angry—furious, really—that he had fallen for her ploy. He had really wanted her as a friend—no, more than that—but he should have known better. He'd never meant anything to her. Perhaps Eddie was right about some aspects of fate. He and Jasmine were meant to be enemies. He slowly relaxed his hands and adjusted his tie.

Mrs. Mathew entered the room. "You have your regular hints of course," she said, placing the messages on his desk.

"Thank you." He opened his window. "Could you take some of these flowers and deliver them somewhere?"

"I tried, but more kept coming."

He sat behind his desk and glanced around the room with a scowl. "Call someone from the adult day care program to pick these up."

"Okay." She hesitated. "I take it that you didn't have a good weekend?"

He rubbed his chin. "The worst."

"How would you like me to order you a large breakfast?"

"Thanks."

Mrs. Mathew nodded then nearly bumped into Nathan as he entered the room.

Nathan took a stunned look around the room then burst into laughter.

"Shut up or get out," Kenneth growled.

Unaffected by Kenneth's mood, he picked up a flower and stuck it to the lapel of his jacket with a pin. He sat down. "I had to see it to believe it."

Kenneth checked his email.

"I would love to have women fighting over me like that."

He didn't reply. He knew being a trophy had its downside too.

That evening, Kenneth sat in his car and stared at his house before he got out of the car. This was his home, but the word made him feel empty. He had accomplished so much in his life, yet he felt he had accomplished nothing. Ace had no father and Jasmine only wanted him as a trophy, just like the other women. Funny, he hadn't expected betrayal to hurt so much. He should have known better than to trust her. All day her deception hung on him like a virus, causing his mind and body to ache.

When he opened the door, a familiar scene greeted him. Ace sat on the ground working on a puzzle and Jasmine sat curled up on the sofa engrossed in a book with an image of a bloody dagger on the cover. In a perfect world this homey scene would be a pleasure, instead it was a burden—another game to play. To think he'd been foolish enough to consider getting the pendant for her when that had been her plan all along.

Syrah jumped up when she spotted him. "Hi, Uncle. How was your trip?"

"It was fine." Kenneth took off his jacket and rested it on the back of the sofa. "Come over here." He sat down next to Jessie, deliberately crowding her space. He wondered how much she would hate him when he made her lose. He said, "You don't look happy to see me."

Jessie closed her book. "Probably because you don't look happy to be here."

Syrah sat down next to him. "Okay."

He sent Jessie a curious look then turned to Syrah. "I bought you something."

"What?"

He handed her a small box.

Syrah looked down at the purple high-tech looking object, one of the latest electronic games. "Oh, Uncle, it's beautiful!" Syrah started hitting buttons.

"Turn the sound off," Kenneth said.

"I will in a second."

He snatched it from her. "Now!"

The echo of his voice hung in the room. She stared at him with wide eyes, her hands paralyzed.

Regret assailed him. "I'm sorry."

"No, no," she said quickly, backing away. "I'm sorry. It was my fault." She ran upstairs.

He stood to run after her, but fell back on the couch instead. He held his head.

"Your talk with Eddie didn't go well?" Jessie asked.

He desperately wanted to share. He wanted to share how helpless he felt and how angry, but he couldn't trust her. He couldn't trust anyone.

He let his hands fall in his lap. "No, it didn't." He looked at her and raised a brow. "Surprised? Kenneth Preston failed at something."

"About the other night--"

"It's over." He reached in his bag and placed a box of colored pencils on her lap.

"What is this for?"

"To color your jewelry designs." He rose and picked up his bag. He didn't want to make an issue of it. He didn't want to think of the half hour he'd spent searching for the perfect selection.

"Kenneth, I have something to tell you," Jessie said in an urgent tone.

"Forget it," he said and disappeared upstairs.

He owed Ace an apology. Never in his life had he spoken like that to a child. The graying darkness of evening filled her room as he entered. He heard the violent rush of sheets being rearranged as he approached the bed. He shook his head and sat down next to the hiding form.

"Ace, I'm sorry."

"It was my fault," a small muffled voice said. "I should have listened the first time."

He pulled the sheets down. "I didn't mean to shout."

She nodded then turned to the window where a bee was banging against the glass.

"Dove, please don't be scared of me."

She turned to him and her face dissolved into tears. "You were so angry."

He pulled her onto his lap and held her. "Not at you. Don't cry. I'm sorry."

"I'm sorry too."

He wiped her tears. "Do you forgive me?"

She nodded.

He looked around the room. He could give her everything, but she didn't belong to him and with his temper he wasn't good for her. "You know your father loves you."

She stiffened alarmed. "You want to send me back, don't you? I didn't mean to make you mad. It won't happen again," she said with growing panic. "Please, Uncle Kenneth. I--"

He framed the side of her face as her eyes filled with tears. "Shh, dove. You're not going anywhere right now. I'm just telling you that your father loves you."

Her bottom lip trembled. "You love me too, right?"

"Yes, very much." He sighed as her little arms wrapped around his neck.

Kenneth surveyed the elaborate layout of the room: the Moroccan red damask window drapery, plush dark carpeting, and black iron bed covered in a maroon bed sheet. His eyes fell on the woman whose warm, dusty brown body stretched out on the pillows with an easy seductive grace, her black hair cascading about her mature face. Her dark brown eyes regarded him with concern. She pitied him, he knew that much. She knew she was the only type of woman he could get. This was the only place he could be himself and it cost him three hundred a night. "You're still tense, Kenneth. Do you want to do it again?"

"No, I'm fine."

"Are you sure? You know I always make it worth your while."

He drummed his fingers on the glass table and studied her. "Yes, and you did. I just don't feel like going home yet."

She rolled on her stomach and kicked up her legs. "That's fine, sugar. It's your money."

He turned to the window.

Leticia watched him. Kenneth was one of her favorite clients. The most gentle and sweetest one she'd ever had. She'd never been able to figure him out though, even after all these years. It was strange. In her profession she'd gotten to know men pretty well. Some had sexual problems and wanted a boost. Some wanted to do kinky things they couldn't imagine doing with their wives and others were either deformed or lacked the social skills to get a woman. Kenneth didn't fit any of these categories.

Okay, so his body was a shock to see at first. Even she had to control a grimace when she'd seen them, but he had the face and the money to make up for them. His scars were something most women would overlook. So why did he pay for it when he could get it for free? She gathered a pillow underneath her chin. There was something sad about him—something guarded. Even though he had shared some things about himself, she still felt as if she didn't know him at all.

"What's wrong?" she asked.

"Nothing."

He was lying, but she was used to men lying to her. Something was wrong. Something about him had changed and after knowing him for so many years she knew what it was.

"So what's her name?" she asked casually, careful that her Midwestern accent didn't slip through.

He turned to her so quickly she knew her suspicions were correct. "Who?"

She ran her fingers through her hair. "The woman you're seeing."

A muscle twitched at his jaw. "I'm not seeing anyone."

"How long do you expect to keep this up?"

"I've been wearing a mask most of my life. I wouldn't know how to function without one."

True. His mask had kept her going for over ten years, but she could see it slipping. She was about to lose him. And she couldn't afford to. She was getting older and had to look out for her retirement. She wanted to save enough money to go to Rome.

She crossed the room and saddled his lap. He immediately responded; she could feel a hard bulge pressed against her bottom. His mouth captured hers then he moved his lips down her chest. He abruptly stopped then sat back.

"What's wrong?"

He shook his head, lifted her off his lap and stood. "I have to go."

After the door closed, Leticia glanced around her room. She'd come too far from the pathetic Ohioan town she'd grown up in to turn back now. Kenneth was her investment. She remembered when he had first come to her as a young college student: eager, fresh, and desperate. The best kind. With one look she knew he would change her life. He was her ticket to a new future and she couldn't lose him now. All she needed was the right information and Jack could get it for her. Jack

Alton was an unscrupulous writer who had been fired from a major newspaper for unethical behavior, but he still had grandiose dreams of winning the Pulitzer.

She picked up the phone and dialed. "Hey," she said when he answered. "I got another job for you."

"Good. What do you need?"

"I want you to find whatever you can on Kenneth Preston."

"He doesn't need a puppy," Jessie said, unsure of Wendy's solution for Kenneth's withdrawn behavior.

"A dog is man's best friend." She gestured to the basket she had brought with her. "I wasn't able to give him away so I'm going to take him to the pound."

Jessie looked at the sleeping brown ball. "What's wrong with him?"

"He limps and has a lazy eye so his vision isn't the best. But he's still adorable."

Jessie chewed on her nails, thinking of how Kenneth had fed the squirrels. She probably shouldn't, but she would. "I'll take him."

Wendy looked relieved. "I thought you would. I really didn't want to send this fellow to the pound."

"Let's see if he can work a miracle."

Syrah was ecstatic when she saw the puppy and she was eager to surprise her uncle. Her enthusiasm died when he didn't come home.

This time Jessie wasn't angry, she was worried. There was something else keeping him from coming home and it wasn't work. She needed to know what. She placed the puppy in the basket and headed for his office.

She got off the elevator and listened to the quiet *swooh* as the doors slowly closed. She marveled at the strange quietness the office had in contrast to the day. She could only see outlines of the desks and chairs and the backup light bouncing off the computer screens.

She stood in front of Kenneth's office and raised her hand to knock, but decided to open the door and peek inside. She carefully opened the door like a grounded child, seeing if her parents were gone. The room was dark except for the red glow from the fireplace, the only sound of biting and crackling flames pierced the silence. She opened the door wider and saw a silhouette on the couch—only one, thank goodness.

"Kenneth?" she called in a soft voice, hoping not to startle him.

"*Qui est là?*" He turned his eyes to her, two biting black orbs full of such hostility that she took an involuntary step back.

"I shouldn't have come," she stammered.

"No," he agreed. "But since you are here, you might as well come in." He returned his gaze to the fire.

Jessie closed the door and gingerly walked to the couch. She placed the basket on the ground behind it then noticed three empty beer bottles on the table. She watched as Kenneth brought the fourth to his lips. She grabbed his wrist before he could drink.

"No, don't," she pleaded. "It's not worth it. Nothing is."

His eyes meet hers. She expected to see a glazed sheen but they were remarkably clear.

"You're worried about this?" He gestured to the bottle. "It's nothing. I don't drink alcohol."

His words weren't slurred, but she still didn't trust him. Some men could handle alcohol surprisingly well.

Seeing her disbelief, he held the bottle out to her. "Come then, taste it."

Jessie took a small sip, gasped and began coughing. It was like swallowing heated gasoline that rested in the middle of her chest to burn. Kenneth fetched her some water and rubbed her back.

"Ginger beer?" she finally managed, tears in her eyes. "I hate that stuff."

"Yes, pure Jamaican ginger beer." He took a long swallow then placed the bottle on the table. "Keeps me awake."

She wiped the tears with the back of her hand. "I can imagine." She sniffed. "Funny the place smells like flowers."

He decided not to comment, glad that the bouquets were hidden from view by the darkness. "What are you doing here?" he asked. "Is something wrong at home?"

"No. I was worried about you."

"Worried about me." He repeated the words as if trying to decipher the meaning. "Worried about me?"

"Yes."

"Strange, I've never heard that before." He shook his head, remembering something. "No, I'm wrong. I had a teacher say that to me once in elementary school: 'Kenny I'm worried about you,' she said."

"Did she have a right to worry?"

He glanced at her then turned back to study the fire.

Jessie refused to be afraid of his silence. She decided to tease him. "I can't imagine what she could have worried about. Did you get a B plus or something? Perhaps a wrinkle in your trousers or—"

"You see those flames, Jasmine?" His voice, though thick, was barely a whisper. "When I was a little boy I once thought they were so beautiful that I wanted to touch them. So I did and ended up with blisters on my hand." His eyes captured hers. "Have you really ever played with fire?"

"No."

"Then I don't suggest you start."

"I just want to help."

His tone was bland. "That's just great because help is what I need. See I've got this tiny little problem. My brother is dying and there's nothing I can do. My niece wants to stay with me and I know that she can't."

"Why not?"

He ignored her. "And then there's this woman who is trying to seduce me so that she can throw me over her shoulder like a chewed bone." *And then of course some board members want to sell the company or see him out of office.*

"That's not true. I wouldn't do that."

He didn't look at her. "How did you know I was talking about you?"

She didn't reply.

He turned to her. "I wasn't talking about you, Jas. You could never seduce me." Her gaze fell. Good. One point for the home team. He was surprised she didn't argue...didn't challenge him. It was rare for her to back down from a challenge. "Why are you here?"

"I thought you needed a friend." She reached out to touch him. He grabbed her wrist before she could. "I am not in the mood to play your games do you understand? You will lose."

"You're hurting me."

He immediately let her wrist go, amazed he'd been holding it so tight. "Sorry," he muttered.

She rubbed her wrist. "I'm not playing a game. You were wrong at the cottage. I don't see you as a trophy."

Damn, she was good. One point for visitors. He returned his gaze to the fireplace. She came to him as the seductive Delilah, ready to use his weakness to destroy him and claim him as her prize. He knew she would do anything to win, he'd seen her play before. Fortunately, he was used to games. He'd played them all his life. He could feel the air tightening around him; the heat of the flames burned his skin.

Jessie slapped him on the back. He took a gulp of air.

"Damn it. Why do you do that?" she asked.

He had learnt the habit as a child to keep himself from crying. He had perfected it to keep himself from feeling pain, dreaming that he would pass out one day and never wake up. He always did. "You're still here?"

"I'm not leaving without you. You need to go home and get some sleep. Your foul mood is probably a direct result of sleep deprivation."

He shook his head and stared morosely at the flames. If he allowed himself, he could actually believe that she cared.

"Kenneth—"

He threw his hand up in an angry gesture and burst into *patois*, speaking so fast it sounded like gibberish, but Jessie understood every word.

She stared at him stunned, not by his words, but that he spoke *patois* at all. She never would have suspected perfect Kenneth Preston spoke, what her mother had called, the gutter language of Caribbean society. Her mother had banned them from speaking it at home, even though she and their father would slip into it when certain guests arrived. But Kenneth spoke it as fluently as a Kingston vendor selling jerk chicken by the roadside. She bit her lip, fighting the need to giggle.

Kenneth narrowed his eyes. "Don't laugh."

She covered her mouth with both hands her eyes beginning to water. "I'm warning you."

That did it. She threw her head back and laughed, slapping her thigh.

He frowned. "It's not that funny."

"Me never did tink—" she couldn't finish, a fresh wave of laughter washed over her.

Kenneth rested his head back and covered his eyes, chuckling a little to himself. "Damn."

She finally quieted. "I'm sorry."

"No, you're not."

She decided not to argue; she reached behind the couch and picked up the basket with the puppy. She placed it on the space between them. "Here."

"What is it?"

"Isa gift fi you," she said playfully. "Tek it nuh."

The corner of his mouth lifted in reluctant amusement. He glanced down at his watch and frowned. "Did I forget me birt-day again?"

"No, I just thought you'd like it."

Kenneth opened the lid, half expecting rubber snakes to leap up at him, but instead he found a curled up ball with brown fur: a sleeping puppy. He felt warmth ripple over him. He reached down to touch it then changed his mind. He closed the lid. "I don't want it."

"Why not?" Jessie lifted the puppy out of the basket and set it on her lap. It yawned, blinked its eyes then went back to sleep. "You were wrong the other night. I did learn things about you and I remembered them. I remembered how you always wanted a house surrounded by trees, that you loved summer storms and that you feed the squirrels because when you were little you weren't allowed to have a pet."

Kenneth inwardly groaned. Score two for the visitors.

"It may have been a crush, but I did care about you as my friend." Jessie held the puppy out to him. "Come on. Give him a chance."

The puppy looked at him with sleepy golden brown eyes.

"I don't want him," he said trying to be firm though his voice was not.

Dara Girard

Jessie sighed dramatically. "Then I guess he'll have to go back to the pound. His original owners weren't able to sell him because one of his legs isn't fully developed so he limps."

Kenneth flashed her a glare of disbelief.

"I'll show you." She placed the puppy on the ground, sat on the couch and called him. He came bounding towards her like he'd fallen into a distillery, weaving to and fro until he reached her. "I'm sure as he grows he won't be as awkward."

Kenneth felt himself weaken, but still said nothing.

"All the other dogs will probably recognize his weakness and terrorize him."

The thought of the little puppy being bullied tore at him. "Give him to me." Kenneth took the puppy and examined its crooked leg. "I'm sure that this leg just needs to be mended properly then he'll be fine."

"Right," Jessie said. There was no need to mention that there was nothing a veterinarian could do.

He began to stroke the puppy's fur, delighting in the soft feel. "I'll only keep him until his leg gets corrected. Then I'll give him away."

"Okay."

As if recognizing his new father, the puppy began licking his face. Kenneth held him out at arms length and stared at him. "I'm a busy man. I can't own a dog."

"What are you going to name him?"

"I'll let Syrah decide."

Jessie shook her head. "No. He's yours for now, you decide."

"Dionysus."

"No."

"I thought you said—"

"You are not naming him after the god of wine."

"Dion then." He put the puppy down and watched it explore the room, but it tripped and bumped its head on the leg of the coffee table. It laid down and began to whimper. Kenneth picked him up and rubbed where it had hit its head. "Silly thing." He put the dog down again and it bumped into the couch. Kenneth turned to Jessie.

He sent her a black look. "Let me guess, he's blind too."

"Only mildly. They think he has a slow eye or something. The room is probably too dark for him."

Kenneth shook his head and swore. "Figures you would give me a deformed mutt."

"He's not deformed."

He frowned. "That's true. Right now he's using my coffee table as a toilet."

"He just needs to be housebroken."

"Just what I was looking for," he muttered. "Something else that needs me." The puppy came up and stared up at him, his gaze a little cross-eyed. Kenneth instantly loved him.

"If you really don't want him, I'll take him back."

"You knew damn well when you brought him in here that I would keep him. Nuh try fi mek a poppy show of me."

"No, when I saw him I thought of you."

His brows shot up. "You see me as a partially blind puppy with a limp?"

"No, someone who needs a friend."

"And you're one of my friends?" he asked sarcastically.

"Yes."

Shit. The problem was he wanted to believe her. Hell, if she planned to use him then he would use her too.

He knew once he placed his lips against hers that she was his addiction. She was the one thing he could not seem to deny himself no matter how harmful she was. His body craved her touch, craved her acceptance, craved entrance into her secrets so that he could divulge his own. His lips descended to her neck: a proud column of rich cocoa skin. He knew he was overwhelming her with his need—displaying and admitting his weakness for her—but he didn't care. He delighted in the sweet torture as her body rubbed against his erection, that tormenting ache to be inside her. He groaned in delight and despair, knowing she would soon pull away.

She didn't. She held him tighter. "Kenneth, what's wrong?"

It unnerved him how well she could read him. He used to be so good at masking his feelings. He lifted his hand to caress her cheek and tell her he was fine. He was horrified to see his hand trembling like his brother's had. He didn't answer her, just opened her blouse and captured her breast in his hand, rubbing his thumb over the nipple. He pulled down her jeans and placed his hand between her thighs, feeling the gathering moisture. He felt her hands on his zipper. They were ready for each other.

He abruptly stopped. "Shit."

Jessie looked at him alarmed. "What?"

"Are you taking anything?"

She hesitated. "No."

"And I don't have any condoms." He let out a low growl.

She shifted underneath him. "Look I—"

"For God's sakes don't move," he ground out between his teeth. "I need a minute." He took a deep breath, gathering whatever control he had left. He straightened, adjusting his trousers. Damn, he was still hard. How could he chastise his brother when he put himself at the mercy of someone who could destroy him? Wasn't he being just as suicidal, knowingly tearing out his heart, risking his secrets for a few moments of pleasure?

"What you have can be treated," she said.

He stared at her. "What *I* have?" He glanced down. Hell, was he showing that much?

"Yes. I've seen it before."

He narrowed his eyes. "What are you talking about?"

"Big Sibling Syndrome. You feel it is your duty to repair the lives of your family. Don't worry. You're not alone. Michelle has it too. You help people, but you never ask for it. You offer advice, but you rarely take any. You fear failure more than death."

"What's the treatment?"

"Sharing. Opening up and letting others help you carry your burdens."

Kenneth turned to the fire. "You don't know very much about men."

"What?" Jessie stood.

"If you knew what I was thinking, you wouldn't be lecturing me right now."

Jessie could tell by his tone that he was offering her a warning. He had controlled his body, but there was still a hunger in him that he wanted satisfied. She grabbed Dion and left.

The Sapphire Pendant

He stared at the flames that mirrored the anger in his eyes.

Chapter Twenty-one

Nathan glanced around the bar, taking in the cigarette smoke filtering through the dim lights. The smell of sweat, too much perfume, and liquor clogged the hot air while the sound of a ceiling fan hummed noisily, but offered no breeze. He looked at the quiet man sitting in front of him. When Kenneth had called him up to meet here, he had expected a lot more excitement than this.

"I know men aren't supposed to be talkers, but you're taking this to a whole new level. At least order a beer."

Kenneth glanced at a woman in yellow fishnet stockings. "I don't drink."

"Then it's strange that you would suggest we meet in a bar." Nathan caught the woman's eye and winked.

Kenneth shook his head. No, it wasn't strange. He wanted to test himself; to prove that he was not weak. Although he was surrounded by liquid and carnal temptations, he would resist them. He was strong, no matter how much Jasmine made him feel otherwise. He glanced at a man lighting up a joint. "I need a vice."

"Why?"

"Because I want to kill a woman and I need something else to occupy my thoughts."

Nathan nodded. "Murder would be a pretty risky vice."

Kenneth wrote letters on the table then noticed he was spelling "Jasmine" and silently swore. "She's playing games," he said in a low voice. "Trying to twist me up inside."

"Who?"

"Doesn't matter. I want to hurt her, make her feel this--" He stopped before he said pain. It wasn't pain, it was something else. "Betrayal."

He rubbed his chin. Yes, that was the right word. That's was what had caused the rage and hurt that fought for dominance inside him. It clawed at the control that had always been his greatest protection.

Nathan tapped the table. "I know. Give her something she really wants then take it away."

Kenneth sat back and began to smile. Perfect. He knew exactly what he could do— Jasmine had given him the rules of the game. He planned to use them to his advantage. He'd let her win the pendant and then set the price she would pay.

Freda was not pleased with the new member of the Preston household. Syrah, however, was thrilled. She set off immediately trying to housebreak Dion. She played with Dion in the yard while Jessie sat in the kitchen and stared at the phone. Three days until the ball. She would have to call Deborah and tell her that she had won. Then she would tell Kenneth. Or maybe she could tell Kenneth first then Deborah.

The phone rang.

"Hello, Preston residence," she said.

"Are you free?" Kenneth asked.

She swallowed, just the sound of his voice did funny things to her. "Uh, yes."

"Good, I need to talk to you."

"Okay."

"In my office."

His office. Her danger zone. "I'll be right there." Jessie hung up the phone. She would meet him, but this time she'd be prepared. She went to Freda in the kitchen. "Could you watch after Syrah and Dion for a while? I'll pay you back."

Freda frowned but nodded. "I don't mind the girl, but the dog will cost you."

Moments later, Jessie stood in a grocery store aisle, chewing her nails while she stared at the selection of condoms. She hadn't realized there was such an assortment: colored, large, extra large. How was she supposed to know his size?

She turned and saw a man about Kenneth's height. She pointed to the display. "Excuse me, sir, which size do you wear?"

His face spread into a leer. He looped his thumbs in his belt holes. "Baby, you want to find out?"

She glanced at him. *A small.* She turned away. "Never mind."

"You don't know what you're missing."

She picked up a box and read the label. "And neither do you."

"You're not pretty anyway," he muttered and left.

Jessie ignored the remark, folded her arms then grabbed the gold brand. Gold signaled the best and Kenneth was Mr. Perfect after all, right? She bought her selection and dumped them in her bag for easy access then headed to his office.

A handsome man in a loud red blazer stopped her on the way to Kenneth's office. "Jessie Clifton?"

"Yes?" she asked cautious, feeling as though everyone could see what she had in her bag.

"I'm Nathan Phillips, a friend of Kenneth's. Are you here to see him?"

"Why? Do I need permission?"

He grinned. "I'm just offering you a word of warning. Mr. Boss is in one of his moods."

"Okay." She gripped her bag. Nathan's warning disappeared when Jessie walked into Kenneth's office.

"What happened?" she asked, looking around the room where various vases and plants sat.

"You happened," he said blandly.

"Me?" She closed the door behind her and stepped further into the room.

Kenneth twirled a pen between his fingers. "Yes, it seems you've started a trend."

"The flowers?"

He nodded.

Jessie laughed. "You mean these are all from women?"

"Let's just say I hope so."

She bit her lip. "You never know."

"I know that the local florist is very happy about this." He tossed his pen down and shook his head helplessly. "I've given some away, but more keep coming."

Jessie read the card sticking out of one of the pots. "To Kenneth. I love you a bunch." She turned to him and smirked. "How original."

He reddened a bit. "Can we get down to business?"

"So this is what I smelled last night."

"Probably."

"You didn't sleep well, did you?"

He rested his elbows on the desk. "Can we get down to business?" he repeated.

She picked up a flower and smelled it. "Certainly, Mr. Boss."

"You've been talking to Nathan," he said grimly.

"Interesting guy. Very charming and attractive—"

Kenneth drummed his fingers on his knee. He didn't want to discuss Nathan. "I need you to do me a favor."

Jessie walked towards him. "What?"

"I need a date for the Hampton Charity Ball and I'd like to take you."

Her mouth fell open. She missed a step and tripped over the rug. This time she didn't catch herself. She fell flat on her face. Her handbag dropped, spilling the condoms like candy from a piñata.

Kenneth stood. "Are you okay?"

She jumped up, gathering the items. "I'm fine."

"What the hell are these?" He lifted one of the condoms and winked at her. "I'm flattered."

She snatched it from him. "You were saying?"

"I'd like to take you as my date for the Hampton Charity Ball."

She stared, speechless. *Oh no.* He was doing the unthinkable. He was asking her to the ball. She could *win.*

"Think of it as your rain check for the prom." He sensed her hesitation. "Don't you want to go?"

"I'd love to go." Her voice cracked. She sank slowly into a chair. The pendant was hers; she'd won back her family's honor. But if Kenneth ever found out... She bit her nails. She would just have to risk it.

"Good." He gave her the once over, taking in her jeans, blouse, and flyaway hair. "You'll need to undergo a makeover of course."

"A makeover?"

"Yes. Important people will be there."

Her voice fell flat. "Are you afraid I'll embarrass you?"

He tweaked her chin. "Mind that temper."

"Why are you asking me anyway?"

"Because it will stop this ridiculous show of bribery."

So she hadn't exactly charmed him, at least he preferred her to the others.

"I hate when women fight over me like I'm the door prize at a raffle," he continued. "It's a relief you're not like that."

She smiled weakly.

"So it's all set."

"You don't need to pay for my makeover. I'm not going to show up in jeans and a T-shirt."

"I like to think of it as insurance." Kenneth lifted the chain off her neck and said in a soft voice. "Just think of me as your fairy godfather."

"I can't believe he asked me," Jessie said, pounding her head against the wall in Michelle's office. "Just when I had set myself up for failure, he asks me. It makes everything worse."

"Will you cut that out?" Michelle demanded. "You're giving me a headache."

"Have a heart, Mich. She is obviously upset," Teresa said.

"She's acting like a twit. Why wouldn't he ask you? He thinks you're his friend."

Jessie fell down into a chair. "I am his friend."

"So just tell him the truth."

"I can't," she said miserably. She couldn't take him being disappointed with her. Plus she was too close to reclaiming the pendant.

"Well, I'm sorry, but I'd prefer that you suffer in silence. I am sick of hearing about him. First you were worried that he wasn't paying you any attention. Now that he's paying attention to you, you fall to pieces."

Jessie stared up at the ceiling. "Oh how I love coming to you for sympathy."

Michelle pointed at her. "It's either Kenneth or the pendant. The choice is yours."

A calm summer wind blew over the park as Syrah played with Dion, during Jessie's tennis game. She loved Dion. He was her best friend. She threw a ball and watched him run after it with his funny walk. Sure she had Denise as a friend, but she was too nice, too good. It made her nervous. Real people weren't that good.

"That's the dumbest looking dog I've ever seen," a boy said as Dion dropped a squeaky ball in front of her, his tail wagging in anticipation.

Syrah glanced up at the boy. He wore a black T-shirt with 'Big Jake' written in large red letters. His long brown legs and arms reminded her of a spider. "No, he's not."

"Why does he walk so funny?"

She patted Dion on the head. "'Cause his leg is crooked."

"So he's dumb and he's crippled."

Syrah rushed to her feet. "Take that back."

"Make me."

She punched him in the face. His head snapped back; blood seeped from his nose. He stared at her stunned then lunged at her. They fell to the ground, clawing and punching each other. A small crowd of kids surrounded them chanting: Fight! Fight! Fight!

A boy shoved his way through the crowd. He picked Syrah's tormentor off of her and tossed him on the ground. The other kids walked away disappointed that the fight was over.

"Only cowards beat up girls," her rescuer said.

Big Jake scrambled to his feet. "She punched me first, Daniel."

"He was making fun of my dog," Syrah said, rising as well.

"'Cause he's dumb."

"Not as dumb as you are."

"Watch what you--"

Daniel pushed Jake back before he could lunge at Syrah again. "Cut it out," he said. "Why don't you go away and leave people alone?"

"Why don't you stuff your face with a pie and leave me alone, fatso?"

"Don't call him fatso," Syrah said, outraged on Daniel's behalf. She clenched her fists ready to fight again.

Daniel grabbed her hand and bent to scoop up Dion. "Come on. Let's go find your mom."

Big Jake pushed him. Daniel fell forward, the impact knocking off his glasses. Big Jake laughed. "Fat and clumsy."

Dion began to growl low in his throat. Syrah gritted her teeth. "You're going to pay for that."

Daniel grabbed her leg before she could go after him. "Let's go."

"But--"

Daniel calmly stood, wiping the dirt from his clothes. He adjusted his glasses. "I said let's go. Get your dog."

"Coward," Big Jake said as Daniel took Syrah's arm. "Just like your dad."

Daniel stood still for a moment then spun around so fast Syrah screamed. Jake started. Daniel jumped on him and another fight began.

Syrah ran to the tennis courts. "Aunt Jessie, come quick!"

By the time Jessie and Sryah returned, a small crowd had formed. The group now included Big Jake's mother.

Jessie jumped between the boys and separated them. Jake's mother raced to him, hugging him close. She glared at Daniel.

"How dare you!"

"It wasn't his fault," Syrah said.

"I don't care whose fault it is. You have no right going around beating up little kids."

Daniel kept his voice low. "He's the same age as me, Mrs. Sims."

"Yes, but you're twice his size. Since your dad ran off you've been a menace. Didn't your mother--"

"You leave my mother out of this."

"If his nose is broken, I'm sending her the bill."

Syrah smiled maliciously. "But that wouldn't be fair 'cause I broke it." Her voice hardened. "And I'm glad too."

Mrs. Sims glanced at Jessie. "Is she legal?"

Jessie folded her arms. "What does that have to do with anything?"

"I know how you like to smuggle them in. I realize your countries are poverty-stricken wastelands, but when you bring them here you should teach them American manners. I'm sure your parents taught you."

"Our country is America. We were born here."

"America is your country when it's convenient," Mrs. Sims said. "Otherwise your councils, clubs, and stores wouldn't exist, right?"

"I'm sorry I didn't realize this was a societal argument. I thought this was about the children."

"It is. You need to raise them right. Your island girls are too fast and too wild and they should be tamed."

Jessie grinned. "Don't worry. We take out their fangs by thirteen."

Mrs. Sims glared at them then quickly ushered her son away.

"Bitch," Wendy said.

Jessie slapped her in the arm. "Not in front of the children."

"She's right," Syrah said.

Wendy shook her head. "She's just angry because her husband was having an affair with a woman from the Bahamas."

"He's sleeping with Mr. Han's daughter now."

The adults looked at her stunned. "How do you know?" Wendy asked.

"Denise told me."

Jessie looked at Daniel who was delicately wiping blood from his lips. "Let me take you home."

He turned. "Nah, that's all right."

She grabbed his shoulder. "I know, because I'm not asking."

On the drive to Daniel's place, the kids took turns explaining what had happened. Jessie silently cheered them, remembering her own childhood fights, but gave them a stern lecture.

"The elevators aren't working," Daniel said, as he opened the door to the stairwell.

They climbed the concrete staircase, the lights buzzed and blinked overhead like defunct lighting bugs. Jessie nearly collapsed with gratitude when they reached the tenth floor.

"Here we are." Daniel opened the door and ushered them inside. The room was the perfect stage setting for an urban drama. A large mattress covered by a dull blue spread took up most of the space, a small metal table and two folding chairs sat in the corner, facing a tiny TV on top of a crate. A small kitchen made up the far wall. A petite woman with childish eyes came out from the shadow of the corner. She held a pair of knitting needles. The damage she had done with those objects was evident throughout the room. Not a window, table, chair or pillow had escaped her.

"Oh, good. Company," she said in a soft, high voice.

"These are my friends Mom. Ms. Jasmine and Syrah."

"I'm Lydia." She gestured to the bed. "Please sit down, Jasmine."

Jessie found it disconcerting that Lydia didn't even notice the bruises on her son's face. She began to say something, but as she gazed into the innocent eyes she thought better of it. She sat down on the lumpy mattress, trying to appear comfortable though a spring was pinching into her thigh.

Lydia put down her knitting and rubbed her hands. "Would you like something to drink?"

Jessie saw a cockroach scurry to safety. She wanted to say no, but knew that would be an insult. "Of course, thank you."

"And we'll fix you a nice snack. Daniel, see what we have."

He hesitated. "But--"

She waved him away. "Go on, hon. I'll stay with our guests."

Syrah noticed the mild look of panic on his face and recognized the problem. It wasn't uncommon for her father not to have enough food in the house either. She took his arm and headed for the kitchen. She opened the fridge and frowned.

"As you can see, we don't have much," Daniel said.

"You have enough." She took out some eggs.

"What are you going to make?" He watched her with keen interest as she took down different ingredients from the sparse shelves.

"You'll see." Syrah put some water in a pot and put it on the stove to boil the eggs.

"I bet you're wondering how I could be fat with no food around."

She gave him a quick glance. "No, I'm not."

"How old do you think I am?"

"Fifteen."

"I'm twelve."

Her eyes widened. "No way."

"Yeah, my dad's side of the family is tall."

"You're gonna be like *huge* when you're grown up."

He shrugged.

"It will be awesome. Nobody can hurt you."

He flexed his fingers. "Nobody hurts me now."

"Where's your dad? Did he really run off?"

"No. He's somewhere trying to find work."

"How long has he been gone?"

Daniel avoided her gaze. "Couple years."

Syrah took the eggs off the stove and emptied out the water. "He's not coming back."

"Yes, he is."

She opened a can of tuna. "Grow up. People leave and they don't come back. That's the way it is. My mother left and for all I know she could be dead."

He leaned against the counter. "My father's not dead and he's coming back for me. You'll see."

"And what if he doesn't?"

His voice hardened. "He will."

"But what if he doesn't?" she pressed.

"He will." He pushed up his glasses in a quick angry gesture. He suddenly frowned. "Why did you flinch like that?"

"I didn't." She made the tuna mix and then arranged the crackers on the plates.

Daniel took a cracker and dipped it in the tuna. "It's good."

She nodded, not wanting to say anything that would make him angry again.

He took off his glasses and swung them from side to side. "There's nothing wrong in hoping is there?" He smiled wistful. "There's nothing wrong with hoping that one day he'll come through that door and say, 'Daniel I've missed you and I've come to take you and your mom out of this place.'"

"No, there's nothing wrong with that," she said quietly.

He tugged on her cap, his smile turning from wistful to friendly.

"Exactly."

Syrah smiled back. He had pretty eyes for a boy. And he wasn't fat; he was chubby like a teddy bear. She felt a strange fluttering in the pit of her stomach and looked away. Annoyed, she shoved a plate of crackers at him.

"Take this food over to your mom," she said gruffly.

"Yes ma'am," he teased then turned and walked away.

They all thanked Syrah for her wonderful meal of deviled eggs and tuna mix with crackers. They ate while Lydia chatted, acting the role of hostess as if she were in a grand palace instead of a gloomy apartment. Jessie shifted uncomfortably in her seat; Syrah tried not to yawn. Daniel saved her by showing her a crossword he was working on and his pen collection.

When the visit was over, Daniel insisted on walking with them downstairs, in spite of their protests.

"Thanks for everything," he said, once they reached the exit. He shook Jasmine's hand and surprised Syrah by giving her a brief hug. He then returned to the stairwell.

"I liked them," Syrah said, as they walked to the car. She shoved her hands in her pocket. Her hands curled over a long thin object. She pulled it out and saw that it was one of Daniel's pens: a heavy silver one with ridges. For a terrible moment she thought she had stolen it without thinking, but then she remembered his clumsy hug and smiled. The boy could be slick. "Yeah, I liked them a lot."

When Kenneth came home that night, Dion rushed up to him and jumped around his ankles. The puppy's tail wagged so much his whole body shook like a toy rocket getting ready for flight. Kenneth picked him up and was rewarded with a bunch of grateful licks. "What have you been up to?" he asked, setting the puppy back down.

The answer was evident. He found Ms. Rose cleaning a stain on the living room carpet, Syrah wiping up paw prints in the hallway and Jessie mopping up a puddle in the kitchen.

He rested his briefcase on the counter. "Looks like Dion's been busy."

"Give him time," Jessie said.

"As long as he doesn't start chewing things, he's fine."

She grimaced. "Well..."

"Well, what?"

She put the mop away and began biting her nails. "I wasn't going to say anything, but you'd probably find out anyway so..."

He waited.

She went under the sink and pulled out a chewed up pair of expensive Italian shoes.

He opened his mouth, but no words came out.

"I'll buy you another pair," Jessie offered, hiding the shoes behind her.

"You obviously don't know how much they cost."

"A hundred?" she guessed.

"Try three."

She raised the shoes to her face, trying to figure out what special feature warranted such a price. "You spent three hundred dollars on a pair of shoes?"

"They'll last forever. Or they would have."

"Perhaps they can be mended."

Kenneth took the shoes and frowned. "Right, the scratches and teeth marks can just be polished over."

Jessie took the shoes away from him. "I really am sorry. I'll make it up to you."

He patted her on the head. "Yes. I know you will. Your makeover starts tomorrow."

"I don't think—"

"Don't worry, you don't need to." He took her hand. "I want you to start using that magic word that will make any man yours."

She looked at him suspicious. "What is it?"

"Yes."

"Yes?" she repeated.

He grinned like a proud professor. "Very good," he said then left the kitchen.

Later that evening Freda approached him as he wrote bills at his desk. "Mr. Preston, I'd like to speak to you," she said.

Surprised, he turned to her and gestured to the couch. "Of course. I always have time for you."

She clasped her hands together in her lap. "I've never interfered in your life before, but this time I must speak my mind. I know you're taking Ms. Clifton to the ball and I know why, but revenge never healed a broken heart."

His eyes darkened, but his friendly mask remained. "My heart is not broken, Ms. Rose."

"She told me about the pendant, its power, history, and what it means to her family."

"How is that of any importance to me?"

"You feel betrayed."

"I was betrayed."

"She betrayed her father first and wants to atone."

Kenneth folded his arms and nodded. "I suppose we should congratulate her for giving such loyalty to a dead man."

"She cares for you."

He let his arms fall and glanced towards the window. His voice was soft. "I see you've been blinded by her lies as well."

"She didn't know whether to forsake the pendant or you. I told her to choose the pendant."

He looked at her stunned. "Why?"

"Her father loved her."

He gripped the armrest. "And I don't?"

She raised her brows. "Is that a question or statement?"

He loosened his grip and kept his voice neutral. "She was my friend or at least pretended to be and she betrayed me. Those are the facts. You know me Ms. Rose. You know I rarely let people close. You see how my family is, how the women in my life are. You know how everyone in my life has a hidden agenda. Why should I forgive Jasmine when she is no different than the rest?"

"Forgive her for your sake not hers. Hatred can destroy a man." She hesitated. "You don't recognize your power."

Kenneth flashed an arrogant grin. "Of course I do. I'm a powerful man. I'm rich, I know the right people--"

She shook her head. "I don't mean that kind of power. Something far more dangerous.

You have the ability to destroy her, but you would destroy part of yourself as well." She spoke slowly. "I don't deny that she needs to be taught a lesson. I just don't think it's the lesson you want to give her." She stood. "Thank you for your time, Mr. Preston. That's all I need to say."

Jessie hated the feeling of anticipation as Kenneth drove Syrah and her to go shopping. She wasn't supposed to care about such frivolous things, but she did.

"Wait! You just passed the mall," she said, watching White Crest Mall whiz by.

"We're not going to the mall," Kenneth said.

She turned to him weary. "Where are we going?"

"Gina's Boutique."

"I can't afford there!"

"That's all right. I can."

She began to rub her temples. "I won't be able to pay you back."

"I don't expect you to pay me back." He captured her hand. "We're friends, right?"

She suddenly felt uneasy. Something in his tone wasn't quite genuine. "We'll work out a payment plan."

He shrugged. "If you say so."

He turned into the parking lot of Gina's Boutique, a little place off of Wagner Road a section known for pricey, quirky art stores and shops. Jessie glanced up at the window display of a reed thin mannequin draped in a chiffon gown.

Kenneth held open the door. "Come on, Jas."

She looked down at her jeans and top. "I can't go inside looking like this. Why didn't you tell me we were going to a fancy place?"

"This is a boutique not a palace."

"I'll hold your hand," Syrah said.

"We both will." Kenneth grabbed her other hand and impatiently pulled her inside.

The owner came out to greet them. "Hello, Kenneth, I see you've brought us another one," the woman said. She could have been mistaken for one of the mannequins with her perfect hair, expertly done makeup, and designer suit draped a gaunt, pale figure.

Jessie turned to him. "Another one? How often do you play fairy godfather?"

He only grinned. "Gina, I want you to take good care of her."

"I will. Come with me." She took Jessie's elbow. "What are you looking for?"

"I don't know," Jessie stammered, looking at Kenneth. "Something pretty, I guess."

"We're going to a party," Kenneth said, taking a seat as though he owned the place. "She needs a dress."

"Ah, I see. A formal affair?"

He looked bored. "My usual."

Jessie stared at him stunned. "Your usual?"

Again he flashed her one of his enigmatic grins, but said nothing. He pulled the owner to the side. Jessie watched him using elaborate hand gestures to describe the kind of dress he wanted as he talked to Gina.

"I'm not sure about this," Jessie muttered as she watched him cup the air. She wasn't quite sure to which body part he was referring.

Syrah squeezed her hand. "Uncle knows what he's doing."

Gina came up to her. "Wait in the dressing room. I know of the perfect dress for you."

"Can I come in with you?" Syrah asked.

"Sure. We girls need to stick together."

Jessie went into the dressing room and marveled at the plush silk brocade covered seats and the large mirror with soft overhead lights. She never would have imagined being in one of these places. How would she pay him back? She rested her head against the wall. No, that wasn't the problem. She was excited; bursting at the seams with so much joy she was worried she might start giggling. She took a deep breath and straightened.

Gina came back with an assortment of dresses and hung them in the booth. Jessie tried on a translucent purple dress that floated around her.

"I feel naked," Jessie complained, trying to lift the low cut neckline.

"The front's all wrong." She felt like her breasts were being pushed into her chin.

"What's wrong with the front?" Syrah asked confused.

"You have yet to worry about the problem, love. I think I should wear the green dress."

Syrah stood in front of the other dresses, preventing her from getting to them. "No. Show this one to Uncle."

Jessie stepped out of the dressing room and stood in front of Kenneth. He sat reading a magazine and drinking coffee. After waiting a few moments, she stomped her foot to get his attention. "Well?"

"Patience is the next thing we'll work on," he muttered, casually closing the magazine.

His eyes trailed up the length of her dress, resting a little longer at her chest than she felt comfortable. His eyes revealed nothing.

Her excitement slowly crumbled. He wasn't impressed. She had been foolish to believe a new dress would change how he felt about her. What did she think this was: a fairy tale? "Don't you have anything to say?" she asked.

Kenneth tossed the magazine down and stood up. "Well, the world will be pleasantly surprised to know that you actually have a figure under all those baggy clothes. No, no don't get mad I'm giving you a compliment. Turn around. Very nice."

Jessie glanced down. *Nice?* Perhaps the dress was as ordinary as she was. "Thank you." She went back to the dressing room and sat down discouraged.

"Didn't Uncle like it?" Syrah asked.

"He thought it was nice."

Syrah lightly touched the hem. "I think you look beautiful."

"Thank you."

Jessie stared at herself in the mirror. All right, so she wasn't going to knock him off his feet with her beauty--the night wasn't about him. It was about her. He might not notice her, but that didn't mean other men wouldn't. She was tired of standing on the sideline too scared to play because she wasn't pretty enough. She was a woman with a great figure and she deserved to show it off. She would get other clothes too, ignoring her sister's criticisms or anyone else. She would wear what she liked, what made her feel good.

She didn't need Kenneth as a fairy godfather. She could do the job herself. She smiled at Syrah. "Tell Gina I want to see her."

An hour later she stood in front of Kenneth with her purchases. "I'm ready."

"It's about time." He glanced at her bags stunned. "What is all that?"

"I put them on your account, but I'll pay you back."

His eyes fell to her new green cashmere blouse. "Yes, I know," he said. "Let's go."

He took her to Kayla's Salon next, a bright and airy place with slick black floors and a high ceiling. Each booth looked like a star's vanity table. Kenneth introduced Jessie to the hairdresser, although no introductions were needed. The owner, Kayla, had tried to convince Jessie since high school to do something with her hair. Kayla was a lean young woman with dimpled rosy cheeks in a creamy complexion and an easy smile. She was considered a hair magician, although she was bald.

"Oh this is a momentous occasion!" Kayla gushed, grabbing Jessie's shoulders and spinning her around in a circle. "You have put her in the right hands," she said to Kenneth. "The girls and I will do wonders."

"Do you have a magic wand near by?" Jessie asked.

Kayla laughed, a light fruity sound. "Isn't she darling?" She pushed Jessie towards a chair. "You can go now, Kenneth," she said, shooing him away. "She's all mine now."

Once Kenneth had gone, Kayla wrapped Jessie in a terry robe and handed her a plate full of fruit. "Just eat and relax, girl. I'll take good care of you."

Two of her assistants toyed and touched her hair. They muttered to each other in that foreign language called "hair fashion" about body, features, tone, and volume. Eventually, they looked at each other and nodded in agreement.

Jessie's hair was washed and conditioned. As Kayla snipped away, she sighed with contentment. "You don't know how long I've waited for this moment."

"To cut my hair?"

"No, to style it, to give it life," she said with passionate conviction. "Hair is alive, you know. After this treatment I'm going to give you the right conditioners to feed your hair and even suggest certain foods to eat."

"Okay."

"What look are you going for?"

"Something different. Something completely unlike me."

"So you're willing to risk a little color?" Kayla said hopefully. "Say, honey brown highlights?"

"Whatever you want."

"My favorite words." She met Jessie's eyes in the mirror, an impish grin on her lips. "So what's going on with you and Mr. Perfect?"

She had been waiting for the question, but it still caught her by surprise. "Um...nothing really. He's just doing me a favor."

"I wish a man like that would do me a favor. Aren't we the lucky ones?"

"I wouldn't say that."

"Not one to kiss and tell, are you? That's a good sign. That means it must be serious. The other women usually talk my head off. That's all right, I was just curious."

"Just how many women has he brought here?" Jessie asked unable to crush her curiosity.

"I'd say about twenty-five."

"Twenty-five?"

"Yes, fabulous ladies. I enjoy them, everyone does. You're different though."

Right. She wasn't as rich, or pretty or pedigreed. "I know."

"You're the youngest."

"How old are they usually?"

"About sixty-five."

"Sixty-five!"

"Don't move your head like that," Kayla said. "I almost cut off your ear!"

"He goes out with women who are sixty-five?"

Kayla laughed pleased with her little deception. "He gives some of the women living alone or at the nursing home a treat when they have their dances. Those are the only women he pays for. The young ones are on their own."

"Oh."

"You know here at the salon we like to gossip, but you can keep your Cinderella story to yourself."

"It's hardly that."

Kayla wrapped Jessie's hair in a cap. "Go to Ana. She'll show you how to put on make up, then come back to me and I'll finish the job."

Ana was a Korean woman who had spiky black hair, two pierced eyebrows and a nose ring. She plucked Jessie's brows and showed her how to accentuate her eyes and develop the fullness of her mouth. She then gave her a load of samples before sending Jessie back to Kayla.

"Oh, you look delicious!" Kayla fussed with Jessie's hair and brushed and combed it. When she was through, she leaned back and clapped her hands in delight. "My best work yet." She handed Jessie the mirror.

Jessie held up the mirror and gasped. "That's not me."

"Yes it is. You look wonderful."

Her hair now framed her face, accentuating her striking cheekbones and her highlights added volume and body to the sleek style. She didn't look pretty, but striking, exotic... mysterious. She never thought her plain features could look so daring. Actually, the woman staring back wasn't plain at all.

Chapter Twenty-two

Jessie waited outside the salon, watching cars go by when Syrah and Kenneth appeared. She smiled at them and waved. Syrah frowned and Kenneth flashed a grin, but they both continued to walk past. Syrah was the first to halt. Kenneth stopped a step later. They slowly turned around like synchronized dancers and stared at her with wide eyes. Syrah ran up to her and threw her arms around her waist.

"You look wonderful!" she cried.

"Thank you."

Kenneth gave her a quick overview. "It's definitely an improvement." He glanced over his shoulder. "Why don't we get some ice cream?" He turned and walked away.

Jessie glared at him. *An improvement?* She wished he hadn't said anything. His vague compliments were irritating.

Syrah grabbed her hand. "Never mind him," she said. "He's been in a strange mood all day."

At the ice cream shop, Syrah and Jessie decided to share a banana split. Kenneth ordered a vanilla shake. While Syrah and Jessie chatted, Kenneth remained silent and spent most of the time staring out the window.

He couldn't look at her. She was even more tempting and dangerous to him than before. He hadn't planned on that. He liked how her hair brushed against her cheeks, the rich purple on her lips and that blouse...

"So do you still want to sleep with me?" she asked.

He inhaled his shake too quickly and began to cough. He glanced at her with watery eyes. "Where's Syrah?"

"At the arcade. Did you hear my question?"

"Yes."

She rested her chin in her hand. "Well?"

He looked down at his glass. "I think I'd better get another one of these."

Jessie watched him leave then scooped up the melted ice cream at the bottom of the dish. Okay, so she was a dandelion trying to be a rose. He could at least show some interest. He offered her more attention when she was her basic self.

"There should be a law against good looking women sitting by themselves," a male voice said.

Jessie glanced up and studied the man. He was clean cut wearing khaki trousers and a green polo shirt. A heavy dose of mousse slicked down his brown hair.

He slid into the seat in front of her. "Could I buy you something?"

Oh god, he was flirting with her and he was actually sober. "No, thank you."

His eyes roamed her figure as if trying to find something else to compliment her on. "Nice bracelet. I like a girl with class."

"Then find one of your own," Kenneth said coldly.

The man stood and stepped back from the table. He held his hands up in surrender. "Sorry, didn't mean to step on your territory."

"Then I suggest you move."

"Right." The man scurried away.

Kenneth sent Jessie an odd glance then turned to the window. "What was that about?"

"He asked me if I wanted to have sex and I said yes."

He looked at her. "What?"

"Surprised another man would be interested in me?"

He watched two kids on skateboards roll past.

"He actually gave me a compliment. Better than you could."

His eyes met hers. "That's because there's not much to say."

She felt like she had been punched in the stomach. For one panicked moment she thought she would lose the banana split she had just consumed.

Kenneth stared at her and suddenly felt ill as if he had used the words against himself instead of her. That's when Ms. Rose's words came to him. He had the power to destroy her. Not just avenge, but destroy. He could use all her insecurities, all his knowledge of her as a weapon to create a kind of hurt and anguish that would linger for years. A pain both mental and physical.

He looked at her defiant eyes. Dark brown orbs he had been so eager to fill with tears, and realized that would be no victory. Yes, he had the power to destroy her, but he wasn't going to. That wasn't the lesson she needed to learn.

Kenneth covered Jessie's hand with his. "I didn't mean that."

She yanked her hand free. "Of course you did," she said, horrified to hear the tears in her voice. "We've always been honest with each other." She clenched her fists and stood. "I have to go."

He rose to his feet and grabbed her wrist. "Jas, please—"

"If you don't let go of me I swear, I'll slug you."

"I'm not letting you go." His grip tightened. "Not this time."

She twisted her arm to free his grip. He grabbed her around the waist. "Jas—"

A young man stood up. "Lady, is this man giving you trouble?"

"Yes," she said.

The man glared at Kenneth, flexing his arms, his bulky form at least twice Kenneth's. "The lady wants you to leave her alone, buddy. I suggest you listen to her."

Kenneth looked bored, releasing her. "Why don't you mind your own business?"

The man cracked his knuckles then swung at him. Kenneth ducked and rammed him in the gut, sending the man flying across a table. Suddenly, two of his companions stood up like pit bulls ready to be unchained. Their eyes said *Charge*. Kenneth swore.

"Look, this has nothing to do with you," he said as the two men came towards him.

The larger of the two cracked his neck. It sounded like broads snapping in half. "That's where you're wrong." He picked Kenneth up and threw him across the room. He hit the far wall and fell to the ground.

Kenneth shook his head and stood, his face a cold mask of rage. Jessie suddenly felt sorry for the other man. He lunged at the man, sending him crashing against the counter--bowls and glasses shattered to the ground while screams filled the air.

In an instant, a fight broke out all around the shop. People either fought or fled. Those at a safe distance stayed and watched.

"Wait! You don't need to do this," Jessie cried, seizing one of the men's arms.

"Don't worry, lady. We'll take care of him for you." He gently pushed her aside. She knew that it was out of her control now. These guys had been looking for a fight and she'd given them a reason to have one. She picked up a chair ready to bring it down on a guy's head when Kenneth snatched it out of her hand and pushed her towards the door.

"Get out of here!" he ordered.

"But—"

He gave her a hard shove before someone dragged him back into the chaos.

Jessie went outside to get help. She spotted Nathan across the street and called his name.

"Well, *hello* there," he said, coming up to her with an inviting grin. "Have we met before?"

She frowned. "Yes. I'm Jessie, remember?"

He halted and stared.

Jessie snapped her fingers in front of his face. "Nathan?"

His eyes measured the length of her then came back to her face. He whistled in amazement then softly said, "Damn."

She folded her arms. "Thank you…I think. I need your help."

"What's wrong?"

"There's a fight. You have to break it up."

He took a step back as if she'd suggested something vulgar. "Me? Why?"

"Kenneth's in the fight."

Nathan began to grin. "Kenneth's in a fight?" He ran towards the ice cream shop. "This I've got to see."

Jessie groaned. Men. She looked around and saw Syrah trying to see what was going on. She grabbed her hand and began walking away.

"Where's Uncle?" Syrah asked, trying to pull her arm free. "What's going on?"

"He's busy now."

"I don't want to leave without him." She looked through the glass and saw him hold off an attacker with a well placed kick. "He's fighting!"

"He can handle himself."

Syrah wretched her arm free. "I want to watch." She disappeared into the crowd.

Jessie sighed defeated. She knew it was fruitless to go after her. She wouldn't be able to find her. Word of the fight spread quickly. Soon people congregated at the ice cream shop like a mob of crazed groupies who had spotted their favorite rock star. Jessie could hear the whirl of a police car in the distance. She turned a corner and walked aimlessly down the street, trying to put order to her jumbled thoughts. A red Volvo pulled up next to her.

"Hey, pretty thing. I'm willing to pay for it."

She recognized the man from the parlor. "I'm not that kind of girl."

He jumped out of the car and grabbed her arm. "Look, I'm willing to offer you a good price."

"I'm not interested. Let go of me!"

"Who are you holding out for?" he asked in an urgent whisper. "You're not going to get better than me."

Jessie hit him in the face with her bag of cosmetics and ran. She jumped into an idle cab and headed for her house.

"He said what?" Teresa asked, her voice as calm as a raging undercurrent. "I don't believe it." They sat in the kitchen while Michelle set up tea.

"Believe it," Jessie said. "One man insults me and another propositions me."

"That rat. Kenneth is a--"

"Calm down, Teresa," Michelle ordered, handing her a cup. "Perhaps that's not the whole story."

"It is the whole story," Jessie said, putting sugar in her cup. "My fairy godfather turned into a rat."

"He apologized, didn't he? That just doesn't sound like Kenneth. He--"

"That's not the point," Teresa interrupted. "The point is he insulted her--"

"You're both wrong," Jessie said. Her temper covered her hurt. "The real problem is I know how he really feels." She stormed out of the room and slammed the front door.

Michelle met her on the porch. Jessie rested her arms on the railing. Michelle stood next to her and gazed out at the street. The night was heavy with a warm quiet. She leaned against the railing and folded her arms. "Of course you know what happened."

"What?"

"You made him jealous."

Jessie looked at her shocked. "Don't be ridiculous. Kenneth doesn't get jealous."

Michelle rested a hand on her chest. "I'm being ridiculous? You're the one having men fight over you."

"They weren't fighting over me, it was testosterone running wild."

"You don't believe that."

No, but she couldn't dare hope otherwise and risk being wrong again.

The stars hung low over the sleeping house when Jessie returned. She sat staring at it for a while, watching where the moonlight cast shadows and light. She finally got out of the taxi and walked up the front steps, a mixture of conflicting emotions colliding with each other. She didn't know what she would say to him—if he wasn't hooked up to life support.

She opened the door glad that they were all asleep so that she could be alone with her thoughts. Dion came up to her yapping happily. She tried to hush him by lifting him up and covering his mouth, but he just licked her palm. She closed the door, turned on the light and saw Syrah sleeping on the couch. She put Dion down and gently shook the girl awake. "What are you doing?"

Syrah rubbed her eyes and stretched. "I   was   afraid   that   you weren't coming back."

"Well, here I am."

Her eyes danced with relief. "You missed the best fight in the world!"

Jessie wasn't interested in the details, another time perhaps, but not tonight—maybe never. "I assume your uncle won. You can tell me about it tomorrow."

They walked upstairs together. Jessie tucked Syrah in bed then went to her room.

She took off her blouse and found her way to the lamp on her side table. She turned on the lights and covered a scream. Kenneth watched her from the couch.

"What are you doing in here?" she demanded, struggling back into her blouse.

"You know why I'm here."

At least he looked all right. She tossed her keys on the side table. "You already apologized. Now get out."

"Ah, that lovely temper. I was beginning to miss it."

She rested her hands on her hips. "How was your little dance with your boyfriends? I see you managed to escape unscathed."

"You sound disappointed."

"I had hoped you would have managed a black eye or something."

"Sorry. Maybe next time."

She sat on the bed and pulled off her shoes. "What are you doing here?"

"I already answered that question."

She threw her shoes in the direction of the closet. "Your apology was enough for me."

"I'm not going anywhere until you let me explain. Will you?"

"Yes."

Kenneth paused unsure he'd heard correctly.

"That's the magic word today, right? So speak."

He moved his hands in an awkward manner as if they were stiff machines he was learning how to control. He kept them close to his body, shielding them in the shadow of his lap. Jessie figured that the matter was more important to him than she'd thought.

"I want you."

She blinked. "That's your explanation?"

"How can I care about clothes when I want to see you naked?"

She picked up a pillow and threw it at him. She missed seeing him wince. "You're making fun of me."

"I'm making fun of you? You're the one playing the game by pretending you don't know how attracted I am to you. By trying to make me jealous by flirting with another man. You won, okay? Aren't you proud of yourself? You've gotten your trophy. I'm taking you to the Hampton Charity Ball so that you can show me off to all your friends and have your night of celebration. Isn't that enough for you?"

"No, I—"

"The game's up Jas, for both of us. Let's recognize this for what it is: a simple exchange. A night for a night. I take you to the ball. You give me a night in bed. Game over."

She stared at him. He knew. Not about the bet, but that he was being used. She had always wondered why he kept himself guarded, but now it was clear. He had been used all his life, tonight she would change that.

She sat next to him. "You're right. Game over." She kissed him.

He pulled her into his arms and deepened the kiss, succumbing to a hunger burning deep inside him. Jessie didn't attempt to protest. She wrapped her arms around his neck and met his desire with a passion all her own. *"Belle laide,"* he whispered. His hand slid down to cup one of her breast and Jessie trembled at his touch.

"Oh god, you taste and feel so good," he groaned.

Jessie pressed against his groin. "Funny, so do you."

He continued to drink in the sweetness of her lips, letting his hands roam free and explore the hollow of her back and grasp her bottom.

She touched his chest. When he flinched, she drew back. "What's wrong?"

"I'm just a little sore that's all. No, don't!"

Jessie ripped open his shirt and jumped up horrified. His chest and stomach were swollen and colored with bruises and had a stretch of torn, raw flesh.

She thought she would be ill. "Oh, my God."

Kenneth quickly covered the bruises with his shirt. "Don't worry about those; they look worse than they feel." He tried to button his shirt, giving Jessie the opportunity to see his hands clearly.

She swore, grabbing his left hand. The knuckles were cracked, covered with dried blood and swollen. It explained why he had moved so awkwardly and kept his hands out of view.

She knelt down in front of him examining the other hand. "You must be in a lot of pain."

He pulled her close and kissed her. "This is worth it."

She pulled back. "No, we have to get these taken care of."

Jessie went to her drawer and fetched her first aid kit. Her hands trembled from anger and worry. She had never seen bruises look so bad. His calm composure was maddening, but if he wasn't going to make a big deal of it then neither would she.

"That's handy," he said, nodding to the case.

She laid out the items on the couch. "I'm an athlete remember? I'm always prepared for injuries." She put some antiseptic on a cotton ball. "Now this will sting a little." She winced for him when the solution made contact with his raw wounds, but he didn't respond. She wouldn't have thought it bothered him either if his jaw wasn't clenched. When she finished, she wrapped his hands in gauze then opened his shirt. Tears of rage filled her eyes. He must be in so much pain, pretending it didn't hurt. He was always pretending.

She leaped to her feet and walked to the other side of the room, trying to count to ten, clenching her fists in an attempt to keep her temper in check.

"Are you all right?" he asked.

She spun around and two streams of tears fell down her cheeks. "No, I'm not all right you dope! You could have been killed. Have you gone to a doctor? You might have internal bleeding."

He stood up, stiffly. "I'm fine. Trust me."

She opened his shirt and pointed to his bruises. "You call this fine? I've seen fewer bruises on a rotten apple." She gently stripped off his shirt to review the bruises on his back. "You're an idiot."

"You really need to work on your bedside manner."

"If you weren't injured, I'd hit you right now."

"Why are you angry at *me*?"

"Because I care about you. Why didn't you just let my hand go instead of letting those guys do this to you? Why didn't you let me help you? You know I'm strong enough."

His voice, though quiet, held an ominous quality. "Because if one of those guys had hit you, even by accident, I would have killed him."

A chill raced through her. She took a deep breath. "You should have let my hand go."

"I couldn't." His eyes burned into hers. "I wasn't going to let you go this time, Jas."

She looked away. "You need to see a doctor."

"They're just bruises."

"And they look awful."

He stiffened. "Then don't look."

She studied his bruises and noticed some faded marks and scratches. "What are these?"

He glanced down. "Nothing. I bruise easily."

She turned away. "Damn it."

He sat ramrod straight while she tied gauze around his middle. She finally pulled away, and placed her hand against his cheek and forehead. "You're warm." He also looked exhausted; his eyes were beginning to droop. She sighed resigned, a heaviness settled in her chest. "Looks like we won't be able to go to the Hampton Charity Ball."

His eyes flew opened. "But you have to go."

She stared at him curious. "Why?"

He searched for words, trying to cover his blunder. "Because...because you've never been."

She began putting her first aid items away. "So what? You need to rest, that's the only way you'll heal."

"But my face is fine."

She looked up shocked. "What?"

"I look all right. No one will notice."

She shook her head. "I don't care."

"You don't understand—"

"I said you're not going."

"But what about our bargain?" He hated how desperate his voice sounded.

"Kenneth, I'm willing to sleep with you whether you take me to the ball or not. I want you. Or has that escaped your notice?"

He didn't understand. Why would she want a night with him, if she couldn't use him as a trophy? Where was the exchange? He'd finally figured out the game and she'd changed the rules.

"The ball--"

She covered his mouth, her voice hard. "Hang the ball. The only thing I care about right now is you." She gathered her things.

He didn't know what to say. Jasmine Clifton, the woman who would do anything to win, would lose a bet, was willing to miss one of the most talked about events of the year, because of him. *Him.* He couldn't understand it. It didn't make sense. He was physically capable of going. His face hadn't been injured. Wasn't that all she needed? Wasn't that the only part of Kenneth Preston that mattered?

He looked down at her bent head as she organized her kit in amazement. She really did care about him. She had been willing to fight with him, had tended to his wounds, and would rather lose a bet than see him ill. She truly was his friend.

He clenched his fist. No, it was dangerous to believe that. She had betrayed him—used him—as so many others had. He needed to hold onto his anger, the only shield against his weakness for her. Yet his mind and body were so tired and eager to surrender to her tenderness. He could feel it slipping underneath his armor, stripping the anger that had kept him safe.

He felt her touch his fist and met her eyes. He couldn't describe the expression there—worry, compassion, something vastly more intimate—but it reached to something inside him forcing either his wariness or sanity to slip away. She did care. He believed that now.

Suddenly, his body didn't feel the pain anymore, didn't feel disappointment. His life was no longer a burden. With her he could accomplish anything. He took a deep breath, a healing, soothing warmth sweeping through him. And it was because of her. His decision was made. He was going to take her to the ball and make sure she had a night she would not forget. There'd be other nights as well, many others. He hoped to convince her to stay in his life. He wasn't sure how, but eventually he would. He rested his head back. His body was battered, but he felt as if he could soar.

"Jasmine, I've never felt this way before."

She patted his shoulder. "Don't worry. In a couple of days you'll feel better."

He smiled. "No, I mean...." How could he explain how he felt? What her simple act meant to him? How grateful he was that she was there for him when many others never had been? "Thanks." It was an inadequate word, but all he could think of.

She smiled embarrassed by the admiration that shone in his eyes. "I can return the dress, right?"

"There's no reason to return the dress. I'm taking you to the ball."

Her smile fell. "No, you're not."

"If you won't go with me, I'll take someone else," he said, hoping to spark her jealousy.

She didn't fall for the bait. "Fine. Go ahead."

He stared at her stunned. "What?"

"I am not taking a sick man to a stupid ball. I'll be worried about you all evening."

He held her face and gently rubbed his thumb against her cheek. "I've suffered worse."

"When?"

When his father had beaten him in a drunken rage and bruised his ribs. Or when his father had whipped him so badly that he had to wear his coat all day at school so no one would see the blood through his shirt. "Other times," he said vaguely.

"Then I'm sure the infant would love to go with you." She lifted a brow. "Fortunately, she has a bedtime so you won't have to stay out long." She began to bite her nails. "Why are you looking at me like that?"

"Like what?" he asked softly.

"Never mind. We could rent videos."

He frowned. "What for?"

"The night of the ball."

"We're going."

"No, we're not."

He grabbed her hand, his voice urgent. "Please let me do this for you. Let me take you."

She shook her head.

He squeezed her hand. "It will make me feel better."

She hesitated then sighed resigned. "Okay." She put her kit away. "The night of the ball you have to use the two magic words that will make a woman yours."

"Which are?"

"You're right." She grabbed his arm. "Let me take you to bed."

He perked up. "I like the sound of that."

She led him to his room, pulled down the bedclothes, and then gently pushed him on the bed. He reached for her, but she ducked out of his grasp and began taking off his shoes.

"You don't need to do this," he protested. He wasn't used to such attention and it made him uncomfortable.

"Lie down."

"Look—"

"Lie down. You wouldn't want me to lose my temper would you?"

He laid back and Jessie pulled the blankets up to his chin. He grinned. "Are you going to watch over me and make sure that I don't die in my sleep?"

Her lips thinned. "That's not funny."

His hand escaped from the blankets, slid down her arm and tightened around her wrist. "Today wasn't your fault. I was in a bad mood anyway."

She turned away still feeling guilty. She spotted his chess game. "How long have you been playing?"

"Couple months."

She examined the board for a moment then moved a piece. "Checkmate."

He sat up too quickly and bit back a groan. "I didn't even see that."

She sat on the bed. "Try to go to sleep."

"Are you going to sing me a song?"

"I can't sing."

"I thought all black women could sing."

She rewarded him with a smile. "If you think you're in pain now, just listen to me try to carry a tune."

"Tell me a story then."

"I don't know any."

"Fine. Then I'll tell you one. There once was this guy who hadn't had sex in--"

She covered his mouth. "Go to bed."

"I'm not tired." He wasn't sure he would sleep tonight or even the night after that. "I want to stay up with my friend."

Jessie shook her head. He sounded like a little boy and did a good imitation of looking like one with the covers all the way up to his chin, his brown eyes bright.

"Don't bite your nails," Kenneth ordered, grabbing her hand before it reached her mouth.

"Kenneth, we're not going."

"Not going where?"

"To the ball."

He furrowed his brows. "But you said--"

"I know what I said, but that's not the point." Her gaze fell. "We're not going because I accepted a bet from Deborah that I could charm you enough to get you to ask me to the ball. If I lost, I'd have to be her housekeeper for a year. If I won I'd get the Sapphire Pendant." She traced a pattern on the bed. "Before I thought losing the pendant and working for Deborah would be the worst thing in the world…and it will be awful, but I'd rather…" She gripped the sheets and took a deep breath. "I'd rather have you as a friend." She raised her gaze to meet his. "I'm sorry."

"I'm glad you told me."

She frowned. "You don't sound surprised."

"I'm not. I already knew."

Her eyes widened. "You knew? Since when?"

He lifted a brow. "Does it matter?"

"No." She bit her lip. "Did you ask me out of pity?"

He shook his head. "I asked you out of revenge."

She laughed without humor. "So I guess I hadn't won." The fact hurt a bit, but she brushed it aside. "What was your plan? Were you going to get me all dressed up again and then decide not to go?"

He cupped her chin. He liked her best when she was like this: real, worried, vulnerable. Her eyes a place he could sink into. His voice deepened. "It doesn't matter anymore. Because right now I'd like nothing more than to go to the ball and have you by my side."

Brooke's blood chilled as the man's cool, threatening voice came through the phone line.

"The vote is coming up and I have yet to be persuaded."

"I told you you'll get your money."

"I don't want words. I want cash. You think you can play with me like the others?"

"Don't get brave with me Uncle. Your gambling debts aren't my problem. You should start thinking of this as a favor. Otherwise I just may think you're not worth my time."

His bravado faltered. "I could tell people what you're up to."

"Sure you can," she said sweetly. "But who will they believe?" She hung up the phone and swore. Why hadn't anyone answered the ad? It was a stupid wooden bracelet and the reward money would be worth its return. Brooke took a deep breath. She wouldn't worry. She would have it back soon. She scowled at the phone. She hated old men who tried to be tough. Her uncle was only useful as a puppet, but she needed him. He was respected by the elder members and would be a great support once Stephanie was in power. It hadn't been hard to find a weakness to use against him. Fortunately, everyone had one.

Brooke suddenly clapped her hands. Why hadn't she thought of it before? Kenneth's image was a little too pristine. She knew he had a few skeletons in his closet. The question was what was the best way to use them against him?

Dara Girard

Chapter *Twenty-three*

Jessie glanced at her watch. She was going to be late if she didn't hurry. One of the most exciting nights of her life and she was ruining it. That morning Kayla came by to fix her hair and Ana had helped her with her make up. Unfortunately, hours later she'd ruined two stockings, misplaced her lipstick and a pair of earrings, and she'd broken the latch on her bra. But now she was ready. She stared at the attractive woman in the mirror, draped in a turquoise two-piece halter dress with beaded embroidery. Tonight victory was hers. She grabbed her bag and shawl then ran down the stairs.

"Never run in a dress," Kenneth said, adjusting his collar in the hall mirror. He wore a sharp conservative evening suit that reminded her of the stranger she sometimes met in his office.

"I don't want to be late," she explained, trying to fix her shawl.

He turned and his mouth fell open; he stood paralyzed.

She touched his sleeve concerned. "Is something wrong?"

"That's not the dress you showed me at the boutique."

No it wasn't. It was a fitted velvet-lace dress with off the shoulder spaghetti straps and hand sewn sequins along the hem. She smiled. "I know." She wiggled. "Surprise!"

"Go back upstairs."

"Why?"

He folded his arms and waited.

She mumbled under her breath, but climbed the stairs. "Okay now what?"

"Come down, slowly. I want to enjoy this."

She descended, feeling like a clumsy, awkward teenager going to her first dance. Kenneth's look was so intense she felt her entire body grow hot. "You're embarrassing me."

"No, I'm admiring you." He took her hand and brought it to his lips. "I am charmed indeed."

She felt tingles explode throughout her body. Hypnotized by his eyes she missed a step and crashed into him. Kenneth grimaced when her elbow made contact with one of his bruises.

"Try not to do that when we get there," he grumbled, rubbing his side.

"Damn these shoes. Are you okay? You know we don't have to go. I saw this great movie they're going to have on TV."

"We're going, Jasmine." He reached into his inner jacket pocket and pulled out a long black jewelry box. "It's customary," he said, when Jessie shook her head.

She opened the box, fear and excitement assaulting her. Inside the blue velvet, gleamed a white pearl choker. "Oh! It almost looks real." She did a quick check. "Wait…it is real. I can't wear this. Do you know how much this cost?"

He grinned. "I have a pretty good idea."

"It must be very expensive."

He shrugged. "It's my money." He lifted the necklace. "Turn around so I can put it on you."

She hesitated.

"You're hurting my feelings."

Jessie took off the chain then turned. "I suppose one night won't hurt."

Kenneth draped the necklace around her. The white gems against her skin were as sensuous as cream over bread pudding. He kissed her neck. "Perfect."

She fingered the necklace then took his hand.

The tall sandstone walls of the Hampton Hotel hugged the corner of Catlon Bay in the soft summer night. Kenneth and Jessie strolled up the stone walkway among the other well-dressed guests.

"You can let go of my hand now," Jessie whispered, trying to free herself from Kenneth's grasp.

"Only if you'll promise to stop biting your nails."

"I can't help it, I'm nervous. I feel like I'm visiting royalty. I've never attended anything like this." *Except as a waitress.*

They stopped in the grand entrance hall of the hotel. Flowers burst forth from china vases; elaborate chandeliers hung overhead, and a long burgundy carpet lead a path through the marble floor. Kenneth handed in their ticket while Jessie tried to calm her nerves and tried to remind herself how to breathe.

"I thought you wanted me to let your hand go," Kenneth said, heading towards the ballroom.

"I do."

"Unfortunately, I can't, if you won't release mine."

"Oh sorry." She abruptly let go. "Are you all right?"

He sighed irritated. "For the tenth time, yes."

"You shouldn't have worn gloves. People are going to think you have some sort of disease."

"Perhaps they'll think it's a fashion statement. Besides, if Nathan has anything to do with it everyone will already know what happened."

Jessie looped her arm through his and searched the crowd for familiar faces, particularly Deborah's. A woman in a floral silk dress came up to her. "Excuse me—"

"Yes, the parmesan basket is filled with goat cheese and we do have white wine that is not too dry with a light fruity bite."

The woman frowned. "I was going to ask about your dress."

Heat touched her face. "Of course you were."

"I think it's gorgeous."

"Thank you. Gina designed it."

The woman smiled and left.

Kenneth tried not to laugh. "What happened?"

"I forgot who I was."

His fingers inched up her back until they reach her bare skin. "I don't know how you could in this dress."

She rested a hand against her cheek. "I am so embarrassed."

Kenneth looked around the hallway and dragged her to a corner where they would be hidden by a marble column. He rested one arm against the wall and the other on his hip, successfully trapping her. "Okay, what's the problem?"

"I'm sorry. Were you somewhere else when I made an idiot of myself?" He smelled delicious; she wanted to be closer, to bury herself in his strength and confidence. His eyes trail down her body touching different areas as if he were caressing them. Jessie folded her arms feeling naked. "I wish you wouldn't do that."

He feigned innocence. "Do what? I think you look delicious."

"You make me sound like something to eat."

"That you are." He glanced from side to side then kissed her, rendering her senses nonfunctional for a few moments. When he pulled away, his voice held a husky undertone. "Fortunately, I like to save my desserts for after dinner."

"I thought you said poison was deadly."

"I've developed immunity." He dug into his pocket and pulled out a ring. It had a silver band with a diamond surrounded by amethysts. He slid it on her finger. "Wear this for me, don't ask why."

She wasn't going to. Speech was impossible as she felt the stone casting its magic, whispering its history and importance. The honor and privilege he had given her was clear and soon questions did fill her thoughts. She looked at him for answers. He merely shook his head. She glanced down at the ring, feeling her courage grow.

She looked at him her voice a whisper. "It's beautiful."

His eyes clung to hers. "My thoughts exactly."

Jessie took a deep breath as they entered the main ballroom. Eyes turned and watched them. Admiring eyes, covetous eyes, and inquisitive eyes followed their every move. Jessie felt like dead meat in the presence of vultures.

"This is stupid," she said. "Everyone is watching us like we're a tabloid feature."

Kenneth laughed at the description. "That's pretty precise."

"Is this how it always is?"

"Usually."

A flash briefly blinded her. "What was that?"

"Photographers."

"Shouldn't they ask permission first?"

"That would be nice, but they usually don't."

She lifted her hand, wiggled her fingers and sent him a wicked grin. "I suppose it would be very uncouth to really give them something to photograph."

"Not worth the energy." He glanced around the room, hoping to find something to divert her attention.

"I don't believe it," two women said behind them. They turned and saw Michelle and Teresa staring at Jessie in amazement.

"Hi, Michelle, Teresa," Kenneth said. "You both look wonderful. It's comforting to know beauty and elegance are not in short supply."

Michelle wore a striking blue sheath dress with a beaded jacket; Teresa a gold lace dress. They didn't hear him, their attention focused on their sister.

"You look fabulous," Teresa said.

Michelle lifted her champagne glass. "For once we agree."

"Yes," Kenneth said. "I think Jasmine looks gorgeous."

Michelle choked on her champagne; Teresa's mouth dropped open. They'd never heard someone call their sister "Jasmine" and not face dire consequences.

"Thank you," Jessie said.

"We'd better mingle," he said. "Nice to see you both."

As she left, Jessie winked over her shoulders at her stunned sisters.

Nathan came up to them as they stood near the hors d'oeuvres. He looked handsome in a dark gray suit. "Can I have the opportunity to dance with this exotic creature?"

"No," Kenneth said before Jessie could reply.

Jessie handed Kenneth her plate and offered Nathan her hand. "I'd be delighted." She ignored Kenneth's fierce frown and allowed Nathan to pull her into a dancer's embrace.

"He is not going to be very happy with you," Nathan said.

"I don't care. I needed to give you something."

"What?"

She kicked him in the ankle.

"Ow!" he cried, hopping on one foot. He scowled at her. "What was that for?"

"For watching while Kenneth got plummeted."

Nathan gingerly put his foot down. "Hey," he said in an injured tone. "First of all I kept him out of jail and second I kept the event out of the papers."

"How?"

"Threats work."

Jessie frowned. "I mean, how did you keep him out of jail? He didn't start it."

"Yes, but he did a lot of damage. I'm surprised the officers let him go after he was arrested."

Her eyes widened. "Kenneth was arrested?"

"Yes, he's a man of many talents." He paused. "Would you do me a favor?"

"What?"

"Dance with the kid when this song is over."

"What kid?"

He jerked his head in one direction. "The skinny kid holding up the wall."

Jessie looked and saw a young man awkwardly holding a drink and searching the crowd as though looking for someone. She began to grin. "Your brother?"

"One of them. His name is Rodney. He's a little shy."

Jessie bit her lip. "I'm not sure…"

"He will, just ask him, please. Just—" A woman walking past diverted his attention.

Jessie sighed, disgusted by his bad manners. She turned to leave him alone on the floor.

He grabbed her arm. "Wait. Where are you going?"

"I'm freeing you so that you can gawk at other women."

He shuddered. "At her? Never."

Jessie allowed him to pull her back into a dance pose. "At who?"

Nathan gestured to a column where a woman in yellow stood alone. "Stephanie."

"Oh, her."

"Kenneth needs to watch himself."

Jessie looked at him. "I guess you like her as much as I do."

"Less."

"Why don't you like her?"

"She's too...assuming. She's too smart to be that open. She's ambitious and women like her don't easily let outsiders on their turf. She and that sister of hers are dangerous."

"Personal experience?"

"Unfortunately. That—"

"Quiet. She's coming towards us."

They both pretended to be enraptured by the music and each other.

"Jessie, I owe you an apology," Stephanie said.

Jessie stopped and looked at her.

"I made accusations that I later learned to be false. Kenneth told me that rumors of a bet were a pure fabrication."

She blinked. Stephanie was apologizing? Being cordial to her? "Umm...thank you. It's nice of you to be his champion."

Nathan snorted. "Convenient, I'd say. Where's your sister?"

"She decided not to come." Stephanie hesitated. "You look very nice."

He stared at her with cold brown eyes then turned to Jessie. "Thank you for a wonderful dance." He bent and kissed the back of her hand then left.

Jessie felt embarrassed by his behavior, but it was the fleeting expression of hurt on Stephanie's face that made it worse.

"He'll come around," she said gently.

Stephanie looked shocked then resigned. "I doubt it, but I still..." she let her words trail off.

"I know."

She let her gaze fall and noticed Jessie's bracelet. "That looks familiar. I had one like it once."

Jessie lifted it up. "Syrah gave it to me."

"That's sweet. See you around." She smiled then left to mingle.

Jessie went in search of Rodney, but ended up with three more dance partners before she was able to break free. She went up to the young man and smiled. "Would you like to dance?"

Rodney looked pleased then suspicious. "My brother asked you, didn't he?"

"Does it matter?"

He frowned glancing at the crowd with disdain. "I know there are other guys you'd probably want to dance with more."

"Does that mean you're turning me down?"

He looked embarrassed. "You don't have to do this."

"Look, I know how it is. I have two older sisters myself and I know how hard it is to try and prove yourself."

He folded his arms. "You're not going to leave me alone, are you?"

"That's right."

"Fine."

He wasn't a smooth dancer, but he managed not to step on her feet. After a few moments he said, "You...uh...smell real nice."

"Thank you. I don't bite, you know. You can hold me closer."

He cleared his throat. "I don't think I should."

"Oh come on. What's the harm?" She pulled him closer then realized why he had kept her at a distance. She licked her bottom lip to keep from laughing. "Well, you certainly know how to flatter a girl."

He missed a step and tread on her foot. "Maybe we should stop."

"No, I'm enjoying myself." She gave his shoulder a reassuring squeeze. "Don't ever feel less than just because you're not like everyone else. Take my advice. I' m a fellow misfit."

He looked at her doubtful.

"Don't tell me you haven't heard of one of the crazy Cliftons."

"Yeah, but you can't be..." He looked incredulous then let his gaze trail the length of her. "Whoa."

She grinned then winked at him, which gave Rodney the confidence to hold her with a little less innocence. Soon he was spinning her around the dance floor, keeping Jessie busy with correcting his wandering hands. But once the song ended she didn't refuse when he asked her for another dance

"I can't wait until this thing is over," she said.

"I'm glad you came."

Jessie raised her brows, surprised by the compliment. "Thank you. It looked like you were expecting someone."

He shrugged. "Yeah, she didn't come. I only came to see her. I hate parties."

"Me too."

"I don't like crowds."

"Me too."

"Give me a machine any day," Rodney said warming to his subject.

"I prefer balls of any shape and size."

When Rodney stared at her shocked, Jessie realized what she'd said. They burst into laughter.

Rodney spun her around a few more times then said, "Why don't we get out of here? We could go for a drive or something."

"I'd love to, but my escort wouldn't like it."

"Who brought you?"

"Kenneth Preston."

His expression dimmed. "Oh, I guess I can't compete with someone like that."

"Why would you want to?"

He shrugged. When the music stopped, he said a hurried 'Good-bye' then disappeared into the crowd.

Wendy jumped into her path and shoved a tray under her nose. "You look amazing."

"Thanks."

"You offer hope to all of us little people. Susan stared at you in shock."

"Like she is right now?"

Wendy glanced over her shoulder to see Susan gesturing to get to work. She swore under her breath. "Must dash," she said. "Have fun."

Jessie finally found Kenneth, leaning against the wall like a Byronic hero—gloomy and brooding—with a crowd of women fighting to get his attention. She saw one rather bold woman drop something between her breasts. His eyes lit up. Jessie pushed her way through the crush of women, grabbed his hand and dragged him onto the dance floor.

"Gentle, gentle," he warned, biting back a groan.

"Oh, I'm sorry. Are you—?"

"Don't ask me."

She shut her eyes as he pulled her into a dancer's embrace. She let the music sway over her and rocked to the smooth rhythm of his body, drinking in his scent and solid presence. With Nathan her mind raced on different thoughts, but now she could only think of the man who held her. She could distinguish his footsteps in a crowd; his tone in a cacophony of voices.

His hand slid to her hip. "This dress fits you like a second skin."

"It might as well be. I didn't want a panty line so I only wore stockings."

His voice deepened into huskiness. "There's only you under there?"

"Me and *Color Me Beautiful*." His breathing suddenly became shallow. "Are you okay?"

He abruptly pulled away. "Let's go get a drink." He headed towards the refreshments.

He gulped down two glasses before the fire in him began to die down.

Jessie held out another glass, concerned. "Are those pain pills making you dehydrated?"

He nearly laughed. "No, Jas. I just need to cool off."

She looked confused then her eyes widened in realization. "I am so sorry. I didn't mean to mention about—"

"It's okay."

"Mum would have been horrified. I might as well have said, 'In less than a second you could take me in the garden.'"

"Jas—"

"Or that I'm only wearing pasties too."

Kenneth pulled at his collar and swallowed painfully. "Will you—"

"But to tell a man—"

He pushed her glass to her mouth. "Drink it and be quiet."

Jessie took a sip and watched as a woman dressed in black with amber eyes like a cat, came towards them. She bumped Jessie with her hip, pushing her aside.

"Hey Ken," she purred. "That dance floor looks empty without you."

"Too bad because I'm fine right here."

"*Fine* is right," she murmured, undressing him with her eyes.

"Are you finished with your drink, Jasmine?"

"Yes, thank you," she said.

The woman turned around and looked up at Jessie as if she were a giant, her head barcly reaching Jessie's shoulders. The woman burst into laughter.

"You're with her?" She laughed so hard tears formed in her eyes.

"Yes," Kenneth said.

She pointed a finger at her. "Weren't you one of the waitresses at the Donovan function?"

Jessie nodded her jaw too tense for speech.

The woman's eyes darted between them. "Nice to meet you." She went over to a group of women by the window and whispered something to them. The group looked in Jessie's direction, turned to each other then began to giggle.

Jessie ground her teeth, tears stinging her eyes. "And the clock struck twelve."

Kenneth took the glass from her before she crushed it in her hand. "Temper, temper," he softly warned.

She felt her new found confidence slipping away. "They're laughing at me."

"Jealous women tend to do that."

"Jealous?"

"Yes. None of them have me."

She stared at him. It was an obscenely arrogant statement, but it made her feel better.

"Let's mingle," he said.

By mingle he meant network. To her surprise, she discovered that Kenneth actually *liked* people. His hundred-watt smile wasn't for show, but a genuine display of pleasure, which explained why people were drawn to him. In a world of fake grins and half-hearted compliments, genuineness was a gift and Kenneth definitely had it.

Jessie couldn't match his pace, however. After the tenth series of introductions, Jessie's smile began to wane. She had never had to chat with so many people. Because she was used to moving through a crowd like a ghost, her face was beginning to hurt and she was running out of things to say.

She stopped a passing waiter. "You will love these tarts," she said to the president and vice president of Homebound. They needed Radson's support in their annual fundraiser. She handed them a plate. After a brief hesitation, they graciously accepted their plates and thanked her. The waiter gave her an odd glance and left.

Later, Kenneth suggested walking towards the bay; Jessie agreed, nearly collapsing with relief.

"Kenneth Preston!" a hearty voice called.

He glanced over his shoulder and groaned. "Oh, no."

Jessie followed his glance. "What's wrong?"

"It's Roger Farley. He owns an insurance firm. He's a slapper."

Jessie didn't know what that meant until she witnessed Kenneth stop the man from slapping him on the back. He grabbed Roger's hand and gave it a firm handshake.

"It's good to see you," Kenneth said.

"And who's this?" Roger asked, leering at Jessie through pale green eyes.

"Jasmine Clifton."

He bent over her hand. "A pleasure to meet you."

She forced a smile. "Likewise."

"Hey, I see the gloves, Ken. Heard you got yourself caught up in a fight." Roger swung a playful punch at him.

Kenneth expertly dodged it. "Yes." He quickly switched the topic to business and Kenneth was successful in avoiding Roger's enthusiastic elbow nudges and hearty back slaps from making contact with his bruises. Unfortunately, his luck ran out. After making a rather poor joke, Roger hit him full force in the chest. Kenneth doubled over holding his sides.

"Are you okay, son?" Roger asked concerned.

"I'm fine," Kenneth wheezed, straightening. It was a lie. He had to blink to stop seeing double.

"That's good!" Roger said ready to give him a friendly slap on the back.

Jessie captured his hand before he did so and shook it. "It was a pleasure talking to you. I think I see a woman over there trying to get your attention." Roger turned and went in the direction she pointed. Jessie led Kenneth to a seat in the hallway and knelt in front of him while Kenneth tried to focus.

"You're not okay, we need to go home." She checked her watch.

"We've been here long enough."

He squeezed his eyes shut. "Wow, Roger is stronger than I thought."

"Kenneth, are you listening to me?"

A light bulb flashed. Jessie turned to see the photographer, she'd seen earlier, running away. "If I get my hands on that guy—"

Kenneth focused on her, his brows furrowing. "Jasmine, get off the floor. People are beginning to stare."

Jessie turned around and saw that a number of people were watching them curiously. Kenneth caught her hand before she spoke. "Don't."

She bit her lip, stopping her words. "You're not well."

"Get off the floor, Jasmine. You're going to get dirt on your dress."

"I don't care. We need to leave."

"Have you seen Deborah yet?"

She rose to her feet. "I'm taking you home."

His mouth twisted with amusement. "By force?"

They both knew that was ridiculous. Jessie sat down on a chair and sighed in defeat.

"I'm having too much fun. You wouldn't deny me that, would you? With you I'm able to get things done. I don't have to worry about you feeling neglected, bored or jealous." He grinned. "I wish we'd done this years ago."

He still held onto his side, but he looked so happy she relented. Only she could see the pain mingled with the pleasure in his eyes. She opened up her purse and handed him one of his prescribed pain pills. "Take this. It will help the pain, but for god sakes don't drink any alcohol."

He nodded obediently. "Yes ma'am. Go and enjoy yourself."

She caught a man's eye then flashed Kenneth a wicked grin. "Don't worry, I plan to."

He caught her wrist. "Not that much."

She slipped out of his grasp and laughed.

Jessie enjoyed herself with many different dance partners. She had convinced herself that she was not going to see Deborah then she nearly crashed into her coming out of the ladies' room.

"Well, well, well," Deborah said, giving Jessie the once over. "Look who's actually here."

Jessie tried to keep her voice cool. "Hi, Deborah, Tracy."

Deborah encircled her like a cat trapping its prey. Her silk silver dress hugged her form and revealed a lot of leg. "You look…interesting. Almost feminine. I can't believe you pulled it off."

"Looks like you lost," Jessie said.

"Did you pay him or something?"

Jessie's lips thinned. "No. Is that how you get your dates?"

Deborah narrowed her eyes. "You didn't really win, you know."

Her confidence wavered. "What?"

"Stephanie told him about the bet. He probably asked you out of pity."

"The deal was that *I* never tell him. I followed the rules, he asked me."

"Only because of Stephanie."

"You told her, didn't you?"

Deborah laid a hand on her chest offended. "Now why would I do that?"

"Because you can't get the pendant for me, can you?"

"I can get whatever I want."

"Except some integrity."

Deborah's eyes flashed. Jessie glared back.

"That's a beautiful necklace," Tracy said to break the tension.

"It's just the customary gift," she replied flippantly. She couldn't believe that Deborah wasn't giving her the pendant.

Tracy looked confused. "Customary gift?"

She didn't want to make a big deal of it. "He gives it to all his dates. I'm sure Deborah has one too."

Deborah blinked. "No..." She shrugged her creamy shoulders. "I'm sure that it's fake anyway."

Jessie fingered the jewelry around her neck. Why hadn't Kenneth given Deborah one of these? "Of course," she agreed.

"Oh my God. What's that?" Tracy asked, seizing Jessie's left hand.

Jessie tried to tug her hand free. "It's nothing."

"It's gorgeous. I've seen this ring before I'm sure." She brought it closer to her face. "Isn't that the Preston family ring?" Tracy's eyes widened. "You two are engaged?"

"No, he—"

Deborah snatched her hand. "Let me see that." She closely examined the ring then looked up at Jessie with reluctant admiration. "I guess I'll give you the pendant as a wedding present."

"But, I'm--"

"Hey girls, look at this!" Tracy called, to a group of women near by.

Before she knew it, Jessie's hand was being passed around under envious and admiring eyes. The group finally broke up when dinner was announced. Jessie watched them go, resting her head against the wall.

"What are you doing out here?" Kenneth asked, coming towards her. "I've been looking all over for you. What's wrong?"

Jessie clenched her teeth and gripped the lapels of his jacket. "What's wrong?" She repeated giving him a little shake. "What's wrong?" Her pitch rose. "What's wrong is that they think--"

"I don't care what they think," Kenneth interrupted, taking her arm. "I'm making some really good contacts and there are some people who want to talk to you."

She stood still. "Will you just listen?"

"Later," he promised. "Come on. I've never been able to get so much business done before."

He introduced her to Mr. and Mrs. Davidson. They talked about developing a computer class for both the community center and the homeless shelter. Although she found the endeavor interesting, Jessie couldn't pay attention. What if the women began to talk? Kenneth would be furious if he found out.

"May we speak to you for a minute?" Michelle asked. She formed the statement as a question for the sake of appearances. Jessie knew it was a command.

"Sure."

"Excuse us," Michelle said to Kenneth and the couple. She and Teresa lead Jessie away each holding one arm. They stopped in front of the large doors, leading out to the back garden.

"Okay, what's going on?" Michelle demanded, tapping her foot.

Teresa spoke up. "We heard that you and Kenneth are engaged."

Jessie groaned as if in physical pain. "It's all a mistake. Tracy saw this ring--"

Teresa pounced on Jessie's hand and held it up to her eyes. She opened her mouth, but no words came out.

Michelle nudged Teresa's paralyzed frame. "Why did he give it to you?"

"Because he wanted to give me good luck, I guess," Jessie said. "He doesn't know yet."

"He doesn't know?" Teresa squeaked.

"I didn't get the chance to tell him."

"Well, you had better tell him soon because the news is spreading like a bush fire."

"Michelle, you tell him."

She rested a hand on her chest. "Why me?"

"Because he'll listen to you."

"He's your fiancé."

Jessie scowled. "That's not funny."

"One of you had better tell him quick," Teresa warned, staring in the distance. "Or Deborah will."

Michelle and Jessie turned in that direction. They watched as Deborah made her way to where Kenneth was standing.

"Oh, no." Jessie pushed and shoved her way through the crowd, hoping to get to him first. She failed.

"So when's the happy occasion?" Deborah asked, smiling up at Kenneth.

He rubbed his chin. "What are you talking about?"

"Kenneth, I'm thirsty could you get me a drink?" Jessie asked, tugging his arm.

He patted her hand. "Sure, in a minute."

"Oh, come on," Deborah urged. "No need to keep it a secret."

"Keep what a secret?"

"Your engagement of course."

Kenneth furrowed his eyebrows. "My what?"

Jessie inwardly winced. She looked at the ground, wondering if there was a hole somewhere she could crawl into.

Deborah's smile grew wider. "I couldn't help noticing the beautiful ring Jessie had on. I just assumed..." She let her sentence trail off.

Kenneth lifted Jessie's hand and studied the ring. "It's beautiful, isn't it?"

"So are you engaged or not?"

Jessie held her breath. He met her eyes and an easy smile spread on his face. She couldn't read his expression, but immediately knew he was up to something. "Of course we are. Aren't we darling?" He kissed her lightly on the mouth. "Now what did you want to drink? Something light and fizzy I image. I'll be back in a minute." He turned and strolled away, with a bounce to his step, leaving both women with their mouths open.

Chapter Twenty-four

"**W**hat have you done?" Jessie asked, hitting Kenneth on the arm once they were alone outside. The sound of voices floated through the warm evening, as the calm waters of the bay reflected the hotel's lights and the stars.

"What?"

She fell down on a stone bench. "I can't believe this." She curled her hands into fists. "You told her we're engaged? Do you know what this means? " She paused as a thought struck her. "Oh, I get it. This is my punishment for using you as a trophy."

Kenneth rested a foot on the bench. "Yes and no." He took a sip of her drink.

She grabbed it from him, splashing it over his glove. "That's not alcohol, is it?"

"No, it's not." He shook the liquid off his glove. "I told you I don't drink. It's punch."

"It could be spiked."

Kenneth grinned. "They don't do that at these kinds of parties."

She sniffed. "You'd be surprised. At one party I waitressed, the hostess made a special request to make sure the guests were happy. We made them very happy."

"I see." He took the drink from her. "Well, I'm waiting."

"Waiting for what?"

"Waiting for that temper of yours to lash out at me. Are you going to attack my pride, my ego, or will you make unsavory comments about my parentage?"

She rested her chin in her hands. "No, it serves me right. I was too

284

ambitious. God, Michelle is going to gloat over this one. She thought the bet was a stupid idea." Jessie rubbed her temples. "This is such a mess."

"Don't give yourself a headache." He massaged the back of her neck. "It's not really a mess." He sat down next to her. "We act like we're engaged for a couple of weeks—"

"Weeks?" she choked.

"Then break up."

"With you dumping me?"

"No, you dumping me. Don't worry, my ego can take it."

She groaned.

"Is it really that bad to pretend that we're engaged?"

The guy had three college degrees and couldn't even tell when a woman was in love with him. She began to question his intelligence. "I guess not."

"The truth is I wanted you to win big. Not just the pendant but Deborah's respect. I knew she wouldn't believe I asked you to the ball because I wanted to, so I thought an engagement would be more convincing."

"It would have been, if she wasn't saving the pendant for a wedding present."

He looked crushed. "I ruined it for you."

It was odd, but she didn't feel disappointed. She didn't feel angry with Deborah for being a liar or at herself for falling for Deborah's ploy. She didn't feel annoyed that there was yet another obstacle to getting the pendant. It was as if the sweet evening had calmed all her haunting thoughts. She was quiet then said, "You didn't ruin it. It's just her excuse. She wasn't going to give it to me anyway."

Kenneth sighed. "I could ask Mrs. Ashford how much—"

She stood and glanced down at the amethyst on her finger, remembering it was a spiritual stone. A stone that called to the depth of her soul, shedding off the layers of her past. The Jessie of before: anxious, angry, vengeful, scared. A Jessie full of bitterness and pain whispered the true story of the pendant before vanishing into the sky. "Doesn't matter," she said.

"What?"

She looked at him. "The pendant's center is like the very sky above us. I don't need to hold it in my hands to claim it. It knows to whom it belongs and is already working its magic." Her voice fell. "It gave me you." He looked blank and she laughed at herself. "I sound as crazy as my father and I don't care. It's a night for believing in magic and stories and dreams and..." She stopped, feeling an overwhelming freedom as if her skin had fallen away leaving her soul to fly. She spun around and looked up at the sky. "Look at the stars, Kenneth. Aren't they beautiful?"

Kenneth gazed at her instead and fell in love.

When they arrived home, Syrah opened the door, brimming with excitement. "Is it true?"

"What are you doing up?" Kenneth asked.

"I couldn't sleep. Is it true?"

He began to bend down to pat Dion, who was eager for attention, but a biting pain ripped at his side and he stopped. Jessie watched worried, but said nothing. "Is what true?" he asked.

"That you and Aunt Jessie are going to get married?" Syrah looked at Jessie's hand and jumped up and down with joy. "It *is* true! I'm so happy! We're going to be a family!"

"Wait, wait a minute. How did you find this out?"

"It was simple really. Denise's cousin was a waiter at the party and someone told him that they heard Tracy talking to Wendy about your ring. So Denise's cousin told his girlfriend who called Denise's sister who told her mother who told Denise who told me."

He blinked. "I see."

"So when are you getting married? Can I be in it? Can we have lots of lemon sherbet?"

"There's not going to be a wedding just yet," he said cautiously. "We have to get things in order. We have a lot of things we need to discuss first."

"Like what?"

"We'll tell you tomorrow," Kenneth promised in an awkward tone. "Now it's time for bed."

"Okay." She raced up the stairs.

Jessie shot him a glance. "Nothing to worry about you said."

"I didn't expect her to hear about it so soon."

"What are we going to do about her?"

"She's grown. She'll understand when it doesn't work out." He shoved a hand in his pocket. "Besides...she's going to have to see her father at some point."

"Have you spoken to him recently?"

"No."

She touched his sleeve. "You don't want to send her back, do you?"

He yawned.

"Why don't you adopt her?"

He shook his head. "I can't."

"Why not?"

He yawned again and headed for the stairs. "Because I can't. I'll see you in the morning."

Stephanie laid her gold necklace on the dresser and unzipped her dress. She glanced at Brooke who painted her toenails on the brown tufted ottoman in front of the window. Since girlhood Brooke liked to visit her room, even though her own was more elaborate.

Stephanie let her dress fall and stepped over it. "You'll be sorry you missed the ball." She grabbed her robe.

"I doubt it," Brooke said. "Events like that are so boring."

"Not this time." She tied her robe and sat on the bed. "Kenneth is engaged."

Brooke glanced up. "To whom?"

"Jessie Clifton. Can you believe it? It was a complete shock to everyone."

Brooke's eyes turned shrewd. "To you especially."

"I misjudged her. She seems to care for him."

Brooke wiggled her toenails. "Or his money. One can never know."

"She doesn't seem the type," Stephanie said. "I spoke to her for awhile. She's very insightful and the dress she wore was amazing."

"You liked her?" Brooke asked in an odd tone.

"Yes." Stephanie opened a bottle of lotion and lathered her legs. "Oh, by the way, she was wearing a bracelet just like the one I lost. Brooke, you're about to spill your nail polish."

She righted the bottle. "Jessie was wearing the bracelet?"

"I doubt it was the exact one. She said Syrah gave it to her."

"Then it must be the one." Brooke tightened the top of the bottle. "Syrah must have picked it up when you lost it."

"Are you accusing her of theft?"

"She's just a kid who saw a pretty bracelet. I don't blame her for taking it."

"But she's Kenneth's niece. Prestons always do the right thing. She would have taken it to the Lost and Found."

Brooke wasn't listening. If Syrah was anything like her father, she had fast fingers and a ruthless mind to match. "I want you to get it back."

"How? I can't just go up to Jessie and say it's mine and I want it back now."

"Sure you can. If Jessie is as likable as you claim, it should be no problem. It was lost— not abandoned—so it is ours. Please, Stephanie." She dimpled prettily. "For me?"

An uneasiness woke Jessie from her peaceful slumber. She sat up in bed, certain the feeling was part of her dream until she felt a desperate need to check on Kenneth. She raced down the hall to his room, imagining him writhing in pain as his pills wore off, desperately looking in his medicine cabinet in search of relief. She flung the door open and stopped. He lay asleep. She walked to his bed.

His blankets lay in a violent disarray at the foot of the bed. She stared at him for a few moments his bandage standing out like a wound of war. Though he didn't toss and turn his rigid body made clear that his thoughts were anything but peaceful.

She gently shook him. "Kenneth." When he didn't move, she kneeled on the bed and whispered in his ear. "It's just a dream."

His jaw tightened more.

She shook his harder. "Wake up."

His eyes fluttered open, bright with pain and worry. He fumbled for her hand and seized it, his voice urgent. "You're all right?"

"Yes."

He relaxed. "Good." He closed his eyes again and buried his face in the pillow, sighing like a contented child. She pulled the blankets up and stroked his cheek. He was probably still dreaming about the fight and the pain pills weren't working. Fortunately, she knew an alternative.

Trying to force him to stay home the next day; however, made Jessie want to hurt Kenneth rather than heal him. When she finally persuaded him that Radson wouldn't topple in his absence, she made him tea, sweetening it with a sleeping pill. She then called Teresa.

"I need to borrow one of your potions," she said.

Teresa's voice hardened. "Witches make potions. I create medicinal drinks and ointments."

Jessie rolled her eyes. *Like it matters.* "I need your service."

"I'll be right over."

An hour later, the two sisters entered Kenneth's room as if they were entering the cave of a sleeping beast. Even in sleep he looked formidable—though he didn't face them.

"He's exhausted," Jessie whispered. "Plus, I slipped him a sleeping pill. I don't think he'll wake up."

Teresa still made a wide arch around the bed. Her eyes were fixed on his back, watching for any sudden movements. If he suddenly woke, he may not be pleased to see her. Her hand clutched her large bag.

"Well?" Jessie asked.

"Let's get to work." Teresa dug inside her bag and pulled out a rectangular wooden box. "I brought your stones in case you wanted to use them."

"Thanks," Jessie said, knowing she had no intention of using them.

Teresa opened the window and closed the curtains. She placed candles of various sizes about the room and lit them.

Jessie watched her replace one candle with another, growing impatient. "Is all this necessary?"

"Positioning is important."

"But—"

"Do you want him to heal or not?"

Jessie had to admit the cool scent of a dew filled morning, which permeated the air with the aroma of candles, made her feel calm. Or perhaps it was her sister who moved around so quietly, yet with such purpose that dispelled her worries. It reminded her of how Teresa had taken care of their parents. Unfortunately, the pneumonia still took them away.

Teresa checked to make sure that everything was set. Then she went to Kenneth and pulled down the bedclothes. She recoiled in horror at the sight of the bruises and scars. His body looked as though some hideous monster were trying to take form.

Jessie grimaced. "They look bad, don't they?"

Teresa swept one hand over his back without touching him. "They're horrible. He must have suffered terribly." She clasped her hands together as if in prayer, her eyes filling with tears. "I'm not sure the cream will be enough to heal these."

Jessie sighed disappointed. "I know. Those thugs were enormous."

Teresa stared at her in surprise. "These aren't from them."

"What are you talking about?"

"Look at his back and his arms." She pulled the bedclothes down to his feet. "Jesus, even his legs."

Jessie leaned closer. A series of long, raised scars caught her attention. She pointed to one. "I wonder what could have made that."

"A belt, a rod, a whip." She toyed with her bracelets. "And this looks like a burn mark."

Her gut clenched. She met Teresa's eyes. "You don't think...?"

"I don't know." Her voice fell. "But he suffered, Jessie. He suffered. I can feel it."

"He told me he bruised easily."

"That's possible."

But neither believed that. The sinister marks told their own story.

Teresa took his wrist and felt his pulse. "The mask he wears takes up so much energy. It will take a while for him to heal." She closed her eyes. "He's sad." She suddenly dropped his hands and stepped back.

"What? Did you sense something?"

She continued to stare at him.

"You saw something, right?" Jessie watched as Kenneth's hands balled into fists. "Do something, he's hurting."

Teresa opened a bottle of oil and handed it to her. "Rub this on him."

"Why me?"

"Just do it," she snapped.

Jessie began to lather the oil on his back and immediately felt him relax. She sighed relieved. "It's working."

Teresa shook her head and said in a quiet voice, "It's not the oil. It's you."

Outside Syrah kicked around a soccer ball in the front yard while Teresa and Jessie took care of Kenneth. Her heart began to pound when she saw a gray Mercedes come up the drive. She watched a woman step out, dressed in khakis and a white blouse. She recognized her from the office. She walked up to her before the woman could come any closer to the house.

"Hi," Syrah said suspicious.

The woman smiled. The expression was guarded, but sincere. "Hi, my name is Stephanie Radson. Is Jessie around?"

"No."

She hesitated. "I see. Perhaps you could help me. I believe you found my bracelet at the office and I would like it back."

Syrah clenched her teeth. Ever since she'd seen the ad in the paper she'd been worried. If only the woman had advertised sooner the reward would have been so sweet. But it was too late now. She couldn't have it. If Aunt Jessie found out she would know for sure that it had been stolen. Then she might tell Uncle.

Syrah pulled her face into a worried frown and wrung her hands. "Do you really need it back? I gave it to Aunt Jessie because she was sad about...about her father. He made jewelry you know." Her voice grew soft. "I said I bought it for her. It would make me look bad if you told her I found it." She lowered her eyes. "I don't have much money but--"

Stephanie waved her hand in a dismissive gesture. "Oh, forget it. I can buy another one." She pointed at her, trying to sound stern. "But next time it's better not to claim something that isn't yours."

Syrah fought a grin, keeping her gaze lowered. "I will."

Stephanie returned from her errand with mixed feelings. She slammed her car door and walked up to her house, her heels pounding against the concrete drive. She was a softie and she knew it. When Syrah had looked up at her with those large, round, worried eyes, she knew she wouldn't tell on her. Unfortunately, explaining that to Brooke would be a problem.

Brooke met Stephanie in the foyer, her hand griping the stair post. "Where's the bracelet?" she asked.

Stephanie hung up her jacket. "I'll get you another one."

Brooke's knuckles paled as she tightened her hold. "But you can't."

"Why not?"

"It's one of a kind you--" She moved her hand with impatience. "I'll get it myself."

Stephanie shut the closet and turned to her. "You can't. I said Syrah could have it. She was so proud to give it to Jessie as a gift."

Her voice fell flat. "Was she?"

"I'll buy you another bracelet. Two if you want."

Brooke forced a smile to ease her sister's anxiety. She touched her cheek. "Fine. You did your best."

Stephanie relaxed and headed for the stairs. "We can go shopping tomorrow. Donovan's Antiques if you wish. It will be fun."

"Yes." Brook waited until Stephanie was gone then picked up the phone. Just as she thought, the kid was a shark like her father. She would have to handle things a different way. "I've found the bracelet," she said once someone picked up. "And I want you to get it back. You'll be going to the annual Preston barbecue."

Syrah lay on her bed thinking about Stephanie's surprise visit two days ago. She sat up when Jessie came into her room and handed her a large rectangular box.

She frowned at it. "What's this for?"

Jessie folded her arms and leaned against the wall. "Michelle and I thought you'd like it."

Syrah swallowed, wondering if they would still like her if they knew what she had done.

"Go on. Open it."

She opened the box. "Pajamas!" She raced into her closet to try it on. She quickly dressed and came out to show Jessie, but Jessie had a strange look on her face. "What's wrong?"

"What happened to your back?"

She felt her gut clench. "That boy hit me pretty hard."

"Oh, I see," Jessie said quickly, trying to dispel the panic in Syrah's eyes. But Jessie had been in a lot of fights when she was a kid and had never ended up with marks like those. Jessie had seen Syrah's reflection in the mirror and the marks stamped on the girl's back. They looked eerily similar to the ones Kenneth had. Syrah was lying to protect someone. Who would she try to protect? Jessie felt sick as a horrible possibility froze in her mind of who that person was: her uncle.

Was that what Kenneth had meant when he'd said Syrah wasn't safe with him? Had the tiger she suspected that lurked beneath his cool exterior lashed out in the privacy of his home? Had what had happened to him in the past effected his present actions? She knew abusers could be consummate actors and Kenneth was one of the best. Why else would he want to send Syrah back to an alcoholic father instead of keeping her? *He knew he was a danger to her and these bruises were proof.*

"Jessie, will you please calm down?" Michelle said.

She continued to pace the office and bite her nails. How could she be calm with such thoughts on her heart?

"You're jumping to conclusions."

"I'm not. I saw them with my own eyes. Kenneth has the same bruises too. Ask Teresa about them. She even had a vision."

Teresa quietly organized a bouquet of sunflowers.

"Well, Teresa," Michelle said. "What do you think?"

"I don't know."

Jessie stopped pacing. "But you saw a vision. I know you did."

"What did you see?" Michelle asked.

Teresa threw up her hands exasperated. "What does it matter? You've never believed my visions before. Why would you care now?"

Michelle and Jessie shared a look and sighed. Jessie finally said, "Okay, we're sorry."

"We might not understand them," Michelle added. "But we respect your gifts. Please tell us what you saw."

Teresa shut her eyes, her brows furrowed in pain. "I saw a man hitting a child. I didn't see faces, but I know it was little boy and he was terrified."

"It was Syrah," Jessie said.

"Syrah is a girl."

"She can look like a boy sometimes."

Teresa shook her head. "It wasn't her."

"How do you know?"

"I just do! I know that Kenneth would never hurt a child and it's bad form to accuse him of such a thing. I don't believe it."

"Can you believe that the upstanding Mr. Preston was capable of what he did to Kenneth?" Jessie asked.

"I can't imagine anyone hurting a child," Teresa said.

Jessie bit her lip. "Well, people do and no amount of denial will change that. Something terrible was going on in the Preston household and none of us suspected it. We cannot ignore the facts we have now. I think we should keep Syrah with us for a few days while I figure something out."

Michelle rested her chin in her hand. "I still think you're jumping to conclusions. Why haven't you considered Eddie?"

Jessie leaned against the desk. "Because why would Kenneth send her back to the very man who abuses her?"

"Maybe he doesn't know. Perhaps he's never seen the bruises."

She suddenly felt ill. Michelle was probably right. Kenneth had limited time with Syrah and she never wore halter tops or shorts nothing to reveal the scars…just like her Uncle. He didn't know and she would have to be the one to tell him. "Oh, no."

"First bring Syrah to the house," Teresa said, sensing Jessie's conflicting thoughts. "Then we'll figure out what to do."

Jessie waited until Kenneth left for work. She told Syrah they were going to have a sleepover at her house and Syrah convinced her to take Dion along. The doorbell rang while Jessie dumped their bags in the foyer. She opened the door and stared at the visitor: Mrs. Preston. She was a handsome woman. Her strong, sturdy frame gave her peach summer dress a sophisticated air, while her too small pointed high-heels hinted at her vanity. She had a face that had been beautiful in youth—round mink eyes with a gumdrop nose—but time had turned it harsh and lofty. A cloud of light brown curls surrounded her face.

"I had to see for myself," she said in a rough, yet cultured tone. She lifted Jessie's hand and studied the ring. "So it's true. He got himself a little something to settle down with." She released Jessie's hand and continued her study. "You're dark, but you'll do. I'm surprised he's marrying a'tal. He won't make good a husband."

Jessie felt her skin grow cold, thinking of the torture Mr. Preston had put his sons through. Wondering how this woman could have let it happen. It was at that moment that she understanding the mask's creator.

"Are you pregnant?"

"No." She spit out the word determined not to reveal what she knew.

"Good." Mrs. Preston nodded, satisfied. "This one doesn't need children."

Jessie took a step back from the scrutinizing gaze. "Would you like to come in?"

She sniffed. "And see all his trophies about the house like him a big, big man?" She shook her head. "I'd rather pray for his soul. I'll pray for yours too." She offered Jessie one last glance then turned and headed to her car.

Jessie watched her go. She'd never liked Mrs. Preston's arrogant ways, but she knew her words had truth.

Syrah came around the corner.

She shut the door. "You just missed your grandmother."

Syrah shrugged nonchalant. "I know."

She didn't find the girl's indifference alarming—Mrs. Preston was far from the type of grandmother one could love. "Come. Let's go."

"At last we can get this garage cleared up," Teresa said, trying to be happy about the new situation.

"Give me a couple of hours and you'll get the surprise of your life," Jessie said, glad to be put to work.

"Syrah and I are in the kitchen if you need us."

Jessie looked down at Dion. He stared up at her with his friendly, crossed-eyed gaze. His tongue hung out as though he were smiling. "So, Dion, I guess it's you and me."

The dog wagged his tail, shaking his entire back end.

Jessie hummed to herself as she worked her mind clear as she lifted and carried things. Major cleaning always helped calm her. Michelle would be pleasantly surprised when she got home. She had been complaining about the garage for months. Jessie reached for a pair of shears on top of an overcrowded shelf. Suddenly, the shelf collapsed. Everything toppled to the ground.

Stunned, she stood still for a moment then a searing pain hit her. It felt like a javelin shot through her ankle. She dropped to the ground as blood rushed like a broken faucet from her wound. Her gaze fell on the ceramic pot that had struck her. It now lay in pieces near her feet. The amount of blood scared her and the world grew hazy. She called out her sister's name.

Kenneth heard the scream as he drove up to the garage. It ripped through his ears like nails against a chalkboard. He leaped out of the car as Dion came running towards him, barking with blood on his paws. He rushed to the garage, his heart pounding as images of Syrah injured flashed through his mind. He halted like a unplugged robot when he found Jessie on the cement ground in a pool of blood. He fell to his knees beside her. Teresa and Syrah followed close behind him.

"Aunt Jessie!"

Teresa held Syrah from rushing to her. "My God, what happened?"

she cried.

"Where are you hurt?" Kenneth asked, keeping his voice neutral so that Jessie wouldn't panic, although his insides were twisting into knots.

"My ankle," she said in a faint voice.

Teresa grabbed a hose, turned it on low pressure and began to clean the wound, but Jessie arched her back in pain, begging her to stop.

Kenneth surveyed the garage. "Do you have a towel or something to wrap her foot?"

"Only this?" Teresa held up a dirty towel then tossed it down. She grabbed Syrah's hand. "Come on. Let's see what we can find."

He swore. "That'll take too long." He took a deep breath as if preparing to jump into a freezing lake then tore his shirt off and wrapped it around her ankle. The blood quickly seeped through. He ripped off his undershirt, ignoring the startled gasp behind him. He wrapped it even tighter around the ankle, hoping to stop the bleeding.

Jessie tried to push his hand away. "You're hurting me!"

"I know, Jas, but I have to do this."

She pounded his back; tears trailed down her face. "Let go, you're hurting me."

"Bear with me, Jas. Relax, breathe deep and bear with me."

Jessie fell back and watched as the ceiling spun round and round.

The bleeding eventually stopped and Kenneth opened the bandage to see the wound. He sighed in relief. "The wound is small, but you'll probably need stitches."

He picked her up and headed for his car. Teresa retrieved Jessie's handbag and a jacket.

"I'll take care of everything," Kenneth assured her, as he buckled Jessie in the backseat.

Teresa handed him a small travel pillow and throw blanket. "I know," she said with serious eyes. "I trust you."

Kenneth and Jessie made an interesting pair entering the emergency room: Kenneth shirtless with bloody jeans and Jessie dangling like a rag doll in his arms with bloody shirts tied around her ankle. It was more the appearance than the actual injury that had them serviced quickly, though they had to suffer through the routine questions.

Kenneth was aware of how people stared at him. He felt exposed—naked—as curious eyes tried to understand the ugly marks that marred his body. He shifted uneasily in his chair as they sat in the waiting room, with Jessie's foot elevated on a hard plastic chair.

"What happened to you, son?" an older man with bright silver red hair asked concern in his green eyes.

Kenneth cleared his throat. "Uh, a fight."

"Over a woman, I bet." His voice lowered to a whisper. "They aren't worth it. They get in your blood and torment you. Nasty creatures these women can be sometimes. When I was—"

A young woman came and took his arm. "Come on, Dad. They said we can see Mom now."

The man patted Kenneth on the shoulder. "You take care of yourself, son. Remember what I said."

"Thanks." He ran a nervous hand over his chest, wishing he had something with which to cover himself. He brushed his chin then rubbed his hands together, trying to ease the tension that was building inside him. He hated hospitals. He hated the stale smell in the air, the hushed sound of rubber shoes against the tile floor, the crackling of a white coat as a doctor walked by.

He had been in so many, sitting in a hard chair holding on to various broken limbs while his mother tried to explain it away to hospital staff as a childhood antic. He rubbed his hands together until his palms began to burn. He hated the feeling of powerlessness. Cosmic irony was definitely afoot. Some celestial god was mocking him, showing him that for all his brilliance he was only a man full of weaknesses and that they knew what they were.

Jessie pinched him. "Breathe, Kenneth."

He hadn't realized he'd stopped. He took a deep breath that caused his entire body to shake.

"You can go outside if you wish."

He felt embarrassed that his discomfort was so obvious. "I'm not leaving you here...unless you want me to go."

"No, I'm glad you're here." She suddenly said, "Hold me."

"What?"

Her voice grew urgent. "Hold me."

He pulled her onto his lap and held her close.

"What are you two doing here?" Mrs. Ashford asked.

Kenneth held her tighter. "She had an accident."

"Oh dear--"

"I'm sorry," Jessie said in a small voice. "I don't feel like talking."

"Of course you don't dear. I'll stop your house later to see how you are." She walked away.

He watched her go then said in a low voice, "You didn't have to do that."

"I won't have you exposed because of me."

He didn't understand what she meant by that, but he didn't understand her. She'd left with Syrah without telling him, yet used her body to cover his bruises. Why? He took her hand, surprised at how cold and clammy it felt. He watched as her eyes began to droop. "Jasmine." He nudged her, trying to keep her awake. "Stay with me."

Her eyes continued to close.

"You know Montey was right. You are a walking accident."

She sent him a clear, hard glare before a nurse called them into a room. Once inside the examination room, one of the nurses handed Kenneth a large towel to give him warmth.

The doctor gave Jessie a tetanus shot, stitched her up, handed her pain medication and then sent her home.

Kenneth didn't speak on the drive back.

She tugged on the green scrub top the hospital had given him. "Ever thought of being a doctor? You'd never want for patients."

"Why did you leave without telling me?"

She chewed her lower lip. "I wasn't thinking. I thought Syrah and I could have a sleepover with my sisters."

"For how long?"

"It wasn't going to be long. It was just an impulsive idea." Jessie tried to smile. "Think of it. You get your house back for a few days— quiet and peaceful."

He fell silent then asked, "Are you in pain?"

"Right now my foot is so numb, I forget it's there." She picked up the bottle of her pain pills and pretended to read it. "Have you spoken to Eddie?"

"No, not yet."

She put her pills away.

"You'll need your rest. I'll take Syrah home with me."

"She's fine with me," she said a little too quickly. "My sisters enjoy her."

"Jasmine—"

She rested her head back and closed her eyes. "I'm tired. Can we talk later?"

He reached out and stroked her arm then sighed. "Of course."

"Come on, Jessie," Teresa pleaded as the doorbell rang. "Give the guy a chance. He's been here every day for a week."

"Tell him Syrah is with Denise," Jessie said.

"He came here to see you."

Jessie stared up at her from the couch. "I can't see him."

"Before you were ready to charge him with abuse."

"I'd rather be angry with him than hurt him. I don't want to tell him about his brother, but I can't pretend I don't know."

Teresa looked helpless. "I'm running out of excuses."

"You don't need excuses, just one good reason."

"Personally, I'm sick of this juvenile behavior," Michelle said as the doorbell rang for the fifth time. She headed for the door.

"Mich, don't!" Jessie ordered. It was too late, Michelle welcomed Kenneth inside. He entered the living room with an over stuffed picnic basket under his arm and a large yellow helium balloon with "Get Well" repeated in various languages.

He scanned her critically and beamed with approval. "Well, it's nice to see you're well enough to receive me."

"Actually, I've been well enough for a while, I just didn't want—" Michelle cut off her sentence by yanking Jessie's hair as she walked past.

"Would you like anything?" Teresa asked.

"No, thanks," Kenneth said. "I'm fine."

The two sisters left the room.

Jessie sat up to show him how healthy she was. "So, what did you bring me?" she asked.

He sat down next to her. Jessie tried to ignore the inviting scent of his cologne or the comfort of being near him again.

"It's my own first aid kit." He opened the box. "First, Preston's famous ginger muffins with marmalade." He put a handful of green oval shaped leaves in her lap. "And leaves."

"Leaves?"

"I thought since you were shut in, I should bring nature to you. Smell them."

Jessie inhaled their fresh scent.

"Then I brought glow-in-the-dark stars. I'll put them up on your bedroom ceiling so at night you can have the same view I have. See here?" He pointed to a diagram. "They show you how to put it up properly so you can see constellations and everything."

"But there must be hundreds of tiny stars here," Jessie protested.

"I guess it will take me a while to put them up then, huh?" His gaze traveled her face and searched her eyes. "That's okay, I don't mind."

Her heart began to pound, silencing the warning bells in her mind. She didn't remember leaning forward, brushing her lips with his.

The phone rang.

Jessie straightened. "I think I should get that."

Kenneth held her hand, staying her. "One of your sisters will get it."

She turned away, rubbing her forehead. "Kenneth, I—"

"Don't think." He brushed his lips against her cheek then drew her close and held her with a tenderness that broke through all her defenses. She wrapped her arms around him, burying her face in his neck. She inhaled his musky cologne and reveled in his warmth.

She took a deep breath, gathering strength. "Kenneth, I know how you got your bruises."

He stiffened.

"And I've seen the same bruises on Syrah."

She felt his heart accelerate. "No, you couldn't have," he said.

"I did. She was trying on a pair of pajamas in the closet and I saw them in the mirror."

"But that would mean—" He shook his head. "No, *no*. He wouldn't." He drew away from her, his eyes like hollow pools, but she knew there were emotions running deep. "He wouldn't touch her. We promised each other. We made a vow we'd never." He shook his head again. "You're mistaken Eddie—" He took a deep, steadying breath. "He drinks that's all. I admit that's a problem—"

"Denial won't change the truth. She can't go back to him." She grabbed his hand, sensing him withdrawing from her, feeling the wall he was building against her. "You're not alone on this. We'll think of something."

He rose. His face too composed, his body too relaxed. "I have to go," he said in a neutral tone. "I'll check on you later."

"Kenneth— " She reached for him, but he moved out of reach.

"Wait!" Teresa cried, bursting into the room. She grabbed Kenneth's arm and pushed him down. "Don't go anywhere. Sit straight." She adjusted his collar.

"Have you finally snapped?" Jessie asked.

"No." Teresa tossed her a comb. "Fix your hair."

"She's finally gone nutty," Jessie muttered to no one in particular.

Michelle came into the room carrying a tea tray with biscuits. "No she hasn't," she said, placing the tray on the table. "Our favorite aunt just called saying she's stopping by."

"But we don't have a favorite aunt. Why are you using the porcelain tea set? We only use that when..." Realization struck her. "Not Aunt Yvette! Please tell me it's not her."

"I wish I could, but she feels that it is her duty to meet your fiancée."

Jessie began biting her nails. "This is a disaster. He can't handle this right now."

Kenneth slapped her hand away from her mouth. "Aunt Yvette? That name sounds familiar."

"It should," Michelle said. "She's our mother's sister—the most obnoxious, condescending British Caribbean immigrant to touch American soil. With mother gone she thinks it's her duty to lead us on the right path."

"Kenneth doesn't have to be here for this," Jessie said, trying to pull him to his feet. "He's hurting right now."

"I'm okay," he said.

"No, you're not. Stop pretending."

"He'll be a help," Michelle argued, pushing him back down.

"He'll be in the way."

"It will take the pressure off of us."

"No it won't. He'll be riddled with questions."

"Don't I have a say in this?" Kenneth asked, trying to free himself from this strange tug of war.

"No," they chorused.

He shrugged.

"Kenneth stays," Michelle said, ending the argument.

Teresa rushed to the window when she heard a car drive up. "They're here."

Michelle paused. "They?"

"Yes, she brought Uncle Harmon...and Cousin Olivia."

The three sisters groaned their sounds of despair followed by the doorbell.

Chapter Twenty-five

"**W**hat a surprise!" Teresa said, opening the door. She hugged her relations and welcomed them inside. Aunt Yvette took the main couch. She was a tall, thin woman who had a nose as long as her face. The sisters often wondered if it was solely made for the purpose of being condescending. She had small eyes under thick, heavy eyebrows. She did nothing to counteract this, wearing her gray-black hair in a firm bun behind her head.

Her daughter took another seat. Olivia was a paragon of beauty, grace, and intelligence, the absolute pride of her parents and the entire family on their mother's side. She was a constant thorn to the Clifton sisters.

Uncle Harmon took a seat next to his wife. He was not a particularly handsome man, but he was successful and rich which made up for his features: a round jaw line and big round eyes like one would see in a stuffed toy. His primary job in life was to nod and agree with whatever his wife said, to which, after over thirty some years, he had become especially adept.

Aunt Yvette stared at Jessie. "Good God! What happened to your hair?"

Jessie raised her hand to her head. "Why? Did it go somewhere?"

"Don't be cheeky." She fixed her small eyes on Kenneth. "You must be the intended. I must say that your engagement came as a surprise."

"It came as a surprise to all of us," Teresa said.

"I don't believe I was speaking to you."

Teresa bit her lip.

"So let me see this ring I've heard so much about."

Jessie held out her hand.

Aunt Yvette straightened, offended. "You can't very well expect me to walk across the room. Come here. "

Jessie walked over to her—exaggerating her limp—and held out her hand for inspection.

"Unusual, but exquisite nonetheless. You may sit down."

Jessie restrained from curtsying.

Aunt Yvette glanced at the tea tray. "Where is the brown sugar? You are always supposed to have a selection of white and brown sugar at hand."

"It's right here, Aunty," Teresa said, moving it from behind the cream.

"Much better. It must always be in view. To the greatest extent you should save your guests the effort of requesting anything." She took her tea and sipped it.

"How are you keeping?" Teresa asked.

"Very well, thank you."

Michelle spoke up. "What brings you into town?"

"Olivia is moving here."

"She is?"

"Permanently?" Jessie asked, failing not to sound disappointed.

"Well, yes for the time being." Aunt Yvette suddenly smiled. "And now that you are marrying this young man I am sure that you will be able to introduce her to all the right people."

Kenneth returned her smile. "I'm not sure that I know all the right people."

Aunt Yvette wagged a finger at him. "Oh, don't be modest young man. I know all about you. You're very successful and charitable and a Preston no less." She turned to her husband. "Isn't that advantageous, Harmon?"

Uncle Harmon nodded as if on cue. "Yes, dear."

"How were you two introduced?"

Jessie groaned at her aunt's short memory. "This is Kenneth Preston, Auntie. Remember? He used to live across the street."

"Oh, yes that haughty young man you couldn't stand." Her eyes widened in recognition. "Well, this *is* a surprise, but as they say 'hate is the cousin to love.' When will the wedding be? I must schedule my time so that I can help you organize it. We must not miss off any important people."

Jessie sat forward tired of the charade. "We might as well be honest. We—"

"We haven't worked out the particulars yet," Kenneth interrupted.

Aunt Yvette frowned. Not enough to cause wrinkles, but enough to look disapproving. "I hope you don't plan on conducting one of those dreadfully long engagements."

"No, we don't."

"Isn't it wonderful that Olivia will be around? She'll make an excellent bridesmaid."

They all nodded.

"So graceful, so beautiful...The dresses must be maroon or lavender since those are her best colors." Aunt Yvette stopped and looked at Jessie. "You still have that disgusting habit of biting your nails. With hands as masculine as yours, it does you no service."

Jessie leaped to her feet. She knew she had to leave before she said something rude. "There's something in the kitchen that I need to tend to. I'll be back shortly."

"Swan, dear, swan!" Aunt Yvette commanded as Jessie made her way to the kitchen. "No need to scurry about like a chicken."

Jessie took a deep breath and pushed open the kitchen door.

Kenneth followed.

"What are you doing?" he asked as Jessie frantically opened various drawers.

"Looking for a knife to slit my throat."

He pulled out a butcher knife, grinning. "Will this do?"

"Perfectly. Now all you have to do is--"

He put the knife back and laughed. "Don't worry. Every family has one."

Jessie looked at him surprised. "You have an aunt like her?"

Kenneth shook his head. "No. I'm trying to make you feel better."

She opened a drawer then shoved it closed. "It's not working."

"Your cousin's still the same."

Jessie affected a high proper tone. "Oh, yes, isn't she absolutely *darling*? And wouldn't she be the loveliest bridesmaid in the entire universe? So lovely that you wouldn't even need the bride. She could just walk down the aisle by herself--the picture of grace and beauty—and the ceremony would be over."

"You sound jealous."

"I am jealous. If she wasn't as sweet as candy floss, I'd hate her."

"As much as you hated me?"

Jessie put her hands on her hips. "You two might work well together when we break up. The perfect couple."

"That's too narcissistic even for me." Kenneth touched her cheek, his voice soft. "Besides, I have no desire to break up with you."

She was too preoccupied with the present situation to give weight to his words. "You may have to when I check myself into an insane asylum."

"Why?"

She tugged on her ear. "Were you not listening? My cousin Olivia is moving here! Staying. Putting down roots. Don't you understand the implications? Extra visits from Aunt Yvette, constant comparisons. I'll have no peace until Aunt Yvette has her precious daughter married off."

"Don't worry about it. I'll take care of Olivia. I'm used to introducing young women to the "right people." That way you'll have done your duty and your aunt will leave you alone."

"Your optimism is amusing." She chewed her bottom lip. "But I'll take you up on your offer anyway."

Teresa poked her head in. "What are you two doing? We need back up fast."

Kenneth grabbed Jessie's hand. "Leave everything to me." He exited the kitchen and smiled at the guests. "Sorry to have kept you waiting," he said, returning to his seat. "Jasmine and I were discussing how I could show Olivia around."

"That would be wonderful," Aunt Yvette said. "Isn't that wonderful Harmon?"

He nodded. "Yes, dear."

"There are a great many restaurants around the bay," Jessie said.

Olivia wrinkled her pretty nose. "Oh, I don't really like seafood."

"Excellent, neither does he. You two have so much in common. The perfect—" Kenneth nudged her. "situation."

"Yes, of course." Aunt Yvette went on to pontificate how perfect the situation was. Everyone pretended to listen.

"Does he know what he's getting into?" Michelle asked under her breath.

"He'll find out," Jessie said.

Aunt Yvette stood. "We must be off. Here's where you can reach us." She handed Michelle a card.

They exchanged goodbyes then the threes sisters and Kenneth waved as their guests drove away. Once they were out of view, Michelle and Teresa left, leaving Kenneth and Jessie alone, standing in the doorway. Evening had come upon them, the scent of flowers drifted up the porch steps and into the house. Jessie watched an Irish setter race down the street, chasing nothing but shadows. Kenneth stood quiet. She could read nothing from his face.

"I'm sorry about Eddie," she said.

He sighed.

"What are you thinking?" She paused. "What are you feeling?"

He shoved his hands in his pockets.

"She can't go back to him, her home is with you. You must see that."

He didn't reply, but she knew he wasn't shutting her out, wasn't shutting the world out. He was feeling his pain—he was breathing.

Rodney threw the bouquet of red roses on the ground and stomped on them. He headed to his car. Brooke couldn't do this to him. He wouldn't let her. She wasn't being fair. First she didn't show up at the ball and now she wasn't even home after he'd told her he was coming. He'd done all she'd asked, but she still wanted him to wait a little longer. He could just forget everything, but he still wanted her. And he planned to have her.

He didn't care when. He wanted her and she knew it. Somehow, any time she passed him in the hallway, she found a way to brush her sweet behind against the bulge in his pants and he was lost. She'd gotten into his blood. He thought about her every day, every night. He dreamed about the moment when he would have her legs wrapped around him. But she kept making him wait, teasing him with promises she never delivered, and pulling him along like a damn dog. She'd forgotten who really held the leash; that he could make her plan work or fail. He would have to remind her.

Rodney got in his car and grabbed his prescription sunglasses. The sleek design always made him feel cool. Brooke was getting nervous, that was the problem. She was worrying herself too much about the upcoming vote. She didn't think she would be able to bribe the right members to sell. Hell, he didn't understand why she wanted to. He knew she hated Preston, but Preston was making money—lots of it. For a woman who worshipped cash, he should have been her priest.

He started the ignition and stepped on the accelerator, making the engine roar. Brooke thought that she could use him, push him aside whenever she wanted. He'd show her otherwise. He would demonstrate his power: his power to put the company at the mercy of its creditors and destroy her plan. Maybe then she'd come to her senses and he'd finally get what he wanted.

Rodney adjusted his sunglasses and smiled.

Night hung like a concave blanket of stars. Kenneth gazed up at the sky, willing his mind to forget his past. He tried to reach for the peace that had eluded him all his life. He loved his cottage, its sense of isolation, but tonight the demons slipped past his shield of iron and chipped away at all he had known. Eddie had succumbed. He'd become...Kenneth clenched his jaw. A small part of him still resisted the knowledge.

He couldn't let himself believe Syrah had suffered what he had: the violent blows of someone you both loved and despised, feeling that everything about you is wrong, that something bad had to be beaten out of you and—worse yet—that you deserved it. He squeezed his eyes shut, thinking of the times he'd left her after visiting her father—all the times he'd abandoned her. He hadn't kept her safe. He heard the gentle squeak of the door and opened his eyes.

"I thought you'd be in here," Jessie said, wrapped in his trench coat. "No, you don't have to get up."

Kenneth sat on the edge of the bed. "Did you need something?"

"No, I have a gift for you."

"What?"

She dropped the coat. "A little distraction."

His eyes clung to the black lace teddy.

She stood in front of him. "What do you think? Do you like it?"

He didn't move.

"The material is soft." She took his hand and placed it on her waist. "See?"

His fingers shifted, but he still said nothing.

She gently pushed him back. "That's okay. You don't have to say anything." She leaned towards him, her breast pressed against his chest.

"I have to tell you what happened the night of your prom," he said suddenly.

She halted, shocked. "What! Now?"

"Yes."

"Kenneth, that's the past. You can tell me later."

"No, I have to tell you now." He stilled the hand unbuttoning his shirt. "You need to know the man you're sleeping with."

"I do know him."

"No you don't." His eyes melted into hers. "Nobody does. I want you to know. I need you to."

She flopped onto her back and rested an arm over her eyes. "My seduction scene gone to waste."

"I don't want you to have any regrets."

Always ready to do the right thing. Damn. "All right. I'm listening." When he didn't speak, she looked at him. "I'm waiting."

He cleared his throat. "Could you put your coat on first?"

For a minute he was afraid she would ignore him, but she eventually grabbed the coat and lay on the bed. "Okay."

He rested against the headboard. "Um…" He looked at her helpless. "I don't know where to begin."

"How about the night you didn't show up?"

"Right." He folded his arms then briefly shut his eyes. She watched him saddened that the memory of that night caused him such pain. He opened his eyes then said, "You don't know shame until you look into the eyes of the man you might become." He paused. "The night of the prom, I saw myself in my father's eyes."

She chilled thinking of the distinguished Charles Preston, thinking of all the lies his house must hold.

"You've never seen my father," Kenneth continued.

"Mr. Preston isn't your father?"

"No. His name was Sir. Monsieur."

"Monsieur?"

He nodded. "Sometimes his full name was Ouimonsieur or Nonmonsieur. When he was in a good mood we called him Pierre. For nine years I never knew what his face looked like, I just knew his hands: massive, strong hands with knuckles the size of quarters. My body filled with terror whenever they held a wine glass, curled into a fist or wrapped around a beer can. He didn't drink beer often. His poison of choice was champagne, which conveniently fooled Mom into thinking he didn't have a problem. Drunks drank heavy liquor, not fine wine, and he drank down the best.

"He had a debonair air with a face so deceptive he could put you at ease even as he crushed your throat. Sure he hit us, but Mom left him because of the women. He never tried to be discreet. We would sometimes find his women passed out in our bed or find crotchless panties between the couch cushions. I don't know what made Mom leave him, but she eventually took Eddie and me to her mother's house." He sighed deeply.

"She hated us on sight. She couldn't stand the fact that we were from him—the man who had ruined her daughter's life. I can't say I helped the situation. I was an angry kid and got into a lot of fights at school. Once, when she had to take me home early from school, my mother told me—" He paused then started again. "My mother told me that she couldn't stand the sight of me because I had his anger. I was like him. She said that she was ashamed to be my mother."

"That's terrible."

He shrugged. "She was upset and grandma had poisoned her against me by then. It didn't come as a surprise. Eddie had always been her favorite. The one she showered with hugs and extra treats. I didn't mind, he was the "good one." But those words changed my life. One day, locked in my room with her words echoing in my mind, I decided then what I had to do. Because she didn't want me, and my dad had never wanted me, I would become the perfect son. The son that all mothers craved; the son that all fathers would be proud of.

"The teachers at school were shocked at the transformation and in two weeks I went from being the most feared kid in school to the most liked. I was just getting used to my new status when Mr. Preston came into our lives. He and his young daughter. Mother told us never to talk about Monsieur. She told Mr. Preston she was a widow. She had never married Sir so there was nothing to stop them from getting married. Mr. Preston adopted us and I buried little Kenny X and became Kenneth Preston. After a month, we moved here as a new family, complete with a fabricated background." He cupped her chin. "Then I met you, and you ruined everything."

"Why?" she asked quietly.

He let his hand fall. "Because you knew I was a fraud. Sometimes I felt that you somehow knew I would come home from school and beat my pillow until my knuckles swelled because I was sick of being good, sick of being nice, sick of being perfect. I thought for certain you would tell someone, expose me. I offered to tutor you, just to show you how harmless I was. As I came to know you, I envied your freedom of emotion—from anger to joy to concern. I just wanted to be close to that kind of courage.

"You were the closest thing I had to a friend. You listened to me, made me laugh, which is not as easy as you think. I asked you to the prom because I wanted to. There was no other reason than that. Then one day Pierre showed up on my doorstep." He laughed without humor. "And he looked just like me. From the shape of his face to the shape of his hands." Kenneth stared down at his own hands in memory.

Jessie grasped one and held it. "It's not the same."

He didn't hear her. "As a child I had seen a monster, but standing before me was a tall, handsome, brown- skinned man, dressed in expensive clothes. He didn't look like an alcoholic; he didn't sway like a drunk. That's when I knew that he could be me, that we were both wearing masks and that I still could end up like him."

His grip on her hand became painful, but she didn't complain. He held on like a drowning man, afraid his memories might carry him away.

"Why did he come to see you?" she asked.

"He said, he came to say goodbye. That he was dying. He said he needed money and if I refused to give it to him he would tell everyone that I was the illegitimate son of a drunk. You know the shame that would have caused my mother, especially in our small community."

She nodded.

"I know I was a coward, but I couldn't see you after that. I couldn't face your honesty with my lies. I couldn't smile and pretend to be something I wasn't. I saw Regine and acted like the man I thought I was suppose to be." He shook his head. "I tried to perfect my facade even more after hurting you. I excelled in school, in work, I even considered marriage."

"Why didn't you marry?"

"I thought I'd be honest with this one woman I was going to marry. But when I told her I didn't have pure Preston blood running through my veins, she didn't want me. I couldn't blame her. I have the blood of an alcoholic and that in time I may poison the blood of my offspring."

"That's just a gene, Kenneth, that's not who you are. You're not your father and you're not Eddie."

"But I'm not above them. I have my vices." He pinned her with an intense gaze, watching for any telling action. "I've been going to call girls for over ten years. One in particular."

Jessie was more surprised than repulsed. "Why?"

"They were the only kind of women I felt free with. They had to sleep with me in spite of the scars."

"But they're not that bad."

"One woman screamed when she saw them. She couldn't stand the sight of them and apologized for not being able to service me. You said they were horrible."

"They are but..." She ripped open his shirt, sending buttons flying.

He groaned resigned. "That's the second shirt you've ruined."

"I wanted to see the scars."

He pulled off a button that hung at an odd angle. "You could have asked."

"Take off your shirt, please."

"Why? Okay! Wait, wait I can take it off myself." He stood and took off his shirt, his eyes defiant. "There."

She had prepared herself, but his scars still came as a shock: the discolored skin, the raised marks, the sections where flesh seemed to have been ripped away. And yet because they were his they were no longer hideous. "Can I touch them?"

He gave a terse nod.

Her hands felt cool against him. Their exploration painful, making his scars real--almost alive. No one had ever touched him like this, gently, tenderly. A whisper in his mind told him he didn't deserve it, didn't need it, and reminded him that he hadn't given her anything for her to treat him with such regard. But for once he didn't care, he wanted to be selfish, wanted to believe this was real.

He closed his eyes, fighting back the torment of memories as she touched his back. The scars seemed to speak in his father's voice: *You're worthless trash. You make me sick. No one will want you. You'll amount to nothing because you are nothing.*

"Breathe," she whispered her breath warm against his skin.

His memories slowly faded, his misery vanishing into something else—something beautiful. Her hands felt like magic, a balm to his scars, taking their pain with each gentle, searching touch. He began to feel whole. Like a man, not a trophy with the guarantee of status or a client with the promise of cash, but a man. He trembled at the warm wet pressure of her lips. "What are you doing?"

"Kissing your bruises."

He spun around. "I have something better for your lips to do." He captured her mouth, caressing it more than kissing it.

They fell on the bed a frenzied passion consuming them.

He removed the straps of her teddy. "Dear god, tell me you brought protection."

She dug into the coat pocket, taking out a handful of condoms.

He chuckled. "Expecting a long night?"

"I'm not sure. I'll do it," she said when he reached for one.
"Be gentle."

"I will." She ripped open the package then paused. She'd practiced on a cucumber, but the real thing just didn't seem the same. It was larger, more *there*. She held the condom taut and thought about the best way to put it on him. It suddenly slipped through her fingers like a slingshot, whizzing across the room. It hit the far wall and stuck then slowly fell to the ground.

They didn't speak.

Kenneth tried to keep a straight face. "First bras now condoms. I think you've created a new sport."

Heat burned her cheeks. She'd practiced the seduction scene in her mind for days only to humiliate herself. "I'm nervous. I don't know what I'm doing."

He controlled his face, sensing her embarrassment. "You can try again." He handed her a condom. "Go on."

She opened the condom and held it above him.

He laughed. "You're going to have to touch me eventually. Roll it on."

She hesitated.

He grabbed her hand and put it on him. "Not so bad, see?"

She touched it tentatively then grew bolder, running her fingers up and down. "Very impressive."

He took a deep breath. "Put it on, Jas or I might come before I'm inside you."

She rolled it on then wrapped her arms around his neck. "There."

He pulled her close and kissed her again. He'd had sex before, but tonight his body burned with a different fevered passion, leaving his skin tender, vulnerable to everything about her: her scent, her lips, her body. He remembered when he was young and still allowed himself to feel, he'd climbed a tree enjoying the scent of wet bark and the gentle whisper of leaves and at that moment he had felt he belonged. That it was okay to be alive. That if he could meld his body into its trunk he could live forever.

He felt the same way now. They were one. For one night he was a man without scars, without secrets. He was a man welcomed into the revered garden of the woman he would forever cherish. With every kiss, every touch of his mouth and his hands, he told her how he loved her. Inside her he thanked her for her gift, worshipping her, seeking to fill her with pleasure. When the night began to welcome morning, he finally left the warmth inside her, his body limp with pleasure and closed his eyes.

Jessie lay wide awake barely able to breathe, afraid the man next to her might disappear. He was like a fey and bewitching form of the sky with its mystery and majesty as he lay still next to her. She had never known such ecstasy. She had not known that their physical forms could couple their souls. She had met the true Kenneth, the one without his many masks, and saw how beautiful he was. How much she loved him.

She touched his shoulder, knowing he was still awake. "Tired?" she asked.

He nodded.

"Are you okay?"

He shook his head.

She sat up alarmed. Had she overworked him or something? She leaned over him and saw his eyes were closed. "What's wrong? Are you in pain?"

He nodded. "I'm thinking of all the money I wasted when I could have just waited for you."

She relaxed. "Let's just say they kept you in good form."

He looked at her. "Did I hurt you?"

"No."

"You're okay?"

She saw the spots of blood before he did. She covered herself with the sheets embarrassed. "A little sore," she said lightly.

His eyes grew soft. "Don't be embarrassed with me okay?"

She nodded and allowed him to take the sheets.

He winced when he saw the red smudges between her legs. "Sorry about that, I got a little carried away."

She nibbled on the sensitive part of his ear. "I like when you get carried away. It's quite a ride." She glanced down and saw scattered brown beads. Her bracelet had snapped. She scooped them up and set them aside. "Unfortunately, it has left a casualty," she said.

"I'll get it fixed," he said.

He stood and went to the bathroom and came back with a warm rag and began gently wiping the blood away.

"You don't have to—"

"Shh." He kissed his way up the inside of her thigh. She watched him amazed that this beautiful man was honoring her womanhood in such a way.

"Kenneth, what are you doing?" she asked, feeling his rough check against her thigh. Her toes curled when he kissed her center.

He lifted his head. His eyes dark with a love he could never express. "I'm kissing your bruises away."

Jessie woke to the sound of papers being shuffled and the smell of Jamaican Blue Mountain coffee. She opened her eyes and saw the familiar yellow of her bedroom walls. She blinked and turned her head. Kenneth sat next to her reading, fully dressed. He looked at her then kissed her forehead. "Good morning. I have to go to work."

She tugged on his tie. "Then what are you doing here?"

"I didn't want you to wake up alone."

She rested her cheek on his thigh. "Thank you."

He stroked her hair. "You're welcome." He groaned. "Don't do that Jas. I have to go to work."

She removed her wandering hand from his leg. "Sorry."

"I put your bracelet on the side table. I tried to restring it." He stood. "Meet me for lunch at Rolland's Cafe at twelve-thirty. I'll treat you and Syrah."

He was out the door before she could reply.

Syrah had plans to see Daniel and his mother, so Jessie went to Rolland's by herself. She couldn't believe she was nervous to see him again. She tried to control the trembling hands in her lap as she sat at booth in Rolland's Cafe, but it was useless. She glanced around the cafe; it had large booths made of wood, plush seats and large windows. It was a place popular with young professionals and senior citizens with enough money to splurge.

She checked her reflection in the window, hoping she didn't have any lipstick on her teeth or that her hair wasn't a mess. She wondered if other women felt this jittery meeting their lover after a delicious night of lovemaking. She took a deep breath. Was it really lovemaking? He hadn't told her he loved her, but who cared? A night like that made up for words and she hoped his feelings for her would grow in time. She began to relax, listening to the hum of voices around her.

"Personally, I think it's all a farce," a woman said in the booth behind her. "I bet you that wedding won't even happen. I mean Kenneth doesn't even act like a man in love."

Jessie scowled, recognizing Deborah's voice.

"What do you mean?" Tracy asked.

"I mean, if a man was in love with me, he wouldn't spend every waking moment in the office. He would kiss me at every opportunity and buy me lots of gifts." Her voice lowered. "Jessie doesn't even have any jewelry or a new car."

"He gave her that necklace."

"On loan probably. You haven't seen her wear it recently, have you? And they didn't even attend Marva's party. Anybody, who's anybody, goes to Marva's parties to at least show their face. No, take my word for it, something fishy's going on."

Jessie peeked over the booth. "You know I never realized my life was so interesting. *You* never come up in any of my conversations."

Deborah jumped, dropping her fork into her salad. She rolled her eyes. "You really need to stop listening in on other people's private conversations."

Jessie narrowed her eyes. "If you stopped gossiping people won't be forced to listen in."

"I don't gossip." She dabbed the corners of her mouth with a napkin. "You and I both know that your engagement is a farce. In a few weeks your fake engagement will be over."

Jessie draped her arms over the back of the booth, showing off her stunning ring. "You're absolutely right."

Deborah tapped the table in triumph. "I knew it! He'd never marry you. It wouldn't make sense. He's an important man. He needs a woman of refined breeding, excellent manners, and superb taste in both clothes and decor. You could pass for a while then you'd probably serve caviar on a silver spoon or something."

"Yes, and that would mark him for life."

"Why the pretense?"

Jessie lowered her voice to a conspiratorial tone. "It's rather silly. I told him I wouldn't sleep with him otherwise."

She stared. "You mean you two—"

Jessie put a finger to her lips. "I'm not one to kiss and tell."

A waiter approached the table. He was young, trying unsuccessfully to grow a mustache, and his coffee skin was ruddy like a constant blush. "Was everything to your liking, ladies?" he asked, placing the bill between the plates.

"Everything is absolutely delicious," Deborah breathed, caressing the waiter with her eyes. He tugged at his collar and smiled shyly. "I'm happy to hear that." He backed away from the table, crashing into a waitress carrying a tray. She got a handle on it before it toppled then sent the waiter a disgusted glare.

Jessie shook her head. "Do you get great pleasure in turning men into doddering idiots?" She watched the poor waiter get scolded by his supervisor.

Deborah smiled. "Jealous?"

She straightened her ring. "I have no need to be."

Her lips thinned. "I don't believe you."

"I really don't care what you believe. I've come to learn that the word of a Wester is as nourishing as acid."

Deborah opened her mouth then closed it. "You're pathetic. This is America. Unless you're a Kennedy or the child of some celebrity nobody gives a damn about your name. Besides you certainly have nothing to brag about. Your father was nothing but a strange man who fixed jewelry and your mother was a pseudo-socialite who helped the poor. You can sleep with the Kenneth's of this world and they'll enjoy you for awhile like most men do." She raised a brow. "I don't know if you know this, but lying down doesn't mean you'll climb up the ladder."

Jessie swallowed, but said nothing.

"Oh and *if* you do happen to convince Kenneth to marry you, perhaps Aunt Rhonda will give you the pendant as a wedding present."

Jessie opened her mouth to tell her where the pendant could go, when Kenneth approached the table.

He looked handsome in a gray shirt and black trousers. He appeared so carefree and dashing; Jessie wondered if she had dreamed last night. "Hello ladies."

"Oh, hello Kenneth," Deborah cooed. "Your *fiancée* was just talking about you."

He glanced at Jessie. "All good things I hope."

"The best of course," Deborah said. She abruptly stood. "I'll see you around." She grabbed the bill then left with Tracy trailing behind.

Kenneth slid in next to Jessie. "What did she say?"

"The usual."

He rested his arm behind her head. "Want to tell me about it?"

A jewelry maker and pseudo-socialite? She blinked back tears of anger. "I don't know why I allow her to get to me."

He gently massaged the back of her neck, sensing her controlled fury. "What happened?"

"I told her that the engagement was a fake and that you'd only said it so I'd sleep with you. She found that harder to believe than a real engagement."

"So what?" He pulled her fingers from her mouth. "Stop biting your nails. If you need something to nibble on, you can nibble on me or some food."

She pushed Deborah from her mind. "Your ear looks very tasty, but I'd prefer to look at the menu." She kissed his cheek. "I'll have you for an afternoon snack."

His arm fell to her waist. He brought her close. "You shouldn't tease a man when he's hungry." He kissed behind her ear.

"Kenneth stop," she demanded when he began kissing her neck. "They could kick us out of here for lascivious behavior."

He grinned. "You call this lascivious behavior? I hear the ghost of your mother's upbringing. Let me show you lascivious behavior." His hand inched its way up her blouse.

She pinched his arm, hard.

He jerked away. "Ow!"

"I think you need to move your seat until you learn how to keep your hands to yourself."

He playfully pouted and took the seat in front of her. "I suppose the lesson can wait."

"Yes. Right now I'm starving." She stared pointedly at the menu not seeing a thing. She couldn't believe she was here with him. In this fancy restaurant, flirting with him as if they'd been lovers all their lives and that last night he had...Heat rushed to her face at the memory. No it couldn't have been real.

"Jasmine."

She glanced up from her menu to see him watching her from the top of his, his brown eyes bright with amusement.

"Yes?"

"It was real." He winked then disappeared behind his menu.

Chapter Twenty-six

Days of bliss followed nights of pleasure. Sensing the new tender feelings between them, Syrah and Freda were often absent. This morning was no different. Kenneth watched Jessie prepare her tea. It had become routine for her to wake early and sit with him before he left for work. She was not a morning person, but sat with him anyway while her dark eyes clung to sleep, and her soft mouth in a pout like a toddler woken too soon. Kenneth didn't care. He treasured these moments, the early sunlight crawling through the windows, splashing across the red-brown on the table and the bright chirping of birds.

"Jasmine, will you marry me?"

She burnt her tongue on her tea and swore. She put the cup down and stared at him incredulous. "Did you just ask me to marry you?"

He nodded.

She began to laugh until she realized he was serious. "You want to marry me for *real*?"

He nodded again.

Jessie waited for the rush of overwhelming joy. The man she loved, the man she'd once placed all her hopes and dreams on, wanted to marry her. Wanted her to be his wife. In place of the expected joy was fear. A fear she couldn't quite name. She looked at him knowing he was waiting for an answer.

"Do you want children?"

He hesitated. She saw a longing that he quickly hid. He wanted to be a Dad, but feared his past prevented it. "You don't think that's fair?" he asked.

"I do think you should have kids, but what if they end up looking like me?" She stopped, recognizing how absurd the statement sounded. His jaw twitched. "If you don't want to marry me just say so, but don't start thinking up ridiculous excuses."

She flashed a sly grin. "Well, you have to think about it. Would you really want a little me running around the house?"

He didn't smile. "Yeah."

"Hmm." She bit her lip. Why did she feel this doubt? With him she felt beautiful and powerful and courageous. She glanced down at the ring on her finger. She had the chance to make the meaning of this symbol real. But could she be his wife, the mother of his children? What if she failed to be what he needed? She looked up at him and noticed he was too still. She kicked him. "Breathe."

"I'm waiting for an answer," he said in a tight voice.

Jessie chewed her bottom lip. "Oh."

"Does that mean yes?"

She saw a woodpecker whiz past their window. She smiled. "Do bras fly?"

He nodded slowly then stood. "Okay, I'll see you when I get home." He walked to the door then halted. He spun around and Jessie nearly laughed at the expression on his face. "Did you just say yes?"

She nodded.

He came to her and rested his hands on the table. "Say it."

"Say what?"

"Yes."

She grinned.

He waited.

"Yes, I will marry you. Yes, I will have children with you." She stood and wrapped her arms around his neck. "Yes. Yes. Yes."

Thank you. Kenneth held her close. He didn't realize he hadn't said the words aloud. He closed his eyes and held her close. Praying. Pleading. Hoping he could keep this happiness, that nothing would take this joy away from him, he was close to living the path reserved for other men. He brushed his lips against her forehead. How he loved her and she was going to belong to him. Be his to claim. He was redeemed. She would not blame him for his secrets, did not despise him his cowardice. She would carry his name and share his life when he'd thought he'd always be alone.

Jessie bit her lip to keep from giggling. She wanted to laugh, cry, scream, dance. Joy was finally breaking through, brushing away all doubts, all fears. It mingled with the love she felt for the man in her arms. She was strong, she was brave, she was beautiful, she was his and he was hers.

He drew away and looked at her. "Are you crying?"

Her chin trembled. "I'm trying not to laugh."

"You think this is funny?"

"I think it's hilarious. I mean you and me, married?"

He grinned. "I know how you feel."

Freda walked into the room as they stared at each other like kids up to mischief. "What are you two up to?"

"Jasmine's going to marry me."

"The whole county knows you're engaged. Are you just finding that out?"

Kenneth and Jessie looked at each other and laughed.

Leticia ignored the filet in front of her, her fingers stroking a wineglass. It always amazed her how even candlelight could not soften the blow of disappointment. Kenneth had barely spoken, that wasn't unusual, but the sadness was gone. There was a happiness in him that kept her mesmerized, as if a filter had been removed and she now saw a clear image of him, and at that moment she realized why she didn't want to lose him.

"Is this goodbye?" she asked casually.

He glanced up surprised then chagrined, but his joy quickly replaced the expression. "I'm going to be married."

She tightened her hold on the glass. "Congratulations."

"I had to see you and say goodbye and thank you."

She frowned. "Thank me?"

"This." He gestured to the room then his gaze fell on her. "And you allowed me to dream when I thought I had nothing."

She felt her throat constrict and shrugged his compliment aside. "You paid for it."

He covered her hand. "I know what we had meant nothing to you, and would be considered immoral and crude to the world, but you were one of the few things that kept me from feeling numb." He dug in his coat pocket and pulled out an envelope. He pushed it across the table. "I want you to take this. Put it towards your retirement. May you find your way to Rome."

Leticia had never been speechless—she had a hustler's affinity with words—but for once her mind was blank, filled with something much more: compassion. She knew all her love could not have healed his wounds the way this nameless woman had. He deserved his joy.

He stood and kissed her cheeks. One kiss causing heartache, one giving hope. Then he walked out of her life as simply as he had walked in all those years ago. She ran her hand over the red tablecloth, her mind setting itself. She would not be selfish this time. She wouldn't threaten to tell anyone. She would let him go.

She called Jack. "I want you to forget all that you uncovered on Kenneth Preston."

He laughed an ugly, dirty sound. "Sorry, babe, but what I found out about him is too good to forget."

"I've got money, if that's what you want."

"Wait a minute, what's going on? You getting soft on me in your old age? Blackmailing clients has always been our claim to fame, baby. It's the way we do things. You know that."

"He's different."

"Yes, bigger game."

"I'm warning you, Jack."

His tone hardened. "I suggest you don't, Leticia. You might get hurt." He hung up.

Leticia gripped the phone, feeling bile rise up her throat. She ran to the toilet, losing her meal. Her life had caught up with her. She had finally found one man who had truly cared for her and she had created a plan that was about to destroy him.

Kenneth stretched out on the bed and smiled at Jasmine as she stared at the chess board. He had never realized how dark and masculine his bedroom furniture was until Jasmine came into it. Draped in her platinum nightdress, she added a softness the room had never seen, and the sweet smell of her lotion clung to the sheets and drifted towards him while a standing lamp they'd bought kept the evening darkness at bay. "Why don't you just move a piece so I can beat you?" he said.

"Be quiet."

He yawned.

She frowned at him. "I'm not taking that long."

He glanced at his watch. "I suppose a half hour is adequate time."

"It has not been that long." She studied the board then made a move.

He quickly beat her--again.

"You play with your emotions," he said.

He went on to describe how she could win, she vaguely heard him. Chess had never been her game, but she played because he enjoyed it so much. She was happy, yet something was missing. Somehow the Sapphire Pendant still called to her, especially in quiet moments like this. Not with warning shouts or bells, but as a whisper—a calm plea. She could not deny the fact that she still wanted it, not with the desperation that had driven her in the past, but with a deep desire that was unexplainable. She pushed the thought aside and set the pieces back in place. He took her arm and slid something on her wrist. She looked down and saw a bracelet of glass beads. "Kenneth, you must stop giving me gifts." He'd made it almost a habit to surprise her: a basket of chocolate chips, earrings, perfume. Something about it worried her, as if he were constantly trying to please her.

"I like to give you gifts."

"And I like getting them but—"

He pressed a finger against her lips. "Do me a favor?"

"What?"

He held her hand. "Do a reading for me."

"It's late."

"It's not that late and you have the stones here. Please."

She hesitated.

"Are you afraid of what you might read?"

Jessie chewed her bottom lip. It was silly to be this apprehensive. What harm could there be in a simple reading? She nodded. "Okay, I'll do it."

A few moments later they sat facing each other with a black velvet cloth on the table and the nine stones Kenneth had selected. Jessie stared at them. She didn't like what she saw. She knew stones were only a vehicle for her intuition, but the sight of the nine stones—from the rich red of a jasper stone to the tiger's eye—filled her with dread. She didn't like the shapes he had chosen or the way he had positioned them.

"What do you see?" he asked in a whisper.

She saw devastating betrayal, hurt, anger and aloneness, which could either mean freedom or isolation, she didn't know. She regretted playing this game.

"Well?"

She began to bite her nails then stopped herself. He looked so eager and happy, how could she douse that joy when he had struggled to gain it for so long? "I see many changes in your life," she said vaguely. "You're going to have to make a lot of decisions. It will be difficult, at first, but you'll succeed at the end."

He nodded satisfied. "Good that means the August meeting should go well. Do you see anything else? Anything specific?"

She swallowed. "Someone close will betray you."

A tense silence filled the room. Kenneth broke it by letting out a deep breath. "Well, that's good to know. Don't look like that, Jasmine. I know how to look out for myself." He pushed his chair from the table then patted his lap. "Come here."

She sat on his lap.

"Now let me read your future. I read palms by the way, bet you didn't know that." He held her hand and trailed one of the lines on her palm. "Interesting. I see that you're going to marry a very intelligent, handsome man."

She gasped alarmed. "Oh no! I'm not marrying you?"

He ignored her.

"And you're going to make beautiful jewelry that sells around the world and make your husband very proud." He held her in a warm embrace, but inside she felt cold. "There's nothing to worry about. Together we can face anything."

That was the problem. She didn't see herself in his future. Had she misread the stones? Had she somehow confused her own insecurities with the reading? She could never imagine leaving his side, but something told her she would. She saw him alone. Why? *Why?*

Kenneth didn't give her much time to wonder. He effectively diverted her attention when he kissed her neck then everywhere else. Hours later they lay in each others arm. Kenneth absently stroked her thigh as he stared up at the ceiling.

"I'm hosting my annual summer barbecue next week. You'll be co-host."

"Why?"

He squeezed her hand. "We're engaged remember?"

She rubbed her face against his palm. "Always, but I don't like crowds."

"You'll like this crowd. Besides it will look good to have you there."

"And appearance means everything, right?"

"The Preston credo. You'll do fine."

She chewed her lip. "I hope so. How big will this barbecue be?"

"Don't worry. It won't be big at all."

He was wrong. Cars poured down the long drive, spilling onto the street, as the sun blew its hot breath, soaking the air in a humid heat. It didn't stop the crowd from enjoying itself, however. The kitchen swelled with the aroma of cool, sweet lemonade and sorrel, fruit salad and various casseroles. The backyard entertained a volleyball game, the living room held a mix of characters in a debate on the economic position of various countries and the family room became gossip central. Jessie found solace behind a tree.

She had remained cordial long enough, maintaining a smile even when a clumsy man bumped into her

"What are you doing behind here?" Michelle asked, peeking around the tree.

Jessie glared at her. "Hiding."

"The day is too hot to worry. Why don't you relax and try to enjoy yourself?"

"It's against my nature."

"At least you're not the only one who looks ridiculous," she said, catching a glimpse of Rodney who'd been following Brooke's every move all day.

Jessie shrugged. "Ah leave him alone, he's young."

"And he doesn't have a chance." Michelle glanced towards the house. "I still can't believe you're getting married."

"Me neither."

"I can," Wendy said, joining them. "He loves you so much. I've seen the way he looks at you."

"When you're not hiding behind trees, of course," Michelle added.

Jessie scowled. "I can't believe he invited Deborah and Tracy."

"They're nothing," Wendy assured her. "Deborah's so angry she could scream."

Jessie tugged on her collar. "It's probably because her skin is frying in this heat."

Wendy grabbed her arm. "Come on, your husband is looking for you."

"He's not my husband yet."

"No harm in practicing."

They found Kenneth talking to Nathan. Stephanie stood close by.

Wendy said, "I found her behind a tree." She suddenly began to speak French and Kenneth responded in kind. She then said something that brought color to his cheeks.

"I took French and didn't understand a word of that," Stephanie said.

Wendy grinned. "That's because it's French with an island twist." She winked at Kenneth, smiled at Jessie then left.

Jessie looked at him. "What did she say?"

He cleared his throat. "Never mind."

"How can you wear that shirt?" Stephanie asked. "It's hot enough to melt iron."

Nathan said, "Personally, I hope it gets hot enough even the women take their tops off."

Jessie frowned. "Nice of you to keep this on a wholesome level."

Syrah ran up to her. "I have to talk to you."

She excused herself and went up to Syrah's bedroom. Once there she asked, "What's wrong?"

"Uncle's going to send me back," Syrah said in panic.

"No—"

"He is! I heard grandma talking about me." Her eyes grew wide and she wrung her hands. "How he wants me out of the way once you're married."

Jessie knelt in front of her. "He said no such thing."

"Is he going to let me stay? Can Dad come and get me? I'm not going back. I'm not!"

She held her shoulder, calming her. She met Syrah's eyes, her voice steady. "We know, Syrah."

Syrah stared stunned, a series of emotions distorting her face then she fell into tears.

She drew her close. "It's all right. It's not your fault. You're safe now."

Syrah hugged her tight wanting to stop her tears but unable to. "He hates me. I don't want to go back."

She wiped her tears with a handkerchief. "You won't have to. We'll take care of you."

Kenneth knocked on the door and entered. "Is everything all right?"

Jessie stood. "Syrah's scared you were sending her back. She's worried her father will come and get her. I think we should call child protection services."

"Absolutely not," he said. "This is a family issue."

"When a man hits a child, the matter goes way beyond family."

"I can't afford the publicity."

Jessie rested a hand on her hip and rolled her eyes. "Oh, I'm sorry. I forgot all about the importance of appearances."

Kenneth's eyes darkened. "The Preston name has never had a scandal and it won't start with me."

She threw her hand up exasperated. "So what are you going to do if he won't let you adopt her? Send her back so everything looks good?"

"I will handle Eddie in the best possible manner."

Jessie's temper snapped. She glared at him. "He's an abusive drunk that should be publicly flogged!"

Kenneth's voice grew softer. "He is my brother. A Preston. That name cannot be tarnished."

"At what price?"

"You know the importance of a name."

"Not to this extent."

"It's all I have," he said in a harsh, raw voice. "The only thing of value anyone has ever given me. Mr. Preston gave us his name to honor and protect and I won't do anything to jeopardize that. He's my father and I won't disgrace him. You of all people should understand."

She did understand. She understood that this wasn't about Syrah or Eddie, it was about them—her. It was about whether she was ready to live under the burden of the Preston name. If she married him, she would pledge to become part of his secrets, his deceptions and be forced to wear the same mask he did.

She would have to sit and watch him spoil his mother, a woman who made no effort to hide her abhorrence for him. She would have to witness him protect a brother that used him and deal with the other relations in his life without saying a word. As much as she loved him, she knew she could not do that. She would only fail him and ultimately shame him. Jessie pulled his ring from her finger. "I can't protect your lies, Kenneth. I can't live for the sake of approval and constantly wear a mask under the burden of a name." She held the ring out. "I can't marry you."

Kenneth glanced at his niece. "Ace would you excuse us?"

She nodded then raced out of the room. Kenneth closed the door after her. He kept his voice soft. "I know you're angry, but don't punish me this way."

Jessie's temper slipped into sorrow. "I'm not punishing you. I realize we're too different."

Pain filled his eyes, but his voice remained firm. "Jasmine, don't—"

"I'm freeing you. I'd make you a terrible wife. I'm too honest. It's a Clifton curse and my conscious would get the best of me until I began to despise you for making me become something I'm not."

"I'm not trying to change you."

"What am I supposed to do when I see him? Am I supposed to

pretend nothing's happened? How about your mother who treats you with such contempt? Am I supposed to stand idly by and watch her mistreat you?"

"Isn't there anything in the Clifton past you wouldn't want people to know?"

"No. Nothing." She took a step back, ready to leave.

He reached out and pulled her to him. "Darling."

She closed her eyes, her heart responding to the tender word.

"Please, try to understand. It may be a struggle at first, but you won't need to be involved. I'll handle everything." He smoothed her hair then lightly stroked her face. With each gentle touch she felt herself weakening. "I'll take care of things."

"You can't handle this alone."

"With you by my side I won't be alone."

"I want to be by your side, but I know that I will jeopardize your secrets." Jessie lifted his hand and placed the ring in his palm, closing his fingers over it. "I can't marry you." She brought his hand to her lips. "I'm sorry."

"Don't do this," it was a quiet, primitive plea.

I'm afraid. I'm afraid. I'll fail you. She stared down at his hand unable to look at him. "I'm sorry," she said again then opened the door.

Syrah stood there with her hands balled into fists at her side. "Aunt Jessie you can't leave 'cause of me."

Jessie cupped her chin. "It's not you, we'll still be friends."

Her chin trembled. "It's not the same. Please don't leave."

Jessie felt tears sting her eyes, her heart constricted with a pain that was suffocating in its intensity. She ran out of the room.

Syrah turned to her uncle, tears of anger and despair falling down her cheeks. "You have to make her come back."

Kenneth sat on the bed, forcing himself to breathe, though he felt as if Jessie had ripped out a vital organ, leaving him hollow. He gathered his pain and tucked it away. All that mattered now was Syrah. "I can't."

"This is Grandma's fault. She knows about Daddy and doesn't care."

He covered his eyes. *His mother knew?* "Go tell Nathan that the party's over."

"What about Aunt Jessie?" Syrah asked. When he didn't reply, she turned and left, dragging her feet.

A half hour later, Kenneth forced himself to come downstairs and found his mother clearing up napkins and used glasses on the coffee table. He had explained that straightening up was the job of the cleaning crew, but she never listened.

"Did you know Ace had bruises on her back?" he asked her.

She paused then continued to clean.

"Tell me you didn't know about it. Tell me that you didn't know that her back is covered with bruises, just like mine. Tell me that this is all one huge surprise and that you're heartbroken and sickened by it." He swallowed, a part of him hoping she would.

She kept her eyes lowered. "Kenneth--"

He clenched his jaw. "You knew and you didn't tell me? How could you have watched me take care of Eddie, knowing what he was doing to her?"

"I didn't want to believe it."

"You didn't want to believe it and that meant it didn't exist, right?" He rested his hands on the back of the couch and closed his eyes. "How does it feel to be there? To be in that comfortable shroud of denial?"

"Try to understand, do." His mother touched his arm in a fleeting gesture.

He moved away, holding up his hands to fend her off. "Don't touch me." He took a deep breath. "Just explain to me why he's still your favorite. Why you would do anything to protect him. I'm the one who pays for your holidays, buys you gifts, and never gets into trouble. I'm the one who loves you." He lowered his voice. "I'd do anything for you."

"I'm proud of you, but Eddie has always been so lost. He's never had your strengths or your talents."

"He has his own, which he's never taken the time to develop. Did you know Jessie gave up her scholarship for him?"

"He tries so hard, but he's weak like I used to be. His heart is good."

Kenneth couldn't believe what she was saying. "How can you compare yourself to him? He acts just like—" He couldn't finish. "Why do you care about Eddie more than me?"

Her eyes turned to stone. "Because you look like *him*. You look like that man who crushed my soul and left me as empty as a dried well. Oh, the joy I felt when you moved out cannot be shared." Her lips tightened, her voice sharpened with bitterness. "Sometimes when I see that charming, handsome face of yours I want to slap it. It's so cool, so deceptive. I watch the women throw themselves at you as I once had not knowing the evil behind your smile. You took me young and fed me with lies, all which I believed."

Kenneth picked up a glass and threw it against the wall. It shattered, falling to the floor like icicles. "You're talking to me!" He pounded his chest, trying to break the hateful glare she directed at him. "I'm not him! I'm me, your son."

"You've even got his temper," she sneered. "That blaze of anger that lashes out like a whip. I can see it in your face now."

He could feel it too. He could feel a white-hot fury storm up his back and tighten his hands into fists. He could not speak, the muscles in this throat constricting. To his mother he could never be anything but that man's mirror, and there was no way to alter that.

"A snake can't escape its fate no matter how pretty it is," she said.

"But I'm still your son."

"You're not my son! You're the bastard of some teenage slut your father met before me. I only looked after you because I loved him. When I left him, I knew there was no one else for you. I was the only mother you knew. It was only Christian that I look after you. And I had to watch you succeed at everything my baby failed at...It was hard to pray to a god who was so unfair."

Kenneth stood still, afraid if he moved he'd collapse into dust. *Breathe, breathe, breathe.* "You're not my mother?"

Only she had ever heard that particular note of despair in his tone. He'd used it once before when he'd asked her why his daddy hated him. It reached through her painful memories and awakened her. The horrible realization of what she had done struck her full force. Her eyes widened. "Kenneth, I'm sorry." She touched his hand.

He leaped back as if she had burned him. His eyes darkened and his voice became as dangerous as a viper. "Never touch me again. Ever." He spun on his heel and stormed into the kitchen. His stepfather stood near the door.

"I'm not the enemy," Charles said, taking in his son's murderous glare. "Sit down."

"I can't talk right now."

"Fine, then just listen." He pulled out a chair and sat down. "I couldn't help overhearing what your mother said."

His throat burned. "She's not my mother."

"Be still." Charles smoothed out his mustache. "I've always known about your father. I forced your mother to tell me about him one day when I discovered a letter he'd sent her."

Kenneth's stormy expression didn't change.

"I met him. Yes." He nodded. "Pierre Chevalier was an impressive figure. I let him talk about himself then gave him money to get out of our lives. That day I took claim of you. You became my son." He wiped his glasses with a handkerchief. "I've seen you rage and I've seen you calm. I know you. You're nothing like the man I met." He placed the glasses back on his face. "Perhaps you have some similar facial characteristics, but that man had no heart, his eyes were soulless. In you I see a man haunted by shadows that don't need to exist. You're my son and I raised you to be compassionate and giving. I was glad when you moved out."

Kenneth turned away. "You too?"

"Because your mother and your brother were not good for you. Eddie uses his past as an excuse for failure and your mother uses it as a crutch for guilt. It's not right, but it's the way it is." His voice became firm. "You're nothing like him."

"I have his hands," Kenneth said, looking down at his own.

"Funny, I always thought they looked like mine," he said, resting his own large hands on the table.

Kenneth sat down, acknowledging the similarity.

Charles shifted awkwardly in his chair. "This is hard for a man to admit, but I think it's something you need to know." He cleared his throat. "Matilda is a beautiful woman, but that's not the reason I married her. I took one look at you and wanted you as my own."

Kenneth glanced down, embarrassed by the sudden tears that moistened his eyes. "No, don't say that."

Charles continued. "I wanted that fiery, intelligent young boy to carry my name. I knew he would make me proud. What I didn't expect was that he'd make me love him like my own flesh and blood."

"Don't," Kenneth whispered in a choked voice. He held his hands together and continued to stare at the tabletop, hoping his father would stop so he wouldn't embarrass them both.

Charles grabbed his hands. "No matter your mother, no matter your father in the eyes of God and the law you belong to me. You are a Preston, claim it, own it, it is your right. The blood of the spirit flows mightier than the blood of the flesh and that's what we have. A spiritual bonding." His voice shook with feeling. "You are my son."

Kenneth shut his eyes. He wanted to speak, but his throat wouldn't let words past.

Charles understood the unspoken words. He squeezed Kenneth's hands then stood.

Once his father left the room, Kenneth rested his head on his arms and began to weep, his entire body aching from a pain so deep he didn't know its cause. It clawed at his wounds and ripped at his scars. He continued to weep until the pain subsided, dissipating into a vow to continue to honor his father's name, too make him proud. Soon he cried for what the vow would cost him—his heart, his love, his life. And on the other side of the wall, an old man cried with him.

Jack ducked as a potentially lethal high heel sailed by his head.

Brooke glared at him. "How could you steal the wrong bracelet?!" she shrieked.

He held up his hands in surrender. "It was the one she was wearing."

She tapped her foot with impatience. "Perhaps Stephanie was right and it wasn't the same one."

"I told you I saw a girl wearing a similar bracelet at the ice cream shop. I think it was her. She must have switched them. I wasn't really paying attention. I just took whatever she wore."

"Oh, shut up," she snapped. "I wish you had warned me about your stupidity before I hired you."

Jack smoothed down his hair, letting the insult slide off him. "Watch it honey, I'm not the one in trouble here. You better hope she doesn't open it."

Brooke narrowed her eyes. "That's not your concern."

"Be careful. Luck only lasts for so long."

"Only idiots wait for luck. I make it myself." She took off her other shoe and sat. She pulled her face into a pout. It wasn't fair that there were so many obstacles to getting the bracelet back. It wasn't as though she hadn't earned it. She'd planned everything so well.

"Why don't you just ask for it back?"

"Because I don't like getting my hands dirty." She'd learned early it was best to get other people to do your work for you. It was easier to come out clean that way. You can always lie afterwards. At least her psychological campaign was working with Rodney. Soon Nathan's head would be on the chopping block and then they'd have to deal with something more.

It was good to keep them busy. They might decide to sell, but no she wouldn't give them that opportunity. She wanted them out--gone.

"Too bad your ad didn't work like Mrs. Ostick's did."

She scowled. She wished people wouldn't talk when she was thinking. "What about her?"

"She'd lost her broach remember? Preston's niece returned it to her."

Brooke jumped to her feet. "Shit!"

Jack watched her wary unsure if he'd given her good news or bad.

She swore again and stomped her foot. "God was giving me a sign and I completely missed it." She pointed a finger at him. "Did you find anything else about Kenneth?"

He rubbed his nose. He'd dug up dirt about Preston and found some things he didn't think any man should have revealed. He'd make a lot more money through blackmail. "You know what you told me about him already sounded pretty explosive."

She tapped her foot.

He cleared his throat. "Yes, I found some things," he said vaguely. He quickly thought of a reason not to tell her. "But I promised Leticia I'd give it to her."

"Let me assure you that I can pay a lot more than some whore can."

"Do you want to blackmail him too?"

"No. We're going to write up a little story." She trailed a finger along his jaw. "Try to remember back to your journalism days when you were fired for shady ethics."

Jack hesitated already reading her mind. "Preston's a real respected person. I don't think we need to take this to the papers."

Brooke fluttered her lashes. "I'm sorry. Did I ask for your opinion?"

"How do you know *The Journal* will print it?"

"Give them the right hook and they'll print anything."

"Remember this is Randall County one of the richest counties in Maryland. We have an image to maintain and like to protect our own."

"Kenneth isn't one of our own. They'll print it and that will get the ball rolling. The other papers will follow like lemmings."

"You have no guarantee that--"

"I will make sure that it's in *The Journal's* best interest to print the story. I know they enjoy their business. It would be very inconvenient if their advertising revenue suddenly dried up."

Jack still felt uneasy. "His dirt might fly out and hit you. I know about--"

She began to smile. He knew that was a bad sign. "You're beginning to get on my nerves," she said softly.

"I just—"

Her smile widened. "I don't want to hear your voice anymore. Just write. Don't think, just write." Her voice hardened. "And only what I tell you."

He sighed and nodded.

She patted him on the cheek then turned. It was going to give Kenneth a one-two punch: one article to set him up and the other to knock him out.

Chapter Twenty-seven

Kenneth stared at the computer screen, seeing nothing. A feminine voice broke into his thoughts. "You have a lovely office."

He turned to Olivia, he'd scheduled to take her to lunch, but he'd forgotten she was there. Of course, if he had been in his right mind, that would have been impossible. She was a painting of perfection. Her rich, dark hair was pulled back from her beautiful honey face. Her light red blouse shifted with every graceful movement. She was gracious in every thing she did, following all social etiquette.

They were alike in many ways, which helped to create an instant affinity between them. They both knew the power of a mask and its many purposes. However, he could sense his mask cracking, years of wear causing fissures. He also wondered if he were losing his mind. Nothing could quell his haunting thoughts--words he could have said, things he could have done to stop Jasmine from leaving him. His mind had become his relentless tormentor and there weren't enough Beethoven symphonies to drown it out.

"Thank you," he said absently.

"I've really appreciated the time you've given me."

Their conversations were always like this: kind, cordial, empty. "It has been my pleasure."

He could feel Olivia watching him and see the family resemblance in her dark eyes. Or maybe he just imagined seeing Jasmine in her face. "What happened with Jessie?" she asked.

"I'm sure you've received an explanation."

Olivia moved her hand in an impatient motion. "But you love her and she loves you."

Then why did she leave? Why didn't she trust him to take care of everything? Why didn't she love him enough. "Livy, let's say that you fell in love with a welder."

She wrinkled her nose. "Okay."

"How would your family respond?"

"They'd be horrified."

"But you love him, right?"

"Yes, but I have to consider other factors like class distinction. We both know that can cause as much of a rift as culture. But you and Jessie don't have that problem. You're of the same culture and class status."

"But as you said there are other factors."

Olivia fell quiet, reading his eyes: love was not enough.

Nathan burst into the room. He slammed the door behind him and stormed towards the desk. "We've got a problem."

His serious tone gave Kenneth no chance to tease him about his dramatic entrance. "What is it?"

"Some files are missing." He jangled change in his pocket. "Basically our receivable ones."

Kenneth swore.

"What's wrong?" Olivia asked baffled by the tension that had entered the room.

"Sit down, Nate," Kenneth ordered. "And stop jangling your change, you're annoying me."

Nathan slid into a chair. "This could bankrupt us."

Olivia stared at them. Nathan looked like a man headed for the electric chair; Kenneth pensive. "Again, what's going on?" she asked.

"Our accounts receivable files are missing," Kenneth explained.

"Basically our lifeblood," Nathan said.

"That file provides us with a complete listing of our customers."

Olivia nodded. "And?"

"And records of money owed are in these files."

"So with the file missing you can't know who owes what," she clarified. "Therefore you can't send out bills."

Nathan again jangled change in his pocket. "Basically, we're thrown on the mercy of our customers, like chickens at the mercy of a fox. I knew things were too good."

Kenneth leaned back in his chair and sent Olivia a look of regret. "Could you please excuse us?"

She nodded and left.

He returned his attention to Nathan. "Calm down. It's expected. It's the second law of thermodynamics."

Nathan stared at him. "What?"

"'The entropy of the universe tends to a maximum.'"

"And I thought English was my first language," Nathan muttered disgusted.

"Entropy is a measure of the total disorder, randomness or chaos in a system," Kenneth explained with grave patience. "The natural way the world works is to go from a state of order to disorder. Fortunately, I prepare for chaos and consequently have a back up system."

Nathan sat up. "You have another file?"

"Yes."

Kenneth looked so sure of himself, so in control, Nathan had a childish impulse to shock him. "Looks like you've done it again Mr. Boss, but I've got another problem for you."

"What?"

"How do you catch a thief?"

Kenneth frowned. "A thief?"

"Yes, someone's been stealing cycles." The time slices on computers that are used to run programs. "My guess is that someone is using the computer lab stations. Those computers sit idle a lot of the time. Someone has been breaking into the password system and using the computers without permission. I think the time is being distributed for commercial purposes."

"How long do you think this has been going on?" Kenneth asked.

"Over a month or two. Hours of computer time have been taken. About eighty thousand dollars."

Kenneth nodded. "Has Rodney found anything?"

"He's working on it."

"The board is not going to like this."

"Trust me. We'll find him."

"Then go ahead. I leave the task to you." Kenneth turned to his computer. "Tell Olivia to come back in."

Nathan jumped to his feet, rubbing his hands together with excitement over the challenge and responsibility. "I will. Thanks." He left.

Olivia entered. "Is everything okay?"

"No."

"Then how can you be so calm?" She frowned. "Aren't you concerned? Someone may be sabotaging the company."

"Nathan will handle it."

"That's very generous of you to let him figure out—"

"I think I know who it is."

"Who is it?"

"When Nathan comes back with the results, I will confirm or disregard my theory. I knew there was something wrong when the programmers complained about unreasonable delays in running their programs. It was as simple as connecting the dots."

Olivia wrinkled her nose. "Oh."

"You don't sound pleased."

"Did you tell Nathan?"

"No."

"You should have told him what you suspected."

Kenneth rubbed his chin. "Nathan wants responsibility and I gave it to him."

"But you're deceiving him. That's not very nice."

He sent her a glance. "I never claimed to be."

Olivia rested her hands on the desk. "You can only be in control for so long, Kenneth. One day your time is going to run out."

"I won't be blamed for someone else's failures. It's imperative that I'm on top of everything. You're a clever woman, I'm sure you understand."

"Of course I understand," she said sadly. "I understand that you trust nobody and therefore nobody can trust you."

Syrah stood in Jessie's empty room, the shadow of trees falling across the bed and sweeping the ground. She wanted to scream and break things. It was all her fault Aunt Jessie had to leave. Soon Uncle would send her back. She sat on the bed and saw the beaded bracelet she'd given Jessie on the side table. She picked it up. The beads slid off the string and dropped on the table. She gathered them up and saw one was slightly cracked. She pried it open and her heart began to race. She finally knew why the beads sounded like maracas: they were filled with diamonds.

"You have to go to the police," Daniel said when she showed him. His mother had gone to work so he and Syrah were alone in his apartment. Light rain fell outside, while the clouds cast a gray hue over the sad little place.

Syrah clutched the sock that held her treasure. "But these are mine. I found them. Don't you see?" Her voice grew eager. "You could move out of this place and I could take care of myself." She shook the sock. "These things will solve all our problems."

"No." Daniel pushed his glasses to the bridge of his nose and shook his head. "Diamonds are not put into bracelets for decoration. They could belong to some mafia group who's selling them on the black market. They could be part of an illegal shipment headed for Europe. Or it could be the loot of some international jewel thieves."

Syrah tugged on her cap and scowled. "You watch too many movies."

"I don't like this at all."

She shifted her position on the lumpy mattress. "Fine. Then you don't have to enjoy them with me."

His eyes slid away. "I can't let you enjoy them either."

She paused. "What?"

"Where did you get the bracelet?"

"I found it."

His eyes caught hers. "Then someone might be looking for it and you as well."

"No one's looking for it. They never placed an ad, so now it's mine."

"It's too dangerous for you to keep it." Daniel studied her face, his eyes sharp behind his glasses. "Who did you steal it from?"

"I didn't steal it."

He adjusted his frames, his eyes never wavering.

"I don't know," she said finally.

"Yes, you do."

She sighed annoyed. "It was at my uncle's office. I think it was Ms. Stephanie's. She came by the house saying she'd lost it."

"I don't want you to get hurt."

"What's wrong with you?" Syrah took off her cap then slammed it back on. "I'm not going to get hurt. Nobody knows I have it. You said it's good to hope. Well, hoping is over. We can do something now. You can find your Dad. Now, do you want some or not?"

Temptation flashed in his eyes. Daniel glanced around the apartment, his thoughts nearly audible. He turned to her, his voice soft. "I once saw a guy beaten to death for his jacket. Someone will do something worse for these, Syrah. I can't let anything happen to you." He touched her hand. "You have to—"

She snatched her hand away. "You're not my damn babysitter, so don't worry about it."

"Tell the police."

"I'm not going to the police."

He held out his hand. "Then I will."

She kept the sock close, her anxiety rising at the determination in his eyes. "You can't. I'll hide them."

His gaze remained steady.

Tears of rage filled her eyes; he knew too much to let her get away with it. She'd told him things that he could use against her. She'd thought he was her friend.

She jumped to her feet trembling. "I hate you," she spat out. "I hate you more than anyone I've ever known. You don't know anything about life. You think life is about being true and honest and good, but you're wrong!"

Daniel stood, placing a hand on her shoulder. "It's the right thing to do."

Syrah backed away from him. She hated how big he was, she hated feeling weak. She lunged at him and pounded him on the chest with her fists. "You're a big bully—a nothing!" He grimaced but didn't fight back; she hated him more for letting her hurt him. "This is my best chance to survive and you don't even care. I hate you. I wish I'd never met you. I wish we'd never been friends." She threw the sock at him. "And I hope your father never comes back." She stormed away, wiping away tears. She shoved people aside as she marched to the bus stop. Suddenly, someone grabbed her arm and spun her around.

Daniel held out the sock. "Take it."

Syrah yanked her arm free. "I thought you were taking it to the police."

"I was going to because I cared about you, but I don't anymore."

His words stung like any slap across the face she'd ever endured. She opened her mouth to retaliate but the look in his eyes stopped her. She'd hurt him. She'd never cared about hurting someone before. She always felt the world was her enemy, that there were people out to hurt her like her father did. She didn't realize she could hurt people too.

She pushed the sock away. "Take it to the stupid police."

"No."

"You don't understand. I just..." She clenched her fist. In the back of her mind she heard the words she wished her father would say, her mother, her grandmother or even the bus driver who didn't listen when she'd told him she'd run away. "I'm sorry all right! I'm sorry. I shouldn't have said anything about your dad. I didn't mean it."

He folded his arms and stared at the ground.

Tears burned her eyes, her voice fell. "I didn't mean to hurt you."

He abruptly turned. "Come on." His tone hadn't softened, but she knew he'd forgiven her. "We won't go to the police right away. They might not believe us since we're kids. We've got to come up with a plan then talk to an adult we can trust."

Jessie listened to the silvery chime of bells as she entered Fedor Malenkov Jewelers. Her eyes adjusted to the cool dark interior then glanced at the lamplight bouncing off the array of gems and metals. The store had the same wonder and enchantment of Ali Baba's cave of riches.

A rude voice cut into her thoughts. "BJ, your cousin's here," the woman said into the intercom. She was a thin woman with haughty features and the inherent lazy attitude of the overindulged. "He'll be out in a minute." She disappeared behind a glitzy novel.

When Jessie heard one of the two back doors open, she held her breath. The past swam through her mind: the many times she'd popped by the store to visit her father, the joy he always greeted her with, his brilliant smile and the ready stories on his lips.

BJ pushed back the metalworker's protective eyeshade on his head. "Hello, Jessie," he said in a low, deep voice. He wore a heavy canvas apron over trousers and an old shirt, which clung to his massive frame. He looked more like a blacksmith than a jeweler with large hands that looked inadequate for his delicate trade. He didn't have a face meant for ready laughter; it was more suited for an ebony sculpture—dark, intense, smooth. He turned abruptly and headed for the shop, expecting her to follow.

In the shop, Jessie peered at the impressive gold Victorian bracelet with locket he'd been working on. He sat and waited.

She chewed her lip. "I don't know what I'm doing here," she admitted. Although she did know what called her there: a desperate need to fill the emptiness of loss, of leaving Kenneth and Syrah. A desire to know she'd done the right thing no matter how painful the outcome. She sought to get comfort from the ghost of the other man who held her heart.

"You want a job," BJ said. "It's in your blood Jess, the stories, the gems. You can't run away from it."

"I'm not a jeweler."

He was quiet a moment. "We could use a reliable clerk. Someone who knows the jewelry, and the history. I could talk to Mr. Malenkov."

She stared at the bracelet, wondering what various owners had hidden inside the locket.

"He loved you more than me," BJ said quietly. Or rather quiet for him, it came across like a low thunder. "I was just a nephew he trained."

Jessie looked at him surprised that she had given him the impression she was jealous of her father's affections. "I admired you. I still do.

You're so talented. I was ashamed of myself. Ashamed that I didn't think my father measured up, that you were proud of him while he embarrassed me. That I didn't want to be anything like him."

"And now?"

"I know the price of shame and I'm not willing to pay it. I don't mind being who I am."

He didn't exactly smile, but she could tell he was pleased.

That evening, Michelle found Jessie in their father's work room. Nothing had been touched. A museum to his memory: a book still open, a picture of New York hung crooked, crumbled tracing paper and his tools. Jessie sat hunched over the drafting table.

"What are you doing in here?" Michelle asked.

"Looking over Dad's designs. I went by the shop today and spoke to BJ."

"How is he?"

"Fine. I'm thinking of working there."

"Dad would have loved that. He'd always wanted one of us..." Her voice faded. She glanced around. "I'm glad you're in this room it needs to be used, not decayed by old memories. He was happy in here."

Jessie sat back in the chair, listening to it softly squeak. All her life she had wanted her father to be big and grand, something to talk about. She had been ashamed of his simple pleasures, his simple dreams, but she understood them now. She had the same ones—a nice job, a home, a family--simple wishes didn't make for insignificant people.

Michelle rested her hand on the back of her chair. "I'm glad you left the house today."

She'd kept to the house for a week, hiding in her room like a wounded animal. "Yes."

"Wendy called and told me that the Garden is catering the Weaver's party this weekend. I told her that you were free. I think you need to get out of the house and face the people you're hiding from."

Not people, Kenneth.

Rodney stared down at the sleeping woman next to him with masculine satisfaction. His plan had worked. Brooke had come to him in a panic begging him to return the files. He'd liked that. It felt nice to have a woman beg: to see her wide eyes plead, to watch her soft mouth saying his name with an urgent appeal. But he finally got her legs around him and that was his greatest victory.

He looked down at the diamond cufflinks Brooke had given him. She'd said no other man had ever made her feel this way. She belonged to him now. Rodney sighed feeling himself grow hard again. He wanted to wake her, but decided to let her sleep. There would be other nights. She wanted him to do one more thing and then promised there wouldn't be anything else. For another night like this, he would do it.

Jessie searched her closet and saw her dry-cleaned tux next to the outrageous outfit Mrs. Ashford had loaned her. She stared at it. It seemed ages ago since she had worn it; it was time to give it back.

She drove up to the Ashford mansion, wondering if she should go up to the front door or around to the servants' entrance. She shrugged and rang the front doorbell.

Ms. Frey answered stone-faced.

"Hello." Jessie held out the package. "It's a bit overdue, but I'm finally returning the outfit."

Ms. Frey glanced at it and stepped back. "Come in. I'm sure Mrs. Ashford would like to see you."

"But I was just dropping this off."

"Wait here." Ms. Frey flashed a mysterious smile and turned away. Jessie stood in the vaulted foyer feeling like a lost orphan.

A loud voice cut through the air. "Jessie Clifton," Mrs. Ashford bellowed at the top of the curving staircase. "You poor girl." She floated down the stairs, draped in a crimson silk dress, a gaudy orange scarf trailing behind her. She stopped in front of Jessie and patted her cheek. "It's terrible, isn't it?"

"I just came to return your outfit," Jessie said confused.

"You don't need to use that as an excuse to see me, my dear girl." She tossed the package to Ms. Frey who had appeared behind her. "I'd like tea in the reading room." She took Jessie's arm. "I just knew you would come to me in this time of struggle."

"I'm afraid I don't know what you're talking about."

Mrs. Ashford patted her hand. Jessie winced as the woman's ringed hand struck her knuckles. "You always were such a brave girl. Take a seat. Now don't be shy to speak to me. I know your heart is aching inside."

"But I—"

She held up a hand. "No, that's wrong of me. I shouldn't force you to share your pain so suddenly. Let me speak first. Just put the tea on the table and leave," she said when Ms. Frey arrived with the tray. "Thank you." She turned to Jessie. "Everybody fails in love once in awhile, but I must say that I'm proud of you...You may go ahead and pour the tea, honey. I don't expect you to stare at me the entire time. My you pour extremely well, some people actually splash the damn thing, getting the saucer wet. I can't stand soggy saucers, can you? But of course you were well trained. Your mother was French."

"British, but she really was—"

"Of course. Plus you're a waitress, which makes all the difference. Two lumps please...excellent. " She took a sip of her tea. "Now where was I?"

"Actually, I couldn't quite follow—"

"Ah, yes. Kenneth. Dear Kenneth. I've very proud of you trying to marry a man like him. He is a worthy effort and you're on the right track. I don't believe in woman trying to forge their own careers like your sister, Melissa—"

"Michelle."

"Is," she continued without pause. "I know it's not politically correct these days to marry for money, but the world does not give women equal pay anyway and as you can see." She gestured to the grand room. "This strategy works out so much better." She pinched Jessie's knee. "I knew I'd rub off on you."

Jessie held the tea and saucer too stunned to reply.

"Now, I know this may sound harsh, dear, but you must move on. There are plenty of other men out there. I know of one who may be perfect. His family is old money, but I'm not completely into the class distinction nonsense and your family is decent enough, besides your sister, Michelle, is it? Right of course. She is still a Winfield, which puts you in good company. Now the man's name is..." She tapped her chin, trying to remember. "His name is..."

"But I'm not looking--"

"It's okay not to want to get out there again, dear, but you can't be on the shore too long or all the big fish will be taken."

"But I don't want a big fish or even a little one. I'm really not interested in men right now."

Mrs. Ashford placed a hand on her chest and shut her eyes. "Oh, you young people are so dramatic. Soon you'll be saying you'll never love again." She opened her eyes. "Don't worry. In time this will all be a memory."

Kenneth would be more than a memory to her. He was her heart. "Of course." Jessie stood. "I really must go. Thank you for your time and advice."

Mrs. Ashford rose also and pinched Jessie's cheek. "I always give out both freely."

Jessie rubbed her cheek as she walked to her car. Mrs. Ashford was a nut, but she couldn't help being fond of her.

The Weaver's had a swimming party. Jessie hated those. She hated the sight of people dripping wet, calling her over to serve them while they lazed in the Jacuzzi or laid out their sculpted bodies--both man- made and natural--in the garden loungers, some snapping their fingers as if she were a pet. At least she was busy, it was better than being at home and thinking. Fortunately, the day was cool so she wasn't forced to melt in her uniform. The Weaver's loved "the help" to be fully dressed while serving, which meant no shorts or short sleeves despite the weather.

"Well...look who's here. What a surprise!" Deborah said. "Now what do we have here?" She surveyed the contents on the tray. "Looks delicious. Does it have any paprika? I'm allergic." She turned to Tracy and said in a low voice, "I'll break out everywhere."

"No," Jessie said.

"Good." She took a stuffed mushroom and popped it in her mouth. Deborah wore a red swimsuit with a yellow wrap and a matching scarf tied around her hair. "I was so shocked to hear about your engagement ending so suddenly and so soon." She fluttered her lashes in mock dismay. "One day you're hosting a barbecue and the next day 'poof' it's all over."

Jessie watched a man dive into the pool.

"And you had to move *all* your bags out. What a shame." She ate another mushroom.

Tracy flashed a weak smile. "Come on Deborah, leave her alone."

"I saw him with a new woman recently. Let me think who it was." She tapped her cheek. "Oh yes, that's right. Your Cousin Olivia. They make a beautiful couple. You should see them together." She leaned closer to Jessie and whispered in her ear. "You didn't really think you were fooling anyone, did you? Sure you had the decent clothes, and the nice haircut, but underneath it all you were still just a nobody."

"Kind of like you," Jessie said. "Somebody who wastes her time only talking about interesting people rather than being one."

"At least I get invited to all the major events as a *guest*. I bet your sister's wedding was just a publicity stunt."

Jessie held out her tray. "Would you like another?"

"No tart reply?" Deborah sniffed surprised, taking another mushroom. "No flare up of the Clifton temper? You must be mellowing or just finally realizing your place in life."

"Yes." Jessie lifted the tray and waved it under Deborah's nose. "By the way I lied. There is paprika." She laughed at Deborah's expression then walked away.

Kenneth prided himself on being calm, but the article in *The Journal* made him want to smash something. His name was being connected with scandal. A priceless bracelet had been stolen the day of his summer barbecue, throwing a shroud of suspicion over his guests. Which one had done it? Why? When? He crumbled up the paper and tossed it in the fireplace. He had a good idea who knew the answer.

"But I didn't steal anything!" Syrah said.

Kenneth rested his hands on the kitchen table. "Mrs. Ostick told me how nice it was that you returned her broach."

"I don't know what you're talking about."

He kept his voice low. "Stop lying to me."

"I didn't steal anything at the barbecue! I swear."

He folded his arms.

"I can't believe you don't trust me!"

"Have you given me reason to? You stole when you promised you wouldn't. I have an awards banquet coming up honoring kids who help the community. How do you think it will look if people find out my niece, a Preston, steals things? I can't afford that kind of scandal."

Syrah narrowed her eyes. "You're not sending me back."

"No, but I know of good schools that may cure you of this habit."

"You're not sending me away. I won't let you!" She pushed herself away from the table. The chair screeched as it scraped across the floor. "I don't need you or anybody. I can take care of myself." She stormed to the door.

Kenneth grabbed her arm before she reached it. She turned around and punched him in the face.

Shock disarmed any pain he might have felt. He could only stare at her. She stared back wide eyed and terrified, with her body poised to strike again. Kenneth knew the look: he'd worn it before.

"Relax, Ace." He kept his voice even. "I just want to talk."

Tears sprung to her eyes, a mixture of relief and dismay. She broke free from his grasp and ran.

Michelle was enjoying her afternoon tea when she heard loud voices in the main lobby. Syrah burst into the room followed by her secretary who said, "I'm sorry, Michelle, I couldn't stop her."

She smiled at the woman. "That's all right."

Her secretary scowled at the girl then shut the door.

Michelle put her tea aside. "What's wrong?"

Syrah rushed through her words. "I hit my uncle and the bracelet's missing, but I didn't take it and I couldn't find Aunt Jessie or Aunt

Teresa and he's going to send me away and I don't know what to do."
She fell into a chair and sobbed.

Michelle grabbed a box of tissues and waited for the tears to
subside. She sat down next to Syrah and squeezed her knee. "Okay,
let's try this again. What happened?"

"I punched Uncle Kenneth." She pressed her palms against her eyes.
"I didn't mean to, I was just so mad. Now he hates me."

"I'm sure he understood it was an accident."

She let her hands fall. "He hates me. He hates me for making Aunt
Jessie go away and he wants to get rid of me. He thinks I stole the
bracelet."

"What bracelet?"

"The one missing in the paper. They think it was stolen the day of
Uncle's party and he blames me, but I didn't steal it, Aunt Michelle. I
swear. But he won't believe me because I stole a broach from Mrs.
Ostick and returned it for the reward and she told him. But that was a
long time ago and I haven't taken anything since. I have to find out
who did steal the bracelet so he'll believe me.

"It sounds like the same bracelet I gave to Aunt Jessie but now it's
gone because..." She hesitated unsure how much to reveal in case she
didn't believe her. "I lost it when Aunt Jessie left it behind. I need your
help. Please." She held her hands together as if in prayer. "Please, I
don't want him to send me away, but I know he wants to. He probably
should because I punched him and I told him I didn't need anyone. And
he said that everyone's going to blame him if they find out I steal
things. He thinks I'm going to ruin his life. Everything is awful and its
all my fault."

"It's all right," Michelle soothed. "Tell me everything from the
beginning. The truth, starting with Jessie's bracelet."

"I did steal it," she admitted. "It was real easy slipping it off Ms.
Radson's wrist. I did everything Dad taught me."

Michelle stiffened. "Your father taught you how to steal?"

"It wasn't like real lessons or anything. He was just bragging. He
knew a lot about jewelry and would talk about it and I picked up things.
Like I can tell your ring's expensive. Emeralds with a pure color like
that are valuable. It has only a slight bluish-green."

Michelle nodded. "Correct."

She grinned pleased with herself. "He'd talk about different gemstones and diamonds. He made it sound interesting and then he started bragging about when he was younger. He said he had been the best thief around and then he'd show me what he did."

Michelle tucked a strand of hair behind her ear, keeping her voice neutral. "Did he tell you why he stole?"

"Oh yea. He said he had to teach this girl he called Dimples a lesson 'cause she thought she was the moon and the sky; the bun and the cheese."

Michelle took a deep breath. *Dimples.* That's what some of the guys used to call Brooke. "I want you to tell me everything your father told you about her and what he used to do."

Once Syrah explained everything, Michelle phoned Teresa to pick her up. Then she called her secretary. "Please see if Stephanie Radson is free for lunch."

The banquet hall for Kenneth's award's dinner was a large dome-shaped room with the grandeur of a cathedral, but the warmth of an estate. Jessie wasn't sure she wanted to be there, but curiosity was a powerful drug. She wanted to see Kenneth again. She wanted to see how Olivia would look on his arm, hoping that he was happy even though she was miserable.

News cameras and photographers filled the room aiming their lens on the mayor and top community officials who had come to commend the project Kenneth had funded for young people--an after school program that acted as a surrogate family for neglected children aged five to eighteen. The twenty young people selected today had helped the community by volunteering at animal shelters and visiting homebound residents.

"You shouldn't have come," Wendy whispered.

"Why not?"

"I've seen two photographers take pictures of you."

Jessie shrugged. "They wanted to know if the rumors were true."

"What did you say?"

"Nothing."

"I heard the mayor was going to give Kenneth an award."

Jessie sniffed. "He doesn't need another trophy telling him how wonderful he is. He doesn't believe it anyway."

The lights dimmed and they both watched Kenneth approach the stage, a commanding figure in a gray cashmere sweater and dark blue suit. He looked good, so together, she felt her insides falling to pieces.

Jessie heard Wendy softly sigh and said, "Cut that out."

"That wasn't me, it's them." She gestured to Carole and Amy who were staring at the stage as though a favorite teen idol had appeared.

Kenneth rested his hands on the podium and began to speak. His powerful voice gathered everyone's attention. "I would first like to thank you for coming tonight to honor the young men and women who have taken the time to enhance our community through their efforts. Let me take this opportunity to introduce them to you."

He began to read off their names, handing each child a trophy and whispering something special in their ear. Each recipient glowed as they exited the stage.

Jessie felt her regret subside. She couldn't have been his wife, couldn't have worn his family's mask, because she did not understand the need for it. But she knew he wasn't a fraud. He was a man who had tried to carve out an existence free from the one society wanted to pin on him. He had accomplished that.

After the last young person had received an award, the mayor approached the podium with a plaque.

"Now it is my distinct pleasure to give this humanitarian award to a man who not only gives the community jobs, offers solace to the lonely and activities to the young, but continues to set an example for all of us. Please help me in honoring Kenneth Preston."

He looked embarrassed, but received the award with grace and elegance. "I accept this award if only to show young people what they can aspire to and achieve." Thunderous applause followed his simple statement.

He was glad it was over. The room looked hollow now, most of the lights were off and he heard the shuffling footsteps of the cleaning crew. Kenneth looked down at the wine glass he held, it had been given to him during a toast. He touched the liquid and rubbed it between his fingers. He wondered what it was like. Wondered what the allure was that drove men to destroy themselves like the Sirens calling sailors to their doom. He swirled the golden liquid imagining how it would taste: sweet, bitter, dry? Would it truly, for a moment, ease his pain, ease his memories; ease the hollowness as Eddie said? Could one drink really be terrible?

"Don't you dare," a voice ordered.

He spun around, placed the glass down and looked into Jessie's fiery eyes. An unexpected jolt of desire and longing rendered him speechless as his eyes swallowed her up. God, she looked beautiful. He wanted to tell her what his father had said, talk to her about his company, and ask her advice on Syrah who hadn't spoken to him in three days. He wanted to hold her, kiss her, tell her how much he loved her, beg her to come back to him, but all that came to his mouth was, "What are you doing here?"

Jessie rested a hand on her hip. "Do you notice we're back where we started? I see how familiarity does breed contempt."

No, he silently disagreed. They weren't back where they had started. They were both different people now.

"I see you decided to get a tux that fits," he said, trying to maintain a casual tone. He folded his arms to refrain from touching her.

"Yes, I decided fitted wasn't so bad."

"Shame you couldn't do something with your hair."

She narrowed her eyes. "Are you trying to provoke me?"

"Sure. I could use a good slap."

"I wouldn't dare. You'd have good reason to hit me back."

He lowered his gaze.

"I'm sorry," she said quickly. "I forgot."

He shoved his hands in his pocket. "Do you have a moment?"

"Sorry, I left it in my other jacket."

He groaned. "If your singing is as bad as your jokes, I'm glad you saved me the agony."

"What do you want?"

356

"I didn't really get a chance to eat."

She sighed. "Let me see what I can do. Wait here." She walked away then stopped. She returned to the table and grabbed the wineglass.

Kenneth laughed. "I wasn't going to drink it."

Jessie only sniffed. A few moments later she came back with a plate full of food and apple juice. She placed the plate in front of him with expert aplomb, going so far as to place a napkin on his lap. Once her performance was over she turned to go.

"It's no fun to eat alone," he said.

"Kenneth, I can't—"

"Please," he said gently.

She sat.

An awful, painful silence fell between them. Jessie watched him eat, looking at his hands and his mouth, remembering the first time he'd kissed her, the moment she felt she belonged to him. She brushed those thoughts aside.

"How's Olivia?" she asked.

He nodded. "She's fine."

"Do you like her? She's—"

"Don't insult me. Or yourself."

"I want you to be happy."

"Why?" His eyes burned into hers. "So you won't feel sorry for me? Did you suddenly realize you deserve better than a man who's half a freak show?"

"Don't talk about yourself like that." She lowered her voice. "You know why I can't marry you."

"You mean *won't* marry me."

Jessie clenched her hand into a fist. "I will not marry a man who'll sacrifice everything for just a name."

"What am I without my name? Nothing! If I hadn't been Kenneth Preston you wouldn't have been interested in me in the first place. No, don't shake your head like that. You and I both know the name means something. It's all I have and no matter how much I—" He bit his lip and abruptly stood. "If you don't understand that you don't understand me."

She also stood and grabbed his arm. "I do understand. That's why I can't be with you."

They had nothing more to say, but neither moved.

"I don't know what hurts more," he finally said. "Being with you or being away from you."

Jessie hugged herself and looked down. Kenneth made a move towards her, then stopped. She closed her eyes as she listened to his footsteps fading away.

Jessie didn't cry when she got home. She went into her father's studio and touched all his things to gather strength from his memory.

She remembered her father and his shy grins, his infectious laugh and dreamy eyes. She remembered the way he used to get on her mother's nerves so that they could make up later. She remembered her mother—now with fondness instead of guilt—a woman who bristled at bad manners, created elaborate dinners as if expecting royalty, and scolded her children with tears in her eyes.

Jessie rested her head against the gray stone wall. All of a sudden, she felt a stone shift from the weight. She stared at the moved stone for a moment her heart pounding with anticipation. She moved it aside and saw a small hiding place. Inside sat a black box. It looked familiar. No, it couldn't be. She remained still waiting for it to disappear like a hallucination. It didn't.

Her fingers tingled as she grabbed the box and opened it. She carefully removed the cloth surrounding the object inside. Her heart stopped when a sapphire eye winked back at her: The Sapphire Pendant. Her fingers caressed the rope-chain as her ancestors once had, feeling its special allure. The pendant was here. Her father had owned it all the time!

Fury nearly strangled her. Rage crawled up her skin and heated her eyes. He'd lied to them. He'd made them suffer. Made her suffer with guilt never easing her pain with the truth. Him and his stupid stories of power and magic. The pendant was nothing but a piece of stone that at that moment she would have loved to see melted or crushed.

Jessie stared at the sapphire eye, its beauty penetrating some of her anger and her bitterness. Here it was. The fabled pendant. In the Clifton possession where it belong. She scoffed at the words then suddenly stared at it in horror.

Which meant the Ashfords had a fake. Her father had sold them a copy. Oh God! The deception was an anvil, crushing all that was left of her revered memories of him. His sense of honesty and integrity crumbled at her feet. He was as fraudulent as the pendant he had sold. Did she continue the lie? Did she let generations of Cliftons hold onto this secret shame?

Did she let them carry the burden of possible exposure and humiliation? How could he have done this to her? For years she had agonized about how to get the pendant back and he'd known the truth. She'd been on a yellow brick road to an ineffectual wizard. Everything had been a lie. She didn't know what to do or think or say. So she did the only thing her chaotic mind could think of. She screamed.

Michelle and Teresa rushed into the room.

"What happened?" Michelle asked.

"Are you hurt?" Teresa asked.

Jessie held up the pendant. "Dad sold the Ashfords a fake."

Michelle took it from her. "I don't believe it."

Jessie wrung her hands. "Here I am telling Kenneth the virtues of living honestly; lecturing on high ideals and my father actually sold the Clifton integrity for cash!"

"Calm down."

"Calm down? I risked the man I love for my father's sense of honesty and he's a forger!"

"Look there's more," Teresa said, pulling out a box and list of names, descriptions, histories and prices.

Jessie squeezed her eyes shut. "There's more and we can't tell anyone. He's forcing me into the very secrecy I abhor."

"Let's not panic," Michelle said. "We have time."

Teresa nodded. "Right. Let Mrs. Ashford think she has the original."

Jessie bit her nails. "What if she gets it appraised?"

"Then we have to steal it back."

Michelle sent Teresa a look of disgust. "Oh, that sounds brilliant. Let's correct forgery with thievery."

"Well, it gets worse." Teresa held out her hand. "Tell me this is not the Arand necklace. The very one Mrs. Donovan is giving to the Historical Society Museum."

They stared at each other. If they didn't do something fast, their father's forgery would be exposed for the world to see.

Chapter Twenty-eight

Nathan had never believed in the power of the pen until it stabbed his best friend in the heart. Nathan paced, watching Kenneth who sat at his desk with the newspaper spread out in front of him. He hadn't moved in half an hour. Nathan wasn't sure he was breathing.

"It's just a story," he said casually, hoping to get a response. "All you need is an unscrupulous reporter and a slow news day and 'Bam.'" He punched the air with his fist. "It becomes news."

And it was big news. It had made the front page of the *Caribbean Times* and *Daily News* and had a significant write up in *The Journal*. Mr. Kenneth Preston wasn't the honored son of Charles Preston, but the illegitimate son of Pierre Chevalier a repudiated womanizer, drunk and con artist and the teenaged girl he'd raped. The article exposed Kenneth's early childhood run ins with juvenile authorities and even revealed that he had recently been seen in the company of legendary call girl, Leticia Mason. Now the board members had the ammunition they needed to remove him as CEO.

Nathan read his thoughts. "I know the meeting's in three days, but there's no reason to worry. I'm sure this will die down. Rodney's still searching for our thief, our accounts are on track." He stopped pacing and stared helplessly at his friend. "You've done a lot for this company. They can't hold this against you."

Kenneth knew they would. He knew the true nature of people. They were as fickle as the wind. The one person he'd allowed himself to trust had betrayed him. But what more could you expect from a hooker who probably remembered one's dollar amount rather than one's name?

Someone knocked on the door.

"Come in," Nathan said.

Brooke walked in, a cool figure in dark blue. "I've solved our computer problem."

Nathan shoved his hands in his pockets. "If you're expecting applause, you're going to be disappointed."

Kenneth pushed away his own concerns. "Who's our thief?"

Her eyes slid to Nathan then focused on him. "Rodney."

Nathan blinked. "No, he's not."

"It's true. I found him last night at one of the terminals and he confessed everything."

"He wouldn't do that. He's been relentlessly searching for--" Nathan stared at her cold impassionate eyes. He pointed at her. "You're lying."

She dimpled prettily. "You can ask him yourself. Come in Rodney."

Rodney lumbered into the room, his lanky form draped in loose trousers and a large ill-fitting shirt. He hung his head, careful not to meet anyone's eyes.

Nathan sat down and watched him.

Kenneth put his hands together in a steeple and pinned Rodney with an assessing stare. "You've been busy."

Rodney shrugged. "Yeah."

"Why did you do it?"

He swallowed and shifted awkwardly. "Because Nathan asked me."

Nathan exploded from his chair. "That's a lie!"

Kenneth studied him, his voice quiet. "You always wanted to have more responsibilities. What better way than to create a problem then fix it?"

"You know I'm not like that. I'm your friend. "

Kenneth looked at Rodney.

Nathan leaned against the desk. "He's lying."

Kenneth narrowed his eyes. "Why? Why would he lie about you? The very person who helped him get his position?"

He glared at Brooke who was watching the scene with studied disinterest. "Because he's covering for that bitch--"

"Careful Nate."

"Who's had her eye on your job for years," he finished. "Don't you see? She's trying to divide and conquer. She knows how you feel about loyalty. She's using it against you."

Kenneth glanced at her then him, but said nothing.

Nathan tapped the desk. "I'm going to prove that she's behind all this. You don't have to trust me or even believe me, but if you put your trust in her you'll find yourself bleeding from the back." He pushed himself off the desk. He grabbed his brother by the collar, lifting him out of the chair. "I hope the sex was worth it because your balls are mine now." He dropped him in the chair then stormed out.

Brooke shook her head as the echo of the slammed door filled the room. "It's a shame how that man only thinks about sex."

Neither Rodney nor Kenneth replied.

Rodney stumbled out the office building. He felt sick to his stomach. The game was no longer fun. Nathan would never trust him again. He'd betrayed his brother. He hadn't expected it to make him feel like shit. He didn't even care that he didn't know what Preston would do to him or that Brooke had promised to take care of him. It was the look on Nathan's face that seared itself on his brain. The look of hurt. His brother had gotten him this job and he had repaid him like this. He was the wretched Cain throwing a stone on Abel's head.

The sky held the heavy scent of rain as he walked across the parking lot. He stopped when he saw a familiar figure standing next to his rusted Toyota Camry.

"How deep are you in it?" Nathan asked, blocking his path.

"I have nothing to say."

He pulled him close. "Speak or squeal. The choice is yours."

"Because you're Mr. Big Shot, right?" Rodney said, guilt making him angry.

Nathan let him go. "So this is about me? You couldn't come to me and fight like a man?"

"I may not be able to beat you in the ring, but you've got to give me credit for what I've done. I broke into the receivable files of a huge corporation leaving it as innocent as a babe. I've stolen cycles costing this company thousands. You're not smart enough to do that. I even got a beautiful woman that appreciates me."

Nathan jiggled the change in his pocket and stared up at the building. "She's not worth it."

His smug confidence tore at Rodney's patience. "Brooke cares about me. The company should have been hers anyway. You and Preston can find other jobs, but it's harder for a woman."

"You're not the first man she's used."

"She's not using me. I'm the one in control."

"You think?" Nathan dug in his pocket and pulled out a pair of diamond cufflinks.

Rodney reached for them. "What are you doing with those?"

Nathan closed his palm. "They look familiar?"

"Yes, they're mine and you know it. She gave them to me."

"She gave you a pair, but not these ones." He glanced down at them. "These are mine. And I carry them around to remind me not to think with the wrong organ." He shoved them back in his pocket and looked at him. "She doesn't care about you. She doesn't care about anyone. You may be clever when it comes to computers, but when it comes to women you're just like the rest of us."

Rodney looked away.

"It's not your fault. She's very good. If you want to protect her, that's fine. That's your choice, but I don't think she's worth it. So I suggest you tell me all that you two have been up or I'll make sure you go down with her."

Rodney's lip twisted into a cynical grin. "You wouldn't."

Nathan clasped the back of Rodney's neck in a grip that made him wince and pushed his face close. "Right now little brother, I'm capable of things you couldn't even imagine. Now what's your move?"

Rodney swallowed, feeling a trickle of sweat slide down his face. Even if he told the truth, Brooke would come out clean. He'd done all the stealing, not her. It was his word against hers. He thought about the diamond cufflinks in Nathan's pocket then briefly shut his eyes, feeling like a fool. "All right."

Nathan nodded and folded his arms. "Go ahead."

"If you want to know everything, I guess I should start with

Stephanie..."

Brooke fell on her bed and laughed aloud. Kenneth's reputation was destroyed! The newspaper tactic couldn't have been more perfect. After she'd read the article she knew it was a the perfect time to reveal the thief—why not kick a man when he's down and feeling betrayed?—and she'd been right. Nathan and Kenneth would soon be out of the picture completely.

Now she just needed to deal with Jessie Clifton and her meddling sisters. They'd caused enough trouble with the bracelet and now were trying to influence her sister. She was sick of hearing Stephanie talk about Jessie, now she was bragging about her lunch with Michelle. She was certain she could find some information about them that would prove useful.

She called Jack. "Find what you can about the Cliftons," she told him without preamble. "What do you mean you don't want to? You got the bracelet? How? Stephanie! I knew she'd come through. Was everything fine? Great! Now I want you...No, you listen if you don't want me to start talking about your recent activities. Good. I'm glad you agree. Now just do as I say. Thank you." She hung up and jumped to her feet. Everything was perfect. She grabbed her handbag. She needed to go shopping. She raced out the door, nearly crashing into her mother.

"Sorry," Winifred said softly.

Brooke headed for the stairs. "Don't worry about it."

If she'd been paying attention, she would have notice the strange expression on her mother's face.

He couldn't remember how he'd ended up there: on a sidewalk in front of a DC liquor store with the smell of vomit and urine swirling in the air about him. Bottles, brown bags, paper cups and matchboxes littered the street. The smells and sights were familiar. Kenneth looked at the wine he'd purchased and held it in both hands as if it were an anchor against the storms of his thoughts. He stared up at the sky.

He had nothing to lose. His business, his reputation, everything he'd struggled to build had crumbled. Now everyone knew of his past, knew of his lies. The response had been swift and merciless.

He'd been politely asked to resign as chair of the Caribbean Council, two other organizations cancelled his membership and another asked him to leave their board. They kindly explained that he was not the kind of image they wanted representing them. He was the typical perception of the bastard Caribbean child with a drunken father and underage mother, stereotypes his community had fought hard to dispel. Overnight, the golden child had become the poster child.

Invitations had dried up as well. People who used to shake his hand now avoided his eyes. Women who had once wanted him now whispered instead of winked when he walked past. Ms. Rose screened calls from angry family members who thought he'd used the article to depict himself as the great American success story. He remembered his mother's call clearly.

"You're a disgrace! How am I supposed to show my face now? How am I supposed to go anywhere now that everyone knows?"

"I'm sorry," he said tired.

"I'm the one who's sorry. I knew I shouldn't have kept you. I knew you would ruin my life."

His temper snapped. "How? You could use this to your advantage. Why don't you tell everyone what a martyr you have been by taking me in? You're not hurt by this. Nobody knows the truth about you and you're damn lucky they don't. But push me enough, woman, and I'll make sure that they do."

Stunned silence buzzed on the other end of the line.

He pinched the bridge of his nose and sighed. It would be so easy to hate her, but he knew he never would. "I know this will probably be the last time we'll ever speak so I want to tell you something."

"What could you possibly want to tell me?"

"That I forgive you."

He didn't know if his words meant anything to her, but he'd needed to say them. He needed to forgive all who had turned their back on him. Ms. Rose still stood by him, but he knew, in time, she would leave him as well.

The image of Kenneth Preston had died leaving only Kenny X.
He opened the bottle and rested his forehead against the lip. He had
no one to turn to. As in the past he was alone. The three people closest
to him had betrayed him: Nathan, Ace, Leticia. He'd failed.
You fear failure worse than death. Hadn't Jasmine said that once?
Fear. He had based his life on fear: fear of being discovered, fear of
being imperfect, fear of being angry, fear of being loved. The
hollowness inside him had always been based on a fear that life would
punish him for what he was: a drunk's bastard trying to pass as a blue
blood. This fear had been his constant companion. It wore different
guises—driving his father and brother into the arms of their liquid
mistresses and him into the arms of a prostitute.
   His hands tightened around the bottle of poison. It was a cool
refreshing drink to some; potentially deadly to him. And into what
world would fear send him now? Into what dark abyss? He threw the
bottle against the wall, gaining strength as it shattered.
   "Thank god." He glanced up as his father approached him. "I've
been searching everywhere."
   Kenneth turned away too ashamed to look at him.
   "Is what you try fi do, man? Kill yourself? God will take you when
he's good and willing."
   Kenneth shut his eyes from the gathering tears. "I'm dead already."
   "No."
   "How can you talk to me?" He tightened his jaw. "I destroyed your
name!"
   "Come. Let's go."
   "Leave me be."
   "Have you forgotten that I am your father?"
   Kenneth sighed heavily then rose to his feet. They didn't speak until
they left the city.
   "We give too much power to our name," Charles said. "To the
actions of those before us. Our heritage does not equate worth. God did
not create you to carry the burdens of your people."
   "Everything I've ever wanted is gone."
   "But your past victories were hollow. An echo of your shame and
sense of worthlessness. You playacted through life. Now you have a

chance to live. To shatter that mask."

"Even though I caused you disgrace?"

"My shame was that I let the deception continue. I cost my son his life for the sake of pride. The burden is lifted, now you are free. You can adopt Syrah. You don't have to pretend anymore. She can be yours."

Kenneth gazed out the window.

Charles was quiet then said, "Michelle Clifton resigned from the Council but not before giving a speech that made everyone feel as sweet as rotten mangoes. Those Clifton women are nice to have at a man's side."

"I won't bring Jasmine into the mess of my life. I don't even know if I'll have a job. I have nothing to offer her."

"Except yourself." Charles glanced at him. "Scared that's not enough?"

"I know it's not enough and I'm tried of reaching for something I can't have."

"I see. I must have misjudged her. I thought she was the type of woman with integrity. The type who fell in love with a man's character rather than his bank account."

"It won't work, Dad. We'll never be together." He glanced at the sky, when he spoke again his voice was barely a whisper. "Somehow I think she always knew that."

"You can't sit by the window all day," Freda told Syrah who'd done just that for three days. "Your Uncle will be back. When he called me he told me not to worry. You're not to worry either. He just needs time alone. The story in the paper really hurt him."

"Why would someone print such a thing?"

She dusted a plant. "Americans like success stories and they also like scandal. You mix the two and it's irresistible."

Dion began to bark. Syrah turned to the window and saw a car drive up. She ran to the door.

Syrah, Dion, and Freda stood as a small welcoming party when Kenneth opened the door. For a moment no one spoke then Kenneth stepped forward and kissed Freda on the cheek. "Have any food ready, Ms. Rose?"

"Of course I do," she said gruffly, annoyed by her gathering tears. "I'll heat something." She disappeared in the kitchen.

Kenneth knelt down and patted Dion then looked at his niece who stood awkwardly, staring at him with happiness and worry.

"Hi, Ace," he said gently.

She wrung her hands behind her back. "Hi, Uncle Kenneth."

"I'm sorry I didn't believe you about the bracelet."

"I'm sorry I lied before." Her gaze fell. "I'm sorry I hit you."

"I know." He watched two tears slip from under her lowered lids and slide down her cheeks. He reached out to touch her then stopped. "Ace?"

"Yes, Uncle Kenneth?"

"You can start calling me Dad."

She glanced up wordless then fell into his arms.

Chapter Twenty-nine

"I don't think we should do this," Teresa said.

Jessie rolled her eyes dismissing her sister's hesitation. She had planned the retrieval of the Arand necklace for a week. It consumed her. It helped her not to think about things—like the article about Kenneth. How he must be suffering and how she could be of no comfort to him.

She now understood why he hadn't been able to face her prom night. She had seen the face of her own father the night she'd held the pendant and looked into the face of a stranger. A stranger whose legacy she must continue to protect. "We don't have a choice," she said. "Dad made a lot of paste jewelry for Mrs. Donovan and others. But the most damaging are the stories."

"Perhaps he thought he was creating fakes for people who didn't want to wear their valuables in public," Teresa said. "That's very common."

"That may be. However, that doesn't explain the Arand necklace. The only person who has the answer is his number one client, Mrs. Donovan. But since we don't have time to chat before the donation, we'll just steal the necklace that could shatter our reputation and be on our way."

"It's risky. Shouldn't we go to the police?"

Jessie shook her head. "Not until we know everything. We have to protect Dad's name—our name—for as long as possible."

Teresa sighed still hesitant. "I don't know. I just think we'll regret this."

Michelle spoke up. "Oh, good. I'm not the only one."

Jessie scowled. "Michelle, this is serious."

"I'm very serious. The only reason I agreed to this ridiculous idea was to keep an eye on you two." She looked out the window at the dark sky with its warning of rain. "This summer storm can't decide whether to come or go." She frowned. "Perhaps we should choose another night. It might rain."

"So?"

Michelle sent Jessie a look of disgust. "If it rains, we'll have to deal with mud and footprints."

"This is the perfect night. The house will be occupied by the Ladies' League. We won't have to worry about any alarms. We'll slip into the library, grab the necklace and leave."

Michelle zipped up her black jacket. "I don't know why you think she'd keep her jewelry in a book."

"Because I saw something hidden in a book one time while waitressing. It makes sense. Lots of people hide things in hollow books."

"No, that doesn't make sense if it's common knowledge."

"Not everyone thinks that way."

"How do we know which book?"

"She doesn't have a big library, remember? It's nothing like Mrs. Ashford's. Mrs. Donovan prefers jewelry and statues. We've been to her house many times before. Do I need to go over the plan again?"

"No, it won't make it any more successful," Michelle muttered.

Jessie headed for the door. "Trust me. We won't have anything to worry about."

An hour later, Michelle sent Jessie a smug look. "Nothing to worry about, huh?"

Jessie stared at the many bookshelves lining the wall. Her flashlight skimmed over the rows of books. Her hopes of an easy retrieval vanished. "I don't remember it looking like this. She must have started collecting books."

"Obviously. The last time we were here was years ago."

"I was here waitressing."

"Yes, but you didn't go into the library."

"I know, but I was sure—"

Teresa hit them. "Will you two stop talking and start looking?"

Each selected a bookshelf then quickly searched the selection of books. A few minutes later they heard footsteps come down the hall towards them. They stopped and listened for the steps to pass. They didn't. The door slowly opened. The lights from the hallway, growing wider ready to expose them as it made a sweeping arch across the floor.

The sisters dashed into a closet just as the lights went on. Fortunately, the new occupant didn't stay long. The lights shut off and they heard the door close.

Jessie sighed relieved. "Good. They're gone. Let's go."

"We can't," Teresa said.

"Why not?"

"The door won't open. There's no knob."

Michelle turned on her flashlight and saw a wooden slab that had been their entrance. She shifted the light around them. "I can't believe this. We're in the old elevator. The second door must have closed on us."

"Strange, I didn't hear it," Jessie said.

"That's because your heart was pounding so loud."

"Push a button or something," Teresa said.

Michelle pressed a few buttons. "They don't work."

Jessie hit the walls. "How do we get out of here?"

"Stop that. We don't want someone coming to get us."

Teresa sat down and pulled her knees to her chest. "I knew we shouldn't have come."

Jessie pulled her hair. "What are we going to do?"

Michelle glanced around the space. "We were locked in here before when we were kids and we escaped, we'll do it again."

Jessie rested her head back and stared up at the ceiling. "And I know how." With her sister's help, she lifted a panel on the top of the elevator and hoisted herself up then helped Michelle and Teresa through. She shut the panel and they stood on top of the elevator looking up into the darkness.

"It's like being trapped in a vertical tomb," Teresa said in a hushed voice.

"Just follow me." Jessie felt the walls and latched onto the bottom step of a metal ring ladder. They climbed it until they reached a tunnel above the second floor bedrooms.

"I assume you know where you're going," Michelle said.

"Good. I'll let you keep that assumption."

"Ow!" Teresa cried, hitting her head on a low beam. "Were people shorter in the twenties?"

"Be quiet," Michelle said. "You don't want them to hear us."

"Sorry, I'll try not to hit my head so hard next time."

"Come on," Jessie ordered. "This tunnel will lead us to the west room. It's usually empty."

Although the room was dark and quiet, they still lifted the vent with care. They lowered themselves to the floor, trying to fall to the ground as softly as possible.

Jessie headed for the window. "We're almost free."

A low deep grumble followed her statement.

"Was that you?" Teresa whispered.

"No, it was him." Michelle nodded and pointed to an old man sleeping in an ornate four poster bed, his arm wrapped around a large Doberman. Its shinning eyes focused on them.

Jessie frowned. "Who sleeps with their dog like that?"

Teresa grabbed her arm. "Who cares? Get us out of here."

The dog lifted its head as they crept sideways to the window.

"Good dog," Teresa soothed.

The dog continued to stare.

"I think he's just curious. He's probably really friendly."

The dog bared its teeth as Jessie slid the window open. They scrambled out as the dog leaped from the bed and ran towards them. Jessie shut the window, just as he jumped.

"Okay, now we're out." Jessie inhaled deeply and stared up at the sky, appreciating the wind and rain on her face. Never had a stormy night sky looked so beautiful.

"Yes, we're out, but we're on the roof," Michelle said.

Jessie chewed her bottom lip thoughtful. "If we could just make it to the mother-in-law house, we'd be okay."

"We can't go running about on top of the roof," Michelle said. "In spite of the storm, it's a bright night and the moon would give us away."

"Fine. There's a trellis by the side of the house near the second servants' entrance. It's not far from here."

"Okay, let's go."

They sprinted across the roof, the rain had softened but the wind acted like a mean spirited child, trying to blow them off.

"This is awful," Teresa said.

"There's no reason to worry."

Michelle sniffed. "Yes, if we fall, death is pretty much certain."

"Cut it out, Mich," Jessie warned.

They reached the trellis and climbed down ready to run across the lawn with the black night as their camouflage. Then the servants' entrance door opened. A stream of light fell on them piercing through the wind and darkness. Two shadows came into view their similar reddish blond hair tossed by the breeze. The sisters recognized them instantly: the Donovan brothers, their past tormentors.

The two men smiled. "Hello girls. Remember us?"

The sisters only stared.

The brother's smiles grew. One stepped back so they could enter. "Come inside. We've been waiting for you."

Chapter Thirty

The brothers ushered them into the dinning room where a meeting was in progress. It looked nothing like the Ladies League, however. The dinning table resembled the Mad Hatter's Tea Party. Porcelain teapots and cups fought for space with gin and other liquor bottles, sherry glasses, half eaten cookies, and tea cakes sat on decorated paper plates.

Three women sat around the table: Mrs. Ashford, wearing a large, extravagant hat more suited for a spring wedding than a summer storm, tsked at the state of their clothes; Mrs. Donovan instructed her sons to leave the room, and Bertha in her large purple turban and intense dark eyes wore an unreadable smile.

"Take a seat," Mrs. Donovan said. "We've been expecting you. Bertha said you would come tonight."

Bertha nodded. "It was the wind."

Michelle took a step forward. "We can explain."

Mrs. Ashford waved her hand. "No need to, dear. We know it all." She giggled. "I must say that you made our evening very interesting."

The corners of Mrs. Donovan's mouth kicked up in a grin. "Yes, I never laughed so hard."

Bertha spoke up, offering an explanation. "We watched your little burglary attempt on the security monitor." She gestured to the large screen on the far wall. It had a picture of every room inside the house and outside on the grounds.

"Nobody lands on my property without being under surveillance," Mrs. Donovan said. "The elevator was a great idea. I'm afraid the boys thought it would be fun to close the elevator on you. We were about to release it when Jessie had her idea." She clapped her hands. "How inspired."

Mrs. Ashford watched them. "They're not smiling. Perhaps we should explain."

"Yes."

"First things first, would you like anything to drink? No need to make a face Jessie we're perfectly sober. Now what would you like?"

"We're fine thank you," Michelle said, answering for all of them.

Mrs. Ashford clasped her hands together. "So you found out about the necklace?"

They nodded.

"And the pendant?"

They nodded again.

"I bet you're thinking some very unkind thoughts about your father right now."

Teresa toyed with her sleeve; Michelle folded her arms while Jessie bit her nails.

"Your father was a true artist," Mrs. Ashford said. "He created the best imitations this coast has ever known. Everyone in the Ladies' League just adored him. Many of us don't like to wear our valuables in public so we use a substitute."

Teresa hit Jessie as an 'I told you so.'

"He was brilliant." She studied them. "You've seen the list, haven't you?"

"Yes," Michelle said. "Why did you do it? Why did he?"

"What exactly do you think we've done?"

"Bought and sold forgeries."

Mrs. Donovan spoke to the other two women. "They have such an imagination." She turned to them and shrugged. "That's not it at all. I took a few courses in antiquities and the like and became enchanted with the history of things, especially expensive things." Her blue eyes twinkled. "That's why I had my husband start the Historical Society. I noticed how an object could make a place famous or rich. However, I soon grew tired of looking at other people's possessions and started to acquire my own, telling their stories and capturing people's interest."

She poured some tea adding a drop of sherry. "Isn't it interesting how you can take any ordinary thing and give it a story and then it's worth something? That concept has always fascinated me. It gave me the idea for the museum."

"So you asked my father to help you fill the museum with fakes?" Jessie asked.

The women gasped. Mrs. Ashford shook her head. "Everything in the museum is genuine, dear. We would never do that."

"Or be that stupid," Mrs. Donovan said. "The Historical Society helped make Randall County one of the richest in the state. Think of all the revenue from tourists."

"But the histories are fiction. I saw my father's drafts." Jessie said. "Are you telling me the story of the Arand necklace is real? If it is, why did my father have a copy?"

"A young Scottish man was enslaved by the British and sent to the Caribbean for pledging loyalty to Charles II. He finally immigrated--"

"That doesn't answer my question. Is the necklace real?"

Mrs. Donovan shrugged. "What is the truth, but something we chose to believe? What is history but records of someone's point of view?"

Michelle shook her head. "That's dangerous thinking."

"That's the kind of thinking that has kept this community strong. We are connected. We protect each other. The Historical Society gives pride to all the diverse cultures of the county and shows the connections of people we chose not to see. Our children are brought up with a sense of history that carries them all through their lives."

Bertha rested her hands on the table. "You are not only insulting us but also your father by your accusations. We have done nothing you need to worry about. Sometimes the actions of one generation cannot be understood by the next, but trust us you reap the benefits of what we do."

Michelle frowned. "And the burdens."

"Your father listened to the elements—the stones and the metals—and heard their stories then he told us and we believed them. Naturally we had the stories confirmed, but his word usually was enough."

"So everything is legit?"

"What do you think?"

"Just tell us," Jessie said.

"We would hope you would have the faith in your father and us to just believe us," Bertha said. "If you'd have held the necklace in your hand real or fake and just taken a moment to listen to your inner truths, you would have known."

Mrs. Ashford adjusted her hat. "Your father was a complicated man, but he was a man with integrity. I can't tell you *all* that he was up to, but I do know he never did anything you need to be ashamed of." She smiled. "I asked your daddy to make me a copy of the pendant because I wanted it so bad. I wanted to be part of its history. A little nobody from Louisiana like me part of a jewel that has traveled the world and through time. I just wanted to pretend for a while. So I bought it. For appearances, of course."

Jessie sighed. *The sake of appearances...* "Yes, of course."

"And don't worry. When I die, it's in my Will that the pendant is returned to your family. Then you can proudly display it again."

She shook her head confused. "But why did he lie? Why didn't he tell us?"

Bertha stood and came over to her. "Because you had to learn its importance. You had taken it for granted too long. Come." She took Jessie's hand and led her to the sitting room. A shot of lighting lit the large windows.

"Why are you still afraid when you know the truth about the pendant?" she asked.

Jessie stared at her. "I'm sorry?"

"You know it's not about vengeance, you know what it truly means." She squeezed her hand. "You are everything you need to be. Never be afraid of your strength. You must decide for yourself what a woman is. Don't let the world's ignorance stop you from creating your own definition.

"You have a man who loves you. He has suffered, yes, but it is not your job to heal him or to be the paragon wife and mother to please him. You know inside your heart what he needs and it doesn't matter if no one else understands." She grasped Jessie's other hand and stared into her eyes. "The sapphire is a stone of holy blessings. Are you ready to claim yours?"

The sisters sat in the car, silent. Eventually, Teresa said, "You realize they were lying."

Her sisters turned to her. "What do you mean?" Jessie asked.

"Some of those jewels in the museum are fakes."

Michelle sighed. "There's no way we can prove that unless we get them all appraised."

"Of course, we could choose to believe that they were telling the truth."

"I guess that's all that truth is," Jessie said. "What you choose to believe." She bit her lip. "So what do we believe?"

Michelle started the ignition and Teresa just smiled. "Whatever we want to," she said. "And I want to believe them."

Michelle nodded. "We'll just believe what they said is true."

At home, Jessie discovered something else to believe as she walked to her room. She stopped in front of a mirror and saw the woman Kenneth loved. And she knew she was beautiful.

Chapter Thirty-one

Kenneth walked into the plain conservative office Radson had used as a boardroom since the company began. This was the room where all the decisions for the future of the company had been made. Today it would decide his future.

"Here he is," Stephanie announced. She sat at the round table in the middle of the room. "We've been waiting."

One of the older members, Uncle Lamar, glanced at his watch. "I have a game at three."

Kenneth glanced at Nathan then Brooke and took his seat. "Don't worry. I won't delay you."

Stephanie looked around the table. "I believe we're ready to begin." They nodded.

Her gaze scanned the group. "I hope that I can count on everyone to vote with their conscious and in the best interest of the company. As we know we are at a crossroads. Brooke believes that it is time to sell Radson while our present CEO Kenneth believes that with proper management we can take Radson to the next level. The line of division is clear, let us cast our votes."

Kenneth spoke up. "I understand if some of you do not feel that an outsider should be running this company. I am willing—"

"You don't need to say anything young man," Winifred said softly.

Uncle Lamar added, "Yes. Let's vote and get out of here."

Everyone cast their votes. Those wanting to sell included Brooke, Uncle Lamar, and her cousin Trent. Winifred, Stephanie and Kenneth voted to stay. They were in deadlock with one swing vote. All eyes turned to Nathan.

Kenneth looked at his friend, a knot formed in his stomach. After the way he'd treated him, Nathan had no reason to vote in his favor. By selling Nathan could make all the money he wanted and start his own company.

Nathan leaned back in his chair and glanced around the room. "Selling of course would be a quick solution to some of the problems Radson has faced recently."

"Selling is the best solution," Brooke said. "We all know that. This is business, not a time to be sentimental. You know that it is in the best interest of everyone in this company to sell. We all know that Kenneth is a good person and has good vision for the company but we also know that some things have come to light that may reflect badly on us."

"Brooke," Stephanie warned.

"No use hiding it, Sis. We can all read." She leaned forward giving Nathan a significant look. "Aside from the bad publicity we know Kenneth has a tendency to overstretch himself and make rash decisions that are sometimes wrong."

Nathan sent Kenneth a pointed glance. "I guess he's not perfect." He folded his arms. "But none of us are." He fell silent and stared down at the table.

After a few seconds Stephanie asked, "So what's your vote?"

"I think we should sell." He kept his head bent, his voice low.

Brooke gave a little squeal of delight.

Nathan lifted his gaze and sent her a cold look. "But I vote we stay."

A tense silence followed then Uncle Lamar stood. "Well, that's that," he said then left.

Brooke slowly stood, her features perfectly composed. "Oh, well." She looked at her mother and her sister then left. Kenneth tried to catch Nathan's attention, but he left before Kenneth had the chance. Soon only Kenneth and Stephanie remained.

"Thanks for your support," he said. "You really covered my back."

"I'd like to take all the credit, but you had a lot of help. Especially from Nathan."

"I owe him an apology."

"I'm sure he'd like that."

"I'm not sure he'd listen." He rubbed the back of his neck

uncomfortable with being in someone's debt. "I can understand Brooke wanting to sell the company. It must have hurt that your father wanted me to be CEO, handing the position to an outsider instead of keeping it in the family."

Stephanie sent him a small, tentative smile. "It never left the family."

He stilled. "What are you talking about?"

"Dad's sister was about sixteen when she met this sexy French Caribbean guy on vacation. She thought she was in love and ended up pregnant. After the baby was born, the man persuaded her with his legendary charm to let him keep the child. Her parents encouraged her to do so since she was young. She later regretted the decision, but the baby was gone. Heartbroken she chose to forget it.

"My dad was too stubborn to do so. He searched for the child of his beloved sister and had about given up until a young man came up to him and asked to mow his lawn. He turned around and saw his sister in the boy's eyes."

Kenneth could feel the blood rushing through his veins. Frank Radson was his uncle? "Why didn't he tell me?"

"He didn't want to cause your family pain. You were the child of Mr. and Mrs. Preston and he didn't want to destroy that." Her smile grew. "But once he found you, he wouldn't let you go. You gave him joy and he loved you very much. He didn't tell Brooke and me the truth until near the end of his life. I think he knew then that he wanted you to run the company."

Kenneth folded his arms as Frank Radson's granite chin and serious eyes flashed through his mind. He remembered their fishing trips, the drives to DC, sitting in his office as he explained the world of business.

Stephanie's smile faltered. "His love for you angered Brooke. She couldn't believe our father could love us all equally. I understood Dad. I knew he felt he could redeem himself by taking care of the son of a sister he hadn't seen in years. When Dad passed I made it my duty to protect you."

"From husband hungry vipers?"

She laughed. "Among other things."

"Nathan thought you were jealous."

"No, proud. You've got the drive and will to succeed and that's pure Radson." She held out her hand. "Hello, cousin."

Kenneth shook her hand and held it. His eyes clung to hers. "I'm not Mr. Perfect anymore. That article—"

"I'm glad that article came out. I never knew when I could tell you the truth. Keeping it a secret left a gaping hole in me. It was awful knowing we were family and not being able to say anything." She tossed away formality and hugged him. "Now we're free. We can be cousins and friends."

"I'd like that." He drew away and studied her. "Now it's my turn to look out for you."

She turned away embarrassed. "I can look after myself."

He hesitated. "Do you know where my mother..."

She looked sad. "Nobody knows where she is. But I do know that she was a free spirit and loved you for the little time she knew you. That kind of love carries you a long way."

They left the conference room and spotted Nathan about to step into an elevator.

"Nate!" Kenneth said.

Nathan stopped and looked at him then swore when he saw the elevator doors closing. "Do you know how long I've been waiting for that damn thing?"

"I can make it up to you."

He lifted a brow. "You plan to carry me down the stairs?"

"I'm sorry."

Nathan blinked looking bored. "Yeah?"

"Thanks for all your help. I couldn't have done it without my brother watching my back."

Nathan hit the Down button again. "I have enough brothers, man. I don't need another one."

Kenneth took a step back, he wouldn't push the issue. "Right."

"But I could use a friend with a BMW I could borrow."

"Your car is in the shop again?"

"No, I just want to borrow it."

Kenneth grinned and patted him on the back. "Just tell me when."

Nathan shoved his hand in his pocket and jangled his change. "I will."

"So all is forgiven?"

He shrugged. "Yeah, well you aren't the only man who's been screwed by Brooke." Kenneth glanced at Stephanie. Nathan had the grace to look embarrassed. "Sorry about that."

"That's okay," she said lightly. "I'm not the only one with a sibling who has to face the consequences."

Nathan nodded solemnly thinking about Rodney. "Yes. You and I need to talk about that. I think there are some things you should know." He glanced at his watch. "But it will have to be another time." The elevator doors opened. He stepped inside and waved. "I have a lunch date. Bye Ken." He winked at Stephanie. "You handled that meeting well. Good job, Ms. Radson. I'll talk to you soon."

"Okay." Her face lit up with such joy Kenneth stared at her. She blushed. "I should go."

They shared a special smile then parted.

Brooke stood near the French doors watching the evening sky. Three days after the meeting and she still couldn't believe she'd lost. She had calculated everything—except Nathan's loyalty to Kenneth. Why? She'd been certain that the way Kenneth had treated him would make Nathan vote to sell the company just to spite Kenneth. But he hadn't. That man was a constant enigma. Damn. She would have to come up with something else.

"Hello, dear," her mother said, entering the room.

She glanced at her, briefly wondering if she could put her in a home somewhere. She watched a lightening flash.

"The game's over."

She spun around. "What are you talking about?"

Winifred sat down, crossing her legs at the ankles. "Poor, Brooke. Do you really think I didn't know what you were up to?"

"How could you possibly—"

"I know a lot of things."

She held her mother's gaze sensing an intelligence more devious than her own. Brooke felt her insides shriveling. "Don't ruin this for me. Everything can be perfect. If you give me the time, the company will be Stephanie's and the town's balance will be maintained. Don't you realize all the good I'm trying to do?"

"I realize that you're scared. You're scared that there will never be enough for you: enough respect, enough money, enough love. If Stephanie even talked about someone besides you, you quickly got rid of them. You hated your father for the same reason. But with a heart as small as yours, I suppose it's difficult to realize there's plenty for everyone."

"You can't—"

"It's too late. I told Stephanie about your phone call, I talked to your cousin and uncle about your attempts at bribery and I learned a little something about diamond smuggling from a young man named Jack."

Brooke laughed. "So what? What could you possibly do to me? It's all hearsay. There's no proof."

Stephanie entered the room. "There's proof and a lot of people willing to talk."

Brooke's throat constricted as she stared at the sadness on her sister's face. "Oh, Stephanie," she said gently. "You don't understand. Just let me explain."

"Explain why you became a traitor? Why you sought to destroy all that my father had struggled to build?"

Brooke clenched her teeth. "Yes, and he left us nothing! How dare he put that woman's bastard son in a place of such prominence?

"That woman was our aunt," Stephanie said quietly.

"I don't care." She pounded her chest, her voice rising. "We're his flesh and blood. It should have been ours. All of it. Not the crumbs he left us."

Stephanie took a deep breath. "Nathan told me how you used his brother."

"No, I did not."

"You seduced him."

"And you believe that?" she scoffed. "Of course you do. You'll believe whatever Nathan says because you're still in love with him."

She narrowed her eyes and pointed a finger at her sister. "Let me tell you something. He is a conniving, manipulative womanizer who would never look at you twice. He would say anything to smear my name because I was the only woman who has ever tossed him aside. He wants to get between us, but you can't let him. You can't let them win. His brother is no better than he is. Why would I want to seduce such a pathetic excuse for a man?"

"Because you wanted him to steal computer cycles for a South African company in exchange for diamonds. Then with the help of an antiques dealer you sold the diamonds, in order to make enough money to bribe people into selling the company." Stephanie folded her hands. "I know how you got that article about Kenneth too. It's over Brooke." She blinked back tears. "I'm sorry." The sisters stared at each other: one with bitterness, one with sorrow. Finally, Stephanie turned and walked to the door.

"You love me too much to let anything happen to me," Brooke called after her. "You don't have it in you to do this."

Soon sirens pierced through the air, Stephanie kept walking until she disappeared out the door.

"You don't!"

"No," Winifred said. "She doesn't. I do."

Brooke sent her mother a withering glare. A layer of ice chilled her words. "You can't let this happen to me."

"I'm sure you'll get off easy. I always thought you used that deceptive little face of yours too well." She sighed. "But you underestimated me." She tilted her head to one side and dimpled prettily. "Who do you think gave you that face in the first place?"

Autumn hinted of its coming, cooling the air and touching the trees with a palate of colors.

Jessie sat by the window of her parents' home and watched BJ walk up the front porch steps, looking no less large and intimidating in a brown bomber jacket and jeans. For a moment she remembered a chubby woman in tatty clothes with a solemn looking, fatherless boy behind her, something her Aunt Yvette would describe as a hoodlum-in-progress. Her father had introduced the pair as his sister Joan and nephew BJ.

"He doesn't look very nice," Jessie whispered.

Her father smiled and patted her on the head. "No, but he's family so I want you to look out for him."

Jessie sighed, she hadn't looked out for him and since her parents' death she'd hardly seen him. She remembered that dreadful night at the prom when she'd spent half of the night in his car crying. He'd awkwardly pat her on the back and offer her tissues not understanding why she was so upset. Then she told him about Kenneth and Regine, but she asked him not to tell anyone and he never did.

She opened the door for him and gestured to a seat. He sat down and stared at her. The way he tugged on his jacket was the only indication of his unease.

"Would you like anything to drink?" she asked.

"No thanks."

"You don't have to have tea, we do have beer."

His face split into a grin so wide Jessie gaped at him stunned. It changed his entire face, revealing a very handsome man. "You just read my mind." He leaned back. "I think I will have drink."

Jessie gave him his drink then sat down. "Michelle, Teresa, and I have been talking and we've decided that there's something that you need to know."

He suddenly looked uneasy.

She rested a box on his lap. "Dad loved you very much and he would have wanted you to have it." When he just stared at the box, she nudged him with her elbow. "Go on."

He opened it. The Sapphire Pendant gleamed up at him. He looked at Jessie incredulous, his sense of unworthiness clear in his gaze.

"It took us a while to understand the turn meaning of the pendant, but now that we know we want you to guard it. It needs to always carry the Clifton name." She held up her hand. "Before you say another word. Let me tell you a story..."

BJ listened. Once she had finished he said, "Before I take this, I want you to do something for me."

"What?"

When he told her, Jessie shook her head. "It's no use. I already know the future."

He glanced at the pendant then her. "You're not the only one who can read stones, Jessie. We both know that the future isn't set there. I want you to do what I say."

She rubbed her hands together and bit her lip. "No, I can't."

"Yes, you can." He lifted a knowing brow, a light twinkle in his eyes. "Even if I have to make you."

Two weeks later Jessie stood in front of Kenneth's house with her hand raised to knock. She let her hand fall to her side and briefly shut her eyes, listening to the autumn storm raging behind her. She probably shouldn't have come, but she had promised BJ. She knocked on the door then rang the doorbell.

"Who is it?" a small voice asked.

"It's Jessie."

The door swung open. Syrah stood there smiling. Dion stood next to her his tale wagging. "Aunt Jessie! I knew you would come back."

Jessie pushed back the hood of her mackintosh and patted Dion. She stood and glanced at Freda who was coming around the corner. "Well, I'm not exactly back. I just needed to say a few things to your uncle."

"He's upstairs listening to some loud music."

"Beethoven," Freda added.

Jessie nodded. "I see."

Freda folded her arms. "I'm sorry you came all this way. I don't think he'll want to see you."

Syrah grabbed Jessie's hand and pulled her inside. "Oh, please Ms. Rose can't she stay just a little while so that she can play with me?"

"But that's not why she came." She let her hands fall to her side, softening her tone. "Not that we're not glad to see you. We don't want to waste her time."

"Being here is never a waste of time," Jessie said slipping out of her coat. "I can spare five minutes."

Freda nodded then left the room.

Syrah watched her go then whispered to Jessie, "I can go get Dad for you if you want."

"Dad?"

She grinned. "Yea, he's going to be my dad now. Isn't that great?"

Jessie hugged her. "I'm so happy for you both."

Syrah looked up at her some of her joy fading. "I'm sorry about all the trouble I caused."

"You haven't caused any trouble. Michelle told me that if you hadn't convinced Daniel to go to the police about the diamonds they wouldn't have had enough evidence against Brooke."

Syrah swallowed, looking a little guilty. "Oh. Daniel likes to say that, but it's not true. I wanted to keep the diamonds."

Jessie laughed then gave her a little squeeze before releasing her. "You wouldn't have been Syrah if you'd thought otherwise."

They sat in the living room and Syrah showed Jessie her electronic game. Jessie told her about her job at the jewelers and Syrah shared about starting at a new school. Suddenly, Syrah jumped to her feet. "Let me go get Dad for you."

Jessie stood as well. "Actually, I think I should leave." She reached into her pocket. "But I want you to give him something for me." She stopped when she heard keys inserted in the doorknob. "Who else has a key to the house?"

Syrah shrugged. "I don't know."

They went into the foyer and watched the door swing open. Eddie walked inside.

Chapter Thirty-two

Shock left them paralyzed. Jessie watched Eddie stroll into the room as though she were observing an experiment volunteer behind a one way mirror. He was an attractive young man with teasing dark eyes, firm features and a confident set in his shoulders. His tailored clothes and arrogant gait gave no hint to the demon he was fighting or the anger he could not control. For a moment, Jessie believed the lie he projected, but it was the slight trembling of his hands as he put his extra key in his pocket, that alluded to the truth. Dion growled, breaking the silence.

"You'd better keep that dog away from me," Eddie said.

Syrah grabbed the dog by its collar. "Come on, Dion." At first Dion refused to move then he allowed her to lead him into another room and close the door. When Syrah returned, Eddie raised a brow. "It's time to come home, Ace."

She didn't move a look of terror clear in her gaze. Jessie stepped in front of her. "She is home."

Eddie shrugged, nonchalant. "I see you've gotten attached to her. You can visit some time. Ace, go get your things."

She still didn't move.

His tone hardened. "Did you hear me?"

Syrah's breathing increased, she clenched her fists and she looked up at Jessie not knowing what to do. Jessie sent her a gentle smile. "It's okay."

"Ace."

"She's not going with you."

"Yes, she is." He shoved Jessie aside and grabbed Syrah's arm. "I said go pack your things. Now do it." He tossed her in the direction of the stairs. She stumbled and caught herself on the railing.

"She's not going anywhere with you."

Eddie spun around his eyes a piercing black. "Where's Kenneth?"

"Doesn't matter."

He smiled. "I'm asking because you really don't want to upset me," he said with chilling politeness.

"Why should I be afraid of a coward that hits children?"

"What has she been telling you? She likes to tell lies."

"I always wondered what my brother saw in the Clifton sisters. You're the one who thinks she's a man, right?"

"I'm not going to fight you."

"Good then you'll stay out of my way." He turned to Syrah. "I'm not going to ask you again. Go pack."

"No," Syrah said in a small voice.

Eddie chuckled. "You always were stubborn." He looked at Jessie. "You should have seen her as a baby."

"Why don't you go home?"

He nodded. "I will once Ace packs." He looped his thumbs through his belt loops. "I'm through discussing this."

"Me too," Jessie said softly. "We both know Kenneth will make a better father than you ever could."

He grabbed the front of her shirt and shoved her against the wall with such force she saw stars. Fear—vivid and dark—coursed through her. "Let me go," she said.

Eddie flashed a bitter smile. "Do you honestly think she's better off here? Do you think Kenneth hasn't got a temper too? He just hides it better." He shoved her head back with his forefinger. "You're not taking Syrah from me. And never compare me to Kenneth again." He swallowed. "I could never live up to Kenneth's perfect image. No one could."

"You're pathetic," Jessie said, disgusted. "You took the path already chosen because you were too afraid to fail at something else. I gave you my scholarship, you had a chance and you blew it. You ruined your life because you were too afraid of failure to do anything. Well congratulations, because you didn't fail. You succeeded at become as useless as your father and worthless as a man."

Eddie tightened his grip until Jessie could barely breathe. She clawed at his hand, dots forming in her eyes.

Syrah rushed up to him. She tugged on his jacket. "Let her go, Dad. I'll come with you. Please, please."

"Tell her how much you love me," he said in a calm even tone.

"I love you so much Dad, I really do," she said her face wet with tears.

"Tell her how much you want to be with me."

"I want to always be with you. Forever. Please let her go."

Eddie smiled. "Did you hear that?"

Jessie nodded. Then she spat in his face. His smile fell. Syrah saw the look on his face—she's seen it before—and raced upstairs.

She ran down the hall and burst into Kenneth's room. He jumped to his feet when he saw her and turned off the music. "What's wrong?"

"He's downstairs and he's going to kill her."

Kenneth knelt in front her and grabbed her arms. "What are you talking about? Are you watching a scary movie?"

"No. It's Aunt Jessie. Dad's got her because of me. You've gotta help her."

A chill went through him. "Eddie's here?"

She didn't get a chance to reply. The sound of shattering glass filled the air. He fled down the hall like a rabid dog.

"They're in the living room," Syrah said.

Freda met him at the bottom of the stairs.

"Where is he?" he demanded.

"I'm sorry Mr. Preston."

"Where is he?"

Her voice shook when she spoke. "I called the police."

"Where. Is. He?"

She took a step back. "He's in the kitchen...with her."

He gave a terse nod and walked past her. "Take Ace with you into your room and lock the door."

She nodded then took Syrah's hand and left. Kenneth stormed into the kitchen with gathering fury, but nothing prepared him for the scene he saw. He'd seen the same scene once years ago. He'd walked into the kitchen late one night and found his mother on the floor with her blouse ripped open, while his father saddled her waist and slapped her until she was as limp as a rag doll. He'd wanted to grab a knife and kill him. He grabbed that knife now.

When Jessie saw him, she widened her eyes. "Kenneth, don't!"

Eddie spun around then leaped to his feet. He stumbled back when he saw the rage in his brother's eyes. "What the hell is wrong with you?"

"Nothing," Kenneth replied softly, taking a menacing step closer.

"Shit, Kenny. Put the knife down."

He shoved Eddie against the wall then lifted him off the ground.

"Don't Kenneth," Jessie said, trying to reach him through his anger.

He couldn't hear her. He was a little boy with the strength of a man, finally holding his father captive so that he could instill the pain and fear that had tormented him for years. He tightened his grip. "You knew I could forgive anything but that."

"I can't breath," Eddie squeaked.

"Don't worry," he growled. "It won't matter in a minute."

"No," Jessie said, seizing his arm, feeling the power. "This isn't the answer. Stop it."

"He shouldn't have hit you," he said in a distant tone that made her shiver.

"But I'm okay. Look at me. I'm okay."

He slowly turned to her. No, she wasn't okay. Half of her face was swollen and blood seep from a cut on her mouth and above her eye. But it was the look in her eyes that stopped him. Right now she wasn't afraid of Eddie. She was afraid of him. He'd become the monster. A fierce pain pierced through him that he'd finally revealed the side he'd never wanted anyone to see.

He looked away and pushed Eddie towards the door. "Let's go. Ms. Rose called the police and we need to get our story straight." He spoke to Jessie though he couldn't look at her. "Stay here," he said then followed Eddie out the door.

Jessie slid to the ground with her back against the wall and drew her knees up to her chest. Every part of her ached, but she fought back tears of relief. Syrah was safe; she'd succeeded. It was a victory she would never forget. Minutes later Kenneth entered the room. She stared up at him as he stood in the doorway soaking wet with grass and mud smearing his clothes. The tears she had fought so hard against now fell from her eyes.

He knelt down in front of her and tilted her chin with his forefinger. She opened her mouth to ask what he was doing when she noticed the first aid kit in his hand.

"You're getting good at patching me up," she said desperate to fill the silence. He didn't reply. He looked composed—too composed as though what had just happened was an unfortunate diversion. "I'm sorry."

"It's okay."

It wasn't okay and he knew it too, but she didn't wish to point that out to him. "Where's Eddie? Did the police take him?"

Kenneth brushed away her tears with his thumb then gently patched the cut above her eye. "In a way," he said vaguely.

"What do you mean 'in a way'?"

He applied antiseptic on a cotton ball. "They called for an ambulance."

"So he decided to check himself into a program or something?"

Kenneth glanced at her then the cotton ball. "No...um...I lost my temper."

"You didn't."

"I'm afraid I did. I accidentally broke his right hand, maybe his arm too." He dabbed the scratch marks on her cheek, his voice low. "He hit you with his right hand, didn't he? It'd be a shame if I accidentally broke the wrong hand."

She nodded woodenly.

He tossed the soiled cotton ball aside then nodded too. Once he finished cleaning her wounds, he sat down beside her, drawing his knees up and rested his arms on them. He leaned his head back and closed his eyes. "I don't know why you came back, Jasmine. My life is not the same now." He sat up and looked at her. "You don't know what it's like. Although I still have my position at the company, I'm not as admired as before." He rubbed his chin, trying to make light of the situation though it still hurt. "You could say my value has dropped." He shrugged. "My value has always been an illusion." He hung his head then said in a low voice. "I scared you, didn't I?"

"No."

His head snapped up. "Don't lie to me, Jas. I saw the look on your face." He briefly shut his eyes. "I'll never forget it. You shouldn't have come back."

Jessie wrapped her arms around herself, but she couldn't stop from trembling. "I had to," she said in a quiet voice.

"Why?"

"Because I love you Kenny Chevalier."

For a moment he didn't breathe, he only stared at her. He never thought he'd hear those words. She loved him. *Him*. Kenny Chevalier. Even though right now he was coarse, dirty and wet. She still loved him. It was a joy so painful he couldn't believe it was real.

"Before I was so terrified that I would fail you." She continued quickly before he could speak. "You had suffered so much and I didn't want to be another disappointment. I thought you had settled for me because you felt I was all you could get. No, don't say anything. I know it's not true, it was just my excuse—my mask. I was focusing too much on myself. But my love for you is unconditional. You don't have to do or be anything it is always there." She dug inside her pocket and pulled out a velvet pouch. "BJ wanted me to show you this. Hold out your hand." He did and she spilled the contents of the pouch into his palm.

Kenneth's eyes widened at the beauty facing him. "The pendant. You got it back."

Jessie sighed. "It's a long story. I'll explain it another time. I just wanted you to hold it. I wanted you to be part of its history."

He didn't ask why because he didn't care. He held the pendant with reverence and ran his fingers over the chain and the sapphire center. He understood her loyalty to it and her father, wishing for a moment that loyalty could be his. Then he glanced up and his heart stopped. She wasn't looking at the pendant, she was looking at him. In her eyes he saw love. *He* mattered. Her loyalty was his.

The rush of emotion he felt was too much—tightening his throat, moistening his eyes. He clasped his hands and rested his forehead against them, the pendant dangling from his fingers. It whispered to him, drowning his father's voice and his mother's bitterness and replacing them with a new mantra. He looked at her and the mask shattered, there would never be that barrier between them. There were no more demons to chase away. He held out the pendant and watched as Jessie placed it back in its pouch. She'd seen a side of him he'd been afraid to let anyone see. She knew about his scars, his past and his flaws and yet she still loved him. Just as how though bruised, red eyed, and trembling, he thought she looked beautiful.

"We'll have a big wedding," he said. "BJ will walk you down the aisle and you'll have a beautiful gown and lots of family and friends around us."

She lifted her chin. "I'm not doing a big wedding. I want something nice and quiet."

"We'll have a symphony."

"No we won't."

He stared out in the distance lost in thought. "We can hire the Garden catering company and rent an old mansion with a large garden."

She grabbed his chin and forced him to look at her. "I'm not doing a big wedding."

He smiled, one of the special smiles he reserved just for her. "Is that a bet?"

They had the biggest wedding Randall County had ever seen. It happened on a day when the sun was merciful, the sky clear and everything that could be bright and lovely was. The mansion where the ceremony and reception was held welcomed and echoed the shouts of cheer and good wishes, reverberated with the love of family and friends and also in rare quiet moments offered forgiveness to those who could not yet forgive.

And as the evening settled with a gentle darkness, it was said later that the stars had never looked so bright.

*E*pilogue: late 1800s

Markus Jahne read the note left where his pendant should have been. *I stole your heart,* it said written in Sonya's bold script. He shook his head, unable to stop a smile. He glanced out at the cool Jamaican morning inhaling the scent of the sea and the ackee and saltfish waiting on his table.

He could feel no anger towards the woman who'd left him while he slept. He would always remember her and how she looked at twilight.

He replaced the floorboard and stood. She was right. She'd stolen his heart. He'd left it there for her to find.

About the Author

Dara Girard is the author of four previous novels, *Table for Two*, *Gaining Interest, Carefree,* and *Illusive Flame.* She loves to travel and hear from readers. Visit her online at:

www.daragirard.com

Or write her at:

Dara Girard
PO Box 10345
Silver Spring, MD 20914

Please enclose a self-addressed stamped envelope if you wish to receive a reply.

Keeping In Touch

To find out more about Dara Girard, sign up for *Dara's News,* a monthly newsletter where readers can learn about:

- What Dara's up to
- Receive sneak peeks of Dara's upcoming books
- Be eligible for special contests and prizes
- Find out what's on Dara's mind
  And much more....

To receive the newsletter electronically sign up online at www.daragirard.com

Or

If you would like to receive the newsletter by mail, complete the form below and mail to: Dara's Newsletter, P.O. Box 10345 Silver Spring, MD 20914

PLEASE PRINT

Name _____

Address_____

City _____

State/Zip _____